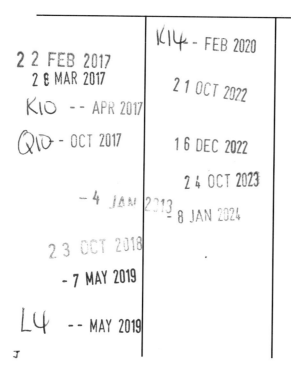

Praise for Rory Clements' acclaimed John Shakespeare series

'**Does for Elizabeth's reign what CJ Sansom does for Henry VIII's**'

Sunday Times

'**An exuberant plot** that hums with Elizabethan slang, profanity and wit . . . a bawdy, **engaging** romp of a book'

The Times

'**Enjoyable**, bloody and brutish'

Guardian

'An **engrossing** thriller'

Washington Post

'A world **spiced with delicious characters** . . . The novel **wears its historical learning lightly**, and Clements seasons it with romance and humour'

Mail on Sunday

'An historical thriller to **send a shiver down your spine** . . . atmospheric . . . the evocation of the filth and debauchery of London is quite **exceptional** . . . demonstrates the **compelling** eye for detail and character that **Bernard Cornwell** so memorably brought to Rifleman Sharpe. **I could not tear myself away, it is that good.**'

Daily Mail

'Clements has the edge when it comes to creating a **lively, fast-moving plot**'

Sunday Times

'**Faster moving than CJ Sansom**'

BBC Radio 4

'A **colourful** history lesson [with] **exciting narrative twists**'

Sunday Telegraph

'**Beautifully done** . . . alive and **tremendously engrossing**'

Daily Telegraph

'**Sharp and challenging**, this book is missed at one's peril'

Oxford Times

CORPUS

RORY CLEMENTS was born on the edge of England in Dover. He was an associate editor at *Today* newspaper, followed by stints at the *Daily Mail* and *Evening Standard*.

Since 2007, Rory has been writing full-time in a quiet corner of Norfolk, England, where he lives with his family. He is married to the artist Naomi Clements-Wright. He won the CWA Ellis Peters Historical Award in 2010 for his second novel, *Revenger,* and three of his other novels – *Martyr, Prince* and *The Heretics* – have all been shortlisted for awards. A TV series of the John Shakespeare novels is currently in development.

Find out more at **roryclements.co.uk**

RORY CLEMENTS
CORPUS

ZAFFRE

First published in Great Britain in 2017 by

ZAFFRE PUBLISHING
80–81 Wimpole St, London W1G 9RE
www.zaffrebooks.co.uk

A CIP catalogue record for this book is available from the British Library.

Hardback ISBN: 978-1-785-76261-1
Trade paperback ISBN: 978-1-785-76262-8

Also available as an ebook

1 3 5 7 9 10 8 6 4 2

Typeset by IDSUK (Data Connection) Ltd
Printed and bound by Clays Ltd, St Ives Plc

Zaffre Publishing is an imprint of Bonnier Zaffre,
a Bonnier Publishing company
www.bonnierzaffre.co.uk
www.bonnierpublishing.co.uk

For Naomi

BERLIN, AUGUST 1936

CHAPTER 1

The man was grey-haired, about fifty, and carried a black briefcase. He wore black trousers, a brown linen jacket, white shirt and striped tie but no hat. He might have been an office worker, except for the white socks and brown, open-toed sandals. *White socks and sandals.* In the middle of a working day, in the traffic-mad tumult of Potsdamer Platz, in the centre of Berlin. He was standing beside her at the edge of the pavement, waiting to cross.

Nancy Hereward turned her head and caught his eye. She stared at him hard and he looked away. She felt like laughing, but her mouth was dry and she had a terrible thirst. Surely, if he was following her, he wouldn't have made eye contact? Nor would he have dressed so distinctively. If you were tailing someone, you had to meld into the crowd, not stick out. A gap opened up between the trams, the buses, the cars and the horse-drawn carts, and he made a dash for the other side of the road by way of the clock tower island. Nancy waited.

Ahead of her, a policeman with white gloves was directing the onrush of vehicles. To her left, two young women in sunglasses were examining postcards at a newspaper kiosk. They wore flat slip-on shoes and short-sleeved, calf-length summer dresses, one polka-dot, the other floral, revealing healthy, tanned forearms. Through the fog of her brain, Nancy's first thought was that they must be tourists like her, but they seemed too confident for that, and their shoes were not designed for tramping across miles of an alien city. She caught the soft burr of their spoken German. Their easy sophistication marked them down as bourgeois Berliners, not provincials.

Nancy realised that she was doing the same to everyone she saw; assessing them, deciding who they were, what they might be concealing. Suddenly everyone looked like plainclothes officers. She had an urge to confront everyone in the crowd and demand of each of them, 'Are you secret police? Are *you* secret police?' She pulled her sun hat down over her hair. Her hands were sweaty and her dress clung to her body. She clutched her slim shoulder-bag closer to her side and walked on.

It was late afternoon but the heat of the day had not yet relented. She and Lydia had taken the U-Bahn from the Reichssportfeld station at the Olympic Stadium in the west of the city and had spent two hours shopping and sightseeing in the broad avenues and boulevards around Friedrichstrasse and Unter den Linden. Now she had slipped away and was alone, the map of the streets she must walk down memorised.

The city was full of thousands of tourists, here for the Olympics and all the fun surrounding the games. *No one is following you.* She said the words under her breath. She gripped her hands into fists, then released, then gripped again. She took deep breaths to calm herself and increased her pace, trying to make herself look businesslike, less foreign. Less interesting.

God, she was a fool, a bloody novice. She had been told what to do, of course, how she must lose possible pursuers with backtracking, circling and stops. How to spot a tail. But that was theory; this was reality.

The man with the sandals had disappeared into the heaving mass of people. Perhaps he had been one of many; perhaps someone else was now on her case. Nancy had attempted to dress as anonymously as she could, in a shapeless green frock, with her hair braided and pinned up around the top of her head. In their shared hotel room, Lydia had looked at her oddly. 'I know what you're thinking,' Nancy had said. 'You think I look like a bloody little Waltraud.' Lydia had raised an eyebrow. A Waltraud was their private derisory name for the sort of Nazi girl who belonged to the BDM, wore dirndls and eschewed make-up and cigarettes. Was there anyone in the world less like the clean-living *jungmädel* ideal than Nancy Hereward? They had both fallen about laughing.

She headed south and westwards. On every corner and from every public building, the swastika banners fluttered in the warm breeze, black on a white circle in a sea of red. Every one of them seemed like a personal threat. Turning right into a side street, she stopped at a butcher's shop window and gazed at the cuts of meat and the endless varieties of sausage without really seeing them. She tensed as an old woman bustled up to her elbow and put a letter in the red Reichspost box fixed to the wall at the side of the shop, then ambled away at snail's pace. No one was following. She carried on, walking further away from the main arteries of the city. At the end of the street she turned right then, quickly, went left. The area was residential now, a respectable mixture of smart tenement blocks, parks and churches, very different from the regimented grid of streets bordering Friedrichstrasse.

She knew that Lydia would be getting worried. Nancy had told her she would only be gone twenty minutes; she should wait for her at the Victoria with a coffee and cake and her book. 'I just want a little time on my own,' she had said. Lydia had shrugged, clearly puzzled, but seemed to accept it. This was going to take a lot longer than twenty minutes; Lydia would just have to wait.

She turned again into the road she had been seeking. Narrow and cobbled with a half-timbered tavern, which must have been old when Otto von Bismarck was young. She looked around once more. The street was almost deserted, save for a boy of about twelve. She stopped three houses to the left of the tavern, outside the front door of a three-storey building. Number six, one of the flats at the top of the house. She pressed the button twice, waited three seconds, then pressed again.

A dormer window opened twenty feet above her and a face peered out. '*Ja?*'

'*Guten tag, Onkel Arnold!*'

He hesitated no more than two seconds, then nodded. '*Einen moment, bitte.*'

Half a minute later, the front door opened.

'Come in,' he whispered. His English was heavily accented, but precise. He was a balding man in his mid-thirties and he was frightened.

Nancy stepped into the gloom of the hallway. On either side of her there were doors to apartments. In front of her was a staircase. 'Here?' she suggested.

'No, please, not here. Come upstairs.'

As soon as he had closed the door to his flat, she removed her hat and tossed it on the table. Then she opened her bag and took out a brown envelope. She thrust it at him. 'It's all in there.'

He slid the papers out and studied them, then gave her a strained smile. It would take a great deal more than this delivery of forged papers to wash away the stresses of his life. 'Thank you, miss. Truly, I don't know how to thank you or repay you. You have risked a great deal for me.'

'Not for you, for the cause.'

'I thank you all the same. Can I make you a cup of tea? Or coffee perhaps? It is ersatz, I'm afraid.'

'No, I must go.' She hesitated. She was shaking. 'Do you have a lavatory?'

'Yes, it is shared. Across the landing.'

No, not here. It would be too risky. She had to get to safety. She tried to control her shakes. 'Forget it. I have to leave now.'

'I think if you were really my niece you would stay a little while, don't you? Having walked all this way?'

'No one saw me coming.'

'My landlord would have seen and heard you ringing the bell and calling out my name. He sees everything.'

'I'll stay ten minutes.' Nancy took a grip of herself. 'I am thirsty. Perhaps you have something a little stronger than tea?'

'Peach schnapps. It is the only alcohol I have, I'm afraid.'

She made a face. 'Better than nothing.'

They sat together in the man's sweltering, badly furnished sitting room, the ceiling sloping acutely beneath the eaves. The open window let in only warm, dirty air. Arnold Lindberg was a physics professor from Göttingen, but in this house he was Arnold Schmidt, unemployed librarian. She could smell the sweat of his fear. His pate was glistening and there were beads of perspiration on his brow and on his upper lip. He lit a cigarette and she could see that his fingers were trembling. As an afterthought, he thrust the packet towards her, but she shook her head. 'A glass of water,' she said. The sugary-sweet peach schnapps stood on the table in front of her, untouched. Perhaps she could wash it down.

He went to the basin and filled a glass. She drank it quickly, then asked for another.

'So tell me, miss, what do you think of the new Germany?'

'You mean the National Socialists?'

'Who else?' He gave a hollow laugh. 'But please, do not name them.'

Don't say the devil's name for fear that he might think you are calling him. 'I loathe them,' she said. 'That's why I'm here.' At last, she threw back the schnapps. It was not as sweet as she had feared. Not what she really wanted or needed, of course, but that would have to wait.

'I pray you never learn what it is like to live here like this,' he said. He began talking of his fugitive life as both a Jew and a communist, spurned by the university where he had been both student and professor. 'The *Deutsche Physik* make it impossible. They take our jobs for the crime of our race. In the twenties I worked with the great names – Einstein, Bohr. I counted them as friends, you know. Leo Szilard, too. Such a funny man. So many others – hundreds of us swept away by men without brains. Lise Meitner is still here, still working because she is Austrian. I want only to be with my friends and colleagues again and to continue my studies and teaching. Leo has said he will find me work and accommodation, if only I can get to England.' He shook his head. 'But a warrant is out for my arrest. All ports and railway stations have been alerted to stop me leaving. My crime? Insulting Himmler, the bastard. I will not embarrass you by telling you what I said, for I confess it was obscene.'

She already knew what he had said. Something about Himmler being promoted to Reichsführer in return for sucking Hitler's cock. One of Arnold's students had denounced him.

Nancy stood up. 'I have to go,' she said.

'Yes, of course. I have kept you too long – but it is safer, you see.'

'I hope the papers are what you want.'

He nodded. 'Thank you again. Thank you.'

She picked up her hat and went to the door, pulling it open. She looked down the empty staircase. She was about to go when she turned round. He was standing there, clasping the envelope she had brought him. He looked pathetic. 'Good luck,' she said. *You'll need it.*

She took a more direct route back, across the Tiergarten towards the Brandenburg Gate. She looked at her wristwatch and saw that she had already been well over an hour. Beneath her frumpy green dress, her body was as slippery as a wet eel.

'I was about to send out a search party for you,' Lydia said when Nancy, sweating and hot, finally came round the corner and slumped down on the seat opposite her at the Victoria café. 'You're soaked! You look as though you've been running.'

Nancy was frantic now, upturning her bag on the table. From the debris, her scrabbling fingers clutched at a silver syringe.

Lydia's mouth fell open. 'Not *here*, Nancy! For pity's sake, not here in front of all these people!'

Nancy ignored her and with a shaking hand thrust the tip of the needle into a small vial and filled the syringe. Lydia looked round anxiously; Nancy stretched her left arm out on the white tablecloth. A thin vein bulged from the white flesh on the inside of her elbow. The needle slipped in, a speck of blood seeped out. She pushed in the plunger of the syringe and let out a low moan.

Neither woman saw the boy looking in through the café window.

ENGLAND,
MONDAY NOVEMBER 30, 1936

CHAPTER 2

He drove the little MG two-seater into a large village in south Cambridgeshire. He was hungry and thirsty and the local inn looked inviting, the sort of place he would have visited on a summer's afternoon in the old days. Rural English. Wholesome food and strange beer.

His assessment was accurate. The Old Byre was a traditional coaching inn with rooms, good food, a log fire and a selection of half a dozen ales and beers. He ordered a steak and kidney pie with potatoes and peas and a pint of bitter. He ate the food hungrily, but he barely drank.

'Is there something wrong with your beer, sir?'

'It's fine.'

'The keg's new on today. Can I get you something else?'

The waitress was a woman in her late thirties with loose curls, a figure that hadn't succumbed to gravity, and a wanton eye. There was a warmth to her, enhanced by the glow of woodfire in a broad open hearth. She was flirting with him.

'I've got to stay awake. I still have a long drive ahead of me. Perhaps a coffee?'

'We don't do coffee, sir.'

'Not even in the landlord's own accommodation?'

'I could ask him.'

'That would be kind of you.' He flashed his best Hollywood smile. 'Black, no sugar, please.'

A few minutes later she reappeared with a cup of coffee. As he took it, she said, 'Beg pardon, sir, might I ask if you are travelling far this evening?'

Had she blushed as she spoke? No, far too brazen for that. It was merely the heat of the fire that brought colour to her cheeks. 'A little way yet,' he said. 'Thank you for the coffee. I am sure it will do me very well.'

'Have you really got to drive on, sir? They say there'll be a fog. It's very late and we have some comfortable rooms to rent. Not many travellers at this time of year, you see. I'm sure if I had a word with the landlord, he'd do you a favourable rate.'

She had touched his hand, deliberately, as she handed him the cup. His initial suspicion was correct. If he stayed, she would come to his room. One of that lost generation blighted by the war, perhaps she took her pleasures where she could among the travelling salesmen who stayed here. On another night he might well have obliged, but he could not stay, and anyway he did not want to leave too large a footprint. As the shutters came down, he paid the bill, took his leave of her, and drove on into the night.

He depressed the throttle. The car was low to the ground, had power and held the road well. The drive was not quick, however, not in late November. These country roads were small, unlit and mostly unmarked. Too many ruts and potholes, some deep. Roads from another century. England had not awoken from the self-satisfied torpor of its Victorian age.

Half an hour later, on a deserted stretch, a mile outside another typical English hamlet – pub, church, green, war memorial and duck pond – he turned left on to a small farm track, where he killed the car lights and switched off the engine. A stranger would never have found this place, even with an Ordnance Survey map, but he knew it well. He lit the last of his Swiss-made Parisiennes, then got out of the car and stretched his legs. The night air was chilly but not cold, and stank of fox. A low mist clung to the ground between the hedgerows. A quarter of a mile away, across a field, he could see a single upstairs light in an uncurtained window of a remote manor house. As he watched, the light was switched off and the house plunged into darkness.

He climbed back into the car, covered himself with his greatcoat and settled down to wait, staring into the darkness. The only light was the glowing red tip of his cigarette. From now on, he'd smoke Players Navy Cut. Apart from the soft, slow sigh of his breathing as he sucked in the smoke, the only sound was the distant hoot of an owl. A little while later, he opened the car door, pushed the cigarette butt into the soil and covered it with a layer of earth. He slumped back into the driving seat, closed his eyes and fell asleep.

On waking, he was uncertain at first how long he had been out. He reached to his left and dragged a small leather case from the footwell onto the passenger seat and flicked it open. He clicked on the electric torch which lay on top of a couple of shirts, then pulled out a flask of water, drank deeply and gasped before pouring some of it into his cupped hand and splashing his face. He looked at his watch. It was twelve thirty.

Pulling aside the shirts, he found his tools: a handgun, two lengths of mountaineer's rope, a large paintbrush, a long and curved hunting knife, its blade honed so sharp he could have shaved with it. He climbed out of the car again, without his greatcoat, and tucked the blade and gun into his belt, coiling the ropes around his chest bandolier-style. He switched on his electric torch. He was ready.

The house was easy. He had anticipated breaking a window, but a side door was unlocked and so he was able to enter in silence. He removed his English brogues and left them by the back door, then padded deeper into the house. In the pantry, he found a galvanised bucket and mop. He removed the mop and took the bucket.

He went through to the drawing room. Years ago, he had spent pleasant evenings here on exeat from college, drinking fine wine and Cognac with Cecil and Penny Langley and their rather staid friends, plus, of course, their beautiful daughter, Margot, who was in love with him. He recalled the old upright piano against the wall closest to the garden window. Penny had loved to play Chopin to entertain her guests, blissfully unaware of how badly she performed and how out-of-tune the instrument was kept. Now it had been replaced by a Bechstein grand, which held pride of place in the middle of the room. Such a magnificent piano was wasted here.

Slowly, he examined the familiar space, playing the torchlight across the furniture and walls, into all the crannies of the curtained room. One corner of a wall was given over to sports photographs from another age; pictures of a young man in climbing gear with peaks soaring behind him, pictures of young men with cricket bats and balls. Some of the sports pictures were draped with faded caps, won by Cecil who had played for county and varsity in the days of his youth. The torch beam alighted on a side table holding silver-framed photographs. At the forefront, in pride of place, was the Führer, his signature scraped in black ink in a downward sloping arc along the bottom of the photograph. Behind it were various other well-known faces: Mosley, Ribbentrop, the Marquess of Londonderry. The King's picture was directly behind Hitler's. The man smiled thinly. So the German corporal took precedence over the British monarch. The world turned upside down.

Another table held family photographs. Aunts, uncles, mothers, fathers, distant cousins, but most of all Margot, the beloved daughter: Margot on the beach in Devon with friends, Margot tanned and glowing with tennis racquet on the lawn, Margot riding side-saddle with high hat and hunting jacket at the Easter meet, Margot in the Alps with her father, Margot in her wedding gown being kissed by her bridegroom in front of the lychgate of a small country church. And then there was another picture, from Cambridge. Four of them, outside the arched college entrance in Trumpington Street: a young man in college gown, standing between Margot and Nancy Hereward, with Lydia Morris at the side. They had their arms about each other, four friends and lovers. His eyes stayed on Margot a moment. Someone had once said she was like a Newmarket filly. Jittery. Likely to snap a leg. Poor Margot.

Turning away, he set to work. He put down the torch on a side table and removed all the equipment he had brought: the ropes from his shoulder and the weapons from his belt. He laid them on the floor, then undressed, leaving his clothes in a neat pile on a wing chair. With the residual heat from a coal fire, the room was warm enough, even naked. He slung the ropes over his bare shoulder and picked up the weapons, the pistol in his left hand, the knife and torch in his right. He would come back for the bucket and brush.

The building was a large manor house from the seventeenth century. It had been refurbished and carpeted throughout. And yet still the boards creaked as, barefoot and naked, he climbed the stairway to the first floor. He paused on the landing. There were five doors. He wondered whether they had a maid. They had always had someone from the village, but perhaps that had changed. He would deal with that matter later, if necessary. From behind the door at the back of the house, he heard breathing – light, comfortable snoring. Slowly, he turned the handle and pushed the door open an inch at a time.

It was a perfect bedroom, well-proportioned and airy, with a high ceiling dominated by a long supporting beam.

His tread was soft. Standing at the foot of the bed, he directed the torchlight at the two sleepers. Cecil was on the left, Penny on the right. Cecil was lying on his side, head beneath a pillow, grunting in his sleep; Penny was on her back, her head on the pillows, her lips parted.

He put the torch on a chest of drawers and approached her. Looking down into her placid face with its yellow teeth just showing, he recalled how pleased she had been when Margot brought him home. She had wanted to know all about him and his family. Her husband had seemed less enamoured. Cautious, distant, unwelcoming. What had gone wrong? It was the picnic by the river, of course. He smiled. The long summer had ended then and they had gone their separate ways, Margot to marry her decent young farmer or whatever he was.

Whether it was his breathing that awoke Penny Langley or some sixth sense was unclear, but her eyes opened and met his. He saw the horror, saw her try to recoil. His face was no more than a foot from hers. Almost instantly, the horror turned to recognition and relief.

'My dear,' she whispered. 'What are you doing here?'

'Sshh.'

'It's so late. You should have teleph–'

She said no more. His blade sliced deep into her throat, releasing a rush of blood. Her dying hands came from under the bedclothes and thrashed the air in uncomprehending frenzy.

From the other side of the bed, Cecil Langley, still asleep, elbowed his wife and pulled the blankets away from her as he snuggled further down. The killer leant over the dying woman's body, his arms and chest slippery with her blood, and put the muzzle of his pistol to the sleeping man's temple.

'Wake up, Mr Langley.'

Afterwards, he went to the bathroom and was pleased to discover a new and efficient hot water system. For a full minute, he gazed at himself in the mirror. The blood was all over him – face, arms, legs, torso. Arminius the warrior, knee-deep in Roman gore at Teutoburg. His eyes were ice blue, atavistic beacons. His hair as pale as the sands of Friesland.

He ran a bath and sank into it, rinsing the blood from his hair under the tap and scrubbing every part of his body, then climbed out and dried himself on a large white towel. After pulling the plug, he wandered the upstairs rooms, listening, looking. Satisfied, he returned to the drawing room where he dressed quickly. Finally, he used the butt of his pistol to shatter the glass fronting the picture frames of Hitler, Mosley, Ribbentrop, Londonderry, the new King. He pulled out the photographs and tore them to shreds, scattering the little pieces in a snowstorm around the room. He took all the pictures of Cecil Langley and hammered the glass into tiny shards.

The first part of his work was done. At the side door, he was loosening the lace on one of his brogues, but then put it back down and returned to the drawing room. From the picture table, he took the photograph of the young man and the three young women outside the college gate, slid it from its silver frame and placed it in his pocket.

TUESDAY DECEMBER 1, 1936

CHAPTER 3

It was eleven in the morning, but Nancy Hereward was still half asleep. The telephone was ringing. Why would anyone be calling her? She wasn't expecting any calls. She wished she had never had it installed.

She crawled from bed and made her way downstairs. Her throat was parched. She hadn't even had a cup of tea yet. Her eyes fell on the silver syringe, but she turned away. The telephone was on a low table by the front door. She picked up the receiver.

'Hello. Nancy Hereward speaking.'

'Nancy. It's Margot.'

'*Margot?*' A voice from years ago. An urgent voice. The last person she would expect to call. 'Margot, where are you?'

'Can you get a message to Mummy for me? Please. I tried calling her, but—'

The line went dead.

Nancy held the receiver tightly to her ear. 'Hello, Margot? I can't hear you, Margot. Is that really you?' Why on earth would Margot Langley be calling her? Where had she got her number? And why had she hung up? Nancy put the receiver down. She should call Lydia. She'd know what to do. Not yet, though; she couldn't face the day quite yet. She felt shaky. Anyone would. Her eyes alighted once more on the glittering needle.

The gyp put his head round the door of Thomas Wilde's room. 'Good evening, professor.'

'Good evening, Bobby.'

'Two young gentlemen are here to see you. They say you agreed to hold their supervision before Hall.'

'Ah – Maxwell and Felsted. Send them in. Oh, and Bobby, some tea if you will. Perhaps rustle up a few biscuits. And you know what for me.'

Bobby grinned. 'I think I might have a bottle of Scotch secreted about my room, sir.'

'You never fail me.'

'Your comfort is my pleasure, as always.'

Professor Thomas Wilde was tall and angular, with high cheekbones and hair that was a little too long for some of the stuffier fellows of this most ancient and venerable of Cambridge colleges. He had spent much of his life in England, but he was American by birth and nationality and even in winter his skin had a summery hue. He had an outdoor face, uncommonly healthy among the morbid pallor of his academic colleagues. His voice was a hybrid that seemed to have washed up from the broad Atlantic; not quite American, not quite English.

He turned towards his old oak desk, remarkably uncluttered save for a typewriter and a two-inch thick pile of foolscap paper, the first three hundred pages of a biography of Sir Robert Cecil, the Elizabethan and Jacobean statesman, successor to Sir Francis Walsingham as the Queen's spymaster. He pushed the manuscript towards the back of the desk.

Though some might have thought his college rooms a little Spartan, Wilde enjoyed working here. He barely noticed the walls, stained yellow from the cigarette smoke of his predecessor, or the cracking and peeling paintwork. Apart from the desk, he had a calf-hide sofa where he read and dozed, two armchairs and a window with a pleasant view over the scuffed lawns, the tall chimneys, the dormers, the mullions and the wintry grey walls of the old court. They were airy, academic rooms, used only for work, not living. There was, too, a smaller room, cell-like and cold, with a narrow bed where he had been known to sleep when he simply couldn't be bothered to trudge home to his modest late-Georgian house in one of the older quarters of Cambridge near Jesus Lane.

The only other sign of domesticity in his rooms was a painting, an oil by Winslow Homer, left to him in his father's will. Occasionally, Wilde would stop and gaze at it, at the young barefoot boy with a straw hat, standing in a meadow, staring away into the distance. The picture seemed filled with yearning, a longing for something lost or not yet found. Wilde imagined his father to have been that strong American boy.

The warmth of the rooms, such as it was, came from a coal fire, which was stoked and refuelled throughout the day by the ever-cheerful Bobby, whose domain was across the stairs, no more than four feet from Wilde's outer door. The gyp room had all the necessary supplies to keep those fellows and students assigned to Bobby warm and watered. Endless supplies of bread for toasting, tea, milk, sugar, butter, jam, coal for the grate, whisky, bottled beer, brandy, cigarettes, tobacco and matches. Bobby was a squat man, whose ever-present smile was marred only by the lack of several front teeth. He had once been apprenticed to a Newmarket trainer and had hopes of becoming a professional jockey, but a bad fall had left him with a limp, a mashed jaw, and had done for his dreams.

Wilde couldn't think of his rooms as homely; he had spent too long enjoying the comforts of North America for that. But he assumed his pupils found them welcoming enough, for they didn't avoid his supervisions. The smoke of the coal, the uneven heat, the soot and grime on the walls; it might have been a railway station waiting room, save for the Homer painting. Well, he wouldn't stay here tonight. All he had to attend to was this supervision and then the irritation of a meeting in the Combination Room. Then home.

Maxwell and Felsted appeared in the doorway.

'Come in, come in.'

'Thank you, sir.' In unison.

'Foggy outside, sir,' Maxwell said.

'Well, Bobby will bring us a warming pot of tea to take the chill from your bones.'

He sat the young men together on the sofa and turned his own desk chair to a ninety-degree angle from the desk so that he could face them. At his elbow was a fountain pen, an ink bottle and a blotting pad.

'Did you hear about the Crystal Palace, sir?' Maxwell said. 'It burnt down last night.'

'Yes, I did hear of that. A great shame.'

'The communists,' Felsted announced. 'After all, they set fire to the Reichstag . . .'

'Oh, nonsense!' Maxwell retorted. 'The Blackshirts did it, sir. Mosley and his filthy gang.'

Wilde raised his hand, but not his voice. 'Enough.' He liked these young men. They were not the best history students he had ever taught, but a long way from the worst. Very raw, with the sheen of school still not washed away. Wilde wanted his undergraduates to take the long view of history, but Roger Maxwell and Eugene Felsted's black and white views on the politics of the twentieth century were intruding on their understanding of the sixteenth. They needed to learn to speak in measured tones and, more importantly, to think.

'The BBC suggests it was started accidentally,' Wilde said quietly. 'I confess I have no idea. But I would also suggest that you two have no idea, either.'

'But, sir—'

'No, don't speak. Not yet. For a moment, simply listen. You might learn something.'

Maxwell and Felsted had the glowing skin, soft hands and well-fed faces of the privileged. Their hair was slicked back with Brilliantine and they were dressed almost identically in flannel shirts, old school ties, Fair Isle sweaters and bags, topped off by their college gowns.

'You must learn not to rush to judgement. None of us here in this room has any evidence regarding the Crystal Palace fire, so how can you possibly reach a verdict? All you have are your prejudices, which are worthless. It is the same with history.'

Bobby knocked on the door and entered with a tray holding a pot of tea, three cups and a plate of biscuits. He deposited it by the fire. 'I'll be back with the Scotch in just a moment, sir.'

'Don't worry. I'll come and collect it before I go.'

'Thank you, sir.'

When he had gone Wilde turned to Felsted. 'Your turn to be mother, I believe. Now then, we were talking about evidence and prejudice. How would it be if a jury, instead of listening to evidence, convicted someone of murder or theft – or arson for that matter – simply because they didn't like his politics?'

'But a Dutch communist was convicted of the Reichstag fire, so there's a precedent, isn't there?'

'Is there? Does that mean because one man with a white beard is known to be a diamond thief, then all diamond thefts are committed by men with white beards? I hope you'll agree that's absurd, because if you don't then I rather think you might be wasting your time at Cambridge. History, I'm afraid, is bedevilled by prejudice. Take the case of Mary Queen of Scots. Was she a saintly figure murdered by the Protestant state and her wicked cousin Elizabeth? Or was she a murdering, scheming witch guilty of every sin known to man or woman? Maxwell, what do you think?'

'I think she was a murdering, scheming witch, sir.'

'Felsted?'

'The same.'

'And which Church were you two gentlemen brought up in?'

'Church of England.' The two undergraduates spoke in unison.

'That does not surprise me in the least. But I can tell you this, there are young men and women of your age brought up in the Roman Catholic Church who would say precisely the opposite. So which version is true? To discover that, we must look at the evidence.'

'But the evidence was presented in court – and she was found guilty.'

'Then why don't the Catholics believe it? I tell you why, because they believe the trial was politically motivated. They believe she was framed. Maybe they have a point. That's for the historians to discover.'

'How then can we tell what is true, sir?' Felsted demanded as he poured the tea.

'By thinking,' Wilde said. 'And by challenging the books you read. By getting dusty in archives. By listening to the evidence of archaeologists and palaeontologists. By using your eyes and ears and brains. And most of all by doubting everything I tell you until you have proved it for yourself.'

The two young men exchanged glances, discomfited. Teachers did not like to be doubted. That wasn't the way the world worked. They would never have dared question their teachers at school.

'Argue with me!' Wilde insisted. 'Make me prove my points, demand evidence, get as near the truth as you can. Re-examine everything you have ever been told and make your own mind up on the evidence you can find. And if there is not enough evidence, then keep an open mind. Become a detective – because if you don't, you'll never become a historian.'

Wilde hoped the talk had done the trick. He used it with all under-graduates and it usually worked, even though it undermined the very foundation of everything they had understood up until then. He looked at the two young men sitting uncertainly on his sofa and felt sorry for them. They needed reassuring. He sipped his tea, then opened his desk drawer and took out an object wrapped in a fragment of cloth. From the cloth he removed a piece of tar-blackened wood, about six inches by three. Without a word he handed it to Maxwell. The young man frowned at it, turned it this way and that, a puzzled look on his face.

'Give it to Felsted.'

Felsted looked equally bemused.

'Well, what do you think it is?'

'A bit of driftwood?' Felsted suggested.

'Not bad. Maxwell?'

'Looks like a chip off a railway sleeper to me.'

'No. Well, I'll tell you.' He took the wood back from Felsted. 'This old hunk of wood is perhaps the most thoughtful present I have ever received. It was given to me two years ago by one of my first undergraduates here at Cambridge. It's a piece of the *Golden Hind*, the ship in which Sir Francis Drake sailed around the world, and the cloth in which it is kept is a scrap of sailcloth from the same vessel.'

'How can you tell, sir?'

'Because it had been in his family for three hundred and fifty years. When the *Golden Hind* returned home, it was brought up on to dry land at Deptford, and became a huge tourist attraction. Unfortunately, every-one wanted to take home a souvenir – and they cut pieces off the hull, the sails and the rigging until the ship fell apart. This is one of those pieces. The rest are probably all lost or forgotten in attics and cellars. Gentlemen, you have just held a piece of history in your hands. That piece of wood was part of only the second ship to circumnavigate the globe.'

'Shouldn't it be in the British Museum, professor?'

Wilde wrapped the wood in the sailcloth and put it back in the drawer. 'I don't know, Maxwell, but perhaps you're right. My feeling at the moment, however, is that it serves more purpose here in this room. I think of it as a time machine, which can transport scholars like yourselves back to the sixteenth century. Anyway, that's where you are now, so let's start talking about that other Sir Francis – Walsingham.'

The hour passed quickly. Maxwell and Felsted were more attentive than they had been in weeks past and they desisted from their usual pastime of baiting each other about politics. At the end of the supervision, Wilde set them a task for the Christmas vacation: 'Like Hitler and Stalin, Walsingham used torture as a tool of statecraft. I won't ask you whose side he would have been on today, because I think I know what your answers would be. But I *will* ask you whether his use of torture helped his cause or hindered it. Remember what he said to Lord Burghley: *without the use of torture, I know we shall not prevail.* Well, we know with the benefit of hindsight that he did prevail – but was that thanks to the use of torture, or despite it? I want your answers, clearly argued, at the beginning of the Lent term. And put a bit of effort in.'

The two young men got to their feet and struggled into their coats. On their way out, Felsted popped his head back round the door. 'That piece of wood, sir,' he said. 'I suppose we've only got your word for its provenance, haven't we?'

Wilde could not suppress a smile and a light chuckle. At last, they were beginning to think. He gathered his papers together and switched off the desk lamp. The truth was he had no proof that the wood had come from the *Golden Hind*, and nor did he care; he liked the story. Not for the first time, it had had an effect on students whose minds were elsewhere. 'There's hope for you yet, Felsted,' he said.

On his way out Wilde looked in on Bobby. 'That Scotch? Just leave the bottle on my desk, if you would.'

'Yes, sir. Oh, and professor, don't forget that tip I gave you.'

'Winter Blood?'

'Ten to one if you get on early.'

Wilde laughed. 'You know I'm not a gambling man, Bobby.'

'This is easy money, Mr Wilde, trust me.'

'Very well. Put me down for five shillings.' He dug into his pocket and handed over two florins and a shilling.

'I'll do half a crown each way. That way you'll make a profit even if it comes second or third.'

'I thought you said it was certain to win.'

'Horses are only human, professor. Things can always go wrong.'

Outside, in the old court, the smoke of the town had gathered and was swirling in a mist, closing down light and sound. The paving underfoot was wet. A group of undergraduates hurried past him. In the grey, foggy light their billowing black gowns made them look like bats. A little electric light spilled from the college windows and lit the way through into the new court. With its high golden stonework, its arches and spires, a little over a hundred years old, it was designed to impress. Wilde preferred the more modest contours and ingrained history of the older court; the beating heart of the college.

The sherry, a fragrant oloroso, was ready in its decanter. A dozen or more glasses, polished to a shine, were laid out at one end of the long oak table that dominated the Combination Room. This was where the fellows met to socialise or to discuss important college matters.

It was a stately room, with a high ceiling on which the college arms were emblazoned in bas relief. The walls were encased in fine panelling that had been fitted in the days of Bloody Mary. It was said that one of the panels concealed a tunnel that led down to the landing stage at the river, near the King's mill, for a swift escape. No one was quite sure whether it had been a getaway for Protestant fellows during Mary's days or Catholics in Elizabeth's long reign.

Horace Dill grinned as he slouched across the room, smoke belching from his cigar like the funnel of a liner. 'Well, well, it's the brilliant and devilishly handsome Tom Wilde! To what do we owe this pleasure?'

'Why, Horace, I wanted to imbibe your wit and choke to death on your cigar smoke.'

'Come on, Tom. A team of six horses wouldn't normally be able to drag you here to take sherry with us lesser mortals.'

'Well, if you must know, Sawyer's asked me to meet him. And I can assure you there is no pleasure involved.'

'What on earth does he want?'

'It's a mystery to me.'

'Sherry?'

'No, thank you, Horace.'

Dill took a sip from his own glass. 'Sawyer is a filthy runt and you can tell him so from me.'

'I suspect he already knows your opinion. Anyway, he's just come in. Off you go, Horace. Go and annoy someone else.'

Dill laughed. 'Up your scabby middle-class arse, Tom.'

'Up yours, too, Horace.'

'You know why I like you, Wilde? Because no one else does. On which thought, I'll leave you to the Nazi's tender mercies.'

As Dill edged away, Sawyer appeared in front of Wilde.

'Ah, Professor Wilde, a rare appearance. Good of you to come. Have you got a glass? Can I pour you one?'

'No, thank you, Dr Sawyer.'

'No? Well, bottoms up anyway.' Sawyer held up his own glass and sipped, then nodded appreciatively. 'Glad something good still comes out of Spain.'

'You wanted to speak to me.'

'Indeed. Indeed. The bursar thought you should be brought on board. Wanted your support. Asked me to have a word with you.'

'And why couldn't he have had a word himself?'

Sawyer smiled. He was a distinguished-looking man with a hint of steely grey in his sideburns. He had a rowing blue from Oxford, had played tennis in the early rounds at Wimbledon, won races at Cowes week, was known as a fair boxer, and had been mentioned in dispatches for a daring action in Mesopotamia in the last year of the war. His subject was German literature and it was said he was a man destined for great things. Wilde had always felt there was something missing in him. A soul perhaps.

'He was called away to London. I believe his father's ill. Asked me to carry on without him. So here we are.'

Wilde waited. He did not spend more time than necessary in the Combination Room. The sherry, the cigars, the port and the undrinkable coffee were all bad enough, but it was the college politics, the tittle-tattle and whispers that he most disliked.

Duncan Sawyer, of course, was already proving himself a master in the art of college politics. Like Wilde, he was a man in his late thirties. He had been elected a fellow two years ago, not long after Wilde's own arrival, and was already thought to be in line for the position of senior tutor when the incumbent moved on in the summer. Sawyer had been a favourite of the old master, Sir Norman Hereward; their politics, both in and out of college, were perfectly aligned. They were both good friends of Sir Oswald Mosley and Lord Londonderry. But even though Hereward had retired, very little had changed for Sawyer; anyone who imagined the old man's absence would harm the younger man's prospects had been wide of the mark. Sawyer was thriving and set for great things. Perhaps a safe seat in the Commons and, if his pal Mosley continued on his upward trajectory, possibly a Cabinet post, and maybe eventually the mastership of the college itself. No hint of doubt or scandal ever threatened the charmed life of Duncan Sawyer.

'Will you be joining us at High Table?' Sawyer asked.

'No, not this evening.'

'And yet you are required to do so three times a week. Once would be a start.'

'Well, there we are.'

Wilde was well aware that some of the other fellows were put out that he avoided dining in Hall. '*Not clubbable*,' was one phrase he had overheard. '*Not quite one of us.*' Or the more straightforward '*bloody Yank.*' He was indifferent.

Sawyer put down his glass and took a cigarette from his case. He didn't bother to offer it to Wilde.

'Do you know Peter Slievedonard, Wilde?'

'Lord Slievedonard? I know of him. I read the papers. But we haven't met.'

'Well, you'll be aware that he is exceedingly wealthy. Did you also know that he has a home not far from Cambridge?'

'I imagine he has homes all over the world.'

'Indeed. Indeed. One in Berkshire, a villa on the Riviera, a place in Knightsbridge and an estate in the Hamptons. Oh, and an estate near Bayreuth, I believe. The point is, he has strong connections with the college and wishes to endow us with a generous benefaction, in the form of a scholarship. To be precise, a history scholarship, which is where you come in. In addition, there will be a handsome sum set aside for us to spend as we choose. It is a most wonderful offer, I'm sure you'll agree.'

'You're not a fool, Sawyer. The man's a Nazi – or at the very least a Nazi sympathiser.'

Sawyer maintained his smile. He was perhaps a shade under six feet, with a pugilist's powerful physique. A middleweight, Wilde reckoned. It would be an interesting match. A love of boxing was, perhaps, the only thing they had in common.

'I rather feared you would say that, but hear me out. Peter's son was here studying history under the supervision of your predecessor. He had just finished Part I, with a first, when he enlisted. He died on the Somme. Lord Slievedonard wishes to endow a scholarship named in his honour.'

'That is admirable, Sawyer, but Slievedonard's politics do not sit well with the traditions of this great institution. The college would be permanently tainted by such an association. Do your own political leanings blind you to such considerations?'

Sawyer sighed and ran a large hand across his elegantly curling hair. 'You are being tiresome, Wilde. The British Union of Fascists, which Slievedonard supports as do I, is a perfectly legitimate political party. It's not as if he's a damned Commie like Horace Dill and his chums. This is not about politics, but the good of the college, a fine opportunity for scholars, both now and in the years to come. We cannot allow personal prejudices to get the better of us to the detriment of the college. Such opportunities are few and far between.'

'Good evening to you, Sawyer.'

Sawyer's mask of politeness slipped. 'We don't need your permission for this, you know, Wilde. It's simply that the bursar and the master were anxious that there be a consensus among the fellows. As a history don, they were particularly keen to secure your support.'

'Well, they and you don't have it.'

'As you wish. But you *will* be overruled, Wilde. You will be the anvil to my hammer.'

'Oh, for pity's sake, don't quote bloody Goethe at me.'

'You're a bad lot, Wilde.' Sawyer gave full reign to his vitriol. 'Remind me – what exactly did you do in the war? Run back to America and hide? And don't go telling me it's because you're American, because I know damned well your mother is Irish and I know, too, that you were at school here. What happened to those boys you were at school with?'

The room was almost full. They had raised their voices. They were making a scene, the ultimate Combination Room transgression. On the far side of the room, fat Horace Dill was watching them with evident pleasure. He grinned broadly at Wilde, gave him an exaggerated wink through his thick bottled spectacles and blew out a cloud of smoke. So Wilde had one friend to stand against Sawyer. The question was: did he really want or need the allegiance of a man like Horace Dill?

Fifty miles away, in another fine old room, three men were meeting over a decanter of brandy. They were in the long room of one of London's premier gentlemen's clubs. A fire blazed in the wide hearth, but they had chosen to seat themselves in the quietest corner, by one of the tall, curtained windows looking out over Pall Mall. They were important men in the life of the nation, a general attached to the War Office, a landowner with thirty thousand acres in the West Country and a senior civil servant in the Foreign Office. None of them was ambitious for himself. None of them had need of more money or property.

Their families had been close for generations and they had known and liked each other since early childhood. They had been at prep school together, then Eton – same house – and Cambridge, where they had all won blues and Firsts. All had served in Flanders in the same regiment. It was only after the war that their paths had diverged into different careers. And yet they met often, both in London and at shoots and meets. When one was invited to a house party, the others tended to be there, too.

Their trust in each other was absolute; their views on Great Britain and its place in the world almost identical, though none of them considered themselves British exactly. They were English. Old English. And their loyalty was simple and inviolable. First came King, then country, then each other.

It was the first of these loyalties that had brought them together this evening: the threat to the King from the prime minister and those in the Cabinet who were trying to force him to abdicate if he refused to give up Mrs Wallis Simpson, the love of his life.

'So we are agreed?' the landowner said. 'I call Cambridge?'

The Foreign Office man nodded slowly. 'Baldwin is implacable. He's not even lukewarm to the idea of a morganatic marriage and believes the King must go. I was with him yesterday and he really means to proceed with this madness, which means we have no option. We have all sworn an oath of allegiance to Edward and an oath is an oath. But time is not on our side.'

'This morganatic idea?' the general said. 'Surely it would be acceptable if she became Duchess of Cornwall but not queen.'

'Baldwin says he's consulting the Dominions on the matter, but it'll be a fix.'

The landowner shook his head. 'Our friends in Munich are certain that Baldwin is about to force an abdication. It's a bloody palace coup! Baldwin should be shot for treason. We must protect the King. He is our only hope for peace.' He paused, then, 'Sophie called. She has been talking to Munich and is at our disposal.'

'And Munich will play its part?' the general asked, stroking his moustache. 'Because Nordsee can't do this alone. And we three cannot be implicated.'

'The Germans already have it under way. Edward is their best hope of avoiding war. They want to work with us, not against us. Edward is like-minded, of course, as is von Ribbentrop and, indeed, the Führer himself. All we have to do is ensure Nordsee is in place, and wait. The Reds will be blamed, of course.'

'Germany should have talked to us first.'

'Things don't work that way in Berlin and Munich these days.'

'I'll call Cambridge,' the landowner repeated. 'I'll keep in touch with Sophie.'

'Of course.'

The general raised his forefinger to summon the steward. 'I think we need more brandy,' he said.

CHAPTER 4

The butler entered the Combination Room and announced that dinner was served, and the fellows began their slow, shuffling progress in the short step to the less intimate grandeur of the Hall and High Table. Outside, the bell was clanging, and the students made their way from their rooms and studies and the library, across the chilly court to the scarcely warmer hall, where they found their tables and waited for Grace to be said.

Tom Wilde walked against the tide. He took a deep breath. God, he needed a proper drink. He loved this place; but in many ways he loathed it, too. Ranged down the south side of the new court, the library with its exquisite Gothic tracery was one of the finest in Cambridge, a repository for books and papers going back to medieval times. But the other facilities left much to be desired, particularly the bathroom amenities. The miserable trudge of undergraduates in their pyjamas crossing the courts in quest of a bath seemed to dwindle to almost nothing in the winter months.

The lack of bathrooms was one of the reasons he lived out of college; but he also had an aversion to the school-like claustrophobia of the place. Some fellows never wanted to leave its limited confines, but a college was a society of men, and Wilde had never been entirely certain that he wished to belong to such a society.

The fog outside in the new court was somewhat fresher than the fug of the Combination Room. No sign of Christmas snow yet and not much in the way of cheer. At the main gate, the broad-shouldered head porter, Scobie, tipped his black top hat, then rubbed his bristling moustache and said there was no chance of ice on the Fens, so no skating for the undergraduates before they went down.

'Nothing like a game of ice hockey to get the blood pumping, Scobie.'

'I can imagine, sir. Never tried it myself.'

'Well, good night.' Wilde removed his square and shoved it under his arm, then walked on, his hands in his pockets.

It was the first day of December. The streets were alive with people on foot and, seemingly, even more on bicycles. Men in coats and hats, making their way home from offices and factories or college rooms and laboratories. Many were smoking, their mouths and fingers busy with pipes and cigarettes, puffing smoke into the grey swirl of fog and smoke from ten thousand chimneys. A town full of smoke, soot blackening the ancient stones.

There was an air of the university winding down for the festive season. Michaelmas term was almost done. Soon the undergraduates would leave their rooms, their gowns and their bicycles and take the train home from the long platform, scattering to the far corners of the realm, leaving the town to those who lived and worked here and the colonial students whose people were too far away to be joined for the holidays. Once again Cambridge would revert to what it had always been: a modest English market town that just happened to have a collection of some of the country's most magnificent buildings and the world's greatest brains.

Town and gown. The host and worm intertwined, and yet the worm grown more magnificent than the host. Living side by side yet separately, a symbiotic relationship. The town did not need the university to survive, for it had prospered alone before the scholars arrived seven hundred years earlier and would do so again if the scholars left. And nor did the university need this particular town. Food and servants could be got anywhere.

But there was something about Cambridge at Christmas, thought Wilde as he pressed on through the crowds. The spires of King's College Chapel against a winter sky, the Backs sharp with frost, the cheerful busyness of a town celebrating on its own account. He'd spend the day with his neighbour, Lydia Morris, and the waifs and strays who congregated at her house on high days and holidays, he decided. He smiled to himself. Which did she think he was? Waif or stray?

At times he wasn't quite sure why he stayed in England. It had been made clear to him that he would be welcomed at Harvard. Or that he could leave academia altogether and join the state department or the diplomatic service like his oldest friend, Jim Vanderberg. Perhaps it was his subject that kept him here, close to the places Sir Francis Walsingham and Sir Robert Cecil knew so well. His mother, now widowed, lived in Boston, preferring the ease of the New World to the privations of the old one. He hadn't seen her in two years and he knew she missed him as much as he missed her. But perhaps he was here in England because America brought back too many memories. The love of his life lost, a child dead at birth.

He stopped at the Bull Hotel, downed a large Scotch and felt a lot better for it. The lounge bar was filling up nicely. It reeked of beer and smoke. Local businessmen argued over the price of corn; college dons discussed the world, the universe and the quality of hall dinners and claret. Most of all, they talked of delicious scandals usually involving ambition or sex or both. It was a masculine place, as were the colleges themselves, all save Girton and Newnham. It didn't occur to these men that their women might like a drink at the end of the day and if they did, well, they could always raid the bottle hidden in the dresser for a sip of sherry.

Wilde stood alone, at the end of the bar, his shoulder turned away from the next man, who wore a cheap suit and looked like a clerk. When he ordered another drink, the barman tried to engage him in conversation about the Crystal Palace fire but Wilde simply smiled vaguely as people do when they have no wish to be rude, but do not want to engage. The clerk inadvertently saved him by calling for a pint of stout. Wilde slid his empty tumbler across the bar and made his escape, slipping back out into the fog. He wanted nothing more than to go home, get away from the crowds, fix himself a ham omelette and settle down with a book and Bessie Smith. *A pigfoot and a bottle of beer*. Heaven on earth. He enjoyed his own company and when he wanted conversational sparring, why, there was Lydia next door to stretch his wit.

Wilde was passing her gate when he spotted her new lodger walking up the path towards him, hands shoved deep in his pockets, flat cap perched on his brow. 'Good evening, Mr Braithwaite,' he said with a cursory nod, scarcely breaking his stride

'Hang on a minute.'

Wilde stopped. 'Yes?'

'Just saying hello, Mr Wilde. Passing the time of day with a neighbour.'

'Good, well, hello then, Mr Braithwaite. Feeling fit and strong for the next part of your journey, I hope?'

'Getting there, Mr Wilde. Getting there.'

Leslie Braithwaite was chewing tobacco. A stream of thin, brown fluid dribbled from the corner of his thin, pinched lips. He was a short man, barely five feet tall, with bowed legs, a clear case of childhood malnourishment and rickets if ever Wilde had seen one. How far removed from the healthy, well-fed figures of Maxwell and Felsted.

His forehead and nose were scarred by blue lines beneath his flat cap: the unmistakable marks of the collier. He had arrived a week ago, throwing himself on Lydia's charity. 'I've come from Yorkshire, miss, walking to the Kent pits. I'm told there's jobs to be had. Someone gave me your name and address, said you'd stand a stranger a meal, perhaps a bed for the night. Cold at the roadside, miss.'

Lydia had responded in the way she always did to those in need and offered him a room, a bath and food. The bath had been particularly welcome; his clothes had been rank and ragged and she had washed those, too, handing him some new socks and a shirt from a charity bag that she kept for such eventualities. Since then, however, he had shown no sign of moving on.

'What do you think of the news, then, Mr Wilde?'

'The Crystal Palace fire? I have no opinion on it, but I'm sure you'll tell me who started it. Everyone else has this evening.' Wilde began to move away towards his own gate but Braithwaite grasped his arm.

'Not the fire, the King of England and his fancy piece.' Braithwaite's little eyes glittered.

'Now you've lost me.' In truth Wilde knew all about the King and Mrs Simpson. He had been apprised of the full facts by colleagues returning from foreign lecture tours and by his mother in her letters. It seemed all the world's newspapers were full of the great romance. All save the British papers. Wilde had heard, too, from the senior tutor that there were machinations in Whitehall; that the prime minister, Stanley Baldwin, had vowed to let the government fall rather than allow Edward to marry Wallis. There was talk, too, of Churchill forming a King's Party so that he could step into the breach and support Edward. To date, however, Wilde had seen not a word in the London press. The British, it seemed, were the only people in the world not allowed to know what their King and government were up to.

'Mate of mine showed me an American newspaper he got sent, Mr Wilde. Edward Windsor's got his grubby fingers in the drawers of a slattern named Simpson.'

Wilde laughed.

Braithwaite grinned, too, then snorted with undisguised scorn. 'Royal bloody family. They're all the same. Leeches feeding off the sweat and blood of the poor. Lenin had the right idea. Line them all up against a wall and let rip with a Vickers.'

'Do I take it you have communist sympathies, Mr Braithwaite?'

'Card-carrying member. Same as anyone with half a brain.'

'Well, you won't be alone in this town. Now if you'll excuse me, I must get home. Essays to mark, a lecture to prepare.' *Novels to read, music to be listened to*. In truth, he was hungry and tired and wanted time to himself.

'Your problem, Mr Wilde, is that you don't know what it's like for the working man. I never used an indoor lav until last week when I came into this house. You haven't seen starving, freezing children scrabbling for coal on the slag heap. Go up to the Yorkshire pits one day, see what it's really like. I tell you this, you'd join the party, too.'

'I shall make a note of your advice.'

'Don't suppose you could lend us a couple of bob for a drink, could you?'

Wilde laughed again, but not so good-humouredly. He took out a shilling. 'That's your lot, I'm afraid.'

Outside the cinema on Market Hill, Lydia Morris shivered in her duffle coat as the temperature fell. The film was about to start and Nancy hadn't arrived. Why could she never be on time?

Not that Lydia cared a great deal whether she saw the film or not. It was *Things to Come*, a nightmarish vision of a second great war and poison bombs dropped from the air onto cities. Not the cheeriest subjects for a dreary December evening. It was Nancy who had demanded they see it. She had said she wanted to see Lydia; she had said she wanted to talk about things, about a call she'd had from their mutual friend Margot, of all people. She was troubled, and, thought Lydia, she had sounded a little afraid.

'Your boyfriend not turned up, miss?' the commissionaire said.

'What makes you think I'm waiting for a boyfriend?' She smiled at the chippy little man in his ridiculous uniform with its Ruritanian epaulettes and buttons.

He eyed her up and down, trying to appraise her figure, hidden beneath her unflattering coat. 'You're a good-looking girl. Bound to have a suitor.'

She held up the tickets. 'Can I get my money back on these?'

'Non-refundable, I'm afraid, miss.'

A shilling down the drain. 'What a surprise.'

'Tell you what, you go in and if your friend comes along, I'll bring him in to you. How does that sound?'

'No, thank you. I'll just wait out here a little longer.'

'Very well, miss.'

She shuffled away and pulled her knitted hat down over her ears. Beneath the old duffle coat, she wore thick woollen stockings and a long paisley skirt, which she hated. Her neighbour Tom Wilde had once told her she dressed to avoid attention while other women rather liked to attract it. She had retorted that he should stop talking in stereotypes and look to his own unkempt appearance. 'It wasn't meant as a criticism,' he had said, laughing. 'I *like* your tattered, somewhat eccentric appearance. You look Bohemian. Just the way a poet should be.'

'You're piling insult upon insult, do you realise that? You're telling me I'm a poet cliché.'

'Well, let's put it this way then. You're the only woman I know who never carries a handbag.'

That had made her laugh. 'You know just how to win a girl's heart!'

'You flatter yourself, Miss Morris.'

To avoid the commissionaire's gaze, she pretended to study the new shoes in the window of Freeman Hardy Willis next door to the cinema. Nancy must be slumped in a doped-up stupor somewhere. That stuff was going to do her no good. She seemed to need it more and more. So much for the career in newspapers she claimed she was looking for.

Nancy had never been reliable, but her behaviour had become even more erratic lately. Lydia was beginning to wonder whether her friend might be on the verge of a breakdown. She said the heroin calmed her down, made her rows with her father more bearable, but it wasn't convincing. Berlin in August seemed to have been a tipping point. Something had happened there the day she vanished, but she wouldn't say what.

Across the road there was a telephone box but she couldn't for the life of her recall the number of Nancy's newly installed telephone. Nothing to do but wait. After another ten minutes, Lydia decided she could wait no longer. 'Here.' She handed the tickets to the commissionaire. 'Give them to someone you like the look of. An early Christmas present.'

Her breath blew vapour trails into the fog as she hurried along Bridge Street and over Magdalene Bridge. Below her, the river was slow and ominous, the punts-for-hire all put away for winter.

Ahead of her, the Pikeling was horribly raucous for a Tuesday evening and she gave the pub a wide berth. She had been pawed too often by stragglers lurching out into the street. Even her roughest clothes didn't seem to put them off. Passing Magdalene College, she turned right into Chesterton Road and walked along the river, the town's artery, bringer of produce from the fertile Fens on sedate, heavily laden barges. This, too, was where the pleasure boats plied their trade in summer, steaming up and down river with laughing, singing bands of men and women on works outings from the Pye factory.

Here were gentle banks of grass leading down to the water's muddy edge, in the shade of willows. It was all deserted now, but in the summer months young men and boys dozed here, keeping half an eye on the procession of punts. Lydia had known many such days, and had more than one reason to remember them. She shook the memories away; this was winter and all was forlorn and quiet and cold and the smell that rose from the river was very different from the warm, reedy aroma of summer.

The walk was no more than twenty minutes, but it felt like over an hour before she arrived at Nancy's rented house. It was at the end of a small Victorian terrace in the suburb of Chesterton. Hardly the sort of place a girl like Nancy, brought up in a country manor and a college master's lodge, was used to, but nice enough.

The curtains were open and the lights were on, so Lydia knocked at the door and waited. There was no reply. She tried the door handle, but it was locked. She peered in through the bay window; books and newspapers piled up on the bare floorboards, but no sign of Nancy. Suddenly Lydia was angry: couldn't she have rung to cancel the film? She had her own telephone, for heaven's sake.

She called through the letterbox. Nothing.

The stout, elderly woman who lived next door came out and stood on her step, arms folded across her bosom. 'I think you're wasting your time, love. I haven't seen hide nor hair of Miss Hereward all day,' she said.

'We were supposed to be going to the cinema. I don't suppose she leaves a key with you, does she, Mrs—'

'Bromley. And yes, we have a key. The landlord asks us to keep it.'

'I thought she might be ill in bed. Perhaps a fever. She might need a doctor.'

'Fever? Is that what they call it these days? You know she has men in there? The noises I hear . . .' She pursed respectable lips. 'I'll get it for you.'

Mrs Bromley bustled off and came back with a key. 'Here you are, love. You go in. I don't like to intrude.'

Lydia didn't want to go in alone. 'I'm sure Nancy will understand if you'd like to come with me.'

The woman glanced in through the bay window and grimaced with distaste. 'No, I'll wait out here if it's all the same to you. Wouldn't feel right.'

Lydia shrugged. She put the key in the lock and turned it. Her heart was pounding. She turned to Mrs Bromley but the woman wouldn't meet her eyes.

'Mr Bromley said he heard a noise early this morning while I was out at Woolworths.'

'Noise, what sort of noise?'

'A *loud* noise. Like someone crying out.'

The door opened and Lydia stepped inside. She took off her hat and stuffed it in her coat pocket. 'Nancy,' she called. Nothing. The sitting room smelt of dust and damp. In the little kitchen she spotted a full cup of tea and put her hand to it. The cup was cold. There was a bottle of fresh milk, which showed that someone had, at least, been here recently. She called again, her voice quieter now and beseeching. 'Is anyone there?'

She walked up the bare staircase. The boards creaked and echoed beneath her feet. All the lights were on up here, too, naked bulbs with no shades. On the right was the bathroom. Directly ahead of her was the lavatory, its door open, the chain hanging from the cistern like the rope on a gibbet.

On the left was the only other room. The door was open. Relief washed over her. Nancy was lying on her side facing her, eyes closed, fast asleep. But hope dissolved as she realised there was no sound of breathing, no movement. And then there was the faint unwholesome whiff of vomit, and two flies began to buzz.

Nancy was in a powder-blue silk slip, nothing more. Her dark hair, cut shorter since Lydia had last seen her, fell across her slender throat. Her left hand was trapped beneath her body; her right hand was bent back, fingers splayed, as though she were about to catch a ball. Lydia took hold of the wrist. The skin was cold and clammy. There was no pulse. Lydia put her hands to her friend's dead face but there was no one there.

Nancy was lying on rumpled sheets and blankets. The sheets were good white linen, but stained. Vomit, blood, semen? A glint caught Lydia's eye. Nancy's silver syringe. She looked again at Nancy's clawed hand, her eyes following the line of the muscles and dried blood down along her arm to the place where needle holes clustered like blots on a pad.

She had warned her often enough. Everyone had. She had wanted to change the world, to slough off the Victorian gloom of England, to break down borders and barriers. She had burned too bright and it had killed her. The bile rose in Lydia's throat and she turned away.

CHAPTER 5

The telephone was ringing in the hall. Wilde tried to ignore it. On the gramophone, Bessie Smith was singing, her voice as sweet as raw molasses. The gas fire was throwing out an oppressive heat that scorched his knees. Reluctantly, he rose from his armchair, put down his novel, turned off the fire, made his way to the hall and picked up the telephone.

'Hello.'

'Is that Professor Wilde?'

'Yes, it is. Who's calling?'

'Sergeant O'Brien, Cambridge police.'

'Has something happened?'

'Would you mind coming down to the station on St Andrew's Street, sir? We're right by the fire station, if you know it.'

'What's this all about?'

'It would be easier to explain when you arrive. Miss Lydia Morris has asked for you. She's not hurt and nor is she in any trouble but we think it would be best if she had a friend with her.'

As he hurried down Jesus Lane, Wilde couldn't get the Bessie Smith song out of his head. It had been sounding all evening and he hadn't been able to concentrate on his novel. Whenever he read Waugh, he found himself thinking how very odd the English were. Particularly the English upper classes. Mr Beaver, Lady Cockpurse, Lady Chasm . . . Who were these people? What did they represent?

He had his hands stuffed in his coat pockets. Not cold enough for snow or skating perhaps, but winter – *real* winter – couldn't be far off. Now he was in St Andrew's Street. Through the smoke-scented fog, the hazy blue light over the police station was an icy harbinger.

Wilde had never liked this building. Soot-blackened, monolithic and intimidating, it was four storeys high, broad-fronted and just as deep. He entered through an arched double doorway, carved in thick oak with discs and panels that seemed designed to suggest the iron bolts and straps on a cell door. *Enter at your peril.* Even the windows, with their heavy lead latticework, spoke of prison bars.

What on earth had Lydia got herself into?

She was standing by the front desk, wrapped deep into her capacious duffle coat. Her eyes were haunted and her cheeks were drawn, and smudged with tears. Wilde couldn't imagine Lydia weeping. Or calling on him for assistance, for that matter.

'What's happened, Lydia?' He spoke gently.

'The bloody sergeant insisted on calling my husband. Well, as you know, I haven't got a sodding husband, and you were the closest thing to a friend I could think of. Nancy's dead. I found her body.'

Back home, she told him she couldn't be alone. Not tonight.

'I thought your coalminer friend Braithwaite was still here.'

She threw him a contemptuous look.

'I'll sleep on your sofa then.'

'Would you? I know it's a lot to ask. Mr Braithwaite locks himself away in his room.'

Wilde nodded. When the miner first arrived, she had defended him to Wilde. 'He's not so bad, you know.' He had been doubtful. 'Perhaps not, Lydia, but don't be too trusting. One day one of your good deeds might bite you.'

She brought out the whisky bottle and they sat together in the kitchen, facing each other across the table, a glass each. 'The police won't have it that it's anything but an accidental overdose or suicide,' she said, voice still shaky.

She was repeating herself. They had been through all this on the way back from the station. And from what she said, it seemed the police had reached the obvious conclusion. A known addict is found dead in her own bed, her syringe at her side. The front door locked. Case closed. The only remaining question would be decided by the coroner: accident or suicide?

'I think she was killed.' Lydia continued.

'On what evidence?'

'What she said.'

'Which was?'

Lydia sighed. 'She telephoned me, said she wanted to go to the cinema. Said she wanted to see me so we could talk.'

'Is that it?'

She shook her head. 'No. I can remember the exact words. She said, "I think I've upset someone." I asked her who and all she said was, "I'll tell you about it." I told her I didn't know what she was talking about, *who* she was talking about. Her voice was fading, Tom. All she said was, "Later." But there wasn't any later.' Lydia sniffed. Wilde passed over his handkerchief and she blew hard.

'Did you tell the police about the call?'

'Of course.'

'What do you think was worrying her? You knew her better than anyone, Lydia – you must have had some idea about her concerns.'

'Her political friends, I suppose.' She hesitated. 'Oh God, I might as well tell you what I think, but you'll probably decide I'm unhinged.'

'Go on.'

'Well, you know we went to Berlin together in August? She was pretty worried that the German authorities might get wind of her politics before she even got there and bar her at the border. They didn't, but the thing is, I'm pretty sure she did some secret work for the party while she was there.'

'The communists?'

'Yes.'

'Tell me more.'

'She was being awfully odd the whole trip. But it came to a bit of a head when we went into the centre of town to go shopping together. After a while she said she wanted to go off and explore on her own. We agreed to meet at a café half an hour later, but she was gone a lot longer than that, and when she eventually turned up she was a nervous wreck, but rather excited, too, as though she had done something clever. And when I asked her where she'd been, she wouldn't say.'

'Have you told the police this?'

'Yes. Well, I tried to, but they weren't very receptive. They seemed to think I was imagining things. In fact, I saw them smirking at each other when they thought I wasn't looking.'

'Well, I'm not laughing, Lydia. But your Berlin trip was months ago.'

She lowered her eyes, then held her head in her hands, looking down into the amber depths of her whisky. 'I don't know,' she said, her voice barely audible. 'The police surgeon has already said he has no reason to believe Nancy died of anything but an overdose, and the other officers took no notice of Mr Bromley next door when he said he'd heard some sort of cry. They said it could have been anything . . .' She trailed off miserably. 'And I suppose they're right about that.'

Wilde knew Nancy from college, but not well. They had passed the time of day once or twice and he was aware of her reputation as Hereward's wayward daughter, but the former master was not a man with whom Wilde had ever seen eye to eye, and he had rarely been invited to the master's lodge. There had been fleeting meetings at Lydia's house, and his instinct had been to like Nancy and be amused by her, but she lacked Lydia's warmth.

'When did she start using heroin?' he asked.

'It began about a year ago, not long after the scandal broke. She was full of it at first, urged me to try it. Said it was better than making love, better than alcohol. I wouldn't touch it.'

'Where did she get it?'

'I don't know, Tom. I really don't know. Nancy was never afraid to go where I wouldn't like to tread. The Pikeling, perhaps? They say you can get anything there if you have the money.' Lydia sighed heavily, her eyelids drooping. 'Oh God, I think I'm done for.'

'Finish your drink. Let's talk more in the morning. It will make more sense then. You need sleep, Lydia. Go to bed.'

She got up from the table and turned her exhausted face to him. 'She said something else, too, Tom. She said she'd had a call from Margot.'

'Do I know Margot?'

'No. She was at Girton with us. We did everything together in those days. But it's a strange thing. No one's heard from her in eighteen months. She got married in rather a hurry and then she ran off – she was always a bit wild – but none of us heard from her after that and we rather thought she must be lying low somewhere. But I would have thought Nancy would have been the last person she wanted to talk to because they fell out badly.' Lydia paused, aware she was rambling.

'This isn't meaning much to me, I'm afraid.'

'No matter. It's not important. I'll tell you about it some other time, perhaps. Oh God, I'm so tired, but I don't think I can sleep.'

She went off to fetch him blankets for the sofa, then went to her room. A little later, she returned and climbed onto the sofa beside him, fully clothed save for her shoes, clinging to his back without a word. She was still there when he woke in the morning.

WEDNESDAY DECEMBER 2, 1936

CHAPTER 6

They slept fitfully and the night left them drained. Dawn came so late in winter. Wilde lay with his eyes open.

'I hardly slept,' Lydia said. 'I wish I hadn't slept at all.'

'You have to sleep.'

'I had a dream, Tom. I was trying to fly, out of a maelstrom, but it was pulling me down. It wasn't water, it was a huge, jagged wound, full of swirling, silvery-red blood. I woke and shook you; you just grunted and tried to move away.'

'It doesn't take much to interpret that dream, Lydia. Even Herr Freud wouldn't put that one down to your parents.'

They ate breakfast together in her kitchen.

Lydia pushed away her toast, barely nibbled. 'Pour me another coffee, Tom.' She paused to gather her strength. 'I'd like to go back to the house today to see how the police are getting on. Do you think you could come with me? Maybe,' she added bitterly, 'you could persuade them to take me seriously. They might listen to a man.'

Wilde smiled. 'They might,' he said. He thought for a moment. 'Can you tell me how she was lying when you found her?'

'Oh God, did I not tell you? She was lying on the bed, her head on the pillow, to one side. Her left hand was trapped beneath her, her right fingers were stretched out like talons, clutching at something. And her stupid silver syringe. She thought it was so bloody special. God knows where she got the thing. Oh, Tom, it was all so cold and sordid. I wanted to be sick. Her face was blank. No fear, no serenity. Nothing. She just wasn't *there*.'

'I understand.'

'Do you?' She looked at him uncertainly, then corrected herself. Tom Wilde had suffered more than his share of tragedy. 'Sorry. Of course you do.'

'Tell me about her. I didn't know her well.' He had no wish to hark back to the pain of his own past.

'She was the brightest of us, the best. We all wanted to change the world and make it a better place, but she was really trying to do something about it. That's why she wanted to get into newspapers – so she could write about what she saw. She was planning to go to Abyssinia, to Spain, to China. She wanted to tell the truth. Did you read that article she wrote on the new Germany?'

He nodded. It had been slightly naive, he thought. Full of sound and fury, but lacking sophistication in its depiction of the harsh reality of German daily life hidden behind the glittering Olympic facade. Not quite there for the big newspapers, and so it had ended up in a small, left-wing publication with a circulation that numbered in the hundreds rather than the millions she wished to reach.

The kitchen door opened and Leslie Braithwaite appeared. 'Morning.' He caught sight of Wilde. 'Fancy you being here, Mr Wilde.' He grinned.

Lydia tried to smile, but it was unconvincing. 'Good morning, Mr Braithwaite.'

'I heard noises in the night. Like the pattering of little feet. Wonder what that could be? You got mice, Miss Morris?'

They ignored him and he approached the kitchen table and looked at the toast rack. 'Any of that for me?' Without waiting for a reply, he took a slice and bit into it. 'Be a good girl, make us a cuppa.'

'The toast *wasn't* for you,' snapped Lydia. 'And if you want a cup of tea, you can make a pot yourself.'

He took another bite. 'Coffee'll do.'

'When are you leaving, Mr Braithwaite?'

Wilde was surprised by her sharpness. However much her patience was tried, it was unlike Lydia to show it. Sometimes it seemed her sense of charity and social justice knew no bounds. Not today.

'Thought I'd go in a day or two. Bit too chilly for walking this morning.'

'I'll buy you a train ticket to East Kent,' Lydia said tersely. 'That will see you on your way. Think of it as an early Christmas present.'

'Very generous of you, miss. But I've one or two things to do before I go.'

'Such as?'

'This and that. Meet some comrades maybe. There's NUWM organising to be done.' Braithwaite touched his cap. 'Power to the workers, eh?
Thanks again but I'll not take you up on the offer. I'm going down the
caff. If you could loan us a tanner I'll be able to have some bread and
dripping, too.'

At college, Wilde sought out Bobby. 'Please don't take this the wrong
way, Bobby, but where would someone get hold of dope in this town?'

Bobby raised an eyebrow. 'Dope, professor? Not sure I know what you
mean, sir.'

'Heroin. Diamorphine. Not for me, I hasten to add – think of it as a
theoretical question.'

'Ah well, yes, tricky one that.' Bobby bared his toothless mouth and
rubbed his chin. 'The chemist would be the place, I imagine. Or the
doctor's.'

'What if it was illegal? Would a man be able to buy the stuff in a bar,
maybe? How about the Pikeling?'

Bobby shook his head and grinned. 'Get you a good second-hand
wireless there, or some cheap whisky. Even French letters if you like – but
never heard of demand for dope as you call it.'

'OK, thanks, Bobby.'

Wilde sat astride the Rudge Special, opened the fuel tap, tickled the
carburettor, closed the choke and applied the lever to retard ignition,
then depressed the kickstart to feel for decompression. Satisfied, he
released the decompressor and kicked hard. The motorbike's 500cc
engine spluttered then roared into life. Even on a December day she
didn't let him down, the beauty. He rode home and found Lydia ready
in her coat at the gate, waiting for him.

'Hop on,' he said.

'Is it safe?' she demanded as she clambered aboard the pillion seat.

'With me steering, what do you think?'

'I'll risk it.'

They rode through Cambridge towards the suburb of Chesterton. It
was almost midday. Outside Nancy's house, Wilde pulled into the kerb

just behind a black Rolls Royce, attended by a chauffeur in peaked cap and livery of grey, with gold braid. It was all so out of place in this modest road, with its rows of small bay-windowed houses. The front door to Nancy's house was ajar and Lydia knocked. When there was no answer, she pushed the door open and peered into the front hall. Through the doorway on the left, she saw a man in his fifties, clean-shaven with thinning grey hair, sitting in an armchair next to the window. He was gazing at a silver-framed photograph he held in his hands. He did not look up at Lydia's approach.

'Sir Norman?'

He raised his eyes from the picture but didn't seem to recognise Lydia, although he knew her well.

'I found her, sir.'

He nodded slowly. 'I heard.'

'You know Professor Wilde, of course.'

Hereward's eyes shifted vaguely in Wilde's direction, but he didn't acknowledge him. Instead, he turned the picture round so that it faced the two newcomers. It showed a strong, slim, dark-haired girl in running shorts, vest and spikes, standing on a hurdles track. She was holding up a silver trophy and smiling triumphantly. 'This is my favourite picture. She was healthy then. In mind and body.'

Tears were streaming down the man's face but he didn't seem to notice or care. He was incongruous in this small room, an Edwardian gentleman scholar in a Norfolk jacket sitting in a modest artisan's dwelling. He held the photograph, taken years earlier at a school sports day, for them to see for a full minute, then turned it back so that he could gaze at his daughter again. He kissed the picture and then put it on the arm of the chair, face down.

Lydia went over and knelt in front of him on the worn boards and clasped his hands. 'I'm so sorry, Sir Norman. She meant a great deal to me. I can hardly imagine what you are going through.'

He seemed to be talking to himself. 'The thing is, everything was all right when she was away at school. It all went wrong when she came up to Girton.' With an effort he looked down at Lydia's upturned face. 'Well, you saw it, Lydia. You saw what happened, how it all began to fall apart.'

Wilde had heard about Girton from Lydia. It was supposed to be as closely run as a prison ship. Girton women were meant to be as modest as nuns and as clever as Einstein. But that wasn't how it had been for Nancy, Lydia and their friend Margot Langley. They certainly had brains to spare – indeed Wilde suspected they were far more intelligent than many of the male undergraduates who were at university simply because they had been to the right schools – but they were a long way from taking holy orders. And the whole thing – last year's scandal – had been further complicated by Nancy's father's position as master of a great Cambridge college.

'We'd had another row,' Sir Norman said. 'Did she tell you that? She told me she hated me and everything I stood for. I sent her a note the day before yesterday begging her to come for Christmas, but I knew she wouldn't. Those people she ran with. That damned stuff she stuck in her arm. I wanted her to get help.'

Lydia thought she had probably heard chapter and verse about the problems between father and daughter. It wasn't just the heroin. It was the politics. Sir Norman was fervent in his hatred of Bolshevism; Nancy was a Marxist through and through.

Hereward turned to Wilde, as if registering his presence for the first time. 'Why are you here?' Hereward had been master of the college when Wilde first arrived. Their relationship had never been warm, but Wilde's academic rigour, his research credentials and his well-received book on Sir Francis Walsingham's role in the downfall of Mary Stuart had overridden other concerns.

'I live next door to Lydia.'

'Ah, yes. Never did care for the college life, did you? I'm surprised you've stayed on as you dislike our traditions so much.'

It wasn't true. Wilde didn't dislike their traditions; he just wished they'd enter the twentieth century: install proper bathing facilities on every staircase, showers even, make the place less monastic. 'Lydia has her doubts about your daughter's death,' he said, but even as the words emerged from his mouth, he wished they hadn't. Why add to the man's misery?

'Of course she has doubts!' The words exploded from Hereward's mouth. 'However far she had fallen, Nancy would never kill herself. Her bloody Bolshie chums did this. They're monsters.'

'What have the police said to you?'

'They won't listen. I've had a word with the coroner, too, and he's made up his mind. Won't even call a jury. He's having a quick inquest tomorrow, and the verdict will be accidental death. Then she'll be released for burial. It's all rot. This bears the hallmarks of the Reds.'

Wilde looked from Hereward to Lydia and back. Sir Norman's suspicions were born of simple prejudice: Lydia was haunted by Nancy's own fears. The same doubts, but different reasons, and neither had any solid evidence to offer the police. As everyone of note in Cambridge would testify, Nancy was a heroin addict; the case was going nowhere. Heroin addicts had a tendency to die young.

'Why would the communists want to kill her?' Wilde asked.

Sir Norman looked incredulous. 'Are you asking me why the Bolsheviks kill people?'

'No. I am asking why they would want to kill your daughter.'

'And I can't think you're that naive or ignorant, Wilde. It's like asking why cats kill mice. Killing is what Stalin's lot do. It's the nature of the beast.'

Wilde said nothing. He wished he hadn't spoken. It was unseemly to have raised voices in this room. Lydia looked bemused and flustered.

'They feed off each other,' Hereward continued, undeterred. 'In their own country – everywhere. They wade in their comrades' blood to clamber to the top. Even Nancy's great hero Trotsky is on their death list. They're all dirty little Jews, you know, all killing each other. They killed Nancy, too. That's what they do. They beat each other with their hammers and when they grow too tall, they cut them down with their sickles.'

Wilde bowed his head. He understood why any father might be filled with rage at the death of his daughter, but he had no wish to hear this. Murmuring his excuses, he left Lydia with the man and set off to look round the house.

First he tried the two downstairs windows, in the front room and the kitchen. The bay window was a sash and had been secured with a latch on the inside. The kitchen window was a metal-framed casement, which had also been shut tight from within. Neither showed any sign of a forced entry. He went upstairs to the bedroom. The corpse was long gone to the mortuary and the bedclothes had been bundled up and dumped on the thin mattress.

He examined the windows in the three upstairs rooms. There was a bay window in the bedroom, similar to the one directly beneath it, a frosted one in the small bathroom and a tiny one in the lavatory, again frosted. All were closed and showed no signs of having been tampered with.

Lydia had said that the front door was locked when she arrived and that all the windows had been closed. She also said that the police had told her that Nancy's key was found on a hook in the kitchen. So if all the windows were shut from the inside, then there could have been no one else involved in her death, unless the perpetrator had a key – either the one from the next-door neighbour, or a third one. It was easy to see why the police had no reason to suspect foul play.

The bathroom was modest and old. There was an iron bath that would certainly not have been big enough for Wilde without his legs bunched up at the knee, and a small basin on which sat a facecloth, a half-used tin of Gibbs dental cream and a worn toothbrush. On the wall, there was a little medicine cabinet, which he opened: a tin of lavender-scented Yardley talc, some Nivea skin cream, nail-varnish remover, shampoo powder and various other feminine products. The sad leftovers of a young life cut short. Whatever the devastating effects of her heroin habit, Nancy had tried to keep herself properly groomed.

As he made his way downstairs, he saw that Sir Norman was leaving. His head was down; a broken man. Through the front window, he saw the chauffeur touch his peaked cap, then open the back door of the Rolls Royce.

By the front door, next to the telephone, which was off the hook, two pairs of shoes were laid out on a copy of the *Cambridge Daily News*, as though ready for cleaning. Wilde picked them up, examined them, then put them back down. He replaced the telephone receiver.

'How long did she live here, Lydia?' he called through to the sitting room.

'She moved here in September not long after we came back from Berlin.' Lydia came out and perched herself on the bottom stair. She was holding the silver-framed picture of Nancy. 'Things were very strained with her father, as you know. She had to get away from him. I offered her a room – the one Braithwaite's in now – but she wouldn't take it.'

'Apart from you, who were her friends?' Wilde checked himself. 'More to the point – who were her enemies? Do you believe this was really something to do with her links to the communists?'

'I was perhaps her only real friend, unless you count her political acquaintances . . .' Lydia looked miserable. 'But sometimes even I needed a break from her. She could drive people away, you know, but I can't think of any specific enemies. I suppose she had political adversaries. She could be a bit fervent, a bit unforgiving. To the puritan, all things are impure, as the saying goes. Not that she was a puritan, of course, but the same holds true: she was an idealist. And everyone fell short of her rather rigid ideals of a socialist world.'

Wilde crouched down beside her. 'Look, Lydia.' His voice was kind. 'The police explanation does seem the most logical, but that phone call to you . . .' He straightened up. 'Something was clearly bothering Nancy and it's bothering you, too. Let's think about your Berlin trip. If she was there at the behest of someone, what do you think she was doing that she would want to keep secret from you?'

'Well, I don't think she was an assassin, if that's what you mean!'

Wilde smiled. 'I agree that's unlikely. Do you think she was a courier, then, taking something to someone – or picking something up? Or perhaps she was spying on something or someone? If – and it is a big *if* – she was on some sort of a mission to Germany, then someone sent her. Someone in England, perhaps even someone here in Cambridge.'

Lydia shrugged, but didn't reply. She turned over Nancy's photograph and stared at it. 'Better get this back to Sir Norman. Did you smell his breath, Tom? He'd been drinking.'

'I don't blame him.' Sir Norman Hereward had always been a heavy drinker, even back in the days when he was master of the college. Wilde sighed. Lydia was running out of steam. 'Just one more thing. What about men? You said the neighbour had something to say about that.'

'Ask her – see if you believe her. I don't.'

*

Next door, Mrs Bromley crossed her arms over her bosom as she had done before. 'This is a sad business and no mistake,' she said.

'Indeed, Mrs Bromley,' Wilde said. 'And I know you have already had quite enough questions from the police. But may I ask one more? You told Miss Morris here that Miss Hereward had entertained various men in her house. When did she have her last visitor?'

'Well, I never saw them, of course.'

Lydia frowned. 'But you said she had had men here. How can you say that if you hadn't seen anything?'

'Well, I heard things, didn't I? Noises through the wall late at night.'

'The wireless for instance?'

'I know what I know.' Mrs Bromley backed away into the dark hallway of her house, glared at them, then closed the door.

Lydia's mouth fell open. 'What did I say?'

'Come on,' Wilde said. 'There's nothing more for us here.'

CHAPTER 7

Leslie Braithwaite spread beef dripping liberally over his thick slice of white bread, then sprinkled salt on it before folding the bread into a malformed sandwich. He thrust it into his gaping mouth, chewing with vigour. Ah, the pleasure. The food of his Yorkshire boyhood. Proper fresh white English bread with a golden crust. The black German stuff wasn't the same.

He put up a hand to summon the waitress. 'Another cup of tea, missus. Make it stewed and strong. This stuff's like cat's piss.'

'Language, if you don't mind.'

Language. He took another large bite of his sandwich. How about German for a language? *Scheisse!* All manner of pork sausage in Möhlau, beef dripping too, but you couldn't get a proper cup of tea for love nor money. *Weissbier* – wheat beer or fart-beer as he called it – was your lot these days, and you could stick it up the Kaiser's arse.

His tea arrived. He spooned in plenty of sugar and stirred it hard, clinking the sides with the spoon and spilling the sweet liquid over the tablecloth. Not that it made much difference; it was already stained with egg yolk, butter, marmalade and dripping. This was a working man's caff, in a side street, away from the hangouts of the bourgeoisie and the intellectuals who infested this hole of a town. This was where the carters, the bargees, the college servants and the factory hands came for their bacon and eggs and sweet tea.

The clinking of the spoon. His teeth tightened, those that hadn't fallen out in the PoW camp. He closed his eyes and the clinking became the rat-a-tat clattering of the machine guns and the spit-spit of the snipers' bullets, the thunder of the big guns and the volcanoes of mud. The Somme in late autumn 1916, in the rain, holding the line against the Boche. God, the rain that autumn. That's where it had all started, the road to Möhlau.

His thoughts turned to his wife and children. One little killing and he would see them again, would slide once more between Gudrun's fleshy legs.

He had made his home in Germany because of Gudrun, and then he had rejoiced as it regained its pride with the rise of the National Socialists. Adolf Hitler had done this, through willpower alone. He had kept his promise of providing bread and work for the common man.

One little killing, Braithwaite owed them that much.

He fished some worn coppers from his ragged pocket. A penny with the face of Victoria almost rubbed smooth, two George V halfpennies and a shiny new silver threepenny piece.

'How much, love?'

'Tuppence to you.'

'How about you make it a penny halfpenny? How about you and me, out back, for another penny halfpenny? Been on the road for weeks, I have. Haven't seen my family in an age.' Didn't tell her that his wife was German, that he lived in Germany. Didn't tell her that he'd only been back in England ten days, that he'd landed at Harwich. As far as this town was concerned, he was English and communist. That was the way he had been told it had to be, and it was easy enough to remember.

'Tuppence. And you can take your filthy language with you.'

He put two fingers in the air, handed over the small coins and put the threepence back in his pocket. Stuffing the last of his plug of chewing tobacco into his mouth, he walked out into the dull December rain.

Across the road, there was a telephone kiosk with a queue of three people outside. He checked his cheap pocket watch. It was five to twelve. Five minutes to go. God forbid those queuing were windbags. Might have to use his elbows. He joined the line, his cap down over his brow, his hands deep in his pockets. Clutched in one of his buried hands was a precious slip of paper; it bore the telephone number of a Mayfair hotel.

'What now, Tom?'

'Lydia, I understand your suspicions, but it is hard to conclude from them that this is murder. One can only go on the evidence. You can see that, surely? We have to leave it to the police and coroner – and we know what they'll say.'

They had ridden back to the college and were now in his rooms. Bobby had stoked up the fire and brought them lunch from Hall, some sort of meat pie with boiled potatoes, gravy and peas. Neither of them had had the appetite to finish it. Now they were drinking tea in front of the hearth.

'She wasn't the suicidal type,' Lydia said.

'Then it was an accidental overdose.'

'People have the wrong idea about her,' Lydia said fiercely. 'It simply wasn't like her. The whole heroin thing was a phase. It would have ended sooner rather than later. She liked to shock people. She always did. That's how it all went wrong when, you know . . . the incident.'

'Ah yes, the *incident*.' He stressed the noun with the gravity that might be reserved for the sinking of the *Lusitania*. The scandal. It had been the talk of the whole university and had brought an early end to Sir Norman's illustrious career as college master. Nancy, having left Girton some four years earlier, had been living with her father in the master's lodge at the time. Their relationship had never been easy, but she had needed to get away from London. It was rumoured that she had been having an affair with a Labour member of parliament and his wife had found out and was threatening a messy divorce. The MP had taken the line of least resistance and sent Nancy packing. She needed to get away from the capital and all the people they had known, and so, with some reluctance, she had asked her father to allow her to stay with him in the lodge. It might have been better if she had gone to his country house nearby, but it was rented out while Sir Norman served as master. With deep reservations of his own, he had agreed to let her stay in college. A good-looking, somewhat wild, young woman among a couple of hundred men was a recipe for disaster.

'It was the bedder that did the dirty on them apparently,' Wilde said. 'Caught them *in flagrante* and made a formal complaint.'

'Those stupid women act like some sort of morality police reporting to the Inquisition,' Lydia said bitterly.

He laughed. 'Some do. Others are more obliging.' Nancy had been caught in bed with two undergraduates, both of whom had been sent down. 'Anyway, it was all a fuss about nothing. Who in God's name was hurt by a little sexual congress? Mind you, I don't suppose the reaction would have been any different at Girton.'

'Girton was like the Tower of London when we were there – I'm sure it still is. Suited some of the Sapphists, of course, including a few of the lecturers. No man would have got in there, although I must say we were quite adept at getting out.' Lydia sighed, got to her feet and walked over to the window. 'God, I hate this time of year. It'll be dark soon.'

Wilde stood up. 'Look, I'm bored silly with college matters, so to put your mind at rest I'm going to ride out to St Wilfred's Priory to have another word with Hereward. I can take his picture back. Let's see if he really does have a reason for believing there's something more to Nancy's death.' He paused. 'By the way, I take with a pinch of salt what Mrs Bromley had to say, but *was* there a man in her life?'

'Nothing serious, I don't think. But you could never be sure what Nancy was up to from one week to the next.'

'She was an attractive woman.'

'I sometimes wondered . . .'

'What?'

'Well, you know, there were men, but it occurred to me that she wasn't too choosy. Boys, girls, I think it was much of a muchness to her. When we were in Berlin, she sort of tried it on with me after a few glasses of wine. It was the night after we had our shopping trip. The one I told you about, when I was going frantic because she went missing. Anyway, we were sharing a room and she crawled into bed with me during the night.'

'And?'

'Well, of course, I didn't have the heart to push her out, so well we, you know . . .'

She gave him a wan smile. He said nothing, raised an eyebrow at her sad little jest.

'All right, all right. I had to tell her it wasn't me. She called me a bourgeois tart.'

'Fair enough description.'

'Thank you very much, Professor Wilde. Anyway, she called everyone bourgeois.'

'And tart?'

'A private joke. She knew all my secrets, you see. The problem is, I obviously didn't know all of hers.'

Wilde recalled seeing her across the college courts. He hadn't known her well, but there had been something in the way Nancy Hereward moved. He could imagine that men – and some women – would have found her difficult to resist.

Lydia hugged her arms around her chest, as she stared out into the gathering darkness. 'I've got to do some work, Tom. I have a deadline to meet, but all I want to do is go home, go to bed and bury my head beneath the covers.'

'What would Nancy say?'

'You know what she'd say.'

'Well, listen to yourself – and to her. Go to work. Keep yourself occupied. I'll ride out to St Wilfred's Priory alone.'

'I take it you know about Nancy's mother?'

'I thought the old man was a widower.' Like me, he thought. What a strange word, *widower*.

'He is. But I mean the circumstances of his wife's death. I think Nancy's mother killed herself.'

'What makes you think that?'

'Something Nancy said once. She said her mother never recovered from the deaths of her sons in the war. Can suicide run in families? It would certainly reinforce those who think Nancy killed herself.'

Wilde rather thought that the children of suicides could well become obsessed with the subject. 'I'll keep an open mind and do a little inquiring for you. Perhaps I'll talk to one or two of her friends. Any names you can think of?'

'Well, I don't know any of her dope addict friends. But there is Dave Johnson, the Socialist Club secretary. He was pretty close to her. We'll see him tonight.'

'What's happening tonight?'

'You haven't forgotten about the rally? I thought you said you were coming. Personally, I don't want to go but I think I have to. I'm supposed to be helping.'

God knows why, he thought, but kept his expression carefully neutral. 'Comrade Kholtov, you mean?'

'Nancy would have been there,' she said. 'Some of her Bolshie friends are sure to be in evidence. Horace Dill, of course.'

'God bless the preposterous old commie.'

'You know he was close to Nancy? Took her side at the time of the three-in-a-bed scandal. Bit of a mentor, I'd say.'

He'd seen them chatting in the college courts but hadn't really given it too much thought. There was never going to be anything untoward between them.

'You never know, a few enemies could also be in evidence.'

He smiled. 'I'll be at your side. What's the dress code?'

'Ha ha. Oh, you are funny, Thomas Wilde.' But Lydia wasn't laughing. Just now she thought she would never laugh again.

Wrapped up in his trenchcoat, Wilde exulted as the Rudge purred beneath him along the Ely road. His coat buttoned, his leather flying cap buckled beneath his chin, his eyes protected by goggles and his hands deep inside thick gauntlet gloves, he twisted the throttle and felt a surge of speed. From Chesterton Lane he headed north and a little eastwards. St Wilfred's Priory was fifteen minutes' ride. The sky was darkening and the tempera-ture was falling. He was wrapped up well and had a scarf tied around his lower face, but neither the trenchcoat nor any of the other layers could keep the wind out of his skin. Even for a man who had endured the rig-ours of north-eastern winters in the States and the unheated dormitories of an English public school, the Fens could be harsh and bitter.

There had been times since returning from the States that he had han-kered after his old Harley Davidson 1200 SV. For a while he had even thought of paying to ship it over, but then he heard about the Rudge from Andy at the garage and decided to give her a go. 'Hundred miles an hour guaranteed, Mr Wilde. Been winning races.'

So far, so good. Though it pained him to admit it, the English had the drop on the Yanks with this one. She was sleek and black with thin trims of gold paint, twin exhausts and plenty of chrome. She also had a pillion seat and was a hell of a sight more reliable than the Harley.

He considered the state of the roads. The tyres were new but fenland highways could become dangerous, with mud or ice or both: a week ago he nearly slid into an eight-foot deep dyke when he went out towards the Wash in search of pochard and Bewick swans. Birdwatching was his secret escape. He was no expert on ornithology, but every now and then he had an overwhelming desire to seek out some bleak landscape and lie amid the grass or the reeds and clasp binoculars to his eyes to watch the birds go about their business: searching for food, building nests, playing in the air. These were days when conscious thought vanished;, when his mind became clear and untrammelled.

The road ahead was almost empty and the landscape was desolate. Through the gloom, he spotted a Humber wrapped around a tree, the tracks of its tyres showing where it had skidded off the road through a mudslide. He pulled up, lifted the Rudge onto its stand and walked over to investigate. A pair of rooks lazily beat their wings and flew away from the dead rat on which they had been feeding. There was no sign of a driver or passengers. Nothing to be done, so he resumed his journey. After a couple of miles, he took a right and rode through an avenue of soaring elms, standing like ghostly sentries in their wintry nakedness, until he came to a gatehouse and a sign saying St Wilfred's Priory.

The land here stood in marked contrast to the bleakness of the Ely road and most of the farm country around. He rode into parkland bound by forest, past a herd of grazing deer, along a straight driveway that led up to the ancient building. It had been one of the religious houses that had been turned into a private home for a favoured courtier of Henry VIII at the time of the Dissolution. The old building had clearly been changed a great deal over the years. Turrets and columns had been added, probably in the eighteenth century, giving it a pleasant Gothic appearance. The mellow stone walls and bays of mullioned and transomed windows could easily have graced the pages of a travel brochure advertising the joys of England's countryside. So this was where Nancy Hereward had been brought up – here, boarding school, Girton and the master's lodge. Most would say she had been lucky, for this was a fine English country house. Wilde wasn't so sure. Houses like these held unspoken history and too many dark corners. It was what went on within the walls that made for a happy home. Or otherwise.

He parked the Rudge on the forecourt and switched off the engine. Cold rain was beginning to fall. He pulled up his spattered goggles and used his sleeve to wipe the the mud from his face.

A man in livery was approaching along the gravel driveway, across the frontage of the house: Wilde recognised the chauffeur he had seen outside Nancy's house in Cambridge.

'Who are you?' the chauffeur demanded. 'Delivery? Courier?'

'My name's Wilde. I'd like to speak to Sir Norman.'

The chauffeur peered through the smear of grime coating Wilde's face. 'You were in Cambridge outside Miss Hereward's house. What do you want?' The tone was unwelcoming.

'Professor Thomas Wilde. Sir Norman knows me from college.'

'He's not available.'

'Let him judge for himself.'

The chauffeur looked Wilde up and down, as though inspecting him for fleas. 'Wait here.'

He opened the large front door, leaving Wilde standing on the stone step outside. From within, Wilde heard a muffled hum of voices and, in the gaudy glow of the electric lights, caught a glimpse of a familiar face crossing the hallway. Duncan Sawyer. And then he was gone. Wilde supposed Hereward's close friends and relatives had arrived to offer condolences. He thought of his own wife's death. Strange how short the condolences and remembrances were; the conversation inevitably veered back to the living.

He turned at the noise of tyres on gravel as a large sporting car drew into the driveway. It was a Maybach, luxurious, lipstick-red with white-wall tyres and an extravagant running board. Even in the dusk and rain, it gleamed. The driver climbed out, snapped open an umbrella and opened the passenger door. An enormous man with a short, neatly trimmed moustache, voluminous chins and a long fur coat stepped from the vehicle and ducked beneath the umbrella. His driver struggled to keep up as his master strode towards the porch.

The chauffeur was back at the door. He ignored Wilde and bowed to the newcomer. 'My lord,' he said as the man's huge bulk swept past like an unstoppable force, entering the house as though it were his own.

Lord Slievedonard, the gold millionaire. Peter Slievedonard, who wanted to endow the college with a scholarship. Wilde had seen his pictures in the newspapers and on newsreels. He made his money from trading in gold and used a lot of his wealth to fund Sir Oswald Mosley's British Union of Fascists. Wilde tried to follow him inside, but the chauffeur's arm shot out and barred his way. 'The answer's no.'

'What's Slievedonard doing here?'

'Good day, Professor Wilde. Use the telephone if you wish to make an appointment.'

Wilde removed the picture of Nancy from his coat pocket and handed it to the servant. 'Well, at least give him this. With my compliments.'

CHAPTER 8

While Wilde rode out to the priory, Lydia walked the short distance to her little office in the attic space above a gentlemen's outfitter in Bene't Street. Her publishing company, LM Books, barely turned over enough to pay the rent, but she was determined to keep it going for as long as she could. She had already published more than twenty volumes of poetry and one day she hoped another publisher might see fit to bring out her own work, if only she could find the words within her to write. She was huddled into her duffle coat, looking down at the pavement, avoiding the cheery Christmas faces. She didn't want to see happiness: not today.

Settling herself at the long table, she worked all afternoon, peering at the proofs until her eyes were sore and her head ached.

The anthology she was editing reflected her dark mood. Death and horror in the mud of Flanders. She knew that many young people of her age, mid-twenties, gave barely a thought to the war. To them it was ancient history, the tragedy of a past generation, never to be repeated. She knew, too, that the survivors wouldn't – or couldn't – talk about it. They wouldn't describe the ripping apart of human flesh, the effect of shrapnel on bone, the obscenity of blood spurting in fountains, the filth of choking to death on gas, the indescribable pain of lying alone in the mud with your guts spilled, waiting for death. They thought they were being brave, stoical, manly, by keeping silent. But their silence simply ensured it would all happen again.

The only people who told the truth were the poets.

She had been a poet, too. Now, she was no longer sure. Her pen scratched holes in paper and she stabbed nibs into the blotter until they broke, but nothing was fully formed any more. Perhaps the poetry was there, in her frustration. Her poems had always been physical things. Ecstasy, passion, skin against skin, the sweetness of a mouth on mouth, the pleasure that must be sought if peace was to conquer war.

Lydia took a swig from a half-empty bottle of beer and laid her head on her arms, her eyes closed. When, a while later, she heard the door opening, she did not look up.

'Lydia.'

Slowly she raised her head. 'Hello, Tom.'

'Are you ready? We should be going.'

'Give me a couple of minutes.'

She didn't move. What was the point?

He picked up the dustcover of her anthology from the table and gazed at it.

'What do you think?' she said with an effort.

'It's good.' The cover he was looking at showed a grainy image of a soldier charging with bayonet fixed, under the title *Prime of Youth*.

'Good?'

'Very good. Powerful. Poignant.'

'I've put half my life into this.'

She looked exhausted. Today, he would definitely call her attire Bohemian rather than tattered. Her hair was tousled and loosely tied back. She wore corduroy trousers tied at her narrow waist with a boy's snake-buckle belt, a voluminous Sea Island cotton shirt – open-necked with rolled-up sleeves and a threadbare collar that had once belonged to her father. A scruffy pullover hung over her shoulders. Her clothes were a reflection of her surroundings, which were an exotic shambles. This was the way she liked to dress and the way she liked to work. And this was the way he liked her.

Looking around the room, Wilde had no idea how she ever found anything in the clutter of books, papers and boxes. He smiled and shook his head. 'Utter chaos, Miss Morris.'

'Mind your own business, Professor Wilde.'

They had known each other for two years now, ever since he moved in next door, and they enjoyed each other's company when their paths crossed. She knew some things about him, about the wife and baby he had lost in childbirth ten years ago, about his ambivalent feelings for Cambridge and the college, the fact that he had American nationality but an Irish mother. These were facts she had gleaned from Nancy, who had taken to him because her father hadn't. Lydia liked Tom Wilde well enough, but that didn't really explain why she had thought of him when the police insisted she call a friend to collect her. Was there really no one else in her life, or was it simply that he lived next door?

Wilde was wondering the same thing. She was the last person he would have expected to seek his help. Looking through Lydia's bookcase very early on in their acquaintance he had seen the volume *Live Alone and Like It* by Marjorie Hillis. Leafing through it, he had come across a chapter headed *Pleasures of a Single Bed*. It had amused him as much as it annoyed him.

'I'm not the marrying kind,' she said.

'You have a copy of *Married Love*,' he had pointed out, as he moved along the shelf.

'So do a million other women.'

'So why not marriage?'

'I wouldn't be able to turn a blind eye to a man's infidelities.'

'And what if you were to marry a faithful man?'

'What if I were to find a unicorn?'

Now he put his hand on her shoulder. 'Have you finished?' he said. 'Shall we go? The rally, remember.'

'Almost done. What happened at St Wilfred's Priory?'

'I didn't see him. The chauffeur was playing the part of bodyguard and gatekeeper. Not at all friendly. But there was an interesting visitor – Lord Slievedonard, complete with fur coat, shiny red sports car and double chins like a bullfrog. He swept in just as I was being ejected.'

'He's rather large and imposing, isn't he? Nancy always called him the Tyrannosaur.'

'Ah yes, his politics. Very disagreeable.'

'Pretty much the same as her father's. Messrs Hitler and Mussolini have a lot to answer for.'

He looked down at her. Her eyes were bloodshot. Stray hairs crawled across her brow. She wasn't as resilient as she liked to make out.

'Nancy's death has taken the ground from under me like a landslip,' she whispered. 'Every time I close my eyes, I see her body and that mass of blotches on her arm. I don't think it will ever leave me.'

It was pointless to contradict her.

'Come on,' he said quietly. 'Your Bolshie friends will want to see you before the meeting gets under way.'

Stanley Baldwin had not felt so energised in months. The sickness and lethargy of the summer was a thing of the past. As he was driven in the back of his official black Rolls Royce to Buckingham Palace he reflected that there was no better man for the painful task that lay ahead: the removal of a king from his throne.

Edward was waiting for him, smoking a cigarette as always. Baldwin lit up his pipe and together they produced a small cloud of tobacco fumes in the uncomfortable vastness of the state room. 'I am afraid, Your Majesty,' the prime minister said, 'that the Dominions are as one in their opposition to your proposed marriage.'

Edward dropped his head and looked at his feet. For a moment Baldwin thought the little man was about to burst into tears.

'Shall I pour you a brandy, sir?'

'I never drink before seven, Mr Baldwin.'

'No. Indeed not.' Baldwin bowed his head. He could wait.

Edward raised his head. 'Then I shall be forced to abdicate, is that what you are saying?'

'You have a difficult choice, sir.'

'Well, if that is what I have to do to marry the woman I love . . .'

Baldwin said nothing, merely sucked on his pipe. The silence echoed around the high ceilings. What Edward would never know was that Baldwin was lying. It was not true that the Dominions were united in their opposition to a morganatic marriage. Australia certainly was, but both Canada and New Zealand had thought it a rather good idea.

The street outside the church hall was packed with protesters, agitators and jeering onlookers. More than a hundred students and activists were facing each other down with shouts and brandished fists. They were split into their tribes, each tribe bearing its placard or banner of belonging: the red flag for the communists, the lightning flash and strong-arm salutes for a handful of Blackshirts, a red and black standard for the Anarcho-Syndicalists, hammer and sickle with the legend *POUM* for the Workers' Party of Marxist Unification, Spain's Trotskyites.

They hurled slogans through loudhailers. Like dogs at bay, they jostled, threatened, intimidated. Half a dozen uniformed police constables kept them apart. The protesters surged towards each other, but the police held them back with a good-humoured wave of the finger or a raised palm. The communists began to sing the 'Internationale'. The Blackshirts responded with the 'Horst Wessel'.

To the side, incongruously, a group of evangelist Christians knelt on the pavement and prayed loudly for world peace.

Wilde observed the strange stand-off for a few moments, then put an arm round Lydia's shoulder. 'Safe enough. Come on.'

She shrugged off his arm. 'I'm not a bloody child, Tom.'

They pushed their way through into the hall, where the organisers were preparing the stage. Spotting them, Dave Johnson, the Socialist Club secretary, hurried over, his expression one of concern. He was a whippet-thin man of middle years with a patchy beard that did little to disguise the burn scars that disfigured the bottom half of his face. He clasped Lydia's hands. 'I'm so sorry. She was one of us. The best of us.'

Lydia nodded. Wilde could see that she was suddenly too choked to speak.

'We'll talk later,' Johnson said. He stepped back and indicated the man who had followed him. 'Let me introduce you to our guest, all the way from the frontline in Catalonia. Comrade Kholtov, this is Miss Morris. She produced the fliers for this evening's event. Lydia, can I leave you with him? I've got to help with the door.'

Johnson nodded to Wilde, then made his way to the entrance. Wilde turned his attention to the Russian.

Though not tall, Yuri Kholtov had presence. He was heavy-set with a thick thatch of hair and Slavic cheekbones. Wilde estimated his age at a little over forty, so he would have been in his early twenties at the time of the October Revolution, when he became respected and feared as one of Stalin's closest comrades-in-arms. In recent months he had been in Spain helping to organise the republican struggle against the nationalist rebels. As he was introduced to Lydia, Wilde noted his eyes: they had creases of humour, as did his mouth, but his smile was not convincing. This, Wilde knew from his friend Jim Vanderberg at the American embassy in London, was a man steeped in blood. He had warned Lydia, but she wouldn't have it. 'You say that about all of them, Tom. You swallow the anti-Soviet line like a bloody trout.'

'Comrade Morris!' Kholtov exclaimed. 'I have been looking forward to meeting you. I am told I must thank you for your assistance.'

She held out her hand, but the Russian ignored it and put his hands to her face and kissed her on both cheeks.

'It was very little, Mr Kholtov. Just a few fliers and leaflets.' She tried to smile at him, but it was not convincing.

He took her hands. 'Miss Morris, I have heard that your friend has just died. That is terrible.'

'Yes. Yes, it is.'

'You have my heartfelt condolences.'

Lydia took a deep breath, pushed back her shoulders and smiled again. 'When Professor Dill suggested this evening's rally, I couldn't believe it was possible, so I am both thrilled and surprised that you are here.'

'Here's the secret, Miss Morris. I have an ulterior motive – to recruit your finest young men and women for the struggle in Catalonia. But first a complaint: do you know they are saying there is no vodka here? What sort of country is this? A man could die of thirst.' Kholtov laughed raucously – a laugh, like his voice, roughened by too many cheap cardboard-tube cigarettes. He bent his hands now round the one he had fixed in his mouth and lit it before discharging a spiral of smoke.

'There is a bar. I am sure we will find something else to your taste, Comrade Kholtov.'

He turned to Wilde, who was standing at her side. 'And who is this?'

'Professor Wilde, my neighbour.'

'Then if he is not your husband, there must still be hope for me.' Kholtov laughed again and shook hands with Wilde. 'It is a pleasure to meet you, comrade.'

'Mr Kholtov.'

'Your accent. What do I detect? Not quite American, not quite British?'

'Half American. The other half Irish.'

'Aha, the general secretary has great hopes for the Irish. They have thrown off the English yoke, now they must complete their revolution. I assume you are a paid-up member of the party, Professor Wilde?'

'Not yours, nor any other.'

'Then I will persuade you otherwise. But first, a drink, yes? Without vodka what do you recommend?'

'Scotch.'

'Whisky is good. I shall have one. And Miss Morris, what will you drink?'

'Whisky for me, too.'

'I shall buy the bottle. A small fraternal offering from the great Soviet peoples.'

The air was thick with tobacco smoke, muted voices, the scraping of chairs being moved into place. It was a large, echoing space with a stage at one end, dominated by a central lectern, like the set-up for a school speech day. The hall had not seen a lick of paint since the turn of the century and the chairs were a job lot, many in need of repair. Dave Johnson had opened the doors and the room was filling up quickly. There was the possibility of trouble here, and not just belligerent heckling: Kholtov had his fair share of enemies.

'Tell me, Mr Kholtov,' Wilde said, 'what have you been doing in Catalonia?'

'Providing support for our friends against the fascist insurrection. You should join us. All right-thinking people are welcome.'

'I mean you personally. What is your role?'

The Russian was putting his glass to his lips, but paused before drinking. 'I am an adviser, professor. Nothing more.' The glass resumed its journey to his mouth and he downed the double Haig in one shot. Then, without a pause, he poured himself another.

Wilde found himself wanting to push the man, for the hell of it. 'I hear reports that Comrade Stalin's team in Spain spends more time killing Trotsky's people than General Franco's.'

'Then you have been listening to nonsense.'

'So there has been no covert action, no assassinations, no abductions outside the Soviet Union?'

'You have been listening to rumours, Professor Wilde. Rumours put about by the western capitalist press.'

'I could name names, if you wish.'

Just for a moment it seemed to Wilde that the apparent good humour was about to vanish from Kholtov's face. A flash of irritation, perhaps? But Kholtov kept smiling. 'I am sure I could prove to your satisfaction that all the deaths of those wanted for trial in Moscow have been due to accidents or natural causes. But perhaps we will talk of it another time, professor. For the moment, I must prepare myself for tonight's speech.'

'And will an accident befall Comrade Trotsky in his Norwegian hideaway?'

'Trotsky? I would happily put a Tokarev to his head and pull the trigger myself. He is a traitor to the revolution.' Kholtov dropped his cigarette and used his well-worn heel to grind it into the floorboards. He took out another cigarette and stuck it, unlit, into the corner of his mouth. 'Who have you been listening to?' He smiled at Wilde, but it was a smile that didn't reach his eyes.

Wilde held his gaze. How many men and women had seen those eyes in the last seconds before the darkness descended?

'I'm a professor of history,' he said. 'My subject is Elizabethan England and I have a special interest in the birth of the English secret service under Walsingham, but I like to keep up to date with modern intelligence methods. History is meaningless unless you discern how the past shapes the present. I am interested, for instance, in your AST.'

'AST?' Kholtov asked politely.

'The Administration for Special Tasks. A division of the NKVD. They kidnap people and take them back to Moscow to be murdered in the Lubyanka prison, or they kill them where they are. Feel free to correct me if I'm wrong.'

'No one is murdered in the Lubyanka. Is this some plot for a novel? Of course you're wrong! The Soviet Union does not stoop to such tactics. We leave such things to the fascists, to Hitler, Franco and Mussolini. *They* are the enemies of the people. They are the criminal elements, Professor Wilde!'

Johnson elbowed his way towards them. 'I think we're about ready, Mr Kholtov.'

Wilde edged through the crowd to the back of the hall where he had spotted Horace Dill.

'Evening, Tom. Didn't know you'd joined the party.'

Kholtov was walking up to the lectern to deafening applause.

Wilde put his mouth close to Dill's ear. 'You knew Nancy Hereward pretty well, Horace, didn't you?'

'Of course I did. It's a desperate tragedy.'

'Do you think she was murdered?'

'*Murdered?*' Dill gave Wilde a strange look through his thick glasses, then lifted his chin and exhaled a cloud of cigar smoke. 'What's this about, Tom?'

'Just asking a few questions. The police have made up their minds, you see, but Lydia Morris is convinced it wasn't a simple overdose.'

'Oh, for God's sake, Tom. Not now.' Dill put a finger to his lips. 'Sssh, the great man is about to speak.'

Kholtov began his speech with some scandalous allegations about well-known names in the Soviet Union and beyond.

'So how did Natalya Sedova come to be with child when Lev Bronstein was in prison?' he demanded rhetorically. 'Are we to believe the sorry tale that she was allowed conjugal visits even though they were not married? Not credible, you will say. Which surely must mean that Trotsky was a cuckold and that little Lev junior was not a Bronstein? Who, then, was the true father?'

Kholtov went through a list of the big names of the Russian Revolution, with details of their supposed sexual preferences and the likelihood of them having fathered Trotsky's first child. He was seeking laughter and familiarity, and it served him well: he kept his audience entranced. There were well-rehearsed anecdotes about Lenin and Krupskaya's bedroom antics, the peccadillos of Kamenev and Zinoviev. But never about Comrade Stalin. Comrade Stalin didn't appreciate humour at his expense. And word, inevitably, got back to him.

Bit by bit, the speech turned from titbits of scandal to the serious business of war and the people's struggle. Kholtov spoke of Spain and the need for volunteers to fight against Franco and his Falangists. This was why he had travelled from Barcelona across France to England. 'I know that many of the brightest and best among you are prepared to take up arms against the fascists. Some of your comrades are already with us. You will have heard of the new International Brigades. I am here to urge you to do your duty and join us. And I can promise every assistance if you need help in making your way to the front. We have routes and we have funds.'

Tom Wilde stood at the back of the hall, whisky in hand, listening intently. Kholtov was a persuasive speaker. At least a handful of those here this night would take his advice and go to Spain, risking lives cut short by a bullet in the brain or a jagged chunk of shrapnel in the gut. He could just make out Lydia at the front of the hall, standing close to the side of the stage, rapt.

'What do you think, Professor Wilde?'

Wilde turned sharply at the unfamiliar voice in his left ear. An elegant young man in a light grey Savile Row suit stood next to him, hands in his trouser pockets.

'Have we met?'

'Philip Eaton. I'm a correspondent for *The Times*.'

'And how do you know my name, Mr Eaton?'

Eaton laughed. 'I'm a reporter. I make it my business to find things out. You *are* Professor Wilde, are you not?'

'Yes.'

'Then I believe we share a common interest in the death of Nancy Hereward.'

Suddenly the thundering voice of Yuri Kholtov became nothing but a background murmur. 'I had no idea the press had any interest in the story.'

'Most of them don't. It's an accidental overdose. Shameful, perhaps, but suicide would be even worse. The father's already suffered enough scandal with his daughter's antics, so the press won't touch it. Sir Norman has some powerful friends.'

'So why is *The Times* interested?'

'Won't you allow me to buy you a drink, professor?'

CHAPTER 9

Philip Eaton handed Wilde his refreshed drink and proffered his cigarette case. When Wilde declined, he snapped the silver case shut and slid it back into his inside pocket without taking one for himself. 'Frightful habit. I only keep them to hand out. Reporter's trick. Cheers.' He clinked glasses.

'What makes you think I might be interested in the death of Nancy Hereward? Are you a friend of Sir Norman's?'

'I've never met the man.'

'Then someone of his acquaintance? Horace Dill perhaps?'

Eaton smiled. 'Let's just say I do my homework. Now, may I ask you a question: what is your interest in the case?'

If this man wouldn't give straight answers, Wilde's inclination was to walk away. And yet he stayed. There was nothing to be lost by listening to him. He shrugged. 'All right, Mr Eaton, it's very simple. Lydia Morris, a friend of mine, has doubts about the death and the police have made their minds up. I suspect they're right, in which case I want to prove to Lydia that this was just a tragic accident. No foul play. No murder. Just set her mind at rest.'

'And what if it *was* murder? Good Lord, the idiotic girl had made enough enemies here, there and everywhere,' he said.

'You sound as though you knew her.'

'I knew *of* her. Our paths never crossed, but as a former Trinity man I spend quite a lot of time up here and one hears things – you know, that story of three-in-a-bed with Nancy as the honey in the sandwich. And then, of course, her silver needle. All very fast for Cambridge. More Riviera or Happy Valley than Trumpington Street.'

By now they were standing in the yard behind the hall in the chilly evening air, the sound of Kholtov's speech a distant hum.

'So what makes you think there is something suspicious about her death?'

Eaton paused. 'I think it had something to do with Berlin.'

'Berlin?' Wilde was careful not to reveal his surprise. 'Then you've lost me. She went to the Olympics, but what could that possibly have to do with her death?'

'I think she had an ulterior motive in making the trip.'

'She was writing an article about the real Germany, behind all the salutes, the marching and the flags. Perhaps you read it.'

'It was more than that. She had orders to do some covert work for the Comintern.'

Wilde didn't respond. Berlin again. The missing hour that Lydia had spoken about. Suddenly, the whole affair of Nancy's life and death had taken on a new dimension. This stranger had approached him as if he knew him and claimed to know the history of a young woman who had died little more than twenty-four hours earlier. How had he discovered so much and what had any of it to do with Thomas Wilde, professor of history, birdwatcher, motorcycle enthusiast and sometime amateur boxer?

There was something about Berlin; that was certain. Lydia had felt it and now so did Wilde. But the *Comintern*? Surely not.

'You are not saying anything, professor.'

'What do you want me to say?'

'I thought you might register surprise.'

'Mr Eaton, if I don't look surprised it might be because I can't keep up with your vivid imagination. Or perhaps you *do* know something, in which case, tell me this: how does a humble *Times* reporter know all this?'

'Do I really look humble, old boy?'

'Anything but, Mr Eaton.' *Old boy.* Philip Eaton had injected a mocking tone, but it was hardly convincing.

'Look,' Eaton continued. 'I hear things.'

'You sound like a spy.'

'Oh, no more than the sort of things you hear, I'm sure. I'm told you like to call in at the American embassy when you're in town. You must pick up some jolly good gossip there, I imagine. And you're not a spy are you, Professor Wilde?'

'Who told you about my embassy visits?'

'I know people. I do my research. I have a lot of friends in Cambridge. Amazing, too, what you can pick up in a London club. My newspaper pays me to keep my ear close to the ground.'

Wilde was tired of the endless fencing. 'So tell me what you want.'

'I thought we could pool resources. Do the police's work for them if you like. You can tell me what you and Miss Morris know of the dead girl and her movements. As things stand, there's no chance of persuading either the police or the coroner that Nancy Hereward's death was anything but an accident or suicide. Case closed as far as they're concerned, but you're beginning to have doubts.'

'If you say so. But what is in it for you?'

'A good story. The true tale of the murder of the girl with the silver needle. And you get some kind of justice for Miss Morris's friend.'

Wilde didn't believe him for a minute. Eaton was altogether too well informed for a reporter, even one who represented a publication as august as *The Times*. There was something more to him – and he intended to find out what it was. 'So, Mr Eaton, what have you discovered so far?'

'Isn't the Comintern line enough? God knows what they were hoping she'd do in Berlin. I can't imagine a young lady with a weakness for theoretical communism and heroin being given a pistol and told to shoot Hitler. So what was she up to?'

'I still find it unfeasible that a newspaper reporter could have discovered such information.'

'Up to you, Professor Wilde. You can work with me or not, as you please. For myself, I'll be looking for whoever it was who sent her to Berlin in the first place. Once we know that, we might discover what she was doing.'

'How will you find this elusive contact?'

'Cambridge is infested with commies! I would hazard a guess that it's one of the dons. They're very happy to send impressionable young people off to do their dirty work in Germany and Spain, while they drink port in the Combination Room. It was ever thus. Old men sending off young men to die. Story of the Great War.'

'You're a cynic, Mr Eaton.'

Eaton raised an eyebrow. 'And you're not, Professor Wilde?'

'So what will we do when we identify this supposed Comintern agent?'

'Get the truth out of him. Therein lies the clue to her death, I suspect. Do *you* have any idea who it might have been?'

Wilde didn't hesitate. 'None,' he said shortly. Then he paused. If he was going to get anywhere with Eaton he would have to give him something. 'Perhaps you should talk to Lydia?'

'Ah, Miss Morris. Bit of a leftie herself, apparently. You don't think—'

Wilde shook his head decisively. 'I don't think for a moment that Lydia has anything to do with the Comintern or anything else remotely secret. She's a free thinker. Believes in a bright tomorrow when all men and women live in harmony in Arts and Crafts houses. But that's it. She's no Bolshevik.'

'I believe they met at Girton.'

'Yes.'

'And Miss Hereward was an aspiring journalist.'

'Just like you, Mr Eaton. Quite a good cover, don't you think? Reporters have an excuse to go abroad. Observe things. Ask difficult questions.'

'You sound like Mr Secretary Walsingham. A devious character, your Mr Walsingham. I read your biography of the great man and the way he did for the Scots queen. Congratulations, Professor Wilde.'

'Thank you. I'm sure Walsingham would use journalists as spies if he were around now. He certainly used merchants, travellers, diplomats and servants in the palaces and great houses.' Wilde finished his whisky. 'Let me think about your proposal, Mr Eaton. I will be in touch.' He turned to go back into the hall where Kholtov was just finishing his speech. 'Do you have a card? Where are you staying?'

'Leave messages for me at the Bull Hotel. I'll be in and out.' Eaton handed Wilde his embossed card. Headed '*The Times*', it said *Philip Eaton, Special Correspondent,* and gave a series of telephone numbers for the London office.

'I'm afraid I don't have a card to give you.'

Eaton patted him on the shoulder. 'I know exactly where to find you, professor. Let's talk in the morning. Oh, and do buy one of the sensational newspapers – I think you'll find there's quite a splash.'

While the hall was being cleared, Wilde cornered Dave Johnson. 'You obviously knew Nancy well, Mr Johnson.'

'I did. It's hit me hard, Professor Wilde, just like Lydia. To tell the truth, I wasn't really expecting her to turn up tonight.'

'I take it you knew Nancy and Lydia through the Socialist Club.'

'Nancy and I both believed in the cause, if that's what you mean. Not Lydia. She's not really committed, I don't think.'

No, thought Wilde, there's more to her than that. 'Do you think Nancy was the type to take her own life?'

Johnson shook his head vigorously. 'No. Must have been an accident. Too much dope, though God knows she knew what she was doing. Shouldn't have made such a mistake.'

'Did she have enemies?'

He gave a bitter laugh. 'You mean apart from the whole British ruling class? They hate us and they fear us. They think we're going to take their vast estates and wealth from them. And do you know what, Professor Wilde? They're right.'

Wilde smiled. 'Actually, I mean someone who might have wished her personal harm?'

Johnson pulled at his beard, massaging his jaw. Wilde's eyes were drawn to the scars.

'Flying Corps,' Johnson said. 'The plane was on fire. Somehow I landed it with flames licking at my face. Top of my face was saved by my goggles and cap. You can't imagine the pain.'

'I'm sorry, I didn't mean to stare.'

'Everybody does and so I tell them what happened. Makes it easier for them to look at me.' There was a brief pause. Johnson collected himself. 'But we were talking about Nancy. You've got my opinion. Accidental death. Tragic.'

Outside the hall, the police were breaking up a fight between a band of Blackshirts and a group waving the red flag. 'Don't worry,' Wilde said when he emerged with Lydia. 'They're play-acting.'

To Lydia, it looked very much as if a full-scale riot was about to break out. She couldn't stomach the thought of violence. 'How do you tell the difference?'

Wilde pointed across to the front line of the Blackshirts. 'Look at that one. He's one of my undergraduates, a boy called Eugene Felsted. His father owns half the coalmines in Yorkshire and he went to Eton. It's all a game to him.' He jutted his chin in the direction of the communist banner-waver.

'As for him, that working-class hero over there with the bloody nose is Roger Maxwell. I believe his people own one of the smaller African colonies – almost all the farmland, at least. You've probably drunk quite a lot of their coffee. With a bit of luck, they'll beat each other to a pulp and leave me alone until the New Year.'

She wasn't entirely comforted.

'They try to act like men, Lydia, but they're boys, nothing more. Here, watch.'

He strolled over to the Blackshirt lines. The leaders bristled at his approach, but he ignored them and spoke quietly to Felsted, who blushed and looked embarrassed. He then did the same to an ashen-faced Maxwell on the opposite line.

He was smiling when he returned to Lydia.

'What did you say?'

'I pointed out to them that they weren't wearing gowns, and that I had just seen the proctor and two bulldogs. In the circumstances, I said, they might very well find themselves facing a penalty rather more severe than a thirteen and eightpence fine if they didn't hurry back to college. Sharpish.'

'They're probably more scared of you than Stalin or Hitler.'

'I don't think so.'

'Which only goes to show how little you know yourself, Tom.'

From Sidney Street, they turned right into Jesus Lane. There they encountered a choir of children and adults singing 'Silent Night', standing in the glow of a gas lamp, their voices clear and full of hope. They stopped and listened for a minute, then Lydia turned to Wilde. 'You gave Comrade Kholtov a hard time.'

'Yes, I did, didn't I?'

'Well, I liked him. I thought he was an inspiration. He's coming to dinner tomorrow. You're invited if you want.'

'Aren't you worried I might give him an even harder time?'

'I suspect he can take care of himself. And who was that rather smooth man I saw you drinking with?'

'Philip Eaton, Special Correspondent for *The Times*.' Wilde hesitated.

'You were about to say something?'

'Actually, I wasn't going to say anything this evening, but I suppose you'll want to hear this: Eaton thinks there's a story to be had in Nancy's death.'

'Well, perhaps he's right.'

'What really unsettled me, though, was that he seems to know all about me – and you, for that matter.'

'What does he know about me?' Lydia laid her hand on his arm, suddenly disturbed.

'He knows that you went to Berlin with Nancy. And he seems to have some information that she was up to something there other than reporting. Doing something for the Comintern, would you believe.'

Lydia's eyes were fixed on Wilde's. 'Well,' she said at last. 'Well, yes, I would believe it actually. What else did Mr Eaton say?'

'Nothing much. To be honest, he reminded me uncomfortably of the very elegant sixth-former who smacked me hard around the head on the house stairs when I first arrived at Harrow, and then said, *"That's for being new. And foreign-looking."* Then he patted me on the back and said, *"Get along now, old chap."*'

'He really hit you for being foreign-looking?'

'And for being new. He died at the Somme in his second week at the front, but it's still difficult to forgive him. The injustice rankles.'

What Wilde didn't tell Lydia was that it was this incident that had encouraged him to take up boxing. His mother had hated the idea. She said it reminded her of her grandfather who would fight anyone in Galway after half a pint of whisky. 'He was a pig of a man, Tom. You're not like him. Don't be like him. God gave you a fine brain, use it.'

He had. And at first, university life had indeed been good. He had met the woman who became his wife on campus; a college librarian who shared his love of English history. But after her death, the enclosed world of academe had lost its joy. Even the success of his book, even the move to Cambridge had done little to interest him. Now he wondered if the discipline of a local boxing gym might give him the stimulus he craved. He thought again of the ugly stand-off outside the church hall. Yes, it might be a good moment to take up boxing again.

Lydia was looking at him with a wry expression. 'Don't hit Mr Eaton for the crime of reminding you of someone else.'

'I'll try not to.'

'Because if you can arrange it, I'd like to meet him.'

THURSDAY DECEMBER 3, 1936

CHAPTER 10

Wilde woke to a hammering at the front door. He opened it bleary-eyed, a bear disturbed in mid-hibernation. Whisky and a smoke-fogged room had taken their toll. It was Lydia, coated, booted and about to set off for town.

'Ah,' he said, 'it must be morning.'

She eyed his dishevelled hair and dressing gown. 'Tom, it's nine o'clock.' She thrust a newspaper in his hands. 'I thought you might like to see this. Page fifteen.'

'What is it?'

'They're finally writing about the King.' She turned as if to go and then stopped. 'This Comintern thing. You know we were talking about Nancy being good friends with Horace Dill? Well, the truth is she thought he was possessed with god-like wisdom.'

'More divine than Dave Johnson?'

'Oh God, yes. And did you know that Horace put Kholtov up in his college rooms last night?'

Wilde hadn't known, but he knew that Dill had been a paid-up party member since 1920. He was very proud to have had one of the first British cards.

'I must go. Will I see you at dinner? They'll both be there – Kholtov and Dill. Please come. It's all organised. I can't let them down.'

'Then count me in.'

The front of *The Times* was the same as always, with its seven bland columns of births, marriages, deaths and personal advertising. Wilde shook his head and carried on through the paper until he reached page fifteen where he found an article headlined 'King and Monarchy'.

He read it quickly and found himself little the wiser. No mention of Mrs Simpson, nor any suggestion that there was any pressure on the King to abdicate. The possibility of a constitutional crisis was as far as the piece went. *The Times* attacked the 'vulgar' American press for its campaign of 'exaggeration and invention'. Only at the very end did the story contain any meat, concluding that a government statement was urgently needed and suggesting that the King's 'private inclination' must never be allowed to come into open conflict with public duty. It was dry stuff, but it was a seismic shift for the British newspapers. The cat was out of the bag at last.

Wilde put down the paper. He was indifferent to the story. To an American used to changing heads of state as frequently as they bought new shoes, it seemed hopelessly trivial.

Instead, his thoughts turned to Horace Dill, a man he rather liked. Did his friendship with Nancy Hereward have a deeper significance?

There was more to Horace Dill than the crusty, curmudgeonly face he turned to the world: a great deal more – and much of it spoken only in hushed tones. Dill had a lurid reputation among the other fellows and undergraduates. And it was said that he had been among those socialists who profoundly influenced young John Cornford, the Trinity history undergraduate who had recently gone off to fight with the International Brigades in Spain, carrying a volume of Shakespeare and a pistol. Tales of Cornford's daring actions and brilliant leadership were now the talk of the Cambridge Union and he had inspired others to follow him. According to one of Wilde's students, Horace had a standing offer of funds to help with the fare of anyone else wishing to go.

After a breakfast consisting mostly of restorative coffee, the telephone rang.

'Professor Wilde?'

'Good morning, Mr Eaton.'

'Glad I caught you in. There's been a development and I rather think you might be interested.'

'Carry on.'

'Two deaths. Murders. Definitely murder this time. It's just possible there might be a connection to the death of Nancy Hereward. I'm covering it for *The Times*. Do you mind if I pop over and see you?'

'What sort of connection?'

'Let's talk when I see you.'

He had a lecture to deliver, but to hell with it. Let the clever young men do something else with their time. Buy Christmas presents. Get drunk. 'OK, come over,' he said.

'I'll be with you in a quarter of an hour.'

'My address would probably be helpful.'

Laughter at the other end of the line. 'You live next door to Lydia Morris.'

'I must cease to be surprised. I'll get the coffee on.'

'Don't bother. I'm taking you out for a drive.'

By daylight, Philip Eaton looked every bit as smooth as he had the previous evening. His hair was slicked back and his shoes were polished to a military shine.

'Good car,' Wilde said as he pulled open the passenger door and climbed in.

'Austin Ten sports tourer. Decent enough.'

'And where exactly are we going?'

'It's a village called Kilmington St Edmund, a few miles south of Cambridge. Have you heard of Cecil Langley?'

'Should I have?'

'Possibly.'

Langley? Yes, he *did* know that name. 'It rings a bell. Does he have a daughter called Margot?' She was one of the Girton triumvirate: Lydia, Nancy and Margot. Shortly before Nancy's death she had received an unexpected telephone call from Margot, he recalled Lydia telling him. A strange and troubling connection indeed.

'I've no idea about his family,' Eaton said. 'All I can tell you is that he was an MP and junior minister until the last election. Never made much of a name for himself, but there was a bit of a fuss when he quit the Conservatives and joined Oswald Mosley's crew. Anyway, he and his wife have been murdered, it seems. I asked you along because he was very close to Norman Hereward. Very similar world view, both ran in the same circles – county set, that sort of thing. There are some curious elements to the story, so my newsdesk tells me. But I can't imagine it'll get much of a show – not with all this royal stuff beginning to come out. Have you seen the papers today?'

'Only yours. Nothing I didn't know. What are the curious elements in the murder?'

'Come on, let's get going.' Eaton pulled away from the kerb. 'It seems it might be a bit political,' he said. 'Haven't got the details yet, but that's what I'm told.'

Kilmington St Edmund was ten miles due south of Cambridge, along winding country roads and byways, mostly unsignposted. Wilde navigated with the assistance of an Ordnance Survey map, of which Eaton had a pile on the back seat, along with a selection of newspapers. While they waited for a flock of sheep to move out of their way, Wilde picked one of the papers up. The royal story was spread big across the front page: 'The King and his Ministers', 'Constitutional Crisis', 'Cabinet Advice'. It was much harder hitting than *The Times*, yet still there was no mention of Mrs Simpson.

'Do you care about any of this, Mr Eaton?'

'The King? I care a great deal.'

The sheep were shuffled off the road into a field and Eaton drove on.

'It's not looking good for him,' Wilde said.

'No, it's not.'

Two minutes later, Wilde saw the signpost to Kilmington St Edmund. 'Almost there.' The Austin rounded a bend and they spotted two police cars parked outside the entrance to a driveway.

'No press in sight. With luck we'll have it to ourselves for a while.' Eaton pulled up behind the police vehicles and stopped. 'Come on, let's see what's been happening.'

Kilmington stood on the banks of the Cam, not far from the headwaters. It was a timeless village with an ancient church, St Edmund's. The house where the police cars were parked was half a mile outside the village on the north side of the settlement.

Eaton and Wilde introduced themselves to a uniformed constable at the wrought-iron gate to the driveway and he told them to wait. 'I'll get the detective superintendent.'

The house was set well back from the road and hidden from view until one was in the driveway. Square-built and tall, it was the sort of place a local lord of the manor would have owned: a comfortable home. There were good views in all directions over farmland and woods, with a river frontage a hundred yards to the side of the house.

Wilde's attention turned to the front door, a hundred yards down the track, where another two cars were parked. The constable was emerging with an older man in plainclothes, a large shuffling figure who seemed in no hurry to make his way along the path.

'Well, well,' Eaton said in Wilde's ear. 'It's my old chum Bower, up from the Yard.'

'Good morning, Mr Eaton,' the plainclothes officer said as he arrived at the gate. He was puffing from the exertion of his short walk.

'Good morning, Superintendent Bower.'

The policeman turned to Wilde. 'And who do we have here?'

'Let me introduce Thomas Wilde, a Cambridge University history professor,' Eaton said.

They shook hands. 'Detective Superintendent Bower. Scotland Yard. They woke me soon after midnight. I arrived here before dawn. Breakfast is long overdue.'

'I take it you two know each other,' Wilde said.

'Oh, yes, I know Mr Eaton. But you, Professor Wilde, what brings *you* here today? I understand Mr Eaton's interest, of course.'

'He suggested I tag along.'

'Morbid curiosity, eh?' There was the ghost of a smile on Bower's lips. He was a shambling man, aged fifty or so, his silver sideburns just visible below his hat. He had intelligent eyes behind a pair of heavy Bakelite spectacles. Despite his shabby suit and stained tie, Wilde suspected that the rundown Mr Bower was a great deal more important than his appearance might suggest.

'Can we come in?' Eaton said.

Bower looked at Wilde. 'I'm not sure this is a place for those without a professional interest.'

'I'll vouch for the professor. I'm sure he will be discreet.'

'Very well. But be prepared for the worst. It's not pleasant.'

In the drawing room of the house, two constables were picking up scraps of photographs from the floor and trying to put them together like a jigsaw. Wilde could make out Hitler's toothbrush moustache in one of the emerging images.

Bower took a deep breath. 'Go easy on the detail when reporting it, Mr Eaton. These were nasty deaths. Mr and Mrs Langley had their throats slit. As far as we can tell, there were no other injuries. But as you will discover, that's only the half of it. The overtones of the case will become obvious to you. Look around you – photographs have been torn to shreds.' He swept his hand around the room. 'So far we have identified the King and Mr Hitler. How are we doing?' He addressed the two constables.

'Coming together, sir.'

He turned back to Wilde and Eaton. 'There's worse upstairs, I'm afraid. A great deal worse.'

'Could we take a look?'

'By all means, gentlemen. I trust you both have strong stomachs. But please tread carefully and don't touch anything. We don't want to smudge fingerprints or disturb evidence.'

Bloody footprints led from the runner at the top of the staircase to the bedroom and to the bathroom. As he stepped into the bedroom, Wilde felt that he had been transported to an ill-kept slaughterhouse. He had never seen so much blood. The carpet and bed were thick with it, the walls streaked with handprints and blotches.

But the blood wasn't all sprayed haphazardly. By the bed, he spotted a metal pail with a long-handled paintbrush in it. Someone – the killer or killers – had collected the blood of the victims in the bucket and had used it to paint the walls.

DEATH TO FASCISTS

The words were picked out in capitals, in blood, with clotted drips beneath each letter. On another wall there was just one word:

REVOLUTION

Beneath it, there was a hammer and sickle.

A bloody approximation of a red flag with yet another hammer and sickle polluted the wall behind the bed. The window was painted with a bloody drawing of a pig.

The killer had evidently spent a deal of time about his work, for the writing was clear, and the images of the flag and the communist insignia carefully drawn.

'We found Mrs Langley in the bed. We think she died very quickly. He must have attacked her in her sleep, cutting her jugular and carotid.'

'And her husband?' Wilde asked.

Bower grimaced. 'Rather less fortunate, I'm afraid, if that is not to do a disservice to poor Mrs Langley. But I don't want her husband's death reported in all its gory detail. There's the family to think about.'

'Don't worry,' Eaton said. 'Nothing untoward will appear in *The Times*.'

'Thank you, sir. I do, however, want the political nature of the murder reported. Someone must know who's behind it – and reports in the press might be useful.'

'I'm sure space will be found. Tell me what you have discovered, superintendent.'

'Well, I'm afraid Mr Langley's death was both terrifying and pro-longed.' Bower pointed up at the beam. 'We found him strung up there, hanging by his feet with his arms strapped behind his back. Like his wife, his throat had been cut, but he bled to death like an animal at the abat-toir, and his blood was collected in the pail. On his forehead the word *Nazi* had been written in his own blood.'

Eaton met Wilde's eye and they both grimaced.

'Do you have any clue to the killer or killers?' Wilde asked, strug-gling to contain his horror. He was having difficulty taking it all in. 'This is the work of a madman, surely? Someone local with a grudge, perhaps?'

'It is highly unlikely to have been anyone from around here, which is why they've brought me in. The only line we have is the obvious: that the murders had a political motive. There is no reason to suspect that this was a burglary gone wrong. The silver cabinets are intact, as is Mr Langley's wallet, as far as we can see. The one thing I can tell you is this: the killer was very deliberate and methodical. He even went so far as taking a bath to clean himself up.'

'Who found the bodies, superintendent?' Eaton asked.

'The maid. She lives in – and before you ask, I have no intention of giving out her name to you or anyone else. She is a prime witness and her own life may well be in danger.'

'You mean she was in the house at the time of the killings?' Wilde could hardly imagine the woman's terror.

'Indeed, Mr Wilde, that is exactly what I mean. She has a room at the top of the house. In the middle of the night, sometime between midnight and one, she was disturbed by noises directly beneath her on the first floor. She went downstairs in her nightgown and saw a man disappearing into the bathroom. He was naked and covered in blood.

'She crept back up to her room. With great presence of mind, she made her bed, switched out her light and climbed into a cupboard. She stayed there, praying that the killer would not come looking for her. Making the bed saved her life, for the killer *did* come upstairs. He switched on the light, saw that the bed was made and left without searching further. The maid didn't move. She stayed there for almost two days, huddled and shivering with cold and thirst. She was only found when the vicar called to discuss the sermon and discovered the murders and her.'

'Where is she now?'

'She was in a catatonic stupor when she was found and is still in a state of collapse, Mr Eaton, being looked after in a safe place.'

'Did she give you a description of the killer or killers?'

Detective Superintendent Bower had removed his hat. He shook his head. 'Not much to go on. She saw one man, naked, from behind. She thinks he was youngish, quite well built.'

'Complexion? Hair colour?'

'We've got nothing like that from her as yet. All she really saw was blood and bare skin. An overwhelming impression of blood. At the moment she can hardly talk. Perhaps we might coax more out of her in due course.'

'Did she see or hear a motor car?'

'Not that I know of.'

'And do you have any idea how the killer or killers got into the house?'

'Same way the vicar did. The side door was open. I'm told that no one hereabouts bothers to lock up. Why would they? There's no crime in a place like this.' Bower let out a heavy sigh. 'My initial impression is that there was only one killer, because we seem to have only one set of footprints in the blood.' He clapped his hat back on his head. 'Now if you'll excuse me, gentlemen, I have to proceed with my inquiries.'

CHAPTER 11

Eaton and Wilde took their time looking around the Langleys' house. In the bathroom, Wilde picked up a bloodstained hand-towel from a three-legged wicker stool, holding it between finger and thumb. Beneath it, there was a man's wristwatch with a leather strap. Taking it in his handkerchief he showed it to Eaton.

'Could be Cecil Langley's.'

'Or a careless killer's,' Wilde said. 'Mind you, it's a bit pricey for an assassin. Gold casing – and look at the name: *Patek Philippe & Co, Geneve*. They don't come cheap.'

The superintendent put his head round the door. 'Found something, gentlemen?'

'This.' Wilde showed Bower. 'Just discussing how likely it is that a communist assassin would have an expensive Swiss watch.'

'I think I'd better take that. Mind if I keep it wrapped?'

Wilde handed it over.

'I'll get your handkerchief back to you in due course.'

'No hurry.'

While Bower and his men continued to search the house, Wilde and Eaton looked around the Langley grounds. At the back there was a traditional country garden, now bare and wintry, abutting woodland and fields and a stream. The only things of any note were the door through which the killer had gained access to the house and some tyre marks on a track at the edge of the estate where someone, perhaps the killer, had parked a car.

'He's quite astute for a copper, our Mr Bower,' Eaton said, as they strolled back down the garden.

'Is he? He hasn't mentioned the possibility of a connection between these killings and the death of a young woman in Cambridge.'

'Well, we'll have to put it to him.'

Returning to the house, they discovered that Bower's men had finished their photographic jigsaws. 'Hitler, Mosley, the King and two other men,' the superintendent announced.

'The one with his nose in the air is Lord Londonderry,' Eaton said. 'The former Cabinet minister and good chum of Adolf and his gang. And the woman by his side is his wife Edie. The other one is the new German ambassador, von Ribbentrop. When will you have the finger-print results in?'

'Certainly not before tomorrow. Probably longer. They'll have to go up to the Met.' Bower shrugged helplessly. 'As I'm sure you'll understand, there is a great deal of concern about this among the powers that be.'

Wilde could imagine there would be. This was not merely an attack on one man and his wife: it struck at the very heart of those who considered themselves born to run the country.

He took some time looking at the photographs in the room that had escaped the killer's frenzied attack. The girl, he concluded, was the Langleys' daughter, Margot, the friend of Lydia and Nancy. He wondered if the police had yet told her the news. Lydia, too, would almost certainly have known the parents. Another picture caught his eye and surprised him: three men together, two of whom he had seen in the past twenty-four hours. The pic-ture was difficult to spot, almost hidden away in an alcove. Cecil Langley, Sir Norman Hereward and Lord Slievedonard, together on a viewing plat-form at what looked very much like one of the Nuremberg rallies. They were all making the straight-arm salute.

'I don't hold out much hope of any more information from the house,' said Eaton.

Nor, Wilde imagined, would the fingerprints throw up a match. But there was still the other matter. 'Did you know,' he said to Bower, 'that a friend of the Langleys' daughter died in unpleasant circumstances in Cambridge the day before yesterday? Miss Nancy Hereward, daughter of Sir Norman Hereward.'

Bower frowned and peered at Wilde through his thick lenses. 'Yes, Mr Wilde, I had heard something of it. Is there some connection?'

'Well, the obvious one – Margot Langley and Nancy Hereward were friends. And Mr Eaton tells me their fathers were friends, too.'

'But as I understand it,' Bower continued, 'the girl in Cambridge died of an overdose. That's what my colleagues there are saying. Isn't that correct?'

Wilde turned to the reporter. 'Mr Eaton, perhaps you'd back me up on this. Surely it's worth investigating?'

'Indeed.'

'Well,' Bower said, 'I shall bear your thought in mind and talk to my Cambridge colleagues again. I'm not closing any avenues.'

The *Gaviota*, a small steam trawler of a hundred and fifty tonnes, had seen better days. She was a pre-war vessel that had served under several different flags and masters and been adapted for the taking of a variety of different fish, as the markets rose and fell in times of conflict and peace. Now she was floating scrap iron, just about ready for the breaker's yard.

As she limped past the red and white lighthouse into the broad mouth of an isolated East Anglian river, its water churning where it met the sea, no one save the harbourmaster noted her. She was clearly in trouble, low in the water and listing to starboard, chugging noisily, black smoke belching from her single funnel.

The trawler's skipper was a man of about thirty with black stubble and a weatherworn brow. He wore durable blue trousers, tied with string at the ankles as though he were about to ride a bicycle, a baggy round-necked sweater and a waxed waterproof. He was at the wheel, a stinking hand-rolled cigarette of north African tobacco wedged firmly in the corner of his mouth. There were two other men aboard, one of them a creaking mariner in his late sixties, the other a youth. All three were similarly dressed; all were unshaven. Anyone looking at the three of them together would have said they were family, and they would be right.

Juan Ferreira, the skipper, was the only one of the three with any English. As he watched the harbourmaster's vessel approach, he rehearsed his story.

He had another concern, too. The water was shallow here, and rough at the point where the river opened up into the sea. He knew he had to keep between the buoys that marked the navigable channel. But he also knew that there was an ever-present danger of grounding.

In truth, Ferreira was astonished they had got this far, to this lonely stretch of Suffolk coast between Felixstowe and Southwold. The *Gaviota* – Spanish for *seagull* – was scarcely seaworthy and he had felt certain that vessels of the famed and feared Royal Navy would intercept them as they crawled up the channel from Finisterre and the Bay of Biscay. It had been a long journey, more than sixteen hundred nautical miles from Cartagena on the Mediterranean coast of republican-held Spain. They had made no more than seven knots, interspersed with diversions to avoid ships in Spanish coastal waters that might be hostile and, later, to make lengthy stops for coal and repairs, particularly at Bordeaux and La Rochelle. At Brest, on the western tip of Britanny, they had had to be towed in for emergency repairs to the screw, which had been damaged by a half-submerged spar from some long-forgotten sailing vessel. It had been an anxious time, for customs officers came aboard and announced they would search the trawler; such vessels had been used too often for smuggling guns since the start of the Spanish war, they said. A bribe of two hundred francs and six bottles of Spanish brandy had satisfied them and so, after a perfunctory search, they had gone on their way with fraternal grins and jovial cries of 'Vive la Revolution'.

But the autumn weather had been against them. The little vessel struggled against the heavy seas and winds and had to spend more time in port, at one time stranded for more than three weeks, every day fearing that their secret would be discovered.

The *Gaviota* had stopped again for repairs in Dieppe. By that point, Ferreira's nerves were in shreds; he had never smoked so much in his life. He found himself wishing he was up on the front line dodging the bullets and bombs of Franco's men; at least he'd know where he was. This was torment; he could not believe they would get away with it. And yet, they had. So far. Now here they were, forty days out of Cartagena, limping into an English mooring, the gold undiscovered and intact.

What does seven and a half metric tonnes of eighteen-carat gold look like? Gold is heavy and does not take up a great deal of room. These weren't ingots: this was coin. It was neatly packed into a hundred boxes, each slightly smaller than a case for six bottles of wine. Each box held seventy-five kilos in a variety of currencies: American, Spanish, German, French, British, Austrian, Swiss, Belgian, and more. But mostly US dollars and Spanish currency. They were well hidden in a hurriedly built but solid compartment attached to the outside of the boat, beneath the hull. A frogman searching beneath the vessel might spot something amiss, but customs men searching the inside of the old trawler would find nothing. The danger came when the craft was raised from the water for repairs to the screw. They had had to do the work themselves, for a mechanic brought in for the job would soon have asked questions. Any thorough search below the waterline would result in the gold being discovered. Ferreira's fingers were yellow from chain-smoking.

Of course, the French hadn't looked too closely because the new socialist government was on friendly terms with the republican government of Spain in its fight against the rebel brigades of General Franco. But England would be different. Here, in this remote stretch of river, bounded by a shingle spit to seaward and marshland to the west, their voyage would be hard to explain away. And a bribe would not help, because legend had it that British officials were incorruptible.

The harbourmaster's red and white motor-launch was no more than a hundred yards away, cutting a gentle wash through water, calm now that they were away from the sea and sheltered by the spit. Ferreira knew that if anything was out of place, even slightly, the harbourmaster would summon the police and customs without delay.

The skipper did something he hadn't done since his childhood. He made the sign of the cross and asked the Almighty for assistance. The prayer gave him no comfort and he did not expect it to be answered. He placed more hope in the French flag now flying at the vessel's stern in place of the Spanish one.

The motor-launch was almost alongside and the engine was cut to one or two knots. The harbourmaster, greying beard beneath a peaked cap, held a loudhailer to his mouth. 'Are you all right there?'

'We head for Yarmouth, sir. Spend night here.'

'Where are you from?'

'Calais.'

'Stick to the channel markers. There are free moorings upriver. If you need any help, someone will show you to my office. I'll be back later. If you get as far as the town, there's good food and ale in the pub.'

'Thank you, sir.'

'Good man. We'll talk later.' The harbourmaster let out the throttle on his launch and continued with the ebbing tide downriver towards the open sea.

Juan Ferreira watched him go. He had no intention of going to any town. The hand-drawn map told him there was a smaller creek very soon – and that, in turn, would lead him into a yet smaller waterway. Deserted and unknown by most, a tiny, silent lake of brackish water. He only prayed that the water would be deep enough to accommodate them.

Wilde and Eaton walked down from the Langleys' house to the village of Kilmington.

'I've got the feeling that Bower has already filed any connection to Nancy's death away under *to be disregarded*,' said Wilde. 'I need a drink.'

The village pub was an old thatched house and the bar was a small, smoky room with low, beamed ceilings. The morning regulars stared at the two men as though they were beings from a distant planet.

In the corner of one wall, next to the bar, a battered cricket bat, an old cricket ball and a scorecard were displayed like trophies. 'Those are from his glory days,' the landlord said.

'Whose?' Wilde asked.

'Mr Langley. He used to play for Essex before the war. That's the bat he used for his first century – and that's the ball he hit out of the ground the same day. Very kindly gave them to the village.'

'Was he liked around here?'

'Aye, he was. A good man, not well treated by Baldwin. Quite a lot of folk in these parts were behind him when he signed up with Mr Mosley.'

'And you?'

'My politics is my business.'

'Did he have enemies locally?'

'Mr Langley? By no means. He was our squire. Who'll open the fête with him gone? And his missus, everyone loved her. Where will the WI be without her?'

Eaton handed the landlord half a crown and asked him to announce his presence. He gave a grunt of thanks and banged a pewter tankard on the bar. 'This young man is a reporter from *The Times*,' he said. 'He wants to buy you all a drink at this sad time – and to listen to what he has to say.'

The room was hushed. Wary eyes rested on Philip Eaton.

'You will soon find your little village taken over by a horde of reporters from the rag press,' Eaton said. 'You will find them intrusive and some of them will be downright unpleasant, prepared to resort to any means to get you to talk to them. It would be my considered advice that you do *not* talk to them, whatever their grand promises, for they will twist your words – and lie. As a representative of *The Times*, however, I will treat all information you give me with discretion. If anyone has any knowledge of the Langleys or the tragic events that befell them, I would be grateful to hear from you. Thank you for listening.' He took a seat at the bar with Wilde. 'Hopefully that will get them thinking,' he muttered. 'Someone must have seen the car, if not the man driving.'

'So,' said Wilde. 'The revolution starts here in Cambridgeshire. If we take these murders at face value.'

'It's all a great deal too pat.'

'Exactly my thinking. And yet, we can't just dismiss it. The Reds aren't known for their subtlety, for God's sake.' Wilde was silent a moment, then met Eaton's eyes. 'And Nancy Hereward?'

'I really don't know. But that family connection is a hell of a coincidence.' Eaton took a deep draught of his stout. 'Come on, drink up. Let's get in among them, see what they've got to say for themselves.'

CHAPTER 12

Hartmut Dorfen pulled up outside the broad entrance of the Dorchester Hotel, handed his small leather bag to the porter and told him to take it to the apartment of Sophie Gräfin von Isarbeck. 'Park the car,' he told the commissionaire, then rode the lift to the sixth floor where he was met by a butler, who bowed low, opened the door and stood back to admit Dorfen to the lushly carpeted lobby of the Gräfin's apartment.

She was waiting for him, her arms wide in welcome. 'Darling.' She stepped towards him. 'Come to Sophie. Welcome to my humble pied-à-terre.'

The apartment, the Gräfin's permanent London residence, was enormous, with four bedrooms, a dining room, a study and a capacious drawing room facing out across Park Lane to Hyde Park. The Gräfin, by contrast, was tiny, no more than four feet ten inches. Dorfen scooped her up into his arms as though she were a small child. He kissed her on the lips. 'Now, where is the best bedroom?'

'Hartmut, you are as naughty as ever! Put me *down*.'

'And I thought you loved me.'

'Of course, I love you. All women love you. You are the handsomest man in all of Germany, as you well know.'

Outside, the day was grey, overcast and gusty. The bare limbs of the trees in the park across the road shivered and bent in the wind. The weather was changing. It was beginning to feel like winter, not autumn. Dorfen realised he was exhausted.

'Food? Drink?' The Gräfin snapped her fingers and the butler appeared. 'Eggs Benedict and a good Krug,' she ordered.

At the window, Dorfen shook his head in disgust. 'God, this city with its red buses and its smoke. It's so dirty. I never liked it.'

The Gräfin wagged her finger. 'This city is the heart of the greatest empire the world has ever known, Hartmut, and the King is at its very core. You *Müncheners* are so provincial. London is important to us, as is Edward. We need them on our side.' She saw the weariness in his blue eyes. 'You are tired, Hartmut, you have not stopped these past days.'

He patted her cheek. 'There has been much to do, many men to see. Our friends in Nordsee . . .'

'I am sure you charmed them all.'

Sophie von Isarbeck wasn't beautiful. She wasn't ugly. Her body was neither slim nor fat, but pale and soft with a rounded womanly belly and no hint of muscle. A little pudding, or *tönnchen*, she had been called, and yet she captured all eyes in any room she entered. Her magnetism drew in monarchs and magnates, dictators and Hollywood stars.

'And what is the news of the King?'

'He is a mess.' The Gräfin's voice turned confidential. 'Wally was here for over an hour yesterday, in a dreadful state. It is all she can do to console the poor man, and I had to do likewise with her. Soon she'll be on a boat to France and Edward will be left to deal with this crisis alone.' Sadness swept across Sophie von Isarbeck's face: like an actress, she knew how to connect with an audience, whatever its class or gender. She was loved and hated in equal measure, but never ignored.

'Will he abdicate? Is it certain yet?'

'She says he is alternately defiant and meek in the face of Baldwin's bullying. She begs him to stand firm, she reminds him that he is king and emperor, but in her heart she knows he will capitulate, throw it all in. It's out of her hands now, so it is up to us. If we allow the King to follow her to Cannes, the game will most certainly be up.'

'And this is all Baldwin's doing?'

'Not just Baldwin. The whole Cabinet wants him out, as does the Privy Council. But Baldwin is the prime mover.' She smiled. 'You know there are those who say the King should dismiss him and rule alone.'

'The Royal Führer . . .'

'Precisely. But of course he will not do it. He is too timid – so we must be his backbone, Hart, or Baldwin will have his *coup d'état*.'

Dorfen nodded his agreement. 'And the Möhlau man?'

'He is ready. I will have the information you need very soon. If not today, then in the next two days.' She paused and smiled reassuringly. 'It is very simple and daring and it *will* work.'

Dorfen spotted a photograph on an occasional table beneath a standard lamp. It was Heinrich Hoffman's picture of Hitler. Hoffmann had made the Führer looked like a movie idol, a Clark Gable or Willy Birgel. The photograph was framed in solid eighteen-carat gold, etched with the words *Hochverehrte Gräfin* – revered countess – beside a small enamelled swastika, embedded in the gold. A special gift from Hitler.

She touched his face. 'There is a speck of blood on your collar, Hartmut.'

'I cut myself shaving.'

'Careless boy.'

'Cancel the food, Sophie. I want to sleep.'

'Of course you do, *liebling*. I'll tuck you in.'

The reporters were arriving. 'They might as well have hired a charabanc,' Eaton said as he watched the cars screeching to a halt along the length of the village main street. He pointed them out to Wilde, by newspaper not name. '*Herald, Mail, Telegraph, Mirror, Observer, Express, News Chronicle*. Don't know the other ones – probably locals from Cambridge.'

The newsmen began swarming around the village with the aggression and singularity of purpose of a foraging army, all of them accompanied by photographers. Detective Superintendent Bower was happy to brief them, but he would not show them the scene of the killings, which meant that the reporters would have to rely on local gossip and the flashing of nice white five-pound notes. But they were too late: the village and the police had become wary.

Before the arrival of the invasion force, however, Wilde and Eaton had learnt quite a lot about the Langleys from the drinkers in the pub. They had learnt that there had been a succession of visitors to the couple's remote house in the past year, many driving Rolls Royces, Daimlers and other expensive cars with chauffeurs and valets. They learnt, too, that their newly married daughter Margot had not been seen for more than eighteen months. In a small English village, people noticed what wasn't there as much as what was. And they gossiped about everything.

'What about their maid?'

'Aspinall? She wasn't local,' said the landlord, a mutton-chop whiskered old soldier, who had taken more money in an hour than he usually took in a week. He'd have even more when the Fleet Street horde came in. 'She came from Ipswich, I believe.'

'Where is she now?'

'No one knows. I heard Dr Barrow had to give her a sedative before she was taken away.'

'And you haven't heard of anyone seeing or hearing a car late at night?'

'Few enough cars come here in daytime, so a car driving through the village at midnight would most likely have been heard. But if it approached from the west, we wouldn't have heard anything.'

'Didn't the Langleys have a dog?' Wilde had asked. Surely everyone in the countryside had a dog.

'Their Springer died a couple of months ago. I don't think they had the heart to replace her . . .'

'How would you describe Mr Langley?' Eaton put in.

'Oh, he was a proper gentleman with all the old virtues: honour, duty, loyalty. He didn't care much for these modern times. And as a military man, I'd say he was right.'

'Tell me about his politics.'

'They were his own business, as are mine.' The landlord went back to polishing the glasses. 'I was brought up a Liberal, but I don't mind telling you I can see the attraction in some of these new parties. That Mr Mussolini is getting things right in Italy.'

They took a last stroll through Kilmington. It was an almost exclusively farming community of labourers, ploughmen and herders. The middle classes were represented by Dr Barrow and the vicar, with the Langleys at the top of the tree. The only other person who might have had pretensions was the schoolmaster at the little elementary school. Wilde estimated that the population could not have come to more than two hundred. The church, St Edmund's, was medieval, thatched, and built of flint on higher ground. There was, too, a modest little brick-built Methodist chapel that had seen better days.

'It occurs to me,' said Wilde, 'that the killer is likely to have known the Langleys' house. There's no sign on the gatepost and it's set well back from the road behind a screen of trees. I doubt whether anyone would have stumbled upon it. We wouldn't have spotted it if we hadn't seen the police cars parked on the road outside.'

'So family, friend? Former domestic with a grudge?'

'I wouldn't rule anyone out.'

'I agree – but I think I've got just about everything I'm going to get today,' Eaton said. 'I'm pretty sure the answer to this murder does not lie in the village. If you'll bear with me, I'll try to bag the telephone box to file my story before the rats dive in.'

Later, as they were about to drive out of the village, they were flagged down by Bower.

Wilde wound down the passenger window. 'Superintendent?'

'There was one thing I thought worth mentioning to you, in confidence of course, gentlemen. It's the photographs. We pieced together five – Hitler, the King and the other three.'

'What of it?'

'Well, I couldn't help noticing that there were *six* empty frames. Of course it might mean nothing, but it set me thinking. Was the sixth one already empty – or did the killer remove the picture and take it away?'

'You're suggesting it might have meant something to the killer?'

'I have to consider the possibility.'

'Any other leads yet?'

'Nothing substantial, I'm afraid. We're talking to various known troublemakers and rabble-rousers. But I don't hold out much hope. This is very different.'

'A communist plot?' Wilde asked.

'Oh, I'm much too long in the tooth to jump to conclusions, Mr Wilde.'

Although he had not seen service in the Great War, Stanley Baldwin was quite adept at keeping his head down when necessary. But still, there was something fairly ridiculous about the events of this Thursday.

The King had summoned him to Buckingham Palace yet again, but this time he wanted the prime minister to arrive in secret, unseen by the hordes of press reporters waiting outside the gates. Now that the story was in the British papers, the palace was under siege.

And so Baldwin had had to hide himself on the back seat of his Rolls Royce and instruct his chauffeur to drive in through a back entrance. Baldwin, almost seventy years old and not in the best of health, was then required to clamber into the building through a ground-floor window. When, finally, he had dusted himself down he had been confronted by an emotional Edward pleading with him to be allowed to make a radio broadcast to his people, to explain why he must marry the woman he loved.

Baldwin listened with concerned eyes, but gave nothing away. Guile and charm were attributes that he possessed in abundance. With his pipe and homely manner, he liked the world to think he was one of them: an ordinary man, a favourite uncle, the heart of everyone's family. He understood the way they lived. He shared their worries and fears and wanted the best for his people, his country. But in fact the Harrow and Cambridge-educated Baldwin was *not* like them – and nor was he as affable as he liked to make out. His public face hid the truth: he was the bastard son of Machiavelli's prince, a man who would kill you with soothing words and a blade so sharp you wouldn't feel it slide into your flesh.

He looked at the pathetic creature standing before him, frantically smoking one cigarette after the other, and agreed that he would consult his Cabinet colleagues on the matter of a possible broadcast but that he held out little hope.

Edward turned on him like a petulant child. 'You *want* me to go, don't you?'

Baldwin spoke calmly but firmly. A father insisting that his son should do the right thing. 'What I want, sir,' he said, 'is what you told me you wanted: to go with dignity, without dividing the country, in a way that makes things as smooth as possible for your successor.'

The wind was picking up as Eaton drove Wilde back to Cambridge. On the less alarming stretches of the road, they discussed the possible meaning of the empty sixth frame.

'Their daughter might know which picture was missing,' Wilde suggested.

'Then we'd better talk to her, hadn't we? I'd also like to know why she hasn't been home in over a year.' Eaton fished inside his jacket pocket and pulled out a slim notebook with a velvet cover. 'Take a look in there. Bound to find her.'

Wilde skimmed the pages and glanced at Eaton. 'This is Mrs Langley's address book. You stole it from their house.'

'Stole is a strong word, old boy. Just borrowing it to take a quick peek. Reporter's trick.'

Wilde kept his gaze on Eaton's well-bred profile. 'Is this really the sort of training you get in Fleet Street these days?'

Eaton laughed. 'You sound somewhat disapproving, Wilde. I do believe I've shocked you.'

'Reporter be damned! Who are you, Eaton? Or should I say, *what* are you?'

Eaton's eyes stayed on the road. 'Not sure I understand you.'

'I mean who do you work for, really?'

'*The Times*. Special Correspondent. You've got my card.'

'I've no doubt you work for *The Times*, but who else?'

'I'm paid well enough. I have no need to moonlight.'

'Don't be disingenuous, Eaton. I'm not an idiot. I think you work in Intelligence.' In the gloomy interior of the Austin, Wilde thought he could just make out the sliver of a smile on Eaton's unblemished face.

'Stick to the history books, Professor Wilde. I think you've been reading too much John Buchan.'

Wilde laughed. 'You just happen to turn up in Cambridge when three people die. You hint at the possibility of links between the two cases. And you just happen to know about Nancy Hereward's trip to Berlin.'

'Sheer coincidence, old boy. Sheer coincidence.'

CHAPTER 13

When they arrived in Cambridge, Wilde suggested to Eaton that he should meet Lydia. The front door of her house was open and they found her in the kitchen, pots and pans everywhere.

'Lydia, this is Philip Eaton. I mentioned him to you.'

'Ah yes, you're doing a story on Nancy. Pleased to meet you.'

'The pleasure is all mine. It would be good to talk.'

'Well, as you can see, Mr Eaton, I'm up to my eyes cooking. Tell you what, maybe you'd care to join us for dinner? It's only boring old beef stew and dumplings, I'm afraid, but you might find the company entertaining. Apple pie for pudding.'

'Nothing boring about stew and apple pie, Miss Morris. I'd be delighted to take up your offer.'

'About seven then?'

'Can I drive you back to college?' Eaton asked as they stepped outside.

Wilde looked at his watch. Five o'clock. He hadn't realised they had spent so long at Kilmington. He very much wanted to talk to Lydia alone. 'No, thank you,' he said.

'I'm told you have a very good brain, professor. Do you ever wonder whether it might be wasted drumming dates and battles into the heads of undergraduates?'

Wilde laughed. 'I'll see you at seven.'

Wilde went into his own house, splashed water over his face and changed his shirt and tie. He peered out of the window into the gloomy, sodium-yellow street to check that the Austin Ten had gone and made his way back to Lydia's house.

In her kitchen he saw that she had opened a bottle of red wine and poured herself a glass. 'I'm sorry, I really felt I needed it.'

'Don't apologise.'

'Would you like a glass?'

'Actually, I think I probably need a Scotch. What do you think of Eaton?'

'Privilege oozes out of him like sweat in a Turkish bath.'

'I think there's rather more to him than that. But we'll see. It'll be interesting to watch him with Comrade Kholtov and Horace Dill this evening. But, Lydia, I need to talk to you. Do you have any inkling where we've been today?'

She was rolling pastry. 'No. Should I have?'

'The scene of a double murder.' He paused and gritted his teeth. 'I'm pretty sure you must know them.'

Lydia turned to face him. 'Tom, I don't like this.'

'Cecil and Penny Langley. The parents of your friend Margot, if I'm not mistaken.'

She put her hand, all covered in flour, to her mouth. 'Oh my God, not Mr and Mrs Langley. Please don't tell me this. Tom, this is too awful. Are you sure?'

'I'm afraid so. I went there with Eaton. He was reporting on it. It's a big story.'

'This is so, so horrible. I knew them well. I went to their house in Kilmington often – we all did. It's not far from here.'

'That's where they were killed.'

'How? How did it happen?'

He couldn't say the words *their throats were slit*. Those four words conjured up too much horror. 'A knife attack,' he said. 'There were political overtones. Apparently Langley was a good friend of Sir Norman. Similar politics. Hasn't it been on the wireless yet?'

'I was at Bene't Street until lunchtime, then I went to the butcher's and grocer's and came home. I haven't heard any news. God, Tom, what is happening?'

She seemed on the point of collapse. He took her in his arms and helped her sit at the kitchen table. 'I'm so sorry, Lydia.'

'But Margot had just called Nancy for some reason. Nancy was going to tell me about it at the cinema. Tom, this is all so horrible and weird.'

Wilde poured her a fresh glass of wine. She gulped at it.

'We used to be a team, Margot, Nancy and I, back in our Girton days. Clever girls with high ideals and a mission to change the world. Oh, poor Mrs Langley. She was lovely. Our weekends at their house were all walks, horse talk and drinks, but it got us away from our studies for a day or two. And she baked the most wonderful cakes. This is terrible. Poor Margot. If she's been trying to contact them, she must be frantic with worry.'

'Where is she? The villagers say they haven't seen her recently.'

'I don't know, Tom. I haven't heard from her in an age. She's a bolter. Married some ass with a minor title and then she did a runner – and I can't say I blame her because he was completely chinless. I rather thought she must have scooted off to London or the South of France – anything to avoid the trouble she'd have got into at home. Her father was an absolute stickler for good behaviour. He would have been incandescent.'

'Well, the police will find her. She must be told.'

'Do you think it's connected with Nancy's death? It must be. Both Margot and Nancy's fathers knew each other well. They were *friends*.'

Detective Superintendent Bower hadn't seemed interested in the friendship. 'We'll find out,' Wilde said, not really believing it. He clasped her hand. 'I'll cancel tonight, yes?'

'Yes, cancel. I can't bear to see anyone.' Her body suddenly shook. 'No, God no, *don't* cancel. The stew's just about cooked. Anyway, I want to hear what your Mr Eaton has to say. And I want to get sloshed.'

Wilde told Lydia most of what he knew about the murders, trying as hard as he could to avoid the gruesome details. Lydia sat in stunned silence, unable to take in the full horror of these past hours and days. She peppered him with questions, most of which he couldn't answer and others that he wouldn't. At last she poured another large wine, drank it in one, and returned to the pastry.

'I can still cancel this evening.'

'No, Tom. I may as well drink myself into oblivion among friends as alone.' She told him she had invited Peggy Rale and Jean Whiston from Bowes & Bowes. 'We were a bit shy in the female department and they were the only ones who came to mind. With luck, they'll steer you men away from fist fights. I don't think I could bear any trouble tonight.'

*

Eaton was the first to arrive. Lydia immediately latched on to him and began to question him about Nancy and the Langleys. 'Surely there must be a connection, Mr Eaton?'

'The problem is *Corpus Delicti*. Ancient British law. Without proof of a crime, there is no crime. And in the case of your friend Nancy, there is certainly no proof of crime and scarcely any evidence to speak of. Merely her fears, a trip to Berlin and suspicion on your part and my part.'

'And her father's,' Wilde said. *And mine, too, after all that has happened.*

'Indeed.'

'But your suspicion isn't without cause, is it, Mr Eaton?' Lydia said. 'You know something – something about our trip to Berlin. How *do* you know about that, by the way?'

'As I told Professor Wilde, I hear things. I'm a pretty good reporter. And Miss Hereward wrote it up herself.' He brushed her question aside. 'But I'd like to find out more. Someone in Cambridge will know the truth. Whatever she was doing in Berlin, it wasn't off her own bat.'

Lydia wiped her hands down her apron, shook her head and turned to Wilde. 'God, Tom, this is all too much. I'm getting scared. Bloody terrified, actually.'

From everything Wilde knew of Lydia, he guessed it would take a lot to unnerve her. And even more for her to admit it. 'We'll talk more later,' he said.

She nodded. 'You're right. Go and get yourself drinks. I'm keeping this bottle of wine for myself.' She bustled them out into the dining room and retired to the kitchen. Wilde looked at the closed door. She was trying to carry on as normal – working on the book, attending the rally for Kholtov, serving up dinner, keeping herself busy to dull the pain. But everything was mechanical. Must do this, must say that, must be jolly, must get drunk, mustn't admit I'm vulnerable. It didn't fool him for a moment.

He headed for the drinks cabinet. 'Now then, Lydia has a reasonable Scotch and there's gin but no tonic. Hang on, I think there's some angostura here. Yes, here it is. Pink gin? Hah, she's got in some vodka for Comrade Kholtov. What will you have, Eaton?'

'Scotch, no water.'

As he was pouring, there was a knock at the door. The two young women from the Bowes & Bowes bookshop were standing on the doorstep, looking rather awkward. He knew them vaguely, had asked them to order books for him. 'Miss Rale, Miss Whiston, come in, come in,' he said, ushering them inside. 'Let me introduce you to Philip Eaton. And a quiet word in your ear. Lydia's feeling rather shredded tonight. Death of a very good friend.'

Wilde wondered what Lydia had been thinking of by inviting these two. They were presentable enough, but they would be lost in this evening's company. Peggy Rale sparkled like lemonade (though she asked for a port and lemon), and Jean Whiston was as prim as the sherry she drank. Both proclaimed a love for books: Peggy read Agatha Christie and Georgette Heyer while Jean spoke quietly of her love for Tolstoy and Gide and was currently reading *Strait is the Gate*, which she found most profound and rewarding. Wilde smiled and nodded; he had found it deathly.

It was another three-quarters of an hour before Yuri Kholtov and Horace Dill appeared, just as Lydia was beginning to panic. Both of them had been drinking.

'We've been talking about the King,' Dill boomed. 'We know what to do with kings, don't we, Yuri?'

Kholtov laughed and his large body shook. He blew out a stream of toxic smoke from his papirosa 'people's cigarette'.

With introductions made and drinks poured, dinner was ready and they fell into their allotted seats. Peggy began to giggle and Wilde realised that Kholtov was doing something to her leg under the table. The Russian leant across and kissed her throat and she shivered with pleasure.

Horace Dill was a less amiable drunk. He continued to rail against the government, the King, Mosley, Mussolini, Hitler and Franco, then turned to Eaton. 'They're all in a conspiracy against the people. Isn't that so? This man we are supposed to revere as our king and head of state is as Nazi as the Nazis.'

Wilde was surprised by Dill's familiarity but then it struck him. He and Eaton must know each other. Dill had been a history don since before the war, and Eaton, as a one-time history undergraduate, must have attended his lectures, perhaps even been under his supervision. Why had they allowed themselves to be introduced as strangers?

'So you two must already know each other,' Wilde said.

Dill and Eaton met each other's eyes and smiled. 'I once had high hopes for this young man,' Dill said. 'But the bourgeois filth was ingrained too deep in his rotten soul. Now look at him! He's taken the Tory shilling at His Majesty's capitalist press!'

Eaton laughed. 'Glad to hear you still spitting Bolshevik bile, Professor Dill. Good to know some things never change. Now have another drink and pay attention to your hostess.'

Lydia was sitting opposite Horace Dill, breathing in the fumes from his enormous cigar. The table was already littered with ash. A fug of fumes hung over the guests like a city fog. 'Don't bother about me,' she said. 'I'm more than happy listening to everyone else this evening.'

'She's all right, that Lydia Morris.' Dill slurred the words. 'Her heart's in the right place. Bit theoretical perhaps, but we'll have her at the barricades yet.'

'What about Nancy Hereward?' Wilde asked. 'Did you get *her* to the barricades?'

Horace Dill peered through his spectacles, his little pig eyes boring into Wilde's. 'What are you suggesting, Tom?'

'You're a very amusing man, Horace, but you do have a tendency to send young innocents into the front line. Did you do that to Nancy Hereward, perhaps?'

'She was worth a hundred of you, Tom Wilde. I'd have trusted that girl with my life. Her death is a damned tragedy.'

And so there *had* been a closeness between them. Another of Horace Dill's projects, like John Cornford. Wilde wondered about the hapless Roger Maxwell. He had spotted him with Dill, deep in conversation on several occasions, just as he had seen Eugene Felsted coming under Duncan Sawyer's influence. If this was the way the young were going – splitting to the furthest extremes – it boded ill for the future of the world.

So, Wilde thought, perhaps he had the first part of his answer, the identity of the man who had sent her on a mission in Berlin. Now he needed the second part, the nature of her task. 'I'd very much like to discover the truth about her death, Horace. There is a suggestion that when she went to the Olympics in August she was asked to do some covert work for the Comintern. Would you know anything about that?' His gaze strayed from Dill to Eaton, and then back to Dill.

'Fuck you, Tom. I don't like men who dance on graves.'

'What was she doing for you?'

Horace Dill looked away. 'Where's that fucking vodka bottle?'

Wilde caught Eaton's eye. If the reporter was put out that his theory about Nancy's secret work had been mentioned, it didn't show. He was watching and listening rather than joining the conversation. That was what reporters and spies did, wasn't it – watched and listened? Wilde pushed on. 'It occurred to me, Horace, that if her death was not suicide or accident, then you might have an idea who wished her dead.'

The rest of the table fell silent.

'Who wanted her dead?' Dill shouted. 'Who do you think wanted her dead, you imbecile? The fucking Nazis. Ask Mosley or Slievedonard or Londonderry or that creep Sawyer. Ask their fucking lordships. Ask the fucking Pope or the fucking Church of England. Ask Baldwin or Churchill or Ribbentrop.'

Jean Whiston started to rise from her chair. 'I'm sorry, Lydia, I don't think . . .'

Dill hammered the table with the haft of his knife. 'Sit down, you stupid woman. Are you a Christian, is that it? Have I offended your superstitious sensibilities by mentioning His Holiness the fucking Pope? Is that it?'

Jean looked to Lydia for assistance, but her eyes were heavy from drink and she shrugged helplessly. When Horace Dill's tail was up, he could squirt a non-stop flow of noxious bile from his arse. Nothing short of death or earthquake would stop him.

Dill waved the knife at Jean. 'I'll tell you about religion. I'll tell you about the priests with their dirty fingernails up the choirboys' cassocks, the nuns with their cunts all waxy from the altar candle. Power and money – your money – that's what they want, you stupid little whore.'

Jean Whiston was standing now. She stepped away from her chair, pushed it neatly back to the table, fetched her coat and handbag and, without another word, walked from the house.

'That was unforgivable, Horace,' Lydia said, tears beginning to flow. 'You were abominably cruel.'

'Moronic tart. Anyway, I see her friend's still here. You're not offended are you, miss whatever your name is?'

'Miss Rale. And my dad was at Jutland so I know all your dirty words, Mr Dill, and plenty more besides. I know *bugger* and *sodomise*, too. I'm sure you know all about those words, don't you, Mr Dill?'

Horace Dill's elephantine face twisted into a scowl, then exploded into a roar of laughter. 'Your dad would certainly know them, being a Navy man.'

Peggy snuggled closer to Kholtov, her eyes still on Dill. 'Now, eat your food, smoke your filthy cigar and shut up, you nasty old man – you're upsetting my lovely Russian friend here.'

Wilde rose from his chair and touched Lydia on the shoulder. 'I'll go after Jean Whiston.'

'Thank you, Tom.'

Wilde caught up with her at the bottom of the road. 'Miss Whiston, I'm sorry about that.'

She met his eyes. He could see that she had been crying.

'It wasn't your fault, Professor Wilde.'

'Still, it shouldn't have happened. Can I walk you home?'

'I've got a flat near Cat's. I'll be all right.'

'I'll see you home safe.'

She managed a modest smile. 'Thank you. It's nice to know there are still a few gentlemen in this horrible world.'

By the time Wilde returned, Leslie Braithwaite had arrived and was sitting at the table in his place, gorging on a large plate of stew, washing it down with neat whisky. He glanced up at Wilde, then returned to his eating, thrusting large spoonfuls of meat, gravy and vegetables into his hungry maw.

Wilde took Jean Whiston's chair and placed it at the head of the table, beside Kholtov. 'How long are you planning to stay in Cambridge?' he asked the Russian.

'Are you worried that I might start killing people, Professor Wilde?'

'Perhaps I'm too late.'

Kholtov turned to Lydia with a hurt expression. 'Your friend lacks manners, Miss Morris.'

Wilde wasn't having it. 'Oh balls, Kholtov, I just lack your belief that the end justifies the means. That's all. I know what has been happening in the Soviet Union – and I have a very good idea of what is now happening in Spain.'

'Do you? I tell you, Mr Wilde, I learnt much at the Spanish front – about England. Britain. Here.'

'Such as?'

Kholtov's mouth opened then shut, as though someone had kicked him under the table. Wilde looked across the table at Dill, glassy-eyed, drunk and taciturn. Had Kholtov been about to say something that he didn't want revealed?

'Anyway,' Kholtov continued, returning to Wilde's original question. 'I think you are sadly misinformed. I am adviser to the legitimate Spanish Popular Front government of Francisco Caballero. I am not a savage. The people of Spain are fighting for their very existence against Franco's fascist monsters. I ask you this – why you think me some sort of assassin or executioner? I have never heard of you, sir – why do you presume to know anything about me? It is most hurtful. You have an English word for it, *slander*.'

'So how long are you staying?'

He swept the question away with a flick of the hand. 'Not more than two or three days.'

'And then? Back to the killing fields of Spain?'

'The killing fields of Spain?' Dill exploded back into life. 'You bleeding heart Yanks! In the real world, there's a struggle between good and evil – and all the while you drink soda from your electric refrigerator and clean your house with a vacuum cleaner. In Spain and Germany, it's kill or be killed.'

'Oh, I think it's a lot more complicated than that.' Wilde turned his gaze back to Kholtov. 'Well?'

'No, I'm not going back to Spain. To Moscow. I have an appointment there.' He looked across at Horace Dill. 'It will be a great pleasure to see my family again after so long away.'

Wilde pressed him. 'Ah – so your work in Spain is finished?'

The Russian was silent for a few moments. Peggy Rale moved away from him.

'I think we all know what a summons to Moscow means, Professor Wilde. We are not children. We do not need fairytales.'

'You mean a bullet in the head? Have you been denounced? If so, why not stay here – seek asylum in Britain or America? I am sure you must have secrets to sell.'

Kholtov pasted a grin on his face and slammed the flat of his hand down on the table. 'How easy it is to have fun at your expense, Wilde. I am joking, of course. Comrade Stalin loves me like a brother. He would never harm a hair on my head.'

The telephone was ringing in the hall. Lydia pushed back her chair, rose unsteadily to her feet and went to answer it.

'Well, that's all right then. You'll be a hero of the Revolution.'

'Mr Wilde, you take a great interest in the affairs of others.'

'So do you. You travelled all the way to Spain to stick your commissars and weapons into their affairs. But from what I hear, you're so busy shooting the Trots there's no ammunition left to fight General Franco. And now here you are in Cambridge, doing your best to lure yet more young men to their doom.'

Lydia returned. 'It's for you, Tom.'

Kholtov lit another strong cigarette and took a deep drag, blowing a cloud of smoke across the table. 'Go to the telephone.'

Wilde turned to Lydia. 'Why would anyone call me here?'

'Perhaps they don't know your number.'

Wilde rose, still angry, and went to the hall where he picked up the receiver. 'Thomas Wilde speaking.'

'It's Sir Norman Hereward. Forgive me for calling so late, but I wanted to thank you for returning the photograph. It was very thoughtful of you. I'm sorry I couldn't see you.'

'Think nothing of it, Sir Norman.'

'Good. Well, let me know if you hear anything.'

Wilde heard a faint slurring in Hereward's voice. He had been at the brandy, always his drink of choice. 'Perhaps I could call on you tomorrow.'

A heartbeat pause. 'Very well. If you think you can be of use. Say two o'clock?'

'I'll be there.'

By the end of the evening, Braithwaite had finished up all the leftovers and gone to his room, Horace Dill was slumped across the table and Kholtov had disappeared into the night with Peggy Rale.

'I think I'd better make my way back to the Bull,' Eaton said. 'Thank you for a most stimulating evening, Miss Morris.'

'Lydia, please. I'm sorry about Horace—'

'Think nothing of it. I've seen it all before – had three years of the old fool. I also know, of course, that he can be quite charming when it suits him.'

Wilde shook Eaton's hand. 'What did you make of Kholtov, Eaton?'

'Obviously committed to his cause. I think you got to him.'

'What puzzles me is how he managed to enter the country in the first place. Does Britain really allow such men to come and go as they please? Even as an American I have to sign the Aliens register. Perhaps a favour was called in.'

'Horace Dill, you mean?' Eaton nodded towards the comatose figure sprawled across the table. 'I suppose he must know quite a lot of people.'

Wilde doubted he'd get any more out of Eaton. 'You'll have to excuse me. I see spies and conspiracy everywhere.' He wondered what Kholtov had discovered in Spain that could have had any bearing on Britain – and why he had been reluctant to discuss it.

'You're right,' Eaton said. 'A strange, unsettling day altogether. Something's going on. Something nasty.'

Wilde nodded. The horror of the Langleys' bedroom was close to the surface. The obscenity of using a man's blood to make a political point. Eaton had promised that no newspaper would publish a word of it beyond the fact that they had been murdered, but the damage was done: the government, the establishment knew. How would they react? How did governments *always* react when they felt threatened?

'Oh, by the way,' Eaton said. 'Who was the man who joined us – Braithwaite, I believe?'

'An unemployed miner walking south to find work in the Kent coal-field,' Wilde said. 'Lydia offered him food and a night's rest – and now she seems lumbered with him.'

'Very charitable, I'm sure. Shall we talk tomorrow, Wilde?'

'Yes, I think that would be a good idea.'

Eaton turned to Lydia. 'I'll try to get Horace Dill home, otherwise you might find him here at breakfast, his head in the ashtray.' He put his hands under Dill's armpits and pulled him to his feet. Dill allowed himself to be manhandled towards the doorway. 'Night, all,' Eaton said. 'Thank you for a splendid evening.'

Wilde watched Eaton descend the steps, out into the windy night, holding up Dill. They looked like a pair of drunks which, he supposed, was no more than the truth. 'Take good care of him, Eaton,' he called after them. 'Believe it or not, I rather like the old sodomite.'

Wilde closed the door and went into the kitchen where Lydia was looking at the piles of dirty plates and dishes with open-mouthed dismay. 'I can't do anything about this. Not tonight.'

'Leave it for Doris. That's why you have a char, isn't it?'

'I've got to go to bed before I'm sick.'

'Goodnight, Lydia.'

CHAPTER 14

Lydia closed the bathroom door behind her and sat at her dressing table to brush her hair, as she always did before bed. Her face in the mirror was swimming before her eyes. She wore a Chinese silk dressing gown, nothing else. The gown had been her mother's and she fancied she could still smell her scent, even though it was seventeen years since the Spanish flu killed her.

The drink, the deaths of her friends ... she was overcome by an unbearable weight of emotion. But it was her parents' faces that came to her rather than those of Nancy or the Langleys.

They had been so young. Her father was thirty when the shell tore the life out of him in the last year of the war, her mother twenty-nine when the sickness took her in the first year of the peace.

Her beloved father had been a doctor. At the field hospital, he shouldn't even have been in danger, but the artillery of both sides did not always know where they were hurling their missiles. And nor did they necessarily care. The shell had taken out a whole tent ward in one go. Her father's body had, apparently, been found untouched. And yet he was dead. She hadn't seen him; he had been buried in France. She closed her eyes and saw his face as she remembered it. Her mother said he was the best-looking man in Cambridge, even more handsome than Rupert Brooke. Killed by the stupid war he had hated. He had been a Quaker. Lydia had inherited his pacifism, but not his religion. There was no God. There could be no God, because God would not have allowed the senseless death of such a good man.

It was difficult to think of her beautiful mother even now. Influenza. How could a little thing like that take her away? She had been so full of life, so fervent in her desire for the rights of women, so insistent that Lydia should have the education she had been denied by her own Victorian father – an education as rigorous as any offered to a young man. Lydia had been left a nine-year-old orphan in the care of her Aunt Phyllis – her mother's widowed sister – in suburban Surrey. She had also been left a woman of some means and the owner of this house, with all its memories.

Lydia removed the gold ring from the fourth finger of her right hand. It was a simple gold band, the ring her father had given her mother on their wedding day. Though the exchanging of rings was not part of the Quaker tradition, Lydia's mother had not been a Quaker and her father had willingly compromised with a plain ring. Lydia wore it now, every day, and took it off every night.

The dull gold glinted in her hand. She opened the lid of the jewellery box at the back of the dressing table and put the ring in its small compartment, then closed the lid. For a moment she caught her reflection in the mirror, frowning, hazily aware something was wrong. She raised the jewellery box lid again. Her maternal grandmother's gold-chain bracelet wasn't there.

She hadn't worn it recently, but she was certain it had been there last night. She would have noticed if it was missing. She picked through the box again, sure it must be there. She was befuddled, yes, but she would know if she had left it somewhere else.

From outside the door she heard a noise: Braithwaite padding about in his room probably. It was time he went. She looked at the space in the jewellery box where the bracelet should be, then thought of Braithwaite again – and immediately chastised herself for making the connection.

She heard the noise once more. Tying the gown tighter around her slender waist, she went out into the corridor and switched on the light. She didn't feel well; she really had drunk a great deal too much. Braithwaite was at the top of the staircase, looking away from her.

'What are you doing, Mr Braithwaite?'

He turned with the look of a guilty schoolboy, then composed himself and nodded. 'Ah, did I disturb you, Miss Morris? I'm just going down to get a cuppa. Couldn't sleep, you see. Shall I make you one?'

'This isn't working, Mr Braithwaite. I want you to move on in the morning. As I said, I'll pay your fare to Kent.'

'And I thought we were getting on famously, miss.' He wore ragged trousers tied with string. No shirt, no shoes, no socks.

'Goodnight, Mr Braithwaite.'

'Hang on a mo.' He was moving towards her. 'They've all gone, all the others. Time for ourselves now, Miss Morris. Get to know each other a bit better.'

What was he talking about? Instinctively, she edged backwards, suddenly aware of the threat in his eyes. He maintained his leering grin and put his finger to his lips as he moved towards her, bow-legged, small and wiry. And then he was upon her, folding his arms round her, clutching her buttocks and kissing her face.

'I know what you want. I heard you last night with him. Your little sobs. I know what you are.'

She pushed at him, and managed to break away. 'Get your hands off me,' she said and thought how feeble it sounded. Then, without thinking what she was saying, 'I know you've been stealing. You'll be doing twenty years with hard labour if you touch me.'

He laughed and grabbed her again. 'You're as pissed as a rat, miss.'

She couldn't believe what was happening, but his hands were wandering, inside the silk of her gown from front and back, defiling her. His right hand went to her thighs and pressed between her legs. She was trying to pull away, but he had a grip of iron. The grip of a man accustomed to wielding a pickaxe into a coal face and hauling two-hundredweight sacks every day of his life. A squat man with the brute strength of a pit pony. With his left hand he ripped off his string belt, opened his fly buttons and his trousers fell away.

Prising her legs apart with his hand and knee, he pushed her back into her room, to the edge of the bed. She cried out and his left hand clamped her mouth. 'Do you want me to hurt you? Is that it? Think you're too good for me, do you? Oh, I can hurt a woman.' His voice rasped in her ear. 'If you don't want to be hurt, then shut the fuck up and enjoy it. You know you like it, you dirty middle-class slut. Your type always do.' He grunted like a maddened pig.

With revulsion, she felt him forcing his way between her legs and she could do nothing. Her eyes were wide open with disgust and fear. His were closed, his rotten teeth clenched like a dog at bay, growling, grunting. The veins in his face were blue, and pulsing. She sensed a movement of shadow and light and then he was wrenched away from her.

Tom Wilde led with his left, a blow to the body, then came up with a right uppercut. His bare fist connected with the man's jaw. Braithwaite, caught off guard, sprawled sideways across the bedroom floor. He crawled up on to his hands and knees.

He started to rise to his feet, mouth set in a cadaver grin, blood seeping from the corner of his lips. He made no attempt to conceal himself, arching his back to thrust his cock at Wilde, like a weapon of war. 'Think you can take me? All your books and learning and you're soft like putty, Wilde. I'll break every bone in your body with my bare hands, then I'll give the bitch what she wants.'

Wilde towered over his opponent, but Braithwaite would fight like a terrier. 'Get out, Braithwaite.'

Braithwaite launched himself, but Wilde sidestepped and tripped him with an outstretched leg, hammering his fists into his back as he stumbled, pummelling him to the wooden floor. Braithwaite gasped for breath and jumped up; he was kneeling on one leg, a predator weighing up prey.

'Here.' Lydia held out a heavy, long-handled electric torch. Wilde took it and swung it at Braithwaite's scrawny head. He swerved right and the torch glanced his ear, slashing it, then crunching into his naked shoulder blade. Braithwaite yelped with pain, blood dripping from his torn ear.

'Now I'm going to kill you, Wilde.' He lunged upwards, his vice-like hands going for the throat, but Wilde was quicker. He kicked hard at Braithwaite's balls. Very hard. The miner let out a scream, doubled up in agony and emitted a long anguished groan. Wilde kicked again, this time at the man's chin. He rather fancied he could hear the crunch of teeth breaking. Then he grabbed the man by the hair and began dragging him from Lydia's bedroom.

'What are you going to do, Tom?'

'Call the police. Let them deal with it.'

With shaking hands, Lydia picked up Braithwaite's discarded trousers and went through the pockets. 'I think he stole my grandmother's bracelet.' Her fingers touched metal and she pulled the precious object from the rancid depths. 'Well, well.'

'He's going down for a long time.'

He had turned his back on Braithwaite for just a moment. Didn't see the injured man rising to his feet, naked, and stumbling towards the stairs.

'Tom!'

Wilde turned again, but Braithwaite was halfway down the staircase, doubled up and clutching his balls. The miner leapt the last few steps, landed awkwardly, but was at the front door before Wilde could get downstairs after him. Reaching the doorway, Wilde watched him run bleeding and naked down the street. He could have followed him, might have caught him, but he couldn't leave Lydia.

Behind him, she dusted the filth off her gown. It would never be the same, even if she were to have it cleaned a hundred times. She would never smell her mother's scent again, only the foul stink of Leslie Braithwaite.

'Come on, I'll call the police – I don't think he'll get far like that. Then something to drink.'

'God, Tom, I never want to drink again.'

He laughed. 'I was thinking more in the line of cocoa or tea.'

While they waited for the police they sat at the kitchen table. Wilde brewed up a pot of tea.

'So you were right,' she said, her breathing calmer. 'He wasn't worth the effort. I suppose I owe you an apology.'

'Are you all right? Did he—'

'No. No, you arrived on cue. Why did you come back, by the way?'

He hesitated momentarily, then smiled. 'To check you were locked up. You weren't.'

There was a knock at the door. Wilde ushered in a constable. They told him what had happened and gave him a thorough description of Braithwaite. The officer assured them they would find the man. He wouldn't get far unclothed and without transport.

'Perhaps you and Mr Wilde would come to the station and give statements in the morning?' the constable said. *When you're both a bit more sober,* was the unspoken message.

After he had left, Wilde offered to sleep on the sofa again. She shook her head. 'I can't keep asking that of you.'

'I don't mind. A sofa is a fine thing for anyone who has endured an English public school dormitory bed.'

She gave a wan smile. 'It's like some ghastly nightmare, Tom.'

He wanted to fold her in his arms, but he kept his distance. 'Yes, I know.'

She shivered. 'Thank God you came back.'

'The sofa then.'

FRIDAY DECEMBER 4, 1936

CHAPTER 15

Unable to face her cleaner, Lydia fled before Doris arrived. Wilde stayed behind to explain.

Doris looked at the depredations of the dining room left over from the feast and tutted with dismay. She held up a plate and inspected it. 'This is Royal Doulton and it's chipped. Her mother loved this set.'

She was a small woman, smaller even than Lydia, grey-haired and in her fifties, strong and clever. She came to Lydia twice a week; her husband had lost a leg in the war and the farm where he had worked no longer had any use for him.

'Things got a bit out of hand, Doris,' Wilde said, drinking coffee at a corner of the table that he had hastily cleared by the simple expedient of pushing glasses and plates deeper into the middle. 'Lydia asked me to give you her apologies.'

'I've never seen so many cigarette ends or so much ash! As for the booze . . . well, it smells like a working men's club in here.'

'There was a bit of trouble with Braithwaite and I turfed him out. I slept on the sofa in case he came back.'

'Well, good riddance to him. It's a blessing that he's gone, I don't mind telling you, Professor Wilde. Perhaps I can get into his room now. What about you, sir? You look as if you could do with some Sanatogen, or at least another pot of coffee.'

'No, thank you, I've got to get home.'

After shaving and bathing, Wilde picked up the telephone and asked the exchange for a London number he knew by heart.

'American embassy.'

'Jim Vanderberg, please.'

'Putting you through.'

A few moments later a cultured east coast voice came on the line. 'Hello, James Vanderberg speaking.'

'Jim, it's Tom Wilde.'

'Hey, how you doing, pal?'

'Well enough, Jim. And you?'

'Oh, everything here's hunky-dory. We're all just watching with dazed amusement as the British ruling class tears itself apart. What is it that they hate most about Wallis Simpson – her divorces or the fact that she's American and doesn't have a title?'

'All that and more. There's also the unspoken fear that a forty-year-old twice-married woman who has had no children never will. They think she's barren – and a king's first duty is to secure the succession, which means children. The royal family are breeding machines.'

'Well, she certainly doesn't fit that bill!'

'You've got it, Jim. But I think there's something else, as well. They're worried that she's altogether too fond of the Nazis. A severe case of Germanophilia.'

'You know, Tom, there have been whispers that Mrs Simpson and Von Ribbentrop . . . well, you can guess what I mean.'

Wilde laughed. 'Use the words, Jim.'

'OK, the German ambassador is screwing the King's broad. Direct enough for you?'

Wilde and Vanderberg had been friends since Chicago University, where they shared rooms and both studied history under Walsingham's biographer Conyers Read. Their friendship continued at the end of their course, but their career paths diverged: Wilde into academia, Vanderberg into the diplomatic service.

'It's still only a rumour, and I teach my undergraduates to be wary of unsubstantiated gossip. If you recall, Jim, you told me rumours this time last year that Hitler was dying of throat cancer and would be replaced by Goering come summer. Well, summer's come and gone and Herr Hitler's still with us. Not only that but when I watch the newsreels, his throat seems to be in fine form.'

'Maybe he's been replaced by a dummy with Goebbels as his ventrilo-quist,' Jim suggested. His tone darkened. 'But what I do know is that Von Ribbentrop is even more rabid than Hitler, if such a thing were possi-ble. It's said that if the Führer comes on the line while he's in the bath, he stands up and heils him, arm outstretched, in God's own regalia.

It's not healthy to be close to a man like that. Mrs Simpson does herself no favours, even if she's not actually being screwed by him.'

'Whatever the truth, the British Cabinet don't like it. They want their kings to marry fertile virgin princesses without politics or opinions.'

'I'm sure you're right, but you can't explain that back home. The way it's playing in Washington right now is that folks see the British looking down their noses at us. A good American gal born plain Bessie Warfield ain't good enough to be Queen of England. Baldwin would do well to explain things better to FDR. Anyway, I guess you didn't call to shoot the breeze, so how can I help?'

Wilde paused, took a breath. Damn it, he trusted Jim Vanderberg as much as anyone in the world. 'Strange things are happening out here in the sticks. Have you heard of the Langley murders?'

'Hell, yes. There may not be much in the papers, but it's big news where it matters. The wires are buzzing, as are the dinner tables. It's worried people. If the ruling classes aren't safe, then no one is.'

'So everyone agrees it's political?'

'That's what I'm hearing. I was at a banquet last night – influential crowd of diplomats, parliamentarians and industrialists – and there was talk of it being a Bolshevik conspiracy. Who next? That's what they're asking.'

'I went to the house where it happened. The evidence would certainly suggest a communist plot.'

'You went there? Why?'

'It's a long story. I was with a reporter named Philip Eaton and he's covering it for *The Times*. Have you heard of him?'

'Philip Eaton? Can't say I have.'

'He's been nosing around up here, not just around the Langley case, but there's something else going on. He was up here as fast as a rat up a drainpipe, before the murders were discovered. Maybe I'm thinking too much: what I want from you is anything you can find out about Mr Eaton.'

'I've never heard of him, but I'll see what I can find. I'll call you back later.'

'No, I'll call you. Oh, and one more thing – what do you know about Lord Slievedonard?'

'I know plenty. He has big money and powerful friends. Deals in gold. It's said he's manoeuvring to snatch the German gold market from under the feet of the Jewish merchants, buying up their businesses when they're in a hurry to leave the country. I'm told he has the dimensions of a whale.'

'Or a Goering.'

'That's right, and similar politics to Fat Hermann, too. Known to be well to the right. I'll find out what I can.'

'I won't push him,' the prime minister said. 'We all know the King will have to go, but we must afford him the courtesy of going in his own way. We owe him that much.'

Papers were shuffled round the Cabinet table. The atmosphere was tense. 'But this nonsense of his,' the minister seated directly opposite Baldwin said, 'this request to address his subjects on the wireless . . . he's taking us for fools.'

'Well, he won't be doing that, of course. Anyway, you have my position.'

'Give him an ultimatum. Give him until midnight tonight: marriage to Mrs Simpson or the throne. He can't have both.'

Stanley Baldwin sighed. If he were to admit the truth to himself, he would have to say that he had never felt so alive. This crisis was the high point in his life. After this he could step down and enjoy his retirement. But until then, the business would be conducted on his terms. 'No,' he said. 'There will be no ultimatum.' He gazed round the table and met the eyes of every man who made up his government; none demurred. 'Now, go to your constituencies and sound them out. I want to know what the ordinary men and women of this land are thinking now they have read the details in their newspapers. Where do they stand? It will make no difference to our handling of the affair, but it will tell us what reaction we can expect – and we can make preparations accordingly. We do not want civil war, gentlemen.'

The Rudge Special had been pushed over. Wilde cursed out loud. He knew it had been Braithwaite: a last, spiteful act. Should have kicked the little bastard's balls harder. He righted the heavy machine, dusted it down with his handkerchief and inspected it. The tank was dented and there were scratches, but otherwise it seemed sound.

The morning was full of much-needed colour, with brilliant winter sunshine, and the wind had dropped as he rode down to the college. At the porters' lodge, he checked his pigeon hole, but it was empty. In his rooms, Bobby was brushing out the grate. He stood up, putting a hand to his aching lower back.

'You're in pain.'

'Gets worse at this time of year, Professor Wilde. Means the weather's about to turn. Me back's never been the same since that fall.'

'Dangerous beasts, horses. How did our boy Winter Blood fare?'

'Hasn't run yet, sir. The race is tomorrow.'

'So my five shillings is still intact. I suppose that's some sort of good news.'

Bobby had managed to straighten himself out and was standing upright. 'Would you like a cup of something, sir?'

'No, no, I'm not staying. But I wondered whether you've had any more thoughts about where a man could get dope in Cambridge?'

'I tell you what, sir, I did know a man as took the stuff. Jockey, he was. Placed in the Derby one year, but he got this problem with his neck. Terrible pain from a fall. He said the heroin kept him going when other men might have chucked it in. Mind you, he lost his edge in a finish. The dope did that, I think.'

'So where did he get it from?'

'As I recall, a Newmarket trainer gave it him – and the trainer got it from one of his owners who happened to be a doctor. But that was a while back, I'm afraid.'

Wilde sighed. 'So a crooked doctor?'

'Maybe, sir. Maybe not. Not sure of the law myself.'

'Well, it's given me something to think about.'

Sophie Gräfin von Isarbeck kissed Dorfen farewell. He had slept for ten hours, then taken a shave and a long hot shower before sitting down to the Dorchester's best bacon, eggs and fried bread.

'So, Sophie,' he said as he put down his coffee cup. 'The time, the place.'

'Soon, Hartmut, soon.'

'If you fail . . .'

She nodded. She understood only too well. The Führer's favour could come and go like sunshine on a showery day. She sighed and touched Dorfen's arm tenderly. 'The meeting will happen within the next three days. They *must* meet. Baldwin cannot give the Duke of York the keys to the kingdom without a final meeting. When that is about to happen, I will know. I promise you. I understand these people, Hartmut. They are meticulous in matters of propriety and procedure, even as they throw out one king and install another.'

Dorfen kissed her again, full on the mouth. She *was* rather ordinary to look at, he acknowledged, even though he had always been as bewitched as the rest. He had no idea how she did it, but she drew men in and held them. Women, too . . .

'What did he say to you, Hartmut?'

'I was summoned to his apartment, in Prinzregentenstrasse. Teatime.'

She smiled. 'The pink cakes.'

'He was making polite conversation with that awful blonde English girl and one or two others.'

'I loathe her. So do the English.'

'He asked after my mother, then he mentioned the way we did for Roehm at Bad Wiessee. The Night of the Long Knives. With one carefully planned operation, he said, we had turned the *Sturmabteilung* from enemies into sworn vassals. In a few hours and days, he had made his position unassailable. Then he showed me newspapers from around the world with the story of King Edward of England and his courtesan. Von Ribbentrop had told him that the King would be deposed – that we would be losing Germany's greatest British friend. It was a conspiracy that had to be prevented. And he said it *could* be prevented. A great leader did not always need to go to war. A pinprick of blood, he said, a whisper of thunder. Just like Bad Wiessee. And I understood exactly what he meant.' Dorfen began to laugh.

'We will make it work, Hart.'

'We will.' He began to push her back towards the bedroom. 'But now, I want to make love, Sophie.'

'Pah! Nonsense. You are too young and beautiful for me.' She shooed him away with her plump little hand, then pressed the button to summon the lift. She gave him a last kiss.

When she was alone she called her butler. 'I am expecting Major Middlemass in ten minutes. Admit him to the anteroom and give him coffee, but tell him I am engaged on an important international telephone call. If he becomes agitated, say nothing, but let me know. Do not let him go.'

'Very well, your ladyship.'

'And after twenty minutes, you will intimate that my call is from Mrs Simpson.'

The butler bowed.

'Oh – and more coffee, Hansi.'

CHAPTER 16

Major Harold Middlemass was a senior member of the royal household, an aide-de-camp in the private office of the Duke of York at his principal home, Royal Lodge. A large man from an old family, his nerves had been shot to pieces at Passchendaele. He had previously worked for Clive Wigram, Private Secretary to the late King George, but he had been shunted aside because the new King, Edward, could not bear to see the tic in his left eye and the shaking of his left hand, the result of either shellshock or a stroke. No one was sure which.

At one stage Middlemass had hoped to leapfrog to the job of Private Secretary to Edward, but that had gone instead to the next in line, Alec Hardinge, and Edward handed on his disappointed aide to his younger brother, like some old unwanted toy. Middlemass had been devastated at being passed over but now he knew that he had had a lucky escape. It was Alec Hardinge who had to endure the company that Edward kept.

Hardinge despised the louche lifestyle of the new King; he had confided his feelings to Middlemass on more than one occasion. There were few people to whom a member of the royal household could pour out their hearts, but Hardinge knew that Harold Middlemass would provide a sympathetic ear and never betray a confidence.

In fact, Middlemass soon found himself enjoying the company of the Duke and Duchess of York and their sparkling little girls, Elizabeth and Margaret Rose. His role might not have been as senior or as important as he might have hoped at this stage of his career, but there were compensations. The duchess was intelligent, knowledgeable and charming. The job was neither demanding nor stressful and he had time on his hands for outside interests, including the very special service provided by the Gräfin.

'Come in, sir,' her butler said with a low bow. 'Her ladyship is taking an international telephone call but will be with you presently. Can I bring you some refreshment, major? Coffee, perhaps?'

'Thank you.' He looked at his watch, gritting his teeth to try to prevent the inevitable spasm at the corner of his eye. 'I thought she wanted to see me. I'm afraid I can't wait long.'

'No, indeed, Major Middlemass, but you *are* expected. I know that her ladyship is most anxious that you stay.'

The telephone call summoning him here had been unusual and unwelcome. Indeed, it had never happened before. Prior to this, it had always been Middlemass who initiated the meetings, when his need became too great and he could no longer contain his craving. And when it was all over, and he went home to his wife, he always experienced the same desolation and shame and vowed to himself that he would never go to Sophie von Isarbeck again.

As he waited in the grand but rather overblown apartment, the tension in his chest rose with every passing minute. The blood was pumping in his ears, the way it did in the war when he waited for the whistle – the whistle that sent you over the top into the murderous fire of the enemy machine guns. He felt as if he was stranded at a crossroads with vehicles hurtling at him from all directions; his life was about to be destroyed by an oncoming carriage, and he did not know which way to leap.

The coffee cup was empty. He rose from the white sofa and walked to look at the Adolf Ziegler painting on the wall. It depicted two naked women, muscular and not in the least beautiful, the ideal of German womanhood. Why on earth did Sophie have such a ghastly work on her wall? He consulted his Garrards wristwatch again. It had been a fortieth birthday gift from old King George and was his most prized possession. Twenty minutes. The bitch had kept him waiting here twenty minutes. Damn it, he had a lunch appointment at Rules.

The butler came back in. 'I'm sorry you are being kept waiting so long, sir.' He lowered his voice conspiratorially. 'I think her ladyship is talking with *you know who*.'

'I don't know who,' he snapped irritably.

'The American lady. The call came from Rouen in France. Very hush-hush.'

'Ah, Mrs Simpson.'

'Indeed, sir.'

'Well could you pass a note to the Gräfin. I'm going to be late for an appointment. I only agreed to dash in and out.'

But then the inner door opened and Sophie was standing there, her soft face beaming, her arms wide. She waved the butler away with a little flick of the fingers. When he had gone, she turned once more to Middlemass. 'Harold, darling! Come and kiss your nanny. Have you been a good boy?'

'Sophie, I really—'

'Now, now. You don't want to upset nanny, do you?'

'Honestly, Sophie, I'd love to stay but I'm meeting people for lunch.' He held the shaking hand in his pocket. The tic at the corner of his eye fluttered madly.

'Little boys who run away make nanny cross. You know that, don't you, Harold? Yes? Come and kiss your nanny.' Her voice was firmer now. She held out her perfect, peach-smooth cheek and touched it with her plump little finger. 'Here, Harold. Kiss me just here.'

He bent down and kissed her cheek. He very much wanted to defy her, but he knew he couldn't. There was nothing to be done.

'There, now you are your nanny's favourite boy again.' As she spoke, she exaggerated her southern German accent. 'So tell me, Harold, why have you come here today? Do you not know I am busy?'

'I came because you asked me to.'

'Ah, yes, so I did. So many cares, I become forgetful. Indeed, yes. Please, come through to my study.' She put her forefinger in the air. 'Now I recall, I have a favour to ask of you. I promise I won't keep you long. Unless, that is, you wish me to perform any special services.'

He glanced at his watch again and his whole face shook. Beads of sweat were gathering on his forehead.

'Please, Harold, don't make it so I have to punish you. I will keep you five minutes, no more.'

He followed her through to the study.

'I have just had a very long telephone call with Wally Simpson. She is unhappy, Harold. Very, very unhappy. That awful Baldwin man is putting the King in an impossible position. He must either give her up or surrender his throne. Did any monarch ever face such a demand? His people love him, but Baldwin is a spiteful man who wishes him harm. Even Louis the sixteenth was not treated worse.'

'I don't think Edward is going to be guillotined.'

'Wally believes the humiliation will kill him. I am sure that you of all people understand such things, Harold. She is at her wits' end. I could not stop her crying.' Sophie von Isarbeck picked up a manila envelope from her desk. 'And so her friends must do what they can to ease the pain. And I am her friend, Harold. Perhaps her best friend after the King himself.'

'What has any of this to do with *me*?'

'She wishes some information from the Duke of York's camp. He is back from Edinburgh, is he not? That is where you come in. It is clear to Wally that Baldwin will have a meeting with the duke in the next two or three days. If the prime minister is to force an abdication, then he must be certain that his chosen successor is in place. For that, he must have the duke's solemn word that he will accept the throne, even though it breaks his elder brother's heart. Can you imagine a younger brother doing that to his elder sibling, stabbing him in the back like that? It is tragic, Harold. And so before the metaphorical knife is thrust, the conspirators must finalise details. Baldwin and the duke must meet – and it must be a secret meeting.'

'But, Sophie, I don't see how I can help. If Baldwin has his mind set, there's nothing I can do to prevent it.' He could not take his eyes off the large manila envelope. He knew what was in it; how could he not?

'Of course not, darling. But you can tell me when and where this secret meeting is to take place. The precise time and location. Wally Simpson is desperate for this information.'

'Why? It is no business of hers.'

'Ours is not to reason why. She is the King's friend and you have taken an oath of allegiance to the King, so you must do all in your power to assist him and the woman he loves. Therefore, you will find out this information and you will bring it to me – and I will pass it on to Wally Simpson.'

'I can't do it.'

'You know what is in this envelope, Harold?'

He nodded.

'Would you like to see it?'

He shook his head. 'No.'

'Yes?'

'No. Please, Sophie. Don't.'

'You are a naughty boy, Harold.' She laughed and slid the photograph from the envelope. It was foolscap sized and very sharply defined, taken with a high-quality Rolleiflex camera. It showed his face clearly, horribly clearly. He was naked in the bath here in this apartment, lying on his back, his prick erect; above him, squatting barefoot on the edges of the bath, was the Gräfin, her skirts raised, pissing down on him, holding the end of a riding crop to his chin. Her face was turned sideways and her hair fell about her cheek, so she was not identifiable from the photograph, but he most certainly was. The Carl Zeiss lens had captured him as decisively as a gin trap round a polecat's leg. Every pore, every follicle, every splash of urine on his face and chest, every detail of the humiliation and horror.

In the photograph, his eyes were wide in shock, startled by the flash. The photographer had appeared from nowhere and had disappeared as quickly. Harold Middlemass had known that this photograph would be used against him one day. He had considered taking his life, but even that would not solve the problem – for the thought of being dead when that photograph was still in existence brought no comfort. What if his wife or children saw it? What if the Duchess of York saw it? How would his family cope with the shame? It would be their last and abiding memory of him.

'If you do this little favour for me and for your sovereign, Harold, I swear that this photograph and the negative from which it was made will be handed to you so that you can destroy them. If, however, I hear that a treasonous meeting has taken place between Baldwin and the duke without my knowledge, then copies of this photograph will be sent to your wife, to the duke and to the editors of every newspaper in London.'

'Sophie, please, I'm not in the loop. If they arrange a meeting as you describe, they'll have no reason to confide in me. I'm small beer at Royal Lodge.'

'You do yourself a disservice, Harold. You will discover the time and place of this meeting. I know you will – because *you* know the alternative.'

'But—'

She patted his cheek. 'Run along and have your lunch. But don't dally – get back to Royal Lodge as quickly as you can so that you miss nothing. Nanny expects to hear from you very soon.'

Wilde picked up the Rudge and made his way to Bene't Street where he parked directly below Lydia's office. He found her lying on the floor, curled up.

'So this is what passes for work in your business, is it?'

She didn't move or open her eyes. 'Are you suggesting you work harder than me?'

He laughed. 'No.' He studied her closely. 'I wanted to see how you were after, you know . . .'

'I'll be fine if you've brought me a flask of coffee.'

'Afraid not.'

'Beer?'

'No.'

'Then you can go away.'

'I thought we could go to the police station together and give our statements.'

'I've already been. The sergeant seemed a lot more interested in the attempted theft of the bracelet than the attack on my person, once he'd ascertained I wasn't actually raped or injured.'

'I also wanted to know where I can find Dave Johnson.'

Lydia sat up. 'Why would you want to know that?'

'Because he knew Nancy pretty well, didn't he?'

'Well, yes, he did. But you've already spoken to him. I saw you at the Kholtov rally.'

'Something else has occurred to me.'

'Tell me.'

'No, I want to talk to him first. Just a vague idea at the moment. Thought I'd drop in on him before I ride out to Sir Norman.'

'OK. Well, when he's not fomenting revolution, he works as an artist. Lives out at Trumpington and has some sort of studio there. Hang on.'

She rose to her feet. 'I've got his address.' She scattered books and proofs on her work table until she found the contacts book. 'Here it is. I'll write it down for you.'

He took the slip of paper. 'See you later.'

The police sergeant told Wilde there had been no sighting of Braithwaite, though there had been a break-in at a gentlemen's outfitters where a few items of clothing had been stolen. Wilde gave his statement, signed it and then asked whether Detective Superintendent Bower was about.

'I'm afraid not, sir, but I can take a message for him if you like. He has taken over an office here. Is it important?'

'Nothing that can't wait. Tell him I might look in later.'

'With any luck we'll have apprehended Braithwaite by then.'

'There's always hope, sergeant.'

Johnson's thatched cottage was in a parlous state of repair; render was coming adrift from the walls and the roof was badly in need of re-thatching.

When no one answered the door, Wilde walked down the side path. The back garden was in better condition than the house, with a vegetable plot neatly hoed for planting. At the far end of the patch, perhaps a hundred feet from the house, he spotted a large wooden shed with a corrugated roof, hidden in the shade of half a dozen apple trees. Through a grimy window, he saw the dim glow of an electric bulb.

Wilde tapped on the window, then pushed open the door.

His sudden appearance made Johnson start. He was standing in front of a large easel, wielding a paintbrush. Recovering, he welcomed his visitor with a slightly bemused smile. 'Not often I get such esteemed visitors, professor.'

'Hope I'm not disturbing you, Mr Johnson.'

'How can I help you?' Johnson put the paintbrush down.

'It's about Nancy. You knew her better than most, I think.'

Johnson looked as if he weighed less than a bag of coal. Eight stone, nine at the most. He was wearing an old black jacket and knitted red tie, the same clothes he had worn to the Kholtov rally the previous evening.

The only difference was the scarf he wore loosely tied around his lower face, concealing his threadbare beard and the burns. In his left hand, he had a narrow-tipped brush; in his right a palette coated with thick blobs of paint. 'Sorry,' he said. 'Take the handshake as read.'

Wilde looked about the room. A small pot stove was belching out heat in the far corner of the room, but here by the door, the air was chilly. He found the powerful smell of oil paint quite pleasant.

Many pictures were in evidence, hung at odd angles, leaning against shelves or walls or lying flat on the bare boards. Johnson was working on a large canvas that stood almost as tall as himself. It depicted a blacksmith at his anvil, hammer raised. There was something of Stanley Spencer about the work, without being in any way a copy.

'It's good,' Wilde said, meaning it.

'You don't have to say that.'

'Well, it *is* good. I like it.'

'I'm painting all the dying professions. The smiths, the cartwrights, the weavers. The honest-to-God working men. They're all gone or going.' He nodded towards a tea pot on the stove. 'Just brewing up. Would you like a cup?'

'Thank you, yes.'

Johnson found a place for his painting implements, and then poured two cups, adding milk and lots of sugar without asking. He handed the least cracked of the two vessels to Wilde, then began rolling a cigarette. 'The problem at this time of year is keeping the bloody damp out. Damages my work before I can sell the stuff.' He took a sip of his tea. 'What more do you want to know about Nancy? I've been friends with her for years, through the Socialist Club. But as I said last night, I can't see there's any more to say – it was an accident.'

'Last night I found myself wondering about your burns.'

'Really? I don't usually make that much impression on people.' Johnson unwound the scarf. 'I'm not ashamed of them, you know.'

'I suppose some people would call them a badge of honour.'

Johnson snorted. 'Badge of honour be damned. None of us wanted our wounds. None of us wanted our friends to die. Were you there, Mr Wilde?'

'No. My mother took me back to America in 1915, when I was six-teen. That was just after the Germans used gas at Ypres. She's Irish. Her words were, "I'm damned if you're being gassed for an English king, Tom."'

'Sensible woman. But the Yanks brought in conscription, didn't they?'

'I was drafted in August 1918. Never made it out of America.' In his gut, Wilde felt he should have been in the trenches, like so many young men of his generation. There was a vague feeling of guilt that wouldn't quite go away. Duncan Sawyer had known all too well what he was doing when he had asked that bitter question: *what exactly did you do in the war?*

'Well, you missed nothing,' Johnson said. 'There was no glory. And what was our heroes' welcome? Unemployment and hunger.'

'And you?' Wilde nodded towards his face. 'I can only imagine the pain of such an injury. You must have been in agony. Perhaps you still are . . .'

'And your point is?' The welcoming smile had vanished.

'From what I know of such things, heroin – diamorphine – would be the best form of pain relief in a case like yours.'

'Ah, so that's where this is going.'

'Well?'

'Drink your tea, professor. I've a painting to work on.'

'Someone introduced Nancy Hereward to the drug. Was it you?'

'You can think what you like. I really have no more to say to you.'

'And having introduced her to the drug, did you continue to supply her when other sources dried up? What I'm really getting at is this: did she die of an overdose because of you?'

'God, you're an unpleasant bastard!'

'I'm sorry, I'll rephrase that. Was the heroin that killed her supplied by you? That's a straight question, and believe me, if I had been through what you have, I'd use the stuff, too. And I know that once you start it's very difficult to stop.'

For ten seconds the silence was broken only by the faint soughing of the stove. The two men's eyes met and held. 'I think I've got my answer,' Wilde said at last.

'All right, I suppose I did – inadvertently – lead her into addiction. I confess, if you must. She knew I used it and she asked me what it felt like, and so I told her. You know the euphoria, particularly in the early days, is as close to heaven as you'll get on earth. Perhaps I was a little too enthusiastic. She badgered me to let her try some and eventually I gave in. I reasoned that if I didn't do it, she'd go somewhere else, which would not have been a good idea. The problem is, once she started, she wouldn't let it go. But she was all right. She was still working for the cause, still functioning normally. Most of us do, you know. Just talk to a few jazz musicians in America. They're all on it, and still playing like angels.'

'And you gave her the last dose.'

'It was fine! There was nothing wrong with it. I shared it with her and I suffered no bad effects. It was just a damned unfortunate accident, that's all. Absolutely bloody. She must have overestimated her tolerance or perhaps she had some undiagnosed weakness of the heart. You never know, do you? But that's all I can tell you.'

'Where do you get your supplies?'

He hesitated, then shrugged. 'I'm not going to name names to you or anyone else, but there's no crime involved, so I'll tell you this much: I get it from one of the medics who put me back together in the war. Unlike the government, he didn't just abandon me. It's all perfectly legal under the 1926 Act. He's not alone in understanding how difficult it is for some of us to live without it. But I've only ever used properly regulated medical supplies. I don't touch the dirty underground stuff and nor, I think, did Nancy. I drummed that into her.'

'Just because you got it legally doesn't mean it was lawful to sell it on.'

'Sell it? I didn't sell it. No money changed hands. She was a friend.'

Wilde sipped his tea. It was far too sweet. 'There are other matters. You mentioned her work for the cause.'

'Look, I don't really know what all this has to do with you. Are you a government spy or something? Keeping an eye on the commies?'

'I'm a history professor, trying to allay Lydia's concerns.'

'Are we done? I need to get on.'

'Almost.' Wilde paused. 'What do you know about Berlin?' The question took Johnson off guard.

'What do you mean?'

'Berlin. You know all about Nancy and Berlin, don't you? You and Horace Dill. What was she supposed to do there?'

'I know Nancy went to the Olympics with Lydia. What's that got to do with anything?'

'Something happened there.'

'Well, I wasn't there, so I have no idea what you're going on about. As far as I know Nancy and Lydia watched a bit of running and jumping and saw the sights. Oh – and Nancy wrote that piece about the tyranny behind the great games. If you want to know the full details of what went on in Berlin, you'd better ask Lydia. As for Horace Dill, you're both fellows of the same college, aren't you? Why don't you talk to him and sod off and leave me to my work.'

Wilde handed over his empty cup. 'Thank you.'

Johnson hesitated then smiled awkwardly. Because of the burn scars, the creases around his mouth were like parchment so that the smile seemed like a grimace. 'Sorry,' he said. 'I'm a bit wound up. I miss her badly.'

'I understand.'

As Wilde reached the door, Johnson called after him.

'And you know, we do get a hard time from the police and the secret boys. Look, if she was murdered, then of course I want to find out who did it.' He went over and proffered his hand. 'Shake and be friends? We're on the same side, yes?'

CHAPTER 17

Wilde rode to St Wilfred's Priory along dry, fast roads. On arrival, he pulled up outside the front door and pulled the bell.

This time, a liveried footman ushered him in and went off to find his master. Sir Norman Hereward walked slowly down the hall and extended his hand. 'Ah, Wilde.'

'Sir Norman.'

'Thank you for coming. I apologise for your previous wasted trip. I really wasn't up to receiving visitors or talking about Nancy. I'm sure you'll understand that this has hit me very hard.'

'You have my condolences, sir.'

Hereward gave a perfunctory nod. 'I take it you've heard of this new business at Kilmington? Cecil and Penny Langley?'

'Yes, sir.' He wouldn't mention that he had been there, not yet anyway.

'Ghastly. Simply ghastly. They were friends of mine, you know. Damned good friends. Bloody awful affair.' There was a pause and then he muttered almost under his breath, 'I can't bear it.'

Wilde had noted how much the man had aged when he had seen him at Nancy's house, but in the intervening days and hours he had become ancient, stooped and frail. Even this early in the day, the stink of brandy seemed to emanate from every pore. He turned and led the way slowly down the hall.

'Please, come through into my study. I would like us to agree on at least one thing – Nancy's death was neither suicide nor accident. It was murder. And with the police doing damn all, I'll listen to anyone with an idea.'

Wilde followed him through to a large, comfortably masculine room with a view out across the deer park to a tree-fringed lake and thick wintry woodland beyond. Every inch of the walls was packed with shelves, and every shelf was packed with books, many of them leather-bound and old. Three of the corners were occupied by marble Roman busts that looked, at first glance, to be genuine.

'Coffee, Wilde?'

'Thank you, yes.'

The footman, who was hovering, bowed and left, closing the door behind him.

'Do sit down. Tell me what you know and we can go from there.'

There were two leather armchairs by the cold, fireless hearth, the sort of armchairs to be found in the better gentlemen's clubs, well-worn, scratched and much-loved. Wilde sank into the one nearest the window. At first it seemed that Sir Norman would remain standing, but then he, too, sat down.

Wilde took a deep breath. 'You know, Sir Norman, I was rather hoping *you* would be able to help *me*. When we met at your daughter's house, you were insistent that she was murdered and you seemed sure that it had a political motive. I was hoping you might have some reason to suppose that, something I might follow up.'

'Such as?'

'For instance, do you have any reason to believe Nancy's death might be linked to the events at Kilmington?'

'It hadn't occurred to me. Go on.'

'I went to Kilmington, Sir Norman. I saw the room where your friends died. There was writing on the walls.' He didn't mention that the daubs were in blood. 'One said simply *Revolution*. Also hammers and sickles.'

'Good God ! What were you doing there?'

'A friend of mine is a reporter. I went with him.' No names, no more explanation.

Hereward shook his head grimly. 'So you think the Reds killed them too?'

'I have no idea if the Reds have killed anyone. I'm merely laying out the evidence. There is an obvious connection between your two families. Nancy was Margot's friend.'

'Well, she was while they were both at Girton, but I'm not sure they kept in touch after that, and I'm pretty sure she's had nothing to do with Cecil or Penny these past four or five years.'

'But *you* have, sir.'

'Indeed.'

'I'm clutching at straws here, Sir Norman, but you and Mr Langley were both to the right, politically. Is it possible that someone was getting at you both because of those views? Someone trying to get at you by harming Nancy?'

'That is an inhuman notion, but carry on, Wilde. I want to hear where you think this is going.'

A maid arrived bearing a silver tray of coffee, along with fine china cups and bowls of cream and sugar. Sir Norman took his coffee with both. Wilde kept his brew black and unsweetened. The coffee smelt and tasted good.

Sir Norman stood up and went over to the window. 'We're burying her tomorrow morning, here at our local church. She had made her feelings very plain to me – she never wanted to come near St Wilfred's Priory again, but I won't have it. She's one of us and will lie with her mother and our forebears. Her brothers are interred in Flanders.' He dredged up a deep, anguished sigh. 'As you know, Nancy and I didn't see eye to eye on much in recent months. But in death, she is still my daughter, she is still a Hereward.'

Wilde rose from the depths of the armchair. He wanted to get out of this cold room.

Hereward was on another plane. 'You probably think you know it all, Wilde . . . the college scandal, the opium. But there was something else. Horace Dill. That filthy swine Dill poisoned her mind with all his lies about Stalin's people's paradise. Dill and others like him should be hanged for high treason. I cannot think why such men are allowed to roam free, spreading their wicked message to impressionable young minds, sending them off to fight for alien causes. Dill turned her against England and her father. That is what happened. The gallows is too good for him.'

'Might I see her room, do you think?'

Hereward gave an indifferent shrug. 'I don't see why not. Drink your coffee and I'll take you up. Like her brothers' rooms, it hasn't been touched.'

Nancy's bedroom was beautiful, the nursery of an Edwardian childhood. A fine and much-ridden rocking horse stood in front of the large window that, like the library almost directly below, overlooked acres of parkland, lake and woods. Wilde looked out. He heard a sound of buzzing and then realised it came from a yellow biplane circling in the cloudless sky. It came swooping over the house, then turned again and skimmed low across the lake and woodland before climbing and looping in a full circle.

'You will see that I have kept all her books. Her mother died when she was nine and she was taught at home by a governess until she was eleven. Then she went off to boarding school when I became master and had to split my time between college and here. I couldn't be both father and mother to her, you see. I suppose I should have remarried.' He paused. 'I want to see her killer hanged, Wilde.'

'You don't seem to have any faith in the police, yet you must carry a great deal of influence in the county.'

'They've made their minds up. Will *you* help me, Wilde?'

Wilde frowned, puzzled and surprised by the request. 'Surely a private detective would be better, someone professional.'

Sir Norman Hereward did not speak for a few moments and Wilde thought he had never seen a sadder, lonelier face. The man was broken.

Hereward shrugged. 'Perhaps. But you know I have always trusted you. Even though I have not been your greatest admirer, I recognise your intellect.' He turned his gaze to the window. 'The police and coroner have decided it was an overdose, pure and simple. But I don't think *you* believe it was an accident. I saw the way you examined things at Nancy's house. I'm taking a long shot.' He gave a mirthless smile. 'You pity me, don't you, Wilde.'

'I feel for your loss, Sir Norman.'

'You know it's difficult to imagine it now, but there was a time when this house was filled with laughter. I had a wife, two sons and a daughter – and I loved them more than my own life. Now they are all gone.' Sir Norman pushed gently on the rocking horse and watched as it creaked back and forth.

'Did Nancy keep a diary?'

'I've no idea. If she did, she never mentioned it. Why do you ask?'

'So you haven't been through her things?'

'I told you: this is all as she left it. Not that she came here very often recently. To be frank, I don't think I could bear to look. Too many ghosts. I'll leave you now to scratch around on your own. I doubt you'll find anything, but you never know. Tread lightly on my memories, young man. They are all I have.'

'One more thing. When did you last see her?'

'That's easy. The Sunday before last. November the twenty-second. Her twenty-sixth birthday. She came for lunch. I hoped we could make up, forget the past. I offered to find her some sort of treatment. I've heard of a clinic in Switzerland, a psychiatric outfit that claims to be able to cure addictions, but she just laughed and started throwing the usual insults at me – bourgeois pig, that sort of thing. We had a blazing row and then she got her damned syringe out and began preparing her opium mixture. I told her never to darken my door again. She said that was fine – that she had no wish to see me or set foot in St Wilfred's Priory ever again, alive or dead. As far as she was concerned, I was no longer her father. She stuck the needle in her arm, withdrew it, and left.'

'And that was it?'

'That was it. I'm stubborn, she's . . . she *was* stubborn. What a damnable waste.'

'Is there anything more you think I should know?'

'How quickly love can turn to hate . . . God, I wish she were here now so that I could tell her how much I loved her. I'd go down on my knees and beg her forgiveness.'

Wilde could see that the man was about to break down. 'You go, Sir Norman. I'll be finished here in half an hour, perhaps an hour. If you think of anything else that might help – her friends, her enemies, her contacts – let me know. Anything, however obscure.'

The older man nodded towards an open-topped box. 'Those are the bits and pieces the police returned to me, things they found around her in her bedroom at the house in Cambridge. I can't bear to look at them.'

CHAPTER 18

Wilde went through the box. The silver syringe wasn't there; he supposed it had gone to the police surgeon. There were books, including *Das Kapital* and *Mein Kampf*, a volume of Shelley poems, *Wigs on the Green* by Nancy Mitford, a few garments, an old box camera, writing paper, pens, a three-penny bag of lemon drops, a foreign coin. He leafed through the books to see if anything dropped out, but there was nothing.

For the next hour and a half, he looked around Nancy's room, going through her books and jottings with assiduous care and attention. There was a picture of her in graduation gown, looking very serious and a lot more grown-up than the school picture her father had favoured. Here, her hair was cut short, carved like some warrior goddess, her hair itself a helmet; she was quite beautiful.

He opened clothes drawers and shut them hurriedly, initially ashamed of himself for such intrusion, but then opened them again and went through the pathetic collection of long-forgotten underwear and other clothing diligently, not at all sure what he was hoping to find. He might know all about the history and theory of espionage and detective work; but he realised he had a lot to learn about the practicalities. Did spies usually feel so grubby as they went about their business?

In one drawer, beneath a pile of sweaters, he found a bundle of letters tied up with blue ribbon. He hesitated, and then undid the bow. A light whiff of perfume emerged. There were about twenty letters. With great reluctance, he began to read them and quickly stopped. They were all dated by month, not year, and charted a rather poetic and chaste love affair with someone named only as Jack. He tied the ribbon back around the delicate paper and replaced them in the box.

Somewhere, in another part of the house, a telephone rang and rang. When it was eventually picked up, he heard Sir Norman's voice, raised and angry, echoing through the hall, though it was impossible to hear what was said.

In an old school trunk, he found piles of exercise books and reports. He flicked through them but they revealed no clues to Nancy's life and death.

An album of old photographs caught his eye. The book had been neglected and some of the pictures had come adrift, the gum decayed. Nancy from babyhood to the age of seven or eight, with her brothers and mother and father. Her mother was not smiling, but her face was kind. In the fields, around the piano, at the beach. Playing lawn tennis here at the priory, playing croquet, sleeping beneath wide-brimmed hats on deckchairs. The sort of photographs he had seen at the Langleys' house twenty-four hours earlier.

How many families had such collections, almost too painful to look at because of the missing and the dead? On one page a smiling face, on the next nothing, the album abruptly ended because no one could bear to look at it any more. Men and boys lost in battle. Women lost to influenza or childbirth. Children taken by scarlet fever or polio. Commonplace tragedies.

Sir Norman might not be able to look at these pictures of those he loved now, but one day he would. This album needed to be restored and preserved. Wilde put it to one side.

One day, Wilde thought, perhaps he too might be able to look at pictures of his dead wife. They were locked away in a small metal trunk beneath his bed, images of days of joy. What a heavy price a man paid for fleeting happiness. When Tennyson wrote, *"Tis better to have loved and lost than never to have loved at all*, he didn't know what he was talking about.

He turned his attention to Nancy's bed. Gently he pulled back the counterpane, the blankets and the top sheet, clean and white and per-fectly made. It was as if it had never been slept in. He put the single pillow to one side. Nothing. Finally, he took another look at the box of possessions Sir Norman had been given by the police. He found himself picking up the small foreign coin he had spotted before. On one side the figure of a lion and the date, 1930. He turned it over. *Una peseta*, it said. One Spanish peseta. He clasped his hand around it. Time to go.

At the front door, his host appeared with a tumbler of brandy in his left hand. Wilde held out the old photograph album but Hereward did not even glance at it, merely handed it on to a footman.

'Her syringe wasn't in the box, Sir Norman.'

'I told the police I didn't want it. Told them to dispose of it as they saw fit.'

He held up the coin. 'And there was this – a Spanish peseta. Had your daughter been to Spain recently?'

'She's never been to Spain.'

'Did she know anyone who had?'

'I have no idea. Quite a lot of young idiots heading off there at the moment, I believe.'

Wilde offered the coin to Hereward. 'Probably nothing then. Perhaps it was in her room at Chesterton before she arrived.'

'You take it, Wilde. I don't want the bloody thing.'

Wilde put the coin in his pocket. 'There was one other matter . . .'

'Go on.' He was beginning to sound testy.

'When I came here before, your chauffeur said you couldn't see me. As I was leaving, I couldn't help noting that Lord Slievedonard was arriving.'

'What of it?'

'Well, there was a picture of him at Kilmington – he's there with you and Cecil Langley.'

'What is your point, Wilde? We've all been good friends for many years.'

'In the picture you were all at one of the Nuremberg rallies. It struck me as a remarkable coincidence. I had never seen nor met Slievedonard or Langley before. But within the space of a few hours, I saw one of them here at St Wilfred's Priory and then attended the murder scene of the other. And the murder scene had pertinent political references.'

A vein was throbbing in Sir Norman's temple. 'There is no coincidence at all, Wilde. Slievedonard and I are friends – and we were both friends of Cecil Langley, God rest his soul.'

'I was thinking of his politics.'

'I know you were, God damn it. But my politics are my own business, as are Peter Slievedonard's.' Hereward sighed heavily. 'Look, Wilde, you have a precise and interrogative mind, you are fastidious in your research, and you are one of the best historians of your generation. Don't go off at a tangent. Look to bloody Horace Dill and his slimy cohort. And, by the by, they are the ones sticking their damned noses into Spanish affairs. I want my daughter's killer caught.'

Lydia Morris had read Sassoon and Brittain and Graves, but she hadn't needed their memoirs to understand what the generation before hers had undergone in the trenches. Anyone with a germ of imagination should be able to envisage what would happen if a shell tore a limb from your body or if shrapnel or a bullet ripped into your throat or spilled your intestines. *The war to end all wars*, they had called it. Did anyone believe that any more?

She peered at the proofs. Her mind was elsewhere. There were times when she needed company, and times when she wanted simply to be alone. Her thoughts turned to Tom Wilde. She supposed he would want another wife and children. She supposed he would tire of waiting for her. Yet somehow she couldn't see him with a compliant kitchen mouse. She wondered about his late wife. Surely she must have been a scholar? He'd always need intellectual stimulation.

Even as such thoughts crowded in, she rejected them as girlish. She was well aware that she had a lot to be grateful for. She was an independent woman. The money bequeathed to her gave her freedom to pursue her own interests; had given her this publishing company. Today, however, she didn't feel grateful. Nancy's death had shaken her to her core. When her mother died she had vowed never to cry again. She thought of that now as the hot, stupid tears fell, unstoppable, onto the proofs of *Prime of Youth*.

When Tom Wilde hit the Ely road at the end of the drive out of St Wilfred's Priory, he stopped. The yellow biplane was still buzzing overhead, performing a series of stunts. He watched it for half a minute, the engine of the Rudge growling beneath him. And then the aircraft came low, as though it was about to land, somewhere inside the deer park, and he saw it no more.

What had Sir Norman heard over the telephone, he wondered, that had altered his mood? And why had he become so defensive at the mention of Slievedonard?

Wilde twisted the throttle and roared off along the deserted road southwards towards Cambridge.

CHAPTER 19

Back in his rooms, Wilde cleaned himself, dusted down his jacket and trousers and asked Bobby to make him a pot of coffee. He collected his thoughts as the gyp fussed round him. Finally, he put through a call to Vanderberg.

'Did you get anything, Jim?'

'This and that.'

'Is Eaton an MI5 man?'

'No idea. Like you and I have always said. We should have records on stuff like that, but we're way off the pace.'

The lack of an American strategic intelligence office had been a constant refrain of their old tutor at Chicago. 'The wars of the future will be won and lost in small back rooms,' he had told them. 'Espionage and covert action: two sides of the same coin. One means spying on your enemy, the other means working to preserve your national interests and keep your country safe from harm. Walsingham understood that and showed the way. We have to follow him. The world is too dangerous a place in the twentieth century. We've got to know what the other guy is doing. And, when necessary, stop him doing it.' Neither Jim Vanderberg nor Tom Wilde could disagree, but thus far there seemed to be no urgency to do anything about it in the White House or on Capitol Hill. Former Secretary of State Henry Stimson had even closed down the state department's code-breaking operation because 'gentlemen don't read each other's mail'. Yes, there was the Federal Bureau of Investigation, the secret service to protect the president, and the various intelligence-gathering operations of the armed forces, but nothing was centralised. Everyone was doing his own thing. No one was combatting the work of hostile agencies and operatives. No one was undermining the enemy. And this in a world where Stalin and Hitler used assassination as a means of implementing government policy and sent out secret armies to wreak havoc abroad.

'But there are things I *can* tell you. Yes, Philip Eaton is a *Times* reporter. Yes, he went to Eton and Trinity. At one time, when he was an undergraduate in the late twenties, it seems he applied for membership of the

Communist Party – but if he was accepted, there is no record that I can access. Youthful indiscretion, I suppose. Since then he has become a fully paid-up member of the establishment. Belongs to the right clubs, attends social events with the great and the good. One more thing: he recently joined the Anglo-German Fellowship.'

'That doesn't make him a Nazi lover. The AGF has some pretty respectable sponsors.'

'Of course, but I guess it shows him on the right of centre. Not many Reds in the AGF.'

'More importantly, it shows us that Mr Eaton is a political animal.'

'Exactly.'

'What about Peter Slievedonard?'

'Ah yes, now he *is* interesting. I've never met the man, but others here have and from what I'm told I don't like him one bit. This guy is somewhere to the right of Adolf. Slievedonard would happily kill and burn every commie, every Jew, every Oriental, every American, every African, the lame, the sick and plenty more besides, and sell their blood and bones for gold. He would certainly burn you and perhaps me. He is immensely wealthy and as a sideline he has a small limited circulation newsletter called *North Sea*. It's a little like a cross between Henry Ford's *Dearborn Independent* and Streicher's *Der Stürmer*.'

'Not good.'

'Not good at all. This thing is only circulated to those of a like mind. You won't find it on newsstands. The embassy has a copy, which I'm holding on to. In the event of war, I want Slievedonard to be viewed as a hostile alien and forbidden entry to the USA. This edition should be evidence enough of his political sympathies. On the front, it has a picture of that blonde anti-Semite Unity Mitford-Freeman, taken at last year's Hesselberg gathering. Inside, there are lengthy quotes from *Mein Kampf* with the juiciest bits picked out in bold. It's in front of me as I speak and I have to tell you, Tom, it makes me want to go straight outside in the street, find a pile of steaming dogshit and use this rag to clean it up.'

Juan Ferreira found the blue and white house with no difficulty. It was a little way inland from the creek, no more than half a kilometre across open land. Two of them would stay here overnight; they would bring their bedrolls and blankets and it would be warmer than the *Gaviota*. They could even start a fire. One of them would have to stay with the boat, however. You cannot just leave seven and a half tonnes of gold unattended. They would take the sentry duty in turns.

The telephone sat on the bare boards. He picked up the receiver and was gratified to hear a dial tone. Now all he had to do was make a call to a man in a town called Cambridge. And then wait. There was nothing to do but wait.

The wait was not long. Kholtov called him back within the hour.

'You are safe, Juan?'

'Some official saw us, but he went away on other business. We found the place.'

Kholtov chuckled down the line. When he had embarked on this plan, he had never really believed it would work. He thought back three months to the chaos of Barcelona, the anarchists holding sway over the city like Paris during the French Revolution. Full of hope and violence, ruled and divided by factions, both home-grown and imported. Men such as Kholtov and his immediate superior Abram Slutsky had held immense power, courted by every side because they had the force of Stalin and the Soviet Union behind them; because they could provide guns and money and fighting men.

But Kholtov and Slutsky had other work to do, far more important to Stalin than fighting fascists. Together, they had been busy organising the killing of senior members of the Workers' Party of Marxist Unification – the POUM – to eradicate Trotskyite tendencies from the theatre of war. They must not be allowed to gain the upper hand in Spain. It was work that Kholtov and Slutsky knew well. Their ultimate goal, if only it could be done, was the elimination of Trotsky himself. But he was slippery, and protected.

The more he killed, the more Kholtov drank. The vodka or cheap Spanish brandy – whatever he could find in the mayhem of Catalonia – made the bloody work tolerable. The order summoning him home had come from Yagoda in Moscow via Slutsky in Spain. It was early September, the time when the Spanish summer begins to shed its furnace heat and the evenings are pleasant. He was needed to give evidence against traitors at a major trial. 'Then I will be delighted to do my duty and take the next ship home, Kholtov had said to Slutsky, smiling. But he had other ideas. Through the red mist of blood and brandy he knew what the summons meant.

He had sobered up fast. That night, he slept outside town beneath an olive tree. The next morning he took the train to Madrid where he used his influence as a senior Soviet officer and Comintern representative to demand an interview with Negrín, the finance minister of the republic and leader of the Socialist Workers' Party. It was a time of panic: Franco's nationalist rebels were advancing on the capital. It was believed the city could fall within weeks or even days. Kholtov had an idea – an idea that might not only save his skin, but help preserve the republican government in Spain.

'You must remove your gold reserves,' he told Negrín.

The finance minister had laughed at him. 'Do you know how much gold we have in the Banco de España? Perhaps seven hundred tonnes. One of the greatest reserves in the world. We cannot just *move* it.'

'If you do not do so and Franco takes Madrid, you will have precisely no gold.'

Juan Negrín was a worldly man, but he was also brave and honest and intelligent. Within twenty-four hours he had summoned Kholtov back to his offices. 'You are right, comrade,' he said. 'The gold should be moved,' he said. But where?

'Somewhere on the coast,' Kholtov said. 'In case you need to ship it abroad in a hurry.'

'I will talk with the council of ministers.'

Within days the council and Prime Minister Caballero had authorised the transfer of their country's total gold reserves, some ten thousand boxes of coin and bullion, to the naval port of Cartagena, on the Mediterranean coast of Murcia. Perhaps the most strongly defended town in republican Spain, it was also a place from which a swift departure by sea would be possible if it became necessary.

On September the fourteenth, a powerful company of militiamen walked into the central bank in Madrid, accompanied by dozens of finance ministry officials, locksmiths and metallurgists, and began the immense task of removing the crates of gold coin and ingots and transferring them to the city's Atocha railway station where a specially commissioned train was waiting.

All the while, Kholtov watched from the wings. 'You might do well to send some to France for safekeeping and some to Moscow,' he suggested. 'Accounts could be set up – money to be withdrawn to pay for military assistance and war materiel.' He did not mention that he hoped his initiative might earn him the gratitude of Stalin, and a pardon for whatever crime he was supposed to have committed.

The Council of Ministers was not immediately convinced by this suggestion, but Kholtov was given permission to join the train on its three-hundred-mile journey under heavy guard across vast, empty tracts of republican territory south-eastwards to the coast.

Once in Cartagena, he found a room and waited in the cliff-shrouded city, with its natural harbour and its ancient Roman ruins, enjoying the late summer warmth and barely able to resist the lure of the heady Spanish wines. It was the sort of place he might have happily stayed in forever, but even here he knew he was not safe. Soon, his presence would become known to Slutsky and men with guns would arrive to kill him or put him on a ship home.

There were days when his thirst for brandy was too great and he ended up in some sandy gutter. Why not, he found himself wondering, simply exchange the bottle for the bullet? That would end all his troubles.

And then, out of nowhere, he heard that the Council of Ministers had agreed to his idea; the order came from the finance ministry that the bulk of the coins was to be dispatched to the Soviet Union, for safe-keeping and to pay for armaments and military assistance.

Kholtov began to feel the jagged knives of apprehension tearing at his stomach. Yes, Stalin would be delighted by the arrival of so much gold – but Kholtov's fond hope that this would save him turned to bitter reality. The arrival of the gold would not mean that Stalin would extend any gratitude to the man who had conceived the operation. He had heard from a Spanish bank official that the Soviet commercial attaché Artur Stashevsky was taking credit for persuading Negrín to ship the gold abroad. It wouldn't stop there. Slutsky and Yagoda would undoubtedly also take credit for themselves. Stalin would never even hear of Kholtov's part, and there was no way of getting word to him.

He still needed to find an escape route – and he needed a portion of the gold. He began to plan a way to get it.

The gold was to be loaded on four Soviet ships: the *Kine*, the *Neva*, the *Volgoles* and the *Kursk* for the journey to Odessa. Almost six hundred tonnes of it. The remaining portion of the gold would be deposited in France. Somewhere, some of it would have to disappear. It had to be a large enough amount for Kholtov's purposes, but small enough to be easily lost in accounting, and it had to be transferable out of Cartagena in a small trawler.

On the journey from Madrid to Cartagena, Kholtov had got to know the guards and officials escorting the gold. He knew men's weaknesses, knew how best to make use of such frailties. Bribery, blackmail or murder – or all three – were powerful tools for a man with his training. Assuming he could spirit away a small portion of gold from the fortified naval battery where it was stored, Kholtov would then be left with two major tasks: to find confederates and to devise a means of removing the gold from Cartagena and Spain.

As it turned out, those two problems were solved in one move.

Kholtov had taken lodgings with a man named Juan Ferreira, the skipper of an old trawler named the *Gaviota*, which plied the waters to the west and south of Cartagena, avoiding the channels used by naval and larger merchant vessels.

Ferreira was a good man, but he was disillusioned. He had supported the republican government and was glad to see the back of King Alfonso, but he was horrified by the destruction wreaked by the communists and anarchists on the Church, and the murder of the priests, monks and nuns. Nor was he alone in this; his mother and wife were devout Roman Catholics and were appalled by the stories of the killings, church plate being looted, relics of the saints being smashed and Bibles burnt in the squares of cities and villages alike.

In the evenings, when Ferreira returned home with his catch, he and Kholtov discussed the war over litres of wine and dishes of rice and seafood. It became clear to Kholtov that Ferreira's loose tongue would very soon bring death and destruction down on his family. Perhaps he would like a way out?

'I have an idea, Juan. I need a man like you to help me. If it succeeds, it would make you and your family rich – and enable you to leave this filthy war behind forever.'

Ferreira had needed no persuasion. He understood instantly what was being offered and was sure his two crew members, his young nephew and a tough but elderly uncle, would go along with it; they were all of like minds. His only fear was the fate of the family that remained. Would they suffer reprisals?

Kholtov was reassuring. 'There will be no reprisals because no one will know that the gold is missing. If anyone in Moscow notices, which I doubt, they will think it an accounting error; the French will think it has gone to Moscow. Your trawler will simply be marked as *missing at sea, all hands lost*. Even if they believe the gold has been misappropriated, they will shrug their shoulders and put it down to the havoc of war. And when we have sold the gold and we are all wealthy men, your family can join you wherever you wish – France, the United States, Mexico. The choice will be yours. You will be wealthy beyond all imagining.'

The *Gaviota* was kept a few miles down the coast, away from the naval dockyards. Juan and his two crew members spent three days working on the vessel to fix the compartments in which the gold would be stowed. Once or twice, other fishermen and villagers tried to watch them at work, but they were shooed away. No one asked questions. It was never safe to inquire into one's neighbour's activities in this part of the world.

Everything was almost ready. All that was needed was the extraction of a hundred boxes of gold coins. Who would miss a measly hundred boxes out of ten thousand boxes? After that, Kholtov himself needed safe passage to England to find a gold buyer and prepare the way.

And then he heard a strange story in a bar. A story that, at first, seemed improbable, and then possible. It involved a White Russian named Rybakov and a Nazi militia known as the SS Romanov Division.

From Cartagena, Kholtov took a series of trains back to Barcelona. Slipping into the city, he was careful to avoid the attentions of Slutsky and his former comrades. For two days, he made inquiries of the men who made a living smuggling intelligence and goods across the lines.

They told him no more than he already knew. Yes, there was a White Russian Nazi outfit near Huesca. They had seen a little fighting. Nothing much. On the third day, he was told the Russians were being moved out. 'These Germans, they think we are stupid, Comrade Kholtov. Because we are Spanish, they think they can speak in front of us and we will hear nothing. Like servants in the dining rooms of the nobility. But, of course, we hear everything.'

'And what did you hear, Senor Paez?'

'I heard that the Russians are to go to England. Crazy, huh?'

Scobie, the head porter, was at the door to Wilde's rooms. 'Message for you, professor. A Mr Johnson asked if you would call him on the telephone.'

'Mr Dave Johnson?'

'I believe so, sir. He called a couple of minutes ago.' The porter handed Wilde a slip of paper. 'That's his number as best I could get it. Says he'll be in all afternoon. Sounded half-asleep. Couldn't quite get his name or what he wanted at first.'

'Thank you, Scobie.'

Ten minutes later, Wilde got through.

'Dave? It's Tom Wilde.'

'Ah, yes. I called you, didn't I?' He was doped up. The voice was slow, hazy.

'Do you want me to come over?'

'A letter arrived. Second post. I don't know what to make of it.'

Silence except for laboured breathing.

Wilde waited. 'You said you received a letter.'

'You might make more sense of it than me. Be glad of your opinion. Hang on. I'll just go and get it.'

On the other end of the line, Wilde could hear the sound of retreating footsteps, a clattering of something falling, then a muffled curse. Half a minute later, the laboured breathing again as Johnson picked up the receiver once more.

'Well?'

'Here goes. It's from Nancy. A bit of a mad scribble. "Dave," she writes. "In haste, but this is important. Might talk to Lydia about it later, too.

'"A couple of weeks ago, my father, Sawyer and Slievedonard all went up to the Londonderrys' place Wynyard Hall. Wonder why I wasn't invited! The Londonderrys and the Ribbentrops were there. HD says Ribbentrop got the job of German ambassador by poisoning Hoesch. Not Nazi enough for Berlin, apparently. How appalling these people are! But—"' Johnson paused, 'there's a bit here I can't quite make out. It's something like "what's the line between fighting for a cause and fighting for the enemy?", but then she goes on to say, "You know what's been asked of me, don't you? Anyway, I went to his library, and hidden among the *Country Lifes* I found a magazine called *North Sea*, which is the most disgusting fascist publication I have ever seen. I'd think better of him if it had been pictures of naked French tarts.

'"And in his desk, I found a sheet of paper headed *North Sea*. It's a list of names – big nobs – politicians, a couple of generals, some senior civil servants and at least three KCs. Slievedonard and Sawyer of course. I made a note of them all. What does it mean? It wasn't what I'd been asked to look for, so it gave me a shock. One name in particular – that's why I want to talk to you. I think I've made a mistake. I think this is serious. Can I come round? N."

'She never came. Must have sent it just before, you know. She had tried to talk to me on the telephone but, well, it was one of those days when she wasn't quite coherent and nor was I.'

'She said you knew what had been asked of her.'

'I didn't know *anything* had been asked of her.'

'Can I see the letter? Did it contain the list of names?' Wilde wanted that letter even if he had to prise it from Johnson's doped-up fingers.

'I need to lie down . . .' Johnson's voice was beginning to slur again. 'Thought you should know, that's all. Perhaps I shouldn't have called you, but I promised, didn't I?'

'I'll come o—'

The phone was already dead.

CHAPTER 20

There was no answer to his knocks at the front door of the cottage, and the curtains at the small windows were closed. At the back, there was no sign of movement in Johnson's garden studio. Wilde tried the door. It was open, so he stepped inside. He breathed in the familiar aroma of oil paint and looked about. Nothing but paints and paintings and splatters on walls and floor and dozens of brushes and a few unused canvases. No Dave Johnson, no letter.

He walked back to the house and knocked on the front door again. Still no answer, so he went round to the garden once more and tried the rear door. It was unlocked and clearly had not been closed properly in quite some time; the wood had expanded through damp so that it no longer fitted in the frame. Turning sideways, he shouldered it open and stepped inside.

The house had the unkempt feel of a man who lived alone. The smell of damp, the bare and neglected kitchen, the peeling paint. Wilde called out Johnson's name as he went through into the house. The front room was anonymous, cold and unlived-in. There was an armchair, a pile of the leaflets Lydia had designed and financed for the Kholtov rally, a telephone on the floor and a desolate hearth, thick with the detritus of long-dead fires. A threadbare rug partially covered the boards, but nothing could disguise the dust and ash and cobwebs that had accumulated over many months. The next room had a commonplace table and three chairs.

Wilde went upstairs. He recalled Lydia's description of her foreboding as she climbed the stairs in Nancy's house. But he felt no sense of horror here; only emptiness.

There were four rooms off the landing. One had an old bath, two others were storerooms, mostly for paintings, but also some boxes and trunks. It was as if Johnson had never really moved in. The door to the fourth room was closed. He lifted the latch and looked in.

To his surprise, the room was sumptuous and exotic, full of cushions and carpets and candles. Overwhelmingly red, with some faded yellow. There was a hint of incense in the air.

Johnson lay in the middle, on his back, stretched out on a pile of cushions. His lips were parted, his eyes closed and his burnt and ravaged chin tilted towards the ceiling. His breathing was light and peaceful. Wilde was careful not to wake him as he took the letter that lay at his side.

On his way back to his rooms, Wilde spotted Duncan Sawyer on the far side of the new court. He was saying goodbye to a young visitor, a good-looking man in impeccably tailored clothes. The two shook hands, then Sawyer patted his arm and the man walked away towards the main entrance.

Wilde strolled over and graced Sawyer with a smile. 'Ah, Dr Sawyer, can you spare me a moment?'

'What is it?'

'You asked a favour of me. Help me with something and I might yet consider your request.'

'Are you serious?'

'Never more so. You've kept in touch with the old master, Sir Norman, I believe. In fact I saw you briefly when I called at St Wilfred's Priory.'

Sawyer's lips curled into something like a smile. 'You know about the tragic death of his daughter, I think?'

'Indeed. In fact that's what I wanted to talk to you about. Both Lydia Morris and Sir Norman have got it into their heads that Nancy was murdered. You're close to Sir Norman – is he simply distraught or do you think there might be something in it?'

'Good God, Wilde, what's it to you? You're not the bloody police. They say it was an overdose.'

'I'm merely trying to put Miss Morris's mind at rest. What do you think? I'd value your opinion.'

Sawyer appeared to weigh up Wilde's intervention. He nodded slowly. 'Well, overdose or not, she ran with some damned odd people,' he said. 'But you already knew that.'

'Odd?'

'Communists, left-wing agitators like Dill. England's full of them. I despise them. The country is going to hell.'

'That pretty well echoes Sir Norman's sentiments.'

'Well, of course it does! How could a man with brains not be dismayed by the rise of the trade unions? They're all in the pay of Moscow, you know. How long before the empire drifts away and Britain becomes a small offshore island? Or worse, just another soviet, ruled by Kremlin diktat.'

'And you think one of these left-wingers killed Nancy Hereward?'

'Don't you?'

Wilde shrugged. 'I have no idea.'

'Then you'd better leave it to the police, hadn't you. And while we're about it, I'll call you in on that favour.'

'That was Herr Dorfen talking to Dr Sawyer,' Bobby said. After he had parted from Sawyer, Wilde had run into the gyp as he was crossing the court from Hall with a tray of food.

'The tall fair-haired man? Should the name mean something to me, Bobby?'

'Before your time, professor. Used to be an undergraduate here. Quite a one with the ladies, I gather. God knows what they saw in him.'

'How does he know Dr Sawyer?'

'Couldn't say, sir. Before his time, too.'

Wilde met Lydia at Dorothy's. The celebrated café restaurant was particularly noisy and busy, packed out with groups of office workers getting into the Christmas spirit early; paper hats, turkey lunches and dancing in the ballroom.

He ordered coffee for them both, then leant back in his chair. Somewhere a great cheer went up, followed by a raucous rendition of 'God Rest You Merry, Gentlemen'. He told her about Dave Johnson, about his heroin addiction and that it had been he who had introduced it to Nancy.

'I had no inkling,' she said. 'He covers it up well.'

'So did our Victorian grandmothers.'

Even behind her glasses, he could see that she had been crying. He did not allude to it. Instead he handed her the letter Nancy had sent to Dave Johnson. He watched Lydia as she read it.

After a minute she looked up and met Wilde's eyes. 'There's a lot to take in. Obviously it's what she was going to talk to me about.' She paused and looked up at him. 'It's damned alarming, actually. I hadn't realised that Hereward was so heavily involved in the Blackshirts.'

'No,' Wilde said. He had been wondering, too, about the role of Duncan Sawyer. Wynyard Hall was the grand north-eastern seat of the seventh Marquess of Londonderry and his ambitious wife Edith. Interesting that Sawyer and Hereward should have been invited there. Particularly interesting that the Ribbentrops had been there, too. The old master and the young professor were flying in high, if notorious, society.

'But why was Nancy going through his things in his study? It's not like her.'

'Someone must have asked her to look for something. That's the implication, isn't it?'

Lydia removed her glasses and frowned. 'But what?'

'The letter doesn't say. But if Philip Eaton is correct and she had been sent by someone in the Comintern to Berlin, why would that be the end of it? Once they've got her doing things for them, why not use her to spy on a Nazi sympathiser?'

'But surely she wouldn't spy on her own father!'

They were both silent for a few moments. At last Wilde spoke out loud what they were both thinking. 'Should we be wondering whether either of these events – Berlin or the visit to her father's study – led to her death?'

'She was definitely worried about something. The names on the list . . . and, it says here, one in particular. What have we stumbled on, Tom? And where's the list? She says here she wrote it down.'

'I mean to find out. Horace Dill might know a few answers.' Wilde reached across the table and took Lydia's hand. Their fingers entwined. With his other hand he pulled the Spanish coin from his pocket and put it on the table. 'The police found this in her house. Sir Norman said she had never been to Spain.'

'What are you suggesting, Tom?' She removed her hand from his.

He shrugged. 'It's a bloody obvious link, Lydia. Who do we know who's just come from Spain?'

'You can't lay this at Yuri Kholtov's door!'

'You're the one who thinks Nancy's death was foul play, Lydia.'

'That's ridiculous! Everyone has old foreign coins.'

'You're right. It probably means nothing.' He picked up the peseta and put it back in his pocket.

'Is that it? Is that all you found there?'

'There was a bundle of love letters from someone called Jack. Scented, and all tied up with blue ribbon. Very innocent, I thought.'

Lydia laughed. 'She was about twelve. I don't think they even held hands. They met at some gymkhana, as I recall. They're nothing, Tom, honestly.'

'I thought as much.'

The waitress came and asked if they wanted anything more, perhaps some Christmas pudding or a minced pie, fresh-baked at Matthews? Lydia said no, and Wilde asked for the bill.

As they made for the door she clutched his arm. 'What about the letter? Are you going to take it to the police?'

'No. They won't be interested. They'd shrug and say it proves nothing – and they'd be right. And after last night's fracas with Braithwaite, I rather think they'd begin to see me as a bloody nuisance. To tell the truth, Lydia, I don't think they want to know.'

CHAPTER 21

Hereward took five minutes to come to the telephone. He sounded impatient. 'Have you found out something?'

'Possibly.' Wilde was back at college, using the telephone at the porters' lodge.

'What?' The voice was brisk.

'I'd like to ask you a couple of questions.'

'Go on.'

'What can you tell me about a group called North Sea?'

There was silence on the other end of the line. Wilde waited.

'North Sea,' Wilde repeated.

'I'm sorry, the line's not terribly good. What did you say?'

Wilde said it again. 'North Sea. I wanted to ask you about North Sea. Your daughter Nancy mentioned it to one of her friends. She seemed to be deeply troubled by it.'

'Which friend?'

'I'd rather not say.'

'And what exactly is this North Sea?'

'I was hoping you'd tell me, Sir Norman. It seems to be a group of highly placed and powerful men. She discovered that you're involved with this group and the effect on her was profound.'

'Look here, Wilde.' Cold anger now. 'I have no idea who you have been talking to or what you think you have discovered, but it sounds like tripe. Who are these North Sea people?'

'Politicians, civil servants, the judiciary. Familiar names.' It was a good enough guess. A fifth column perhaps; allies of the Londonderrys and Mosley. Wilde could not come straight out and accuse his former master of association with them. 'I'm sure you know them all a great deal better than I do. If you want to talk in private, I'll ride out to the priory.'

'No. Whatever you think you've found, I can tell you it's complete bilgewater. My daughter was very disturbed in the last weeks of her life.

She had delusions. You're looking in the wrong direction. I'll say it again: Dill and his gang, those are the ones you should be looking at.'

'North Sea bears investigating, though, don't you think? Your daughter thought so.'

'I would thank you, Wilde, not to trouble yourself any further in this matter.'

The line went dead.

Wilde made his way to his rooms where he hunted down his bottle of Scotch and poured himself a healthy dram. He slung it down his throat and immediately poured another, and then sat back on the sofa and closed his eyes to think. There was a link missing. If, for argument's sake, there was a connection between Nancy's death and work she was supposedly doing for the Comintern, what could it possibly have to do with the deaths of Cecil and Penny Langley? What was it he was not seeing?

Five minutes later there was a rap at his door.

'Come in.'

It was the head porter, hat under his arm, looking very apologetic. 'You have a visitor downstairs, professor. He was all for marching straight up, but I said I thought you would prefer him to be announced.'

'Who is it?' Wilde pulled himself up from the sofa.

'Lord Slievedonard, fur coat and all. He's parked his bright red motor right in front of the main gate. Like he owns the place.'

What in the name of God did Slievedonard want with him? Wilde shrugged. 'Send him up, Scobie.'

He was already there, pushing Scobie aside and filling the doorway with his bulk.

'Professor Wilde?' he boomed.

'Yes.'

'Is that whisky?'

'It is.'

'Pour me one, there's a good man.'

It was an order more than a request.

Wilde laughed and handed his glass over to Slievedonard, then eased past him and called down the stairs after the porter. 'Is Dr Sawyer still in college, Scobie? I saw him an hour or so ago.'

'I believe he's here, sir.'

'Be so good as to ask him to join us here. Now, if you don't mind.' It was Sawyer who had introduced the concept of a Slievedonard scholarship; he could deal with it.

Wilde was certain he had another glass somewhere, hidden behind a pile of papers or books, but he had no chance of looking for it: Slievedonard's enormous girth, made even greater by his voluminous fur, almost filled the room. Only thing to do; Wilde grasped the bottle and drank from it.

'Damnably cold in here. Doesn't your gyp keep a fire for you?'

'I wasn't expecting visitors.'

Slievedonard didn't bother with small talk; he hadn't even thought to introduce himself. 'I believe you know about my proposition, Wilde. And I want your support.'

'Ah, the scholarship.'

'It will be a bit like Herr Toepfer's new Hanseatic Scholarships, but in reverse, like the Rhodes thing. I want to sponsor a German student every year to study history at Cambridge. I want you to initiate it. I need a history man on side and I'm damned if I'll ask that filthy old Bolshevik Horace Dill. My friends tell me you are the man to help me. You will, of course, be rewarded handsomely for your assistance.'

Was he being offered a bribe for his support? A dull glint caught Wilde's eye. The other glass was on the floor by the sofa. He bent to pick it up, wiped it with his sleeve then poured half a glass, neat.

'Well? What do you say to that?'

'Have my feelings not already been made clear to you?'

'A bargaining ploy, Wilde. You want to know what's in it for you. Quite natural.'

'Some friends of yours suggested me, you say? Which friends? Dr Sawyer, by any chance? Sir Norman Hereward?'

Slievedonard began to pace round the room, the ancient floor creaking with every step. Wilde estimated his weight at three hundred pounds. A human earthquake. 'That doesn't matter. Are you interested? I'm sure you have plenty of time on your hands. This will be something to occupy you and earn you some decent money.'

'I'm never against bright young people being able to come to Cambridge. Especially from abroad. But I can see problems.' One particular, insurmountable problem.

'Not just Cambridge,' Slievedonard said. 'Specifically this college. I want them to come here. It will be worth five hundred pounds a year to the scholar and a great deal more to college funds and to you. It will be called the Slievedonard Scholarship, and my son's portrait will hang in Hall, God rest his soul.'

Wilde took a deep draught. The Scotch burnt its way down his gullet. 'That would be up to the fellows.'

'With your backing, I think we can make up their minds for them.'

'Let's fix a meeting early next term and we can talk about it properly.'

'Let's talk about it now.' Slievedonard took out a large wallet and pulled out a wad of five pound notes. He leant forward and slapped the money down on Wilde's desk. 'This is a down payment.'

'Lord Slievedonard, I won't accept your money.'

'Take it.'

'If you leave it here, it will go to charity.'

'Spend it how you wish.' Slievedonard stopped pacing and deposited his bulk on the leather sofa. He stretched out his arms and legs.

'Before we go any further,' Wilde said, 'it's only fair I should be honest with you. There will be many here, myself included, who would have misgivings about being associated with you or your money. Your politics are not looked on kindly, save by Dr Sawyer.'

'My politics! What have my politics got to do with anything?'

'You give money to the Blackshirts. You cheat the Jews out of their gold. You were at Nuremberg cheering on Hitler.'

'Cheering on Herr Hitler? Is that supposed to be some sort of crime? Adolf's a damn fine leader and a good man. As for cheating the Jews out of their gold, that's a calumny. They are desperate to sell and I give them the best price they're going to get. I am not a bigot. I have met many Jews and some of them are decent enough chaps.'

'Then why don't you say so in your nasty little magazine?'

'That's just politics. This is business.'

Wilde picked up the bundle of banknotes and held them out to Slievedonard. He was just about to order the man out, when he paused. 'I saw you at St Wilfred's Priory.'

'Is that so?' Slievedonard said, ignoring Wilde's fistful of money.

'I knew Sir Norman's daughter, Nancy.'

'As did I. Sir Norman and I go back a long way.'

'And I saw your photograph at Cecil Langley's house.'

'Another friend. My heart goes out to both families. These are tragic days. I imagine I must be a target, too, but I'm damned if I'll let the bloody Bolshies terrorise me.' Slievedonard was not a man to be distracted. 'Now – to the matter in hand. These incidents have concentrated my mind on the matter of the scholarship. Life is short. I must do these things while I can. Charity and good deeds cannot wait. Strike while the iron is hot.'

Wilde, too, was not easily put off course. 'You all shared right-wing views – you, Sir Norman and Mr Langley. You were all at Nuremberg together. You fund the British Union of Fascists. There is a connection.'

A brief, almost jarring, hesitation. 'What are you talking about, Wilde?'

Wilde sensed uncertainty, even fear. 'I am wondering whether there might be some link between the deaths of the Langleys and Nancy Hereward.'

'Well, I'm with you on that, Wilde. All three of them were killed by the bloody commies. Only an idiot would think otherwise. The evidence is clear. And the culprit is obvious – a vicious little Russian agent called Kholtov, presently strutting and preening around Cambridge, I am told.'

'Why would you think Kholtov has anything to do with any of this?'

'You'll see soon enough. Pour me another whisky.'

Wilde gave his visitor the last of the Scotch.

'The problem is, Wilde, that most people don't do a great deal of thinking. The BUF is a movement of the common man, as is the NSDAP in Germany.'

'They are bullies. Violent thugs.'

'It's the Soviet Union that has legalised murder. Have you not heard of these show trials in Moscow? False evidence, then a bullet in the head. Wholesale slaughter. No appeal, no defence. Their crime? Falling foul of Stalin and his paranoid delusions. Germany, by comparison, is a law-abiding country. Herr Hitler has had to use very little in the way of strong-arm tactics to put down his enemies.'

To Wilde, this was like arguing that lions must be tame because tigers were wild. He didn't want to labour the point, but nor could he allow Slievedonard's views to go unchallenged. 'In Nazi Germany, there is an internment camp at Dachau, just outside Munich. You may have heard of it. I have been told of men disappearing into its barbed-wire confines, never to be heard of again. There are Jews living in Cambridge today because they were forced out of their businesses and homes in Germany. Others wander Europe stateless, thrown from border to border. We all know of men and women murdered or displaced for the crime of disagreeing with Hitler or Goering.'

Slievedonard roared with laughter. 'You damned Americans, you're soft in the head.'

Soft in the head. Dill had called him *'a bleeding heart Yank'*. He was being attacked from right and left. Which meant he must be dead centre. Was that a healthy place to be?

'Put your mind to it, Wilde,' Slievedonard urged. 'Drop everything and work with me on this. Join my payroll and I'll set you up. We can do business together – help some young people and do a great deal of good for the prestige of this ancient college, which has a special place in my heart. Do I make myself clear?'

Why him? Wilde wondered. It was almost as if the man was trying to buy him off.

'Name your price, Wilde. Five thousand a year? What's that – five times the salary of a history professor? I want you to be my man. We can do this without you, but I want you on our side.'

There was a knock on the door. Duncan Sawyer was standing outside, anger written across his face. He caught sight of Slievedonard and his expression altered dramatically. Not deferential, nor submissive, but something Wilde couldn't quite put his finger on.

'Ah, Sawyer,' Wilde said. 'His lordship was just leaving. Perhaps you'd show him out for me.'

Lydia was hunched over her desk at LM Books. She had already sent the corrected proofs of the poetry anthology back to the printer, but on reading it through again, she had found a literal on the last page. She had telephoned the printer, but he had said bad-temperedly that it was too late, that the run was more than halfway through. The thing was, the error was horribly obvious and changed the whole meaning of the verse. How on earth had she missed *lead* instead of *led*? It should have been '*the old men led them into the acre of death*'. How had she missed it? Her brain was full of blood and murder. Well, it would just have to go out like this with a correction slip; it might have been a linotype operator's error in the first place, but it was *her* fault that it had not been noticed.

She sat back, staring at the error. What was the bloody point of it all? Here she was, publishing other people's poetry when she couldn't even write her own. Why did she even try to write, spending hours late at night searching for the right word to explain emotions and concepts that were probably impossible to convey anyway? How could ink on paper explain the lost lives of young men? In a sudden fury she hurled the proofs across the room.

'Lydia?'

The voice sent a shiver down her spine. She took off her tortoise-shell reading glasses, wiped her sleeve over her eyes, and turned round in disbelief. 'Hart?'

Hartmut Dorfen was grinning broadly. 'Hello, Lydia. I see I have caught you at a bad time.'

She began to rise from the wooden chair. 'Hart, is it really you? What are you doing here?' Of all the people in the world that she had never expected to see again, none ranked higher than Hartmut Dorfen. When he went down from Cambridge seven years earlier, she had done her best to put him out of mind. But here he was, in her office, in the flesh, looking not a day older. She felt the familiar flutter from which she thought she had broken free.

'It's really me, Lydia Morris.' Dorfen stayed in the doorway, smiling at her. 'And look at you – as beautiful as ever. My perfect English rose.'

She blushed. 'Hart, you really do talk such rubbish!'

He, however, *was* more striking than ever. His blond hair had darkened slightly and his features were more sculpted than she recalled. She got up from her desk. Should they embrace? Kiss cheeks? Shake hands?

'Then everything is as it always was,' he said. 'Hartmut Dorfen, always talking rubbish.'

'Hart, what are you doing here? You gave me such a shock. I didn't hear you come in.'

'Your char lady at Cornflowers told me where to find you.'

'And why are you in Cambridge? You haven't been back for so long.'

His brow creased with sorrow. 'You know why, Lydia.'

'Nancy?'

'I saw the notice in *The Times*. The funeral is tomorrow. Of course I had to come. I dropped everything.' He stepped towards her, his face suffused with sadness and grief. 'Such a terrible thing. I can't understand how such a tragedy has happened.'

'Hart, I don't know what to say.'

'We must talk. First, do I not get a little peck of the lips in welcome? We are old friends.'

She turned her cheek to be kissed, but did not move close enough for him to put his arms round her. He accepted the compromise and touched her face with his lips.

Lydia was still confused. 'Have you come all the way from Munich? How did you manage to get here so quickly?'

He laughed and dismissed the idea with a wave of his hand. 'Munich? I haven't lived in Munich since January 1933 when the bloody Nazis came to power. Do you think I could live under a regime like that? I took the first train out.'

'Really?' Lydia raised her eyebrows. 'Wasn't your father a friend of Herr Hitler?'

'Hitler deceived him. I thank God he did not live to see what has become of his beloved fatherland. The Nazis are a boil on the arse of the world.'

'And your mother?'

He shrugged. 'We write every week. I am hoping she will come over soon, perhaps in the New Year.'

'Then what *are* you doing?'

'Surviving. Scratching a living. I have a modest house in Pimlico. I work for a company that exports engineering equipment, mostly to the Kriegsmarine, I'm afraid.' He winced. 'It pains me to supply anything that might help that bastard Hitler, but a man must eat and my language skills are useful, as you can imagine.'

'Why did you never come to Cambridge? Why didn't you write or telephone? Why didn't you let us know that you were here in England?'

'You know why I didn't call,' he said. 'There are too many ghosts here. And now Nancy. What happened to her, Lydia? Illness or accident? There is nothing in the papers, not even an obituary, only the funeral notice.'

She didn't want to discuss this with Hartmut Dorfen, not the truth anyway. The first frisson of seeing his beautiful face and exquisite body, clad in the finest that Huntsman & Sons could provide, had given way to darker memories. *Ghosts.* They had all been in love with him, of course – Nancy, Margot and, she had to be honest, Lydia herself. Hart's harem, one wag had called them. There were probably others, too, for Hart was devastatingly attractive. It was all a bit of fun. Except in the end it wasn't. Not for Margot, anyway.

'It was a heroin overdose apparently,' she said reluctantly. 'I found her body. Her syringe was at her side. The police say it was accident or suicide. They told me the coroner would be holding a quiet little inquest today and it was certain he would rule it an accidental overdose to spare her father the shame of having another suicide in the family.'

'Heroin? Are you saying Nancy took dope?'

'For some time now.'

'But you also mentioned suicide. She was so full of life. I cannot believe . . .'

Lydia shrugged. 'I don't know, Hart. Do you mind if we don't talk about it? Please.'

'Of course. Of course.'

'It's lovely to see you and everything, but I really have to deal with this.' She held up a copy of the *Prime of Youth* cover.

'Something you have written?'

'No.' If only, she thought. 'The war poets. I'm merely editor and publisher.'

'You're a publisher now? What of your own poetry?'

She smiled. Self-belief was the thing. That was what Tom said. We're all limited by our own self-belief, or lack of it. 'One day I'll write something worthy of publishing. I hope. For the moment, there's this, the work of others more deserving than I.'

He looked across the room to where the proofs lay scattered.

'Oh, that,' she said. 'A bloody literal I missed. I do almost everything myself. Too late now to do anything about it.'

'Can I have a copy, misprint and all?'

She smiled. 'Of course! Give me your address before you go and I'll send you a copy. Are you staying at a hotel?' She hesitated only a beat, then said, 'Perhaps you'd like to come round this evening after supper? We could chat over a drink. Catch up on old times, yes?'

'Thank you. I shall look forward to it, even though the circumstances are so sad.'

'About eight then. And there's someone I'd like you to meet – my neighbour, Professor Thomas Wilde. He's a history don at your old college. After your time, so your paths wouldn't have crossed.' She would very much like to hear Tom's opinion of Hartmut Dorfen.

She put out her hand and Dorfen held it between his two hands for a moment, scrutinising her with his dark blue eyes, as if he was not at all sure what he was seeing.

He smiled. 'I think I would remember a man called Wilde.' But he knew of him, of course. Oh, indeed, he had heard a great deal about Thomas Wilde.

CHAPTER 22

The Foreign Office man was beaming. He swirled the brandy as he held it up to the light streaming in through the tall window of the club's long room. 'A bit of good fortune,' he said. 'It seems there is a Russian in Cambridge, a Russian agent. A very convenient Russian agent.'

His two friends laughed. They understood immediately the significance of this statement.

'Then it is our duty to inform the police,' the general said.

'Oh, that won't be necessary,' the Foreign Office mandarin said. 'Everything is already in hand.'

'Well, well,' the landowner said. 'As you say, very convenient. Very convenient indeed.'

'There was something else,' the mandarin continued. 'It seems there is an American academic taking an interest.'

'Does that matter?'

'Perhaps not. But he has connections with the American embassy. And he seems a little too persistent in his questioning.' He put his glass to his lips and drank, savouring the fine Cognac.

'Then we must do our duty by him, too. No loose ends.'

It was late afternoon. December's over-hasty darkness had fallen and the cloudless sky lent a chill to the air. Wilde left his rooms and crossed the old court to the west side. The staircase to Horace Dill's rooms stank of cigar smoke and sweat. Wilde knocked and waited. He knocked again and from within came an irritated cry, 'Go away!'

'It's Tom Wilde. I want to speak to you.' From inside, he heard cursing.

When at last he dragged himself to the door and opened it, Dill looked angry. Behind him, Wilde could see chaos: furniture, papers and books piled high. The smell from within was even ranker than the staircase. He had never been in here; Dill's only visitors tended to be undergraduates.

'Have I come at a bad time, Horace?'

'Is there a good time?'

Wilde stepped forward. 'Can I come in? I want to talk to you about Nancy Hereward.'

'I don't think I have anything to say to you, Tom.'

'Are you sure? I think we need a civilised – and thorough – conversation about Nancy's little excursion in Berlin.'

Dill looked at Wilde suspiciously. 'I thought I made myself clear at dinner, I don't know what game you think you're playing and I care even less.'

'You made nothing clear. Let me in, Horace, for heaven's sake. Who have you got in there?'

Dill stepped to one side. 'Come in, if you must.' He stopped. 'On second thoughts, let's go for a walk. I'll get my coat.'

They wandered round the old court and then the new court, lit by the lights from dozens of windows, two professors strolling in the dusk, an inconsequential daily sight. They could have been discussing the Glorious Revolution, the degeneration of the nucleus, the price of claret or their plans for the vacation. Anything. World-changing concepts had been born in this grassy space, along with a great deal of scandalous tittle-tattle.

'They listen to me, you know,' Dill said. 'In my rooms. We're safer out here.'

'Who listens to you?'

'MI5, the Gestapo. They're all one and the same. Do you not think they talk to each other?'

'I doubt very much that MI5 talks to the Gestapo. What a preposterous notion.'

Dill threw a sideways glance at Wilde. 'How little you affect to know. I don't believe a man who has studied Walsingham is that naive. But then again, the spied-on rarely realise they are watched until it's too late.'

'All I want to know is the truth about the death of Nancy Hereward. So far I don't have much to go on except Lydia's suspicion. But the one thing I'm sure of is that Nancy carried out an assignment for you while she was in Berlin for the Olympics.'

'Who put this nonsense in your head?'

'That doesn't matter.'

'It does to me.' Dill had stopped in his tracks beside the doorway to the master's lodge. He was bent forward as though examining some speck on the path through his bottle-lens spectacles, but he was, in fact, dusting the blackened ash from the tip of a cigar which he had fished from his coat pocket. He looked at Wilde. 'It matters very much.'

'Perhaps I heard it from MI5.'

'You mean Eaton? No, I don't believe he has told you anything. Much too sly and clever to give stuff away.' He shoved the cigar in his mouth. 'Give me a match.'

'I don't smoke. What makes you think Eaton is MI5?'

'He's not. He's MI6. Far too well bred for Five. I supervised him when he was at Trinity. I know Eaton very well.' Dill was looking at Wilde oddly, a quizzical, almost mischievous curling of the lips. Not quite a knowing smile, but not far away. 'Better than you know him, clearly. Have you not wondered why he sought you out, Tom?'

'We are both interested in finding out how Nancy Hereward died.'

'Naive, naive, naive. Tom Wilde, I thought you were more astute than that. Eaton wants to recruit you, you fool!'

Wilde laughed out loud. 'How could I possibly help MI6?'

'By finding the brightest and best of your undergraduates. This is where they recruit young men. They like to use people like you and me as talent scouts. Trust me, Tom, Eaton wants to sign you up.'

Of course. 'And you, Horace – do you work for him?'

It was Dill's turn to laugh. 'He knows my politics too well. I don't think a paid-up member of the Communist Party of Great Britain would be welcomed with open arms by His Majesty's secret intelligence service, do you?'

The college clock chimed five. Wilde waited, considering how to turn the conversation back to Nancy Hereward. If knowledge was power, it did not always benefit its possessor to reveal it. But one way or another he wanted to provoke a reaction. And at least he had got Horace out of his rooms. More than that, he seemed to be reasonably sober, which was a welcome novelty.

Wilde made his mind up. 'I'll be frank with you then, Horace. I have found Nancy's diary.' It was plausible enough. If Horace refused to believe he had learned of the Berlin assignment from Philip Eaton, he had to invent another source. 'You feature prominently in it, particularly regarding the mission you demanded of her at the Olympics. It is clear you had a large influence on her.'

'Show me this diary.' Dill was far too experienced an historian not to insist on seeing the evidence.

'I don't have it with me – and I wouldn't let you get your hands on it, anyway.'

Dill was chewing the butt of his cigar, which was already a sodden mess. He removed it from his mouth. 'All right,' he said. 'Let's talk about Nancy Hereward. She was very brave, you know.'

'I rather gathered that.'

'But I dispute that I had any influence over her. If she did anything, it's because she wanted to do it. And I would say that it's faintly patronising to suggest that the likes of Nancy Hereward or John Cornford could be *influenced* by me; I merely facilitate matters for them when I can. Nancy hated the Nazis and she wanted to do what she could to help in the struggle against them.'

'But you gave her the Berlin assignment.'

'If you know all this, then why do you need anything from me?'

'Because I don't know all the details. Good God, Horace, the girl's dead – how can it hurt her if you come clean with me?'

Dill met Wilde's eyes, his gaze steady in the yellow light. 'If I speak of this, it goes no further. Is that clear?'

'I'll have to speak with Lydia, but apart from that, you have my word.'

'Very well, but you didn't get any of this from me. Nancy wanted to make a difference – to thumb her nose at Hitler's gang. I merely made a suggestion to her; there was no coercion.' He patted his pockets, looking for something. 'The first thing you should know is that her trip had nothing to do with the Comintern. You know of the SPSL?'

'Of course.' The Society for the Protection of Science and Learning was an outfit to which he had happily contributed. Formerly known as the

Academic Assistance Council, it had been set up three years earlier to help scientists and others fleeing persecution in Nazi Germany.

'They are saving a fair number of academics, particularly Jews and communists who have fallen foul of the Nazis. Helping them find new places and new jobs here and in other countries.'

'Yes, I know that. They do good work.'

'What do you know of Arnold Lindberg?'

'Never heard of him.'

'Physics professor at Göttingen and a prominent member of the underground KPD. Too prominent for his own good; first he was attacked by the Deutsche Physik gang, then Himmler set his attack dog Heydrich on the case. I think it was something Arnold wrote about Himmler's sexual peccadillos. That's enough for the guillotine in Germany these days. Arnold was tipped off and went into hiding. All his friends and family were watched but he was able to get a letter to me.

'He knew there was no way out of Germany without convincing ID papers because Heydrich would have put watches on all ports and border crossings. Getting the papers made was easy enough here in Cambridge. There are more than enough refugees from Germany with the knowledge and skills. But I needed a way to get the papers to him.'

'Nancy Hereward.'

'Precisely. All she had to do was take a tram to the Potsdamer Platz for a bit of tourist shopping and sightseeing. Once in the city centre it was simple for her to get lost in the shopping crowds in case the Gestapo were watching, and from there it was only a mile's walk to the apartment where Arnold was hiding out. A twenty-five minute stroll, taking a circuitous route and checking all the while to ensure she wasn't tailed. Once at the apartment, she handed over the false papers, and left him to it. She had done her bit to save a great man.'

'And did it work? Did Lindberg get out?'

Dill began walking again. 'I need a fucking light. Let's go to the porters' lodge.' The temperature was dropping with every passing minute. 'No,' he said at last. 'No, Arnold Lindberg was arrested on the train before it even left the station. I suspect Nancy was followed, and then the Nazi secret boys followed Arnold to see if he led them to anyone else. But that doesn't reflect on Nancy. She had done all she could and more.'

'What has happened to him? Is he dead?'

Dill shrugged. 'Possibly. Perhaps he's in Dachau or some other hell-hole. It's all bloody smoke and fog in Germany. You are arrested and you disappear and when your friends make inquiries, the officials merely shrug their shoulders. Nothing more is ever heard, except that the names of the friends who made the inquiry go on a list of people to be watched. We only know of the arrest because another member of the KPD was at the railway station by chance. Since then I've used the offices of the SPSL to demand information and request he be allowed to travel to England, but we hear nothing. They simply don't reply to our requests – and the British diplomatic service won't help because Lindberg is both foreign and a communist.'

'So you're saying Nancy carried out this mission on behalf of the SPSL, not the Comintern? There's no communist connection at all?'

'That's precisely what I'm saying.'

'From her diary, I would have said she thought otherwise.'

'Then she was protecting the SPSL. It would not be good for their repu-tation to be seen to be working undercover in Germany. They would be badly compromised.'

'And what of Professor Lindberg? When he was captured he'll have been tortured.'

'Of course, he will. And you have to assume that he will have revealed everything he knew about other dissidents. And he will have told them how the papers were delivered.'

'So the Gestapo will know about Nancy?'

'The Gestapo make the Inquisition look like amateurs. Oh, they'll have learned all about Nancy Hereward. She'd have become a prime target.'

'Surely you're not suggesting that the Nazis got one of their agents in England to kill her in revenge for passing papers to Arnold Lindberg?'

'I think they're capable of it. Don't you?'

Wilde nodded. Yes, Himmler and Heydrich were capable of it, but so was Stalin and his new secret service brute Yezhov. 'It's also a possibil-ity that Lindberg's German Communist Party friends thought she had betrayed him to the Nazis.'

'You have a vivid imagination. That's not the way the KPD thinks.'

'It's exactly how Stalin thinks, Horace, and you know it. What about you? Did *you* have any cause to wish her dead, Horace? Were you obeying orders from Moscow?'

'What is it with you, Tom? You know I was fond of Nancy. I have answered your questions and now you're fucking insulting me.'

But Wilde wanted to push him further. 'What else did you ask of her? Did you ask her to spy on her father?'

'Tom, this is gibberish!'

'Answer me one more question then: where was Comrade Kholtov on the day Nancy died?'

Without a word, Horace Dill spat a mouthful of brown strands from his cigar butt onto the path at Wilde's feet and slowly walked away, back towards his rooms, cigar still unlit. Just before the arched entrance to his stairs, he stopped and turned his head. 'He was with me in my fucking room, if you must know. All day. Discussing the revolution.'

'So where is he now?' Wilde had Nancy's last letter in his pocket and he still hadn't used it. 'Horace,' he called after him. 'She felt betrayed. Why should she feel betrayed?' The words echoed around the court. But Dill had already vanished, shuffling up the stinking stone stairway to his rooms.

CHAPTER 23

Once again, Cambridge was bustling with shoppers and a stream of cyclists. The facade of a butcher's was decorated with the feathered corpses of geese, ducks, turkeys, all hung by the neck from a string across the top of the shop window. Dozens of them, alongside a score of rabbits, great haunches of pork, venison and beef. But there was, too, that feeling of the town closing down for Christmas. The long platform would be packed with young men waiting for trains home.

Tom Wilde watched the passers-by as he walked along Trumpington Street. Three people had died and still the world kept turning. He thought about Nancy Hereward and the huge risk she had taken to help a man in Nazi Germany, a man she had never met. Was her death the price she had paid for her action – or was it connected with what she had discovered later, in her father's study?

Now Wilde knew the truth about Philip Eaton, it begged the question of whether the secret service had been watching Nancy all along. Had they followed her in Berlin? That at least would explain how Eaton knew about her trip. And what of Dill's suggestion that Eaton might have wished to recruit Wilde? He had to admit it was perhaps the most plausible explanation for Eaton's interest in him.

Something was happening; the world was churning, and the police were sitting on their arses. *Think harder*, Wilde urged himself. *The answer is there. Think.*

Philip Eaton was drinking in the taproom of the Bull Hotel. He seemed a little surprised to see Wilde, but greeted him amiably and took out the address book he had stolen from the Langley murder scene and placed it in front of him on the bar. 'There you are,' he said.

Wilde ordered a whisky. When it was poured, he turned to Eaton. 'Did you manage to find Margot Langley?'

'There is a number for her in Germany, but no one answers the telephone. And I gather the police have had no luck in contacting her either.'

'In Germany? Interesting. Well, the parents must have known her whereabouts even if no one in the village did.'

'Maybe she's not there. The address could have been written down years ago. I'll keep trying the number.' Eaton took a sip of his own drink. 'So what's new?'

'I'll get on to that. First, has Superintendent Bower discovered anything?'

'He's made a few arrests. Known troublemakers and would-be revolutionaries, but no one is being held. Plodding along is the best I can say for Mr Bower. Another Scotch?'

'Make it a double.'

Eaton ordered, then folded his arms and gave Wilde a full-on stare. 'Well?'

Wilde took the letter from his pocket and placed it on the bar in front of Eaton.

The younger man placed the palm of his hand on the paper. 'What's this?'

'A letter from Nancy to the Socialist Club secretary, Dave Johnson. It arrived after she died. You met Johnson, didn't you, at the Kholtov rally?'

'Yes, briefly. I believe he found communism in the skies above Flanders. Not alone in that, I suspect.'

'Read it . . .'

Eaton looked down at the handwritten note. A minute later, he raised his eyes.

'This is quite something. Did Johnson just hand it over to you?'

'In a manner of speaking.'

'What do you think she's saying in this letter?'

'I was hoping Horace Dill might know, but he told me to fuck off. It occurred to me that it might be Horace who had persuaded her to spy on her father.'

'Really?'

'I think it's a possibility.' *A possiblity?* Even as he said the words, he realised he was failing his own test. What had he said to Maxwell and Felsted? *Make me prove my points, demand evidence . . . and if there is not enough evidence, then keep an open mind. Become a detective . . .*

'This magazine, *North Sea*,' Eaton said. 'That doesn't help us at all. But this list of names . . . I'd love to know more about that.'

'As an MI6 officer, I rather hoped you might know something already, Eaton.'

Eaton laughed. 'Yesterday it was MI5, now it's MI6.'

'Well, Horace has put me right. He also gave me an explanation for your interest in me.'

'Did he really? Did he also tell you that his telephone is tapped and that every secret service in the world is spying on him? I rather think Messrs Jung and Freud would enjoy a few sessions with Comrade Dill.'

Wilde laughed too. 'He thought you might be trying to recruit me. Can you believe that?'

'How wonderful. Were you flattered or horrified? And tell me, if some mythical secret agent *did* try to recuit you to British intelligence, what would you say?'

'I'd tell him I'm American, so no deal.'

Eaton smiled again. 'I'm sure Six would be sorry to hear it.' He took another sip of his drink. 'Now – to the matter in hand. You might like to know that I've been back to Kilmington. Personal instructions of Geoffrey Dawson, editor of my august journal. It seems that Cecil Langley was one of the King's oldest friends. I would never have thought it – polar opposites in my book, except for the politics. What do you make of that, Wilde? I would never have expected a country gentleman like Cecil Langley to be to our monarch's taste. Cocktails and dodgy divorcees are more his sort of thing.'

'Do you disapprove?'

'They're bores, the lot of them. As for the King and Langley, I simply can't imagine what they ever found to talk about – apart from their mutual admiration for Herr Hitler.'

'One of the torn-up pictures was of the King.'

'You should be a detective.'

'And you should be an MI6 officer.'

Eaton shook his head, downed his drink, then signalled the barman. 'You don't give up, do you?'

'Do you?'

'Yes, I certainly do. If I reach a cul-de-sac, I turn round and look for another road out.'

'And what if the answer lies within the cul-de-sac itself?'

'You're talking in riddles now.'

'No, I'm not. Let's talk about Margot Langley. She marries a man but then bolts. The only telephone number for her is a German one.'

The barman poured two more drinks. Eaton warmed his whisky glass with his hands. '*Cherchez l'homme*. Then I'd guess she went after a man. My lady friends tell me that those SS troopers look remarkably attractive in their black uniforms with silver flashes and high boots. And it's a Munich number. But going to Munich is nothing unusual these days; there are scores of young English men and women in the city, either at Baroness Laroche's finishing school or at university. I think they all go there hoping to catch a glimpse of the Führer.'

'You seem to know a lot about it.'

'None of it's secret, Wilde. Adolf Hitler is more accessible than my plumber. Loves to be seen by his adoring public driving around in his big Mercedes or eating his vegetarian spaghetti at the Osteria Bavaria. He would be remarkably easy to assassinate, but of course that's not the way we do things, is it? Unlike you Americans with your habit of shooting presidents when you tire of them.'

'Whereas you Brits just shuffle your kings away when they think of marrying Americans.'

'Very funny.'

Wilde picked the address book up and flicked through it. 'Are there any other names of note?'

'Scores of them, hundreds. Most of the Cabinet, the King's private number at Fort Belvedere, foreign potentates, dukes and duchesses. Cecil Langley had a finger in quite a few pies, I think. He even had Wallis Simpson's private number. I'm afraid I couldn't see much point in ringing them all. I'd have got very short shrift.'

'No. But I suspect there will be a crossover with that North Sea list. If we knew the names on that, we might start seeing connections.'

Eaton shook his head. 'I don't think we'd get very far. My editor is pretty clear that this is a Bolshevik attack on the British establishment. He tells me that the Cabinet believes Stalin's agents are minded to destabilise the country just at a time when it's facing its biggest crisis since the war. There are real fears of insurrection in support of the King. Spain could happen here. Civil war. When revolutionaries see trouble brewing, they seize the ladle to stir the cauldron all the more furiously.'

Out of the corner of his eye, Wilde caught a face he thought he recognised in the wall mirror behind the bar. He turned sharply but the man had gone.

'Seen a ghost?' Eaton asked.

'Not a ghost – our Russian friend, Yuri Kholtov.'

'What in God's name is he still doing here? I thought he would have gone back to Russia by now.'

Looking for you, probably, thought Wilde. 'Perhaps he's thirsty,' he said. He put his whisky down on the bar and walked briskly towards the doorway where he had spotted Kholtov. A gust of cold wind told him that the Russian had gone from the front door. He pushed it open and stepped outside. Kholtov was hurrying south down Trumpington Street, huddled into his coat. Wilde caught up with him easily.

'Comrade Kholtov, I spotted you in the bar. Let me buy you a drink.'

The big Russian looked startled. 'I was just passing. It seemed a pleasant place.'

'Indeed, it is. And if anywhere in Cambridge has vodka, it'll be the Bull. Come and share a glass with Mr Eaton and myself.'

'I must go. I am expected by Professor Dill. I am staying at his lodgings.'

'Oh, don't worry about Horace. He can wait.' Wilde pulled persuasively at Kholtov's arm. 'Come and tell us more about the war in Spain and what's going on in Moscow.'

Kholtov wrenched his arm away from Wilde's grasp. For a brief moment Wilde saw behind the affable veneer. 'I said no, Professor Wilde. Now if you will excuse me, please.' He nodded sharply and turned to head off again.

Wilde touched him on the shoulder. 'Comrade Kholtov,' he said. 'If it's college you want, you're going the wrong way.'

On her return from the office, Lydia wrote a note asking Tom to come round, and posted it through his letterbox. Then she braced herself to go up to the spare room that Leslie Braithwaite had stayed in. He had succeeded in turning it into a rubbish dump. She stood in the doorway, arms folded across her threadbare pullover. Doris had tidied the room thoroughly, airing it with the window open all morning, but it still didn't feel quite right.

It was one of the better rooms in the house, facing south-east to catch the best of any morning sun on offer through a pair of light, sunflower yellow curtains. There were shelves with books for the use of visitors, including copies of the poetry anthologies she had published. Who wouldn't have preferred to spend the night there – or even a week – rather than camp at the roadside or in the woods?

She let out a weary sigh. Was she really just a soft touch? 'They're not pet cats, you know, Lydia,' Tom Wilde had said to her. 'They won't all purr; some will scratch and bite.' Well, she had been well and truly savaged by Leslie Braithwaite. At least there had been no 'Told you so' from Tom, which was a small blessing.

Lydia felt profoundly depressed about Leslie Braithwaite's attack. She had always believed that good trumped evil and that if you treated people well they would treat you well in return. Braithwaite had disproved her theory in the most devastating way. Surely, he couldn't have had any cause to imagine that his rough advances would be welcomed? She supposed a man alone on the road might be sexually frustrated, but whatever a man's background or circumstances, there could be no excuse for the way he had behaved. He simply didn't care. He had wanted sex and he was going to take it. The shame of it was that she would now look with less charity on any other hunger marcher or unemployed man in need of a meal and a roof over his head. But then she found herself laughing at the very notion; she'd *always* be a soft touch. You don't change your nature that easily.

Doris had stripped the bed and called in the pest man to fumigate the mattress. She had probably beaten the curtains, too. Braithwaite had taken down many of the books, read a page or two, then inexplicably torn them out and screwed them up. Perhaps he hadn't liked what he read. And he had spat the brown juice of his foul chewing tobacco on the floor. Now everything had been cleaned up and put back in its proper place.

On the little table, beside the single iron bedstead, beneath the table lamp, Doris had deposited the few belongings that had been left: the toothbrush Lydia had given him, a spare pair of socks, and the screwed-up pages from her books.

She tossed the toothbrush in the wastepaper basket. The socks could be washed and go to charity. Hating to think of a book incomplete, she began methodically going through the rumpled pages, smoothing them flat, and putting them back into the books to which they belonged.

Among the pages was a scrap of writing paper that clearly had not come from a book. Lydia switched on the bedside lamp and straightened it. A few words were scrawled on the paper in black ink, including a four-digit number preceded by the word *May*. She frowned, then realised it was a Mayfair telephone number. Then there was a name, *Carr*, and another name, *Brandham H*, both written with a pencil. And that was it.

Why would a man like Braithwaite, an unemployed coal miner, have a Mayfair telephone number in his possession? Was it something he had picked up in the street? Perhaps he had used it to wrap his plug of tobacco. She looked at her wristwatch. Tom should arrive soon. He might make sense of it.

The doorbell rang. Lydia took the scrap of paper and went to the front door. It was Hartmut Dorfen, beaming, carrying a bottle of French wine. He threw wide his arms, dazzling her with his blue eyes and offering his lips up for a kiss.

'Forgive me, I'm a little early.'

Lydia accepted the kiss and wished very much that she had changed out of her cords and old pullover into a dress.

In the Bull, Wilde finished his drink and took out his wallet to pay the bill.

'These are on me,' Eaton said. '*The Times* will pay.'

'Very generous, your editor.'

'Not sure I'd go along with that, old boy, but I think you count as a genuine contact. Did you catch up with your ghost?'

'Oh, he was real enough. It was Kholtov, looking very shifty. I told him you were here and offered to buy him a drink, but he rushed off saying he was meeting Horace Dill.'

'Perhaps it was the mention of my name that put him off. A lot of people don't like newspapermen.'

'You could be right.'

Wilde turned to go, but Eaton put a hand on his arm. 'What now?'

Wilde shrugged. 'Perhaps your editor's correct. Perhaps the commies are taking advantage of the constitutional crisis.'

'Well, keep in touch. Not sure how long I'll be up in Cambridge, but you know how to find me.'

Wilde shook hands, and strode out of the pub along Trumpington Street, towards King's Parade. With Great St Mary's on his right, he looked across to the wonder of King's College Chapel. Turning right into Market Street he suddenly stopped.

By now, the shops were all closed and most people had gone home. He stood in a shop doorway and waited in the cold air. Two minutes, five minutes. He looked at his watch. It had to be enough. He turned and retraced his steps.

Kholtov was standing beside Eaton at the bar of the Bull, in the place vacated just a few minutes ago by Wilde. They were deep in conversation; Kholtov appeared to be showing Eaton something. If either of them had looked up they would have seen Wilde in the mirror, but they were too engrossed to notice him.

He walked up behind them. 'Eaton, Mr Kholtov . . .'

They both turned at his voice.

'I lost your card, Eaton,' Wilde said. 'I wonder, do you have another? Some way of contacting you when you leave Cambridge?'

'Of course.' Eaton pulled a card from his inside pocket and proffered it without missing a beat. 'Here you are. Are you going to stay for another Scotch now you're back with us? Mr Kholtov took up your offer of a drink after all – rather disappointed you were gone, I think. Poor chap's stuck with me.'

'No, no. Must be on my way.' Wilde held out his hand to Kholtov. The Russian's right hand was clenched tight. He transferred whatever was in it to his left hand so that he could shake Wilde's hand.

'Another time, Professor Wilde.'

'Indeed, Mr Kholtov.' He patted the Russian on the shoulder. 'Good luck in Moscow. Rather you than me.'

As he walked home through Cambridge, this time at a slower pace, he wondered what an agent of the Soviet Union could be talking about in such a secretive fashion to a member of MI6. He particularly wondered why the Russian was showing a golden coin to the Englishman and why he didn't want Wilde to see it.

A black car drew to a halt beside him just as he was passing Petty Cury. Superintendent Bower wound down the rear window and beckoned him.

'Good evening, superintendent.'

'We're looking for the Russian. Where is he?'

'What Russian?'

'Don't be clever, Professor Wilde. I know very well you were at the rally. I know, too, that he had dinner at Miss Morris's house, and that you were there.'

'Ah, *that* Russian. Yuri Kholtov. What of him?'

'I want to question him about the murder of Mr and Mrs Langley.'

'Is there some evidence against him?'

'We've had a tip-off. He's a communist, Professor Wilde.'

'What sort of tip-off?'

'A telephone call, divulging the man's violent past – and his movements in this area. I don't think there can be much doubt about his guilt.'

'Who made the call?'

'It was anonymous, but I can assure you it added up in every detail.'

'Then I shall keep my eyes out for him, superintendent. Thank you for warning me.'

'I'm told you are a scholar of some renown, Professor Wilde, a man of remarkable intellectual faculties. Might I suggest you use the brain God gave you to help the police in the execution of their duty?'

'What are you implying, superintendent?'

'I'm saying I don't believe you, professor. I think you know very well where the bloody Russki is.'

As he walked away Wilde considered why he had not told Bower that Kholtov was, at that very moment, in the Bull with Eaton. Let the police do their own work. Surely, Kholtov was not a man who would compromise his position in such a crude and bloody way; Kholtov was here in Cambridge for some other reason. The question was, what? Wilde gritted his teeth. The truth was, he had no solid reason to believe Kholtov innocent, even though Horace Dill had insisted Kholtov was with him on the day Nancy died. Wilde's hand went to his pocket and gripped the peseta coin. It was a small clue. But the only person he knew who had been to Spain recently was Yuri Kholtov. Why had he not shown it to Bower?

CHAPTER 24

Immediately Lydia opened the front door, Wilde saw in her eyes that something was not quite right.

'Lydia? You left a note on my mat to come round.'

'Tom, there's someone here – an old friend.'

Wilde gazed over her shoulder.

'He's in the sitting room.' *Help me.* She mouthed the words.

It was a pleasant, elegant room, with sofa and armchairs, Persian carpet, occasional tables and a wireless, but the atmosphere was strained and strange. In the centre of the room was a tall, fair-haired man. Wilde frowned. He seemed familiar. But where from? Then he realised – he had seen him fleetingly earlier that day, in college with Dr Sawyer.

Lydia gave Wilde a strained smile.

'Tom, this is Hartmut Dorfen, or Hart as we all called him when he was up here. He's a very old friend of Nancy, Margot and mine. He's here for Nancy's funeral. I so wanted you to meet him. Hart, this is Professor Tom Wilde.'

The men shook hands.

Somewhat surprised, Wilde smiled at the handsome German. 'Good to meet you, Herr Dorfen. Am I right in thinking I saw you this afternoon with Duncan Sawyer?'

'Yes, indeed, I did call on him. He's an old friend from my Munich days.'

'Such a small world.'

'We met in the early thirties when he was at the Ludwig Maximilian University. I was doing some research there after going down from Cambridge. That was before the bloody Nazis grabbed power, of course.'

Wilde nodded. What did this man Dorfen mean to Lydia? She was like a taut cable in his presence. And why was he in her sitting room if she didn't want him here?

'Lydia has been telling me wonderful things about you,' Dorfen said.

'I can't imagine what.'

Wilde had intended only to stay long enough for a brief conversation and a glass of wine with Lydia, to catch up on the day. Now, though, it seemed she needed him. He studied Dorfen. Despite his country tweed suit and immaculate shoes – Church's or perhaps Crockett and Jones? – Hartmut Dorfen would never pass as an English gentleman. The same could be said, Wilde acknowledged, of himself, but then he wasn't trying. He glanced at Lydia, looking for clues that might explain her discomfort, but she had her eyes down, fiddling with the hem of her pullover. He turned back to Dorfen. 'So, when did you and Lydia meet?'

'The 1929 May Ball,' Dorfen said. 'A wonderful night.'

He ran his flawless fingers through his short fair hair. He was absurdly good-looking, thought Wilde; he could have been a movie star from Herr Goebbels's stable of approved Aryan actors. He put aside his instinctive antipathy; if Lydia needed help, he would offer it.

'They were good days,' Dorfen went on. 'Now I live in London, in a sort of limbo. Neither the joy of my Cambridge years, nor the comfort of my homeland.'

'Are you avoiding Germany? Have you joined the happy band of exiles who have fallen foul of the regime?'

'No, it is the regime that has fallen foul of me.'

'Indeed. There is much to dislike about the new Germany.' Wilde was not totally convinced. Why did so many middle-class Germans sneer at Hitler when they were in England and then salute him when they returned home?

'A man must do what a man must do – which I know will be instantly denounced as a cliché by Lydia. It was always her declared role to improve my English.'

'I'd say you speak excellent English,' Wilde said.

'My mother insisted I learn from an early age and that I attend Cambridge. She has always had a romantic notion about your country.'

'Not *my* country, Herr Dorfen.'

Lydia held up a bottle. 'Hart brought us this vintage claret, Tom. You have to try it.' She was pleading with him: *please stay. Half an hour won't hurt.* 'One little glass. You could keep Hart company while I go and change. He's caught me in my working togs.'

There was an edge of panic in Lydia's voice. Wilde touched her arm reassuringly. 'Then how can I refuse? A really small glass, though, Lydia. I've already had a couple of Scotches at the Bull and I do need to keep a clear head.'

Even as he spoke, she was pouring him a glass. It was a premier cru from a good vineyard. A superb year. He held up the glass appreciatively to the light, noting the deep, rich red. 'Very good indeed. You obviously have fine taste and deep pockets, Herr Dorfen.'

'I learnt everything I know about wine during my time here. We were good friends in the old days. Lydia, Nancy and I . . .'

'And Margot, of course,' Lydia said.

'Indeed, Margot.'

Wilde glanced at Lydia again, then back to Dorfen. Did this man not know the fate of the Langleys? Had Lydia not told him? As casually as he could, he said, 'You must have heard about her parents?'

Dorfen frowned. He, too, turned to Lydia and met her frightened eyes. 'What is this, Lydia? Has something happened?'

'They're dead, Hart. I'm sorry, I should have said something before . . .' She trailed off uncertainly. 'It's all been such a shock – and then you walking in on me unexpectedly . . .'

Dorfen's eyes were wide. He was shaking. 'Dead? Why did you not tell me at once?'

Wilde cut in. 'It's very recent.'

'Was there an accident?'

'No accident,' Wilde said. 'They were murdered. Their bodies were discovered on Wednesday evening, their throats cut.'

Lydia gasped. 'Tom – don't!'

'Forgive me, Lydia, I shouldn't have said that. Absolutely unnecessary.'

'It's bad enough that they died, but to conjure up such an image. Hart knew them well. We both did.'

'I spoke without thinking.' Tom Wilde never spoke without thinking. He tilted his head to one side apologetically. 'Please accept my apologies, Dorfen. What happened to them is a tragedy. A horrible tragedy.'

Hartmut Dorfen looked as if he was about to faint. He clasped the arm of a chair and lowered himself into it. 'This is too much. I cannot believe you are telling me this. Who could do such a thing?' He dug his hand into the pocket of his expensive jacket and pulled out a packet of Players. With shaking fingers he put a cigarette in his mouth and struck a match. He drew deeply, and as an afterthought he offered the packet to Lydia and Wilde. They both shook their heads.

'Can I get you a brandy?' Wilde suggested. He turned to Lydia. 'Go and change. I'll look after your guest.'

Lydia put down the wine bottle, touched Hart's arm, threw a grateful smile at Wilde, and left the room.

Wilde went to the drinks cabinet and poured a stiff measure of brandy for Dorfen, but not for himself. He brought the drink back and handed it to the German. 'They lived not far from here, you know.'

'Yes, I visited them on several occasions,' Dorfen said, taking the drink. He seemed to have got over his initial shock.

'Of course, you must have done. You'd have known their house well.' Wilde looked for a reaction, saw none, and continued. 'I have been wondering whether there might be some link between their deaths and Nancy's.' A second speculative line.

'Nancy died of a heroin overdose, did she not? That is what Lydia told me.'

Wilde shrugged. 'Think of the politics. Sir Norman Hereward, Cecil Langley.'

Dorfen looked surprised. 'Politics?'

'Surely you know that they shared an admiration for Hitler and the Nazis?'

'Really? I had thought better of them.'

'You must realise, though, that your old friend Duncan Sawyer is also rather fond of the regime in Germany?'

Dorfen brushed the suggestion away with a flick of the hand. 'Duncan just likes to outrage sensibilities. Take no notice of him. But as for Nancy and the Langleys . . . well, yes, I can certainly see some tenuous connection. I do not understand what the motive could be, however.'

'Nor do I. And yet . . .' Time to cast the third line with its little feathery fly. 'Do you mind if I try a few thoughts on you? You knew these people; I didn't.'

'I would very much like to hear what you think.' Dorfen got up from the chair and picked up the wine bottle. He had recovered his earlier confidence. 'Here, I see you are not drinking brandy, so more claret, yes?'

'Thank you.' Wilde took the glass but did not drink. 'Now stop me if I'm boring you, but as an historian and sometime mathematician, I try to think both logically and with reference to the past.'

Dorfen smiled. 'The world might be a better place if politicians followed your lead, sir.'

'Have you heard of the so-called Zinoviev letter of 1924, which helped destroy the Labour Party's hopes of election victory?'

'No,' said Dorfen. 'I was not in England in 1924.'

'This letter was discovered by the British press and purported to be the work of the senior Russian official Grigory Zinoviev, writing on behalf of the Comintern. In it, he urged the Communist Party of Great Britain to organise uprisings – just at the time that the Labour Party wanted to do a trade deal with the Soviet Union. The implication was obvious: the Labour government was either being suckered by the Soviets or was treacherous. The letter was published a few days before the election – and the effect was electrifying; the Labour Party was demolished and the Conservatives swept to power.'

'One can understand how such a letter might have that effect.'

'The only problem was that the letter was a forgery.'

Dorfen grinned. 'A clever plot, and very effective, it seems. But what has this to do with the murders?'

'Nothing in itself, but it shows how a power, either inside or outside the country, might influence policy and popular feeling with one or two carefully chosen actions. A small nudge of the tiller, if you like. We still don't know who forged Mr Zinoviev's signature, but he undoubtedly changed the course of British history.'

'Are you suggesting that the deaths of Nancy and the Langleys could have been ordered by someone in England or abroad who was looking for some sort of electoral advantage?'

Wilde shook his head. 'There is no election in the offing. But politically motivated murders will always be destabilising. The question is this: *who* wants to destabilise Britain? These are certainly difficult days for the country with the question of the King's friendship with Mrs Simpson.'

'So you mean a foreign power is trying to use the crisis for their own ends?'

'It's possible, isn't it? Or a radical grouping within Britain itself.'

Dorfen stubbed out his cigarette, grinding the butt hard into the ashtray, so that strands of tobacco broke out around his yellow fingers. 'We are both historians, yes? Then let us examine the possibilities one by one. I cannot see what Hitler has to gain. It is my understanding that he has always hoped for an alliance with the British. Is this not so? Why would he wish to make trouble here?'

'Indeed, he seems very keen to make friends with people in high places in Britain. People of my own acquaintance – including at least two fellows of my college – have enjoyed his hospitality.' He recalled Duncan Sawyer's enthusiastic reports of his days as Goering's guest at Carinhall, his hunting lodge near Berlin. 'Many British politicians think Hitler wonderful. So perhaps you are right. On the face of it, the Nazis have nothing to gain by undermining Britain.'

'Hitler is lower than a dog.' Dorfen spoke with contempt. 'He is a scraping on the shoe of German history.'

'Did something happen to you or your family?'

'You mean apart from his persecution of those who disagree with him – and the burning of books? The Nazis lack class, Wilde. And that is unforgivable.'

Wilde laughed lightly. 'Well, I am glad you think like that,' he said. 'So then, we must consider the Soviet Union. Why would Stalin wish to destabilise Britain?'

Dorfen frowned. 'It is what the communists do, isn't it? Look at Spain.' He glanced down at his hands before raising his gaze to meet Wilde's. 'But as an historian, surely you must need more evidence before you can indulge in such speculation, professor?'

Wilde dipped his head in acknowledgement. 'A fair point,' he said. 'But I'm not really speculating, just asking questions.' He held up his hand as if he had suddenly thought of something. 'You know, there is just an outside chance you might be able to do something to help in this matter.'

'Anything, of course.'

'Lydia and I have been trying to reach Margot Langley. We have reason to believe she still doesn't know about her parents' death. The thing is, it's possible she's gone to Germany, but we can't find her.'

Dorfen raised his eyebrows. 'What would Margot be doing in Germany?'

'I'd very much like to find out. Do you know anyone over there who could help?'

'I really don't know who I would ask. I have no family alive except my mother and I have lost touch with many old friends. My home is England now.'

The door opened and Lydia came in wearing a simple dress and cardigan, her hair still unkempt but pushed back from her face.

'Ah – Lydia,' said Wilde. 'I was just asking Herr Dorfen whether he had any way of finding the whereabouts of Margot.'

'Maybe she will see the news about the murders in the press,' Dorfen said. 'I believe the Munich papers carry major stories from England.'

'She might,' Wilde said. 'Although it would be a terrible way to learn about such a tragedy.'

Dorfen looked at his watch. 'Lydia, my dear, I really must take my leave. I will see you at the funeral, yes?'

'Yes, of course.'

'And you, professor?'

'Indeed.' Wilde shook Dorfen's smooth, dry hand. *But I don't believe I mentioned Margot's connection to Munich to you, Herr Dorfen.*

CHAPTER 25

Leslie Braithwaite was waiting for his companion at the side of the road, by the woods where he had been living and sleeping this past day. The clothes he had stolen were serviceable enough and the cold hadn't bothered him. He was used to it, but he had thought they might at least offer him a horse blanket and a stable to sleep in, up at the big house. But they said he couldn't be seen there. Bastards.

He was looking forward to this. His whole life had been building to this. Strike a blow for the proletariat. Start a revolution. He laughed. 'Fuck the revolution,' he said out loud. He just wanted to *kill* one of the English fucking overlords who'd told him what to do every day of his life. The overlords like the halfwit bloody lieutenant who had nearly got him killed back in 1916: 'Fall in, Braithwaite, you're coming on a patrol.'

It had been a wet, moonless night. The rain had fallen ceaselessly for weeks that autumn. In no-man's-land, you could drown in the mud. Braithwaite, Private Joe Fitzpatrick from Belfast and the lieutenant were supposed to capture a German for questioning. Instead they got caught in the wire, slithering helplessly in the thick wet sludge of earth and blood. Close to the German trenches, the lieutenant took a bullet through the throat. Braithwaite watched him in the yellow light of a flare, gurgling blood, clutching his well-bred neck, for two or three minutes, and then he was gone forever. Joe, paralysed with fear, lying flat on his belly took a single round from a German rifle through the top of his head.

Braithwaite, caught in the wire, knew he was next. But then the firing stopped and a pair of Huns crawled forward. Here it comes, he thought, the bayonet in the gut. But instead, a German officer held a pistol to his face while the other cut him from the wire.

'Hello, little Tommy,' the officer said in perfect English. 'Would you care to join us for a glass of schnapps?'

There was no schnapps but a great deal of interrogation about troop numbers, accompanied by clouts to the head.

The next day he had been taken to some wreck of a train station and put in a closed wagon with more than sixty other men. Packed in tight, they had to endure four days on a slow journey eastwards, with little ventilation, water or food, and nowhere to shit or piss or sleep except where they stood. Nine men died between the Somme and Magdeburg. Braithwaite survived because he had been a miner: he didn't panic and didn't gasp for air; something good had come of his time down the pit.

He had joined the army to get away from the mines. Now he found himself at a place called Möhlau, living in a hut with a load of Russians, Frenchmen and a few Englishmen. And he was there to dig up brown coal, lignite, from the Golpa strip mine. Oh, the sodding irony. He had travelled over a thousand miles, been shot at, shouted at, half-starved, kicked and punched – and he was digging coal again.

He worked in the mine for two years, eating bread that a horse would have turned its nose up at and supping the eternal gruel of cabbage and potato. On 11 November 1918, the guards opened the gates. 'The war is over. *Auf wiedersehen*, Braithwaite, you can go home.' Go home? How? He was skin and bones, a five-foot skeleton.

Braithwaite got no further than the nearby village, where he knocked on a door, begged some food in broken German, and collapsed. He awoke to find a young woman in front of him holding a bowl of hot broth, which she began to spoon into his mouth, like a baby. It was the first kindness he had known in all his twenty-one years.

Even by candlelight, Gudrun was neither pretty nor dainty. She had a coarse face and stood at least half a foot taller than Braithwaite. But she was kind and hard-working and uncomplaining and so he stayed, going back to work at the Golpa mine, this time for money. The life was hard, but beer and tobacco were a solace. So was Gudrun; she warmed his bed and accepted his beatings.

Now here, on this roadside in another country, eighteen years later, he missed her and the children. In his head, he had a picture of them. At just thirteen, in his Deutsches Jungvolk uniform, young Hermann already stood taller than his father. And Clara, sweet Clara, had her mother's sunny nature but was lovelier by far. How had a squat, bow-legged York-shireman and a thick-handed peasant woman brought such children into the world? It was for them that he had come back – for them, and for the workers of Germany and England – doing his duty for the Führer's revolution.

A dark car passed him, then slowed, and stopped.

The door closed on Hartmut Dorfen, and Wilde led the way back into the sitting room. 'What was all that about, Lydia?'

'I was hoping you might tell me, Tom.'

'He doesn't give much away. Not intentionally, anyway.'

'Was he overbearing?'

'A little too eager to please. I didn't find him particularly convincing.' Wilde thought about Dorfen's analysis of Germany's intentions. He was either naive or being deliberately obtuse in suggesting Hitler wished Britain no harm. At the very least it was an analysis a little too favourable to a regime he purported to scorn.

'I know some people can find him a bit high-handed, that's all.'

Wilde didn't think it was all, not for a minute. But he didn't pick her up on it. 'Tell me about him.'

'As he said, we met at the college's May Ball. We were shipped in from Girton because they were short of girls. That's how it was put to us! Not very flattering, but if it was meant as an insult we didn't really care because it suited us very well. Clever, good-looking men, smart clothes and lots of champagne.'

'We?'

'Me, Nancy and Margot. With a chaperone, of course, but we soon lost her. None of us had ever met a man like Hart Dorfen before. We were only used to English boys, all frightfully jolly and well brought up. Hart was a world away from them – he was dangerous and killingly handsome. We found ways to escape college and managed to spend all that June with him. He thought he could have us all. But he couldn't – not me anyway. We all flirted with him outrageously, but in my case that was all. Nancy and Margot were another matter. There was an intense rivalry between them. Margot was obsessed with him, I'm afraid. But then she took everything so damned seriously.'

'So what happened?'

'Stay here.' Lydia left the room, returning a minute later with a photograph that she handed to Wilde. 'That's us outside the college gate on Trumpington Street,' she said. 'Margot Langley, Nancy Hereward, Hart and me.'

'Hart Dorfen and the three musketeers.'

'The three Furies, more like.'

'Well, you all look very happy.'

'Appearances can be deceptive.' She sighed, but it was more like a groan. 'Honestly, Tom – bloody Cambridge. Bloody Girton.'

'I've never heard you like this before.'

Lydia threw herself onto the sofa. 'It cossets you in a womb of cleverness, only to deliver you into a world of brutal stupidity. I just want to go to bed and sleep until 1937. I've really had enough of this year. Too much death and destruction.'

Wilde went over to the fireplace and gave the coals a poke. He wanted to know more about Hartmut Dorfen. 'Listen, Lydia, tell me everything. This thing with you, your friends and Dorfen, it must have all happened four or five years before I arrived. Tell me about that summer.'

Lydia threw her head back and looked at the ceiling. 'I'll tell you about one particular day,' she said. 'One glorious sunny Cambridge day when we all took a punt down the Cam towards Grantchester. Hart, me, Nancy, Margot and two King's boys, whose names escape me and who aren't important to the story anyway. We had a picnic . . .' she trailed off.

'Three boys, three girls.'

She nodded. 'I think the whole university was on the river or in the meadow that day. We all thought we were Virginia Woolf or Byron, I think. At first it was perfect. But it didn't end that way. We had wine and beer with us, a portable gramophone and some jazz recordings. The two English boys wore rowing caps and cricket shirts. We girls had changed into summery dresses at Nancy's room in the master's lodge. Hart, of course, was dressed in boater and striped blazer.'

'I can picture you.'

'Well, you know Grantchester Meadow on a hot, hazy day, Tom. Too much wine, too much birdsong, the sound of the green water drifting by. Your perception changes and you forget yourself. We moored in the pool by the mill and danced on the grass. We had cucumber sandwiches and cold slices of pork pie and champagne. Far too much champagne. We laughed and recited poetry. Hart declaimed Goethe and Schiller and Shakespeare sonnets, and then we dozed. Day turned into evening – a balmy evening – and we woke again. We played jazz on the gramophone and danced some more, then made a little campfire.'

'It sounds idyllic.'

'Yes. But there was tension, too. Hart and Margot had been seeing each other ever since the May Ball, and Nancy didn't like it.'

'Seeing? As in?'

'Of course. We might have been chaperoned, but we certainly weren't all virgins. Don't forget, Margot had already been presented at court before coming up to Girton. At first I was rather envious of her: I thought she and Hart had found true love. Margot was much more beautiful than Nancy and me so obviously I thought she would be the one to get him. But as the weeks wore on, she began to become insanely jealous. If he didn't send her a note every day or was five minutes late for a meeting, she was a wreck.'

'The day of the picnic – something happened?'

Lydia nodded. Even now the memory made her shudder.

'Nancy began to undress. It wasn't so shocking because it was a dark night, but you could see in the firelight that she was naked. "Come on, into the water," she said. "Fainthearts have to walk back to Cambridge." We all began to throw off our clothes and dived in – all save Margot. She tried to cling on to Hart, but he was having none of it. He stripped and dived in with the rest of us. There was a great deal of splashing about and horseplay in the water. Margot sat by the fire, sullen and sulky.

'Eventually I clambered out and grabbed a towel, as did the two King's boys. But there was no sign of Hart or Nancy. We didn't notice at first, but then we began to get worried. After all, we were a bit tipsy and I was worried they might have got tangled in the weed. We called softly, then the two boys jumped back in and tried to find them. I wandered around the bank, calling as I went. And then I heard a low moan and saw wet skin and found them, *in flagrante*. A tangle of limbs, sliding on a bed of grass and leaves. They hadn't seen me, so I turned back – and came face to face with Margot. She let out an unearthly scream of anguish, then turned and ran.'

'Well, clearly, that did for her relationship with Hart.'

Lydia shook her head. 'It was worse than that. We couldn't find her. We guessed that she had run back to Cambridge, so all we could do was chase after her. Within five minutes of Hart and Nancy reappearing, we had piled everything on the punt and set off for home. Halfway between Grantchester and Cambridge, we came across a body lying in the water, hair floating around.' Lydia shuddered.

'But you saved her?'

'Of course. She coughed up lots of water and we took her to Addenbrooke's, where she spent the night. If you ask me now, I don't even believe she was ever in any danger. I think she walked into the water and arranged herself like Ophelia just before we arrived. But at the time, we thought she was dead. It was extremely frightening.'

'What happened to your friendship?'

Lydia sighed. 'That was the end of the triumvirate. Margot left college, went off to marry some chinless wonder she'd met at a debs' ball. And then she did a runner. So there you have it.'

'What of Nancy and Dorfen?'

'It went nowhere. Actually, I think Nancy just did it to get one over Margot. I don't think Nancy was even very keen on him.'

'And Dorfen?'

Lydia smiled, but it was a brave smile. 'Seeing him here has brought it all up again, that's all. And now that Nancy and the Langleys are dead, I simply can't bear even to think about such things.' She sat back on the sofa, and hugged her arms around her knees. 'Hart and Margot are quite alike in some ways – intense, a little aloof, even chilly. But there is more to him than that. He can be funny and warm one moment, like ice the next. Didn't you notice that in him?'

'No.'

'But you didn't see him as we did. We always knew there was something of the cruel northern wastes about him, which only added to his appeal. He was like some bloody Norseman, come with axe and longsword to add spice to our dull little college lives. And at Girton, of course, we were all like a herd of penned-in peahens – and then this gorgeous Nordic peacock arrives.'

'You're mixing your metaphors.'

'Sod it, I don't care. And I really don't like it when you correct my English! Correcting English is my job, not yours.'

Wilde smiled. She was beginning to recover. 'Did you tell Dorfen that we think Margot is in Munich?'

'No – why? I didn't mention Margot at all.'

'I think he knows she's there.'

'*What?*'

'I said she was in Germany and that we wanted to contact her about her parents' death in case she hadn't heard. He said she would probably read about it in the Munich papers. But why say Munich? I hadn't mentioned it.'

'Well, he comes from Munich, that's why.'

'But why assume Margot's there? Germany is a big place.' The answer seemed obvious to Wilde. He knew she was there because he was the reason she had bolted from her marriage. So why hadn't he said so?

'Oh God, Tom, I don't know.'

'There was something else. Did you notice his wristwatch? I spotted it when he reached up to light his cigarette. It's new and it looks rather cheap.'

'Tom, you have many defects but I had never taken you for a snob.'

'It was an Ingersoll – I had one like it a few years back. Cost about ten shillings. Everything else about Hartmut Dorfen oozed money. The lowliest waiter will tell you that expensive shoes and cheap watches don't add up.'

'You're losing me.'

Should he tell her this? 'Look . . . we found a wristwatch in the Langleys' house. A very expensive Patek Philippe.'

The horror in Lydia's eyes was clear. 'You don't think, Tom ... Oh please God, no.'

Wilde tried to smile. 'I don't know, Lydia. I really don't know. For all I know the Patek belonged to Cecil Langley. Perhaps I'm just imagining things.' *Perhaps I just didn't like your German friend.*

Lydia read his mind. 'I could see you didn't like him but, good God, why would Hart have killed Mr and Mrs Langley? Please, I've had enough of these horrors.' She got to her feet, and a scrap of paper fell to the floor. 'Oh!' She bent to pick it up. 'I wanted to show you this.' She handed it to him. 'I found it in Braithwaite's room. What do you think it means?'

Wilde studied it. 'It looks like a Mayfair telephone number. What on earth would Braithwaite be doing with that?'

'I have no idea.'

'Carr and Brandham must be names. I know it's late, but shall we call and see who answers?'

They went to the hall and got a connection within a minute. Wilde put his hand over the mouthpiece. 'It's the Dorchester!'

'Are you sure?' Lydia looked incredulous. 'Ask for those names.'

Wilde asked for Mr Carr, but was told that no one of that name was in residence; he tried Brandham and got the same result. He thanked the concierge and rang off. 'Why would Braithwaite be calling the Dorchester? And who are Carr and Brandham H?'

'Harry Brandham, Henrietta Brandham? And why is the Dorchester number written in ink and the names in pencil?'

'Because they were written at different times? Perhaps someone had given him the Dorchester number – and then at a later date he had to call a contact there to get the names which he scrawled in pencil.' Suddenly Wilde went cold. 'Lydia, this isn't two names – it's one name and an address. It's Sir Vyvyan Carr. He lives at Brandham Hall, just ten miles from here.'

'The general? Of course . . .'

'He's very close to the Chief of the Imperial General Staff. An outspoken enemy of Bolshevism. Now what, Lydia, would Mr Braithwaite want with him?'

*

The telephone number in the directory for Brandham Hall was dead, so Wilde called the local police. 'Sir Vyvyan and Lady Carr spend a great deal of their time in Knightsbridge,' the desk sergeant had said. 'But we'll check the Hall over and I'll get back to you.'

In retrospect Wilde thought he had not explained his concerns well. An unemployed miner named Leslie Braithwaite had left a scrap of paper in Lydia Morris's house with a name and the number of the Dorchester Hotel on it. It hardly made sense. And yet to Wilde it was significant. Three people were dead: three people well known to Lydia. The man Braithwaite was a criminal with a vicious streak. And now Sir Vyvyan Carr wasn't answering their calls.

After half an hour, and with no return call from the police, Wilde decided to take a look for himself. He suggested Lydia might be better off staying at home in case the police called back.

'No, Tom, I'm coming with you.'

The night had clouded over and there was a damp wintry chill. As they hit the road west out of Cambridge, a hail shower came on, beating against Wilde's goggles and lower face. Lydia had hurriedly thrown on her old corduroys, two pullovers, thick woollen gloves, scarf and duffle coat for the ride, and now she sat with her arms clasped tight round his waist, nestling her face into his back, sheltering against the foul weather.

Wilde could feel that the road was becoming slick; the Rudge's tyres were losing traction and he had to reduce speed and corner at a crawl. In twenty minutes, they arrived at the village of Brandham. He had been here before, one summer's day. There was good birdwatching, he had been told. He had spent an afternoon listening to the lark, and following its bold rise into the warm air over a field of corn. He recalled having seen the entrance drive to Brandham Hall off a lane on the far side of the village.

Close to midnight. There were no lights save the motorbike's head-lamp, cutting a beam through the sleet. Outside the old Hall, a car was parked on the circular gravel drive. Had the police been on their rounds yet? If Sir Vyvyan had already been woken by the police on their rounds, he would not be best pleased to be roused from his bed again.

The old house was in darkness. Wilde drew to a halt and left the engine running. 'We'll wake someone. A housekeeper or chauffeur. There must be some staff here.'

She slid from the bike. 'Only one way to find out.'

The doorbell was like a small church bell, suspended from a wrought-iron bracket, with a knotted rope to swing the clapper. She gave it a gentle tug. When there was no response and no sign of movement within the house, she clanged it hard. Still no one came.

Wilde glanced at his wristwatch. 'Midnight.'

'The countryside shuts down at ten p.m., Tom.'

'Let's look around.' He switched off the engine, pulled the electric torch from the deep pocket of his trenchcoat and pressed the switch. It splayed a dull yellow glow around the front of the broad-faced house. 'Damn, the batteries are going.'

'This feels very much like trespass. If the police do turn up on their rounds they'll think we're housebreakers.'

'Burglars,' Wilde said. 'Housebreakers come by day, burglars by night.'

'I'm glad Harrow taught you something.'

Their search was short and grim. Within two minutes, they found the defiled body of General Sir Vyvyan Carr in an open-sided barn at the south side of the house. He was lying flat on his back, his body blood-streaked. A sledgehammer and a rusty sickle had been laid out along his corpse. The haft of the hammer ran from his torso up along the line of his throat and the solid iron head lay wide across his face, like the arms of a crucifix. The sickle lay lower down his body, curved from his belly up across his heart. The emblem of the communist revolution in Russia, the hammer of the industrial workers and the sickle of the rural peasantry, united in the class struggle; here it stood for murder and hatred.

There was a great deal of blood, caused by a massive wound to the skull, which had evidently been crushed by the sledgehammer and by deep cuts to the body caused by forceful slashes with the sickle. But this was no frenzied attack. This had been carefully devised. A single blow to the head would have been enough to render him insensible, leaving him helpless against the vile butchery of the blade.

Wilde tried to push Lydia back away from the gruesome sight, but she was having none of it. She took the fading torch from Wilde and knelt down at the side of the dead man, removed the deadly implements from his torso, and put her hand on his chest and throat. Blood was still oozing from the wounds and the body had lost none of its heat, but the injuries were far too great for anyone to survive.

'This has just happened, Tom,' she whispered. 'The last few minutes. The killer could still be here.'

Lydia held the feeble beam of the torch to the dead face and in the dim light they looked down at the mutilated features.

In his late forties, Carr should have been at the height of his powers. He had fought and survived the most terrible war mankind had ever known, had won the Victoria Cross for single-handedly taking out an enemy machine gun while armed only with a service revolver, had become known in the popular press simply by his fitting initials, VC. And now, most bitter of ironies, he had been killed not by a warrior, but by a skulking assassin. Even in death, he had a military bearing and a soldier's dignity. The killer had not been able to rob him of that.

The roar of an engine broke the silence.

'That's the car,' Wilde said. 'Come on.' He ran from the open-fronted barn round to the driveway. The wheels of the car were throwing up gravel as it turned in an arc and began to head away from the house. Through the sleet, Wilde could see the backs of two capped heads in the front seats; one driver, one passenger.

Lydia was right behind him.

'I'm going after them,' he shouted as he climbed on the Rudge and kicked it into life. 'Break into the house, see if the telephone is working yet. Get the police.' Twisting the throttle, he hurtled forward, momentarily lifting the front wheel clear of the ground. Once in control and out on the road, he saw the car a hundred yards ahead. In good weather he could have out-accelerated it with ease, but tonight the film of ice made the road lethal. He strained to see the way ahead through his misting goggles and it was all he could do to prevent himself losing grip and sliding into the verge.

On a straight stretch, a piece of road he knew well, he let out the throttle. Ahead of him, the car was slowing. He wiped a sleeve across his goggles and saw that the passenger had his door open and was leaning out facing him, clutching a dark shape. A gun.

Wilde saw a flash from the muzzle and heard the sharp crack of an automatic pistol shot. Instinctively, he braked and swerved, fighting to keep control on the icy surface. There was another shot, then a third. They were approaching a series of bends. The car accelerated again, the driver sliding through the curves, knowing that Wilde's motorbike could not possibly match it on the bends. Not in these conditions.

He followed as well as he could, but he had already lost sight of his quarry and could no longer even see the vehicle's lights. The road, too, was increasingly difficult, but he kept on doggedly. A ragged white sheet of damp snow lay in patches. His only hope was that the driver would think he had lost his pursuer and slow down.

A couple of minutes further on, Wilde spotted an animal at the side of the road ahead of him, dragging itself, injured or sick, a curious, desolate heap of life. A small deer or a large fox. He wondered if the car had hit it? As he got nearer he saw the animal's legs were giving way; it was collapsing. He slowed down. It wasn't an animal. It was a wounded man on all fours.

The back doors were all open. The lights were working so Lydia switched them on as she went, calling out softly, hoping to find a family member or servant at home. She trod tentatively, determined but afraid. Perhaps one of the attackers was still here.

The telephone was on a glass-topped table in the front hall. She picked up the receiver but the line was dead.

She heard gravel crunching, outside, somewhere in the drive. She switched off the light and edged open the curtain. Looking out, she glimpsed a figure walking towards the door, the light of his torch cutting through the damp sleet. Her body tensed, then relaxed almost as instantly at the sight of the high helmet and reassuring uniform of a police officer.

Her heart still pumping furiously, she closed the curtain, switched the light back on and opened the front door.

The policeman was tall, well over six feet, with a comfortingly broad chest and a powerful physique. He looked down at her from his great height.

'What's going on, miss? I was asked to look in on the general.'

The words came in a rush. 'He's dead.'

She took him round to the barn at the back of the house. He shone the powerful beam of his torch on the mutilated remains of Sir Vyvyan Carr.

'Bastards.' The constable quickly turned to Lydia. 'Forgive the language, please, miss.'

'Bastards.' She nodded at the corpse. 'That's the obscenity, there.'

'He was one of the finest. Never heard a bad word said about him. Who would do this?'

'I think it was a man named Leslie Braithwaite. A car just drove off. I'm pretty sure he was in it.'

'Was that the car that nearly hit my bicycle? It was followed by a motor-bike. Ridden like a madman.'

'Yes, it almost certainly was.'

'There were two men in the car.'

'Yes.'

'And the motorcyclist?'

'That's Professor Thomas Wilde. I'll explain it all.'

'Before you do, miss, what about the others? Lady Carr and their housekeeper, Mrs O'Brady? Oh, and the general's valet, little John Carpenter. I think he used to be Sir Vyvyan's batman in Flanders. Do you know where they are?'

'Oh God . . .' If Sir Vyvyan had been slaughtered and his wife and two servants were not in evidence, where were they now?

They found them in a linen cupboard on the first floor. They were all gagged with cloth rags thrust in their mouths and were bound hand and foot with narrow cord. Their bindings were tight and painful and their gags barely allowed them to breathe. But they were alive. The housekeeper, Mrs O'Brady, a thin, nervous woman, was delirious and gasping; Lady Carr was staunch and indignant. Carpenter, the valet, was badly injured and in pain. His hair was thick with blood and, once his bindings were untied, his left arm hung helpess, fractured above the elbow.

'My husband and Carpenter took them on, constable,' Lady Carr said. 'Wouldn't give in. They overpowered us but still they struggled, even at the point of a pistol.'

'I'm afraid your husband is dead, Lady Carr,' the policeman said.

'Yes, I feared as much.' The general's wife did not flinch at the news.

'Can you describe your attackers?'

'They had scarves around their faces. One was small and wiry, no more than five feet tall. The other was powerful, well-built. They said little and their voices were muffled, but I heard the taller man's voice.'

'Was there any accent?'

'He was monosyllabic. I'm afraid I would have trouble identifying him from his voice.' Lady Carr shook her head briskly.

For a moment, Lydia thought she would shed a tear, but none came. She was, above all, an officer's wife. If her husband was a general among men, then she assumed the same rank among women. She turned to Lydia. 'And may I ask who you are, young lady?'

'My name is Lydia Morris.'

'And why are you here?'

'I live in Cambridge. We were trying to contact Sir Vyvyan. We had reason to believe he was in danger.'

'We?'

'Professor Thomas Wilde and myself. We believe that one of the men who attacked you was my lodger. We found a note ... I'm afraid it will take some little time to tell the whole story.'

'Then the sooner you start, the better.'

SATURDAY DECEMBER 5, 1936

CHAPTER 26

The minute hand on the wall clock ticked insistently: 3.55 a.m. Wilde had a great desire to remove his shoe and hammer the heel into the glass to stop its infernal noise forever.

Detective Superintendent Bower appeared at the door. He turned to a junior officer. 'Perhaps you'd get someone to brew us a pot of tea.'

The sergeant nodded and was immediately replaced in the doorway by the elegant form of Philip Eaton, who slid in and waited by the door while Bower took the chair opposite Wilde.

'I take it you're happy to have Mr Eaton here, professor,' the superintendent said. It was a statement, not a question.

'Yes, but I'd prefer Scotch to tea, all things considered.'

'Not possible, I'm afraid. And I'm sorry you have been kept here so long.' He held out his hand to indicate Eaton. 'I believe you have already divined that our friend here is more than just a grubby newspaperman.'

'Shouldn't Lydia Morris be here, too? Where is she?'

'We've spoken to her and taken her home.'

'Well, I want to go home, too. It's four in the morning and I've had no sleep.'

'This is wearing for all of us, but time is of the essence – and we really would prefer to talk to you and Miss Morris separately. This is a most complex set of circumstances, with major implications. I'm sure you've worked out that much. We need to hear your stories individually. I trust you'll understand.'

Wilde understood, but he didn't like it. 'You make it sound as though we were suspects, not witnesses.'

Detective Superintendent Bower waved the suggestion away. 'Suspects? Good Lord no, Mr Wilde. But you must understand that a lot has happened very fast and we're falling over ourselves trying to catch up with events. It's fair to say that this is a fine mess, as Laurel or Hardy might put it.'

Bower was trying to lighten the mood. Wilde went along with it; better to have this policeman on his side, perhaps. 'Yes,' he agreed. 'A fine mess.'

'So we now have three murders and a man in Addenbrooke's Hospital fighting for his life after falling from a motor car at high speed.'

'Three murders? I think you have to acknowledge now that there are four.'

'Ah yes, Miss Hereward. We'll come to that in due course. The thing is, if we get ahead of ourselves, we may be doing the murderers' work for them, which we believe to be the spreading of terror and chaos. For the moment, professor, who is Leslie Braithwaite?'

Wilde told him as much as he knew about Braithwaite's background and then went on: 'At least some of it must be true. He was obviously a miner. He had the marks caused by coal-dust. I believe it gets into cuts and grazes and stays there, like tattoos. But I can't say I warmed to him. In fact, I tried to advise Miss Morris against taking him in. You must know about his assault on her?'

'Just say what you know, professor.'

'Well, we reported it, of course. Braithwaite tried to rape her. Quite a violent attack. I'd say he was drunk. Luckily I was on hand to throw him out. I thought we'd seen the last of him. But then, as you also know, I found him crawling at the side of the road a few hours ago. Abandoned by his accomplice in murder, so it seems.'

'And what made you go to Brandham Hall in the first place?'

Wilde explained about the paper they had found in Braithwaite's room. 'In the light of everything that had happened, we both thought it was significant. Why would an unemployed miner be calling the Dorchester Hotel? Why would he have written down the names of Sir Vyvyan Carr and his house?' Wilde threw up his hands. 'You might think it was a great leap in the dark, but we felt we had to do something and fast. And we were right – but not fast enough to save Sir Vyvyan.' Though God knows what they would have done against two armed men.

Lounging against the doorjamb, hands in his trouser pockets, Eaton said nothing.

The superintendent unbuckled his black leather briefcase. He removed a small blue card and laid it on the desk between himself and Wilde.

'Have you seen this before?'

'I don't think so,' Wilde said. He examined it closely. It was Leslie Braithwaite's membership card for the Communist Party of Great Britain, complete with number. 'It looks real enough. Certainly fits in with what I know of Braithwaite's politics.'

'We have no way of knowing if it's genuine. The CPGB leadership don't like the police. They tend not to be very cooperative when we make inquiries. Some members just have a number and don't even fill in their names on the cards, so keen are they to remain anonymous. The world reduced to numbers.' Bower paused. 'Tell me, professor, what are *your* politics?'

Wilde frowned at the question. 'It's none of your goddamned business, Mr Bower.'

'You don't have to answer, of course. You are not being accused of anything, but it seems a relevant question.'

'I'm not a communist and nor am I a Nazi, if that's what you mean. Beyond that, you can stick your question in the backyard.'

Wilde's eyes strayed over to Eaton again. He was observing the proceedings like a cat watching a bird pecking at a wounded mouse; he was deciding which one should be lunch.

'The problem is,' Bower continued, 'we are having trouble making head or tail of our Bolshie friend Mr Braithwaite. We have been in touch with the Dorchester, but have had no luck in tracing where his call went. They have hundreds of guests and even more staff, so we are unlikely to have any joy there. As for our calls to the managers of the Yorkshire pits, they have no record of him being employed anywhere in that county. Mind you, they've had to be got up from their beds, so perhaps their information is not wholly reliable. We're checking Notts and Lancs, too, so something may turn up, but I find myself not expecting anything. Nor has anyone at the National Unemployed Workers' Movement been able to identify him.'

'He did mention doing some work for the NUWM.'

Bower shook his head. 'Well, he didn't make contact with them here in Cambridge. All we've got is the CPGB card. Did he ever mention the town or village he came from?'

'Not to me. I didn't have long conversations with the man. He was more likely to be scrounging money than telling me where he lived. It's possible he said something to Lydia. Ask her.'

'When you found him at the side of the road, before the police and ambulance arrived on the scene, I believe he was still conscious. What did he say to you?'

'He was muttering incoherently. He didn't seem to know where he was, then he sparked out. I guess he was concussed. His head had taken the worst of the damage. I tried to stem the flow of blood. His eyes were open, but he wasn't really seeing.'

On the cold, sleet-swept edge of the road, Wilde had torn strips of cloth from his own shirt to use as dressings. He couldn't seek help because he couldn't leave Braithwaite, and so all he had been able to do was wait and hope for a passing car.

In the end, the police came. Two vehicles on their way from Cambridge to Brandham Hall. He had flagged them down and one had taken the injured man to hospital. Wilde had followed the other car on his motorbike back to the house.

'I believe you have already said that you think the car Leslie Braithwaite was driving was a Ford.'

'Yes, but I don't believe he was driving. From the back of their heads, I would say the driver was a taller man. Braithwaite was in the passenger seat, shooting at me. He was holding the door open and leaning out – which is probably why he fell out. Unless he was pushed, of course.'

'Why would he be pushed?'

'I don't know. You're the detective. But if he fell, why didn't his accomplice stop?'

Bower ignored the question. 'Are you keeping anything back? It seems a strange and foolhardy venture – riding a motorcycle out into the night with a young lady. Don't you think so?'

Wilde turned his eyes to Eaton, but he was examining his fingernails. 'You may be right, but we didn't see that we had an alternative. And, no, I'm not keeping anything back.'

'Good. Because your cooperation is vital to us – and to you. This is all a great deal bigger than you realise. Now, let me put another question to you: did you see Braithwaite's accomplice?'

'No.'

'We have descriptions of the two attackers and although they both wore scarves around their faces, one of the men was small and wiry, just like our man in Addenbrooke's. The other one was stronger, perhaps a little older and certainly taller. Does that mean anything to you?'

'Any accent?'

'Did you have someone in mind? Kholtov, for instance?'

Eaton was still examining his fingers. Wilde shrugged. 'No,' he said shortly. 'Now, can we get on to the death of Nancy Hereward? She's due to be buried this morning and you still don't seem to be including her in your inquiries. I think you should.'

'I think so, too, Mr Wilde, but as there is no suggestion of the presence of any substance other than diamorphine, the coroner has concluded that it was an accidental overdose, and the body has been released for burial.' Bower fixed Wilde with a stern glare. 'But like you, I still have my doubts.'

'That's something. What are you doing about it?'

'Trying to find Comrade Kholtov, mainly. But I'm also wondering whether you and Miss Morris know anything about her that you aren't telling us.'

'Such as?'

'Such as her politics. Her links to the Communist Party.'

'Then talk to *him*.' Wilde jutted his chin in the direction of Eaton. 'I'm sure MI6 knows a great deal more about Nancy Hereward's activities and politics than I do.' Wilde waited for Eaton to respond and when he didn't, he stood up. 'I really have nothing more to say, superintendent. I need my bed.'

Bower wasn't ready to let go. 'Do you think Kholtov was the other man in the car with Braithwaite?'

'What do *you* think, Philip?' Wilde turned to Eaton. 'After all, it was only a few hours ago that you were drinking with him.'

'Is this true?' Bower said, surprised.

Eaton appeared unfazed by the question. 'He wasn't a suspect then. At least, not to my knowledge.'

It felt to Wilde as if he and Bower were in a dark room, surrounded by hazards. Each time they moved, they were assailed by something new.

Was Eaton the only one with a key and a torch to light the way? If so, why did he not produce them?

'But he *is* a suspect now,' Bower said. 'In fact he is our one and only suspect. I have a warrant for his arrest, Eaton.'

'I don't know where he is. He left the Bull shortly after Professor Wilde. You could try Horace Dill. He was supposed to be staying at his lodgings.'

'No,' Bower said, 'Kholtov's not there. But I'll find him. All ports – air and sea – have been alerted to detain him. He fits our bill. He is known to be a Red agent.'

Wilde laughed.

'I don't see what's funny,' Bower said.

' "Red agent" isn't the half of it! Kholtov is an assassin, one of Joe Stalin's favourites – as Eaton will confirm.' Wilde gripped the back of the chair. 'Look – I don't necessarily think that this is a Soviet conspiracy. I'm keeping an open mind, and I think you should, too. The murders of Sir Vyvyan and the Langleys are meant to *look* like a communist plot – the bloody writing on the wall at Kilmington, the hammer and sickle murder weapons at Brandham Hall. So the one thing we can be sure of is that it's political and meant to provoke a reaction. Throw in the presence of Kholtov and I can understand the government's fears.'

'Can you?' Bower said. 'You do realise we believe this is to do with the royal crisis?'

Wilde nodded.

'Our enemies are trying to turn a crisis into an emergency,' Bower said. 'Engender fear. Destabilise the country. I've read enough about the communists to know that when they see a little local difficulty they do their best to stir it into riot, civil disobedience and full-blown revolution.'

CHAPTER 27

At around 4.30 that morning Wilde left the police station. Eaton hurried out after him. Wilde strode on ahead in silence. In the cold night air, the town was deserted and the lights were long since switched off. The dead of night.

'I think it's about time you came clean with me, Eaton,' Wilde said over his shoulder.

'But you were the one holding back. Why didn't you tell Bower about the trip to Berlin and the North Sea list?'

'I thought that was your job. You obviously know the man well. What is Bower exactly?'

'Scotland Yard Special Branch. Public face of the intelligence services, if you like. And I should tell you that the prime minister has been on the telephone to his Cabinet colleagues throughout the early hours. He's spitting tacks.'

'Good. So he should be.'

'More than that, he's desperate to keep this all under the bedclothes. Nothing must interfere with his prime concern, which is the avoidance of a constitutional crisis. He may seem avuncular, but when Baldwin goes for something, he's as lethal as a cat.'

Wilde stopped in his tracks. 'Is he now? Well, his enemies – whoever they might be – seem pretty damned lethal, too. So you tell me, what's your part in all this?'

Eaton reached for his cigarettes. 'I think I probably need one of these after all.'

Wilde waved the case away. Eaton removed a cigarette and lit it.

'Look, Eaton, like it or not, I'm involved now. So is Lydia. You owe us answers. If this has anything to do with Kholtov – and that feels like a frame-up to me – then there must be some connection to Spain. Something he discovered in Spain. He was about to tell me at our dinner. At first I thought Horace Dill had kicked him under the table, but it was you he was looking at, wasn't it?'

Eaton drew in smoke, grimaced, dropped the cigarette and ground it into the flagstone.

'Comrade Kholtov is a loose cannon.'

'Is he involved in these murders?'

'I have no evidence to suggest that he is, but nor do I feel confident enough to say that he isn't.'

'But what is your connection to Kholtov, to Spain . . . to all this? None of it's coincidence, is it? You being here? Kholtov being in town? There's something specific about Cambridge that brought him here – and something a great deal more important than simply inspiring a few undergraduates to join the International Brigades.'

Eaton was not smiling. 'He offered me something. And he wanted something in return. That's all I can reveal. But I'll tell you this, because you understand intelligence: we need men on the inside of the Soviet Union, particularly highly placed ones like Yuri Kholtov.'

'Then tell me what he's offering – and what he wants.'

'He's offering information.'

'I need more than that.'

Eaton's smooth veneer had long since gone. 'Information which, when I have it, might prevent a great deal of bloodshed.'

'Something he learnt in Spain?'

'Exactly.'

'And there's some connection to the murders here in Cambridge.'

'I believe so. But acquiring this information is not easy. It is, let us say, a matter of delicate negotiation.'

'What about the gold? Is that part of the deal?'

'Gold?'

'Don't go coy on me. You know what I'm talking about.'

'Ah, the gold coin. Careless of Comrade Kholtov. He's trying to buy arms for the republican cause which is, of course, wholly contrary to our government's non-intervention agreement.'

'With one gold coin?'

'He says there's a great deal more. If I get him a buyer, he will give me the information I need.'

'Do you believe him?'

'I did. I no longer know.'

'So where is he now?'

'He's in a safe place. Come on, let's get you home. You really have to leave this to the professionals, like Bower said.'

Wilde gave a scornful laugh. 'You know as well as I do that this wasn't something I'm involved in by choice. And that brings me to one of the questions I'd really like answered: why does this all seem to be connected to Lydia? *Her* friend is murdered, *her* lodger kills a man and is then thrown or falls from a car for his pains, and a Russian whose visit *she* helped organise has become a fugitive. Why?' As he spoke, he realised that wasn't all. There were other connections – she knew the Langleys, and she knew the strange German who had turned up so suddenly last night.

'I don't know what Lydia has to do with it,' Eaton said at last. 'But it makes me fear for her – for both of you.'

Lydia's lights were blazing and they saw her silhouette passing across the window in one of the front rooms. They knocked at the door.

'I can't bloody sleep,' she said.

'Can we come in?'

'Tea and toast? Eggs and bacon if you like.' She was doing her best to be bright.

'No to the eggs and bacon, but yes to the tea and toast,' Wilde said. 'Any chance of a Scotch with that?'

'No. We need clear heads.'

'Shame.'

Lydia was still in the clothes she wore on the ride to Brandham Hall, including her duffle coat because the fire in the hearth had died and she hadn't bothered to turn on any of the electric fires. Her hair was a mess.

'It's Saturday,' Eaton said, breaking into Wilde's thoughts. 'Bloody awful day for a funeral.'

'Any day's bloody for a friend's funeral,' Lydia said.

The two men sat facing each other across the kitchen table while Lydia busied herself with the toast. Wilde leant forwards. 'There is one more thing. With a little assistance from Horace Dill, I now know a fair amount about Nancy's trip to Berlin. More than you ever told me. Have you ever heard of a man called Arnold Lindberg?'

Eaton sighed wearily. 'Yes, I know of Lindberg, poor bastard.' He stopped and turned towards Lydia. 'But I have to say I'm a lot more interested in another German. A man called Hartmut Dorfen.'

Vladimir Rybakov sipped the ersatz coffee and grimaced. What was it made of? It tasted nothing like coffee. How could a nation such as Germany, with its technological advances, its artistic history and its excellent beers, produce a coffee substitute that tasted like shit – and pig shit at that – and expect anyone to drink it at breakfast?

He spooned in more sugar and took another sip. Sweet, it wasn't so bad. Anyway, there was little else to do while they waited in this dull and functional messroom. Some of his men played cards, a few read books or leafed through German magazines, which were no use to any of them except Rybakov. They looked more like bandits than military men, for they had all been supplied with scratched and worn leather jackets and rough woollen trousers, sourced, so it was said, from various second-hand shops in Berlin. Most of them had scarfs around their necks and carried caps, either worn carelessly or stowed in their pockets. All eleven of them smoked.

Rybakov was a big man. He was tall with broad shoulders, a thick beard – black flecked with grey – and shaggy hair. Some said he had the look and body of a bear. In Paris he was known as *Monsieur Grizzli*, a sobriquet he was happy to accept, for he was powerful, a natural leader of men.

From outside, the drone of aircraft engines was unceasing, even in the grey dawn. They were at an airfield attached to the giant Focke-Wulf plant, a little way south of Bremen. Every day, there seemed to be more fighter planes on the asphalt, more activity in the immense and burgeoning hangars. Rybakov was impressed. He had been told in confidence that the Third Reich now had almost two thousand warplanes, more than twice the number possessed by the British. And that the gap was growing week by week.

He put his cap on his head and pulled down the earflaps, securing them with a tie beneath his thick beard, wrapped his scarf around his neck, stood up and lumbered to the door. The room was stuffy and smelt of sweat, cologne, tobacco smoke and engine oil, a foul and noxious brew. He stepped outside and closed the door behind him. The fresh cold air of early morning made him gasp and he wrapped his bare hands into his armpits. A bitter wind was blowing in across the runway from the north. The sky was white; there were intimations of snow.

A triple-engine JU-52 was taxiing from the runway in his direction. Rybakov watched it with interest. Behind him, the door opened again. Ivan Chernuk, almost as tall as Rybakov but with none of his presence, appeared at his shoulder.

'It's warmer than Moscow, sir.'

'Are you sure, Chernuk?' He nodded towards the windsock flying above the control tower. 'This wind comes straight from St Petersburg.'

The JU-52 had come to a stop. They continued to watch as the three propellers slowed to a standstill. Two uniformed pilots disembarked and strode across the asphalt towards them.

Neither pilot bothered with the Hitler salute. One of them held out his hand. 'Captain Rybakov?'

'At your service.' Rybakov made a mock bow.

'The famous *Monsieur Grizzli!*' The pilot grinned. 'Standartenführer Baur, your pilot.' He was a handsome man, happy, confident, the sort of pilot to trust with your life, perhaps. 'It seems we are to go on a little trip together, Mr Rybakov.'

'Now?'

'This weekend, almost certainly. Hopefully today. First north, then westwards along the Friesian Islands, coming into England from the north coast of East Anglia. I estimate seven hundred and fifty kilometres, mostly over the sea and in the dark. We will not be seen, but just to be on the safe side, the painters have altered the markings.' Baur laughed. 'I see *Le Grizzli* is worried! Have no fear, captain. There is no pilot in the world better at night-flying than me.'

Rybakov gave the man a hard stare. 'If I was afraid, Standartenführer Baur, I would not have agreed to undertake this mission.'

'I know, I know.' Baur attempted to mollify the Russian. 'I meant nothing by it. I am accustomed to allaying the fears of those who are terrified of flying.'

Rybakov was not interested in Baur's views on his courage. He wanted final details of the operation that lay ahead. More than anything he wished to confirm them with his German commanding officer. 'So then, Standartenführer Baur, perhaps you can tell me where I might find Sturmbannführer Dorfen? We have been waiting at this bloody airfield for a week now. Where is he?'

It hadn't taken courage for Rybakov to be here at this windswept airfield near Bremen, merely the sheer filthy boredom of his existence in the western suburbs of Paris.

Everyone talked about Russia. But no one did anything. Everyone he knew was a Russian emigré, or the child of emigrés, and more than half of them worked at the Renault factory. It was a mindless, unending existence of tea-rooms, vodka, car components, tales of the old days and boasts of the good days to come. But there would be no good days, not while Stalin and his crew of Red criminals ran Russia into the ground.

Oh, they all talked big, these emigrés. They all belonged to the Russkie Obschche-Voinsky Soyuz – the Russian Armed Services Union – the pathetic remnants of the White Army, and they all had courage. But no one had the energy or organisational skills to *do* anything.

Then, in the summer, late August, he had had a visitor. It was soon after the end of the Olympics, civil war had been raging in Spain for over a month and the Moscow show trials had begun with a death sentence pronounced in absentia on that grubby little revolutionary Trotsky, God damn his godless soul. That, at least, had provided the ROVS boys with some entertainment. Old General Peshnia even offered to go to Russia and pull the trigger himself if ever Trotsky was caught and if only someone would pay his fare. One young wag pointed out to the general that as he now worked as a taxi driver, he could hire himself and drive there. It was only three thousand kilometres, after all. Peshnia was not amused.

The visitor had approached him out of the blue after the weekly service at the Russian Orthodox Church. As usual, Rybakov had taken his mother, and they were walking slowly back in the midday warmth, keeping to the shade where they could. The street was dusty and there was a smell of dead cat in the still, dry air. Though she was only sixty, his mother was frail and shrunken and dressed in black, in eternal mourning for her husband, a victim of the Bolsheviks, and for the loss of her homeland. The stranger was also small – hardly taller than the old woman – dark-haired and bespectacled. He wore a fedora low over his brow. 'Vladimir Rybakov?' he said.

Rybakov stopped. 'Who wants to know?' He spoke in French, body tense. As an emigré leader he was a target for Stalin's death squads.

'May I talk with you?'

'I'm walking my mother home.' Rybakov noted the stranger's German accent and relaxed. The little man looked like a Hollywood secret agent or private dick. 'Are you a spy?' he demanded in German, laughing.

The German did not seem to understand the joke. 'May I walk with you? I mean you no harm. My name is Dietrich Mann. I am attached to the German embassy.'

'What do you want of me, Mr Mann?'

'Just to walk and talk. You have been recommended to me as a man of passion and energy. And a man fluent in German.'

'Then let us walk and talk slowly, for my mother cannot move quickly.'

Mann told him that he had been sent on the orders of the German government, in particular Reichsführer-SS Heinrich Himmler. It was believed that there were many among the Russian exiles in France – a refugee population of perhaps half a million – who were willing to fight to win their country back from the heathen Bolsheviks. Germany, he said, would very much like to assist them achieve their goal.

'Of course, it is something we all dream of, Mr Mann, but what can Germany do for us where we have so dismally failed ourselves?' Rybakov patted his mother's arm reassuringly. He had no wish to alarm her.

'I believe you saw some action against the Red Army?'

'I was a captain in the Kornilov Battalion, much good it did us. Now I am reduced to bolting car components into place.'

Mann looked up at the bearded Russian bear. 'You have been commended to us as a man of valour.'

'Hah! I need more than courage to maintain my sanity in this living death.'

'Please, hear me out.'

The German explained that Himmler, after discussions with Goering and Hitler, wished to form a White Russian regiment, under the auspices of the SS. The most modern equipment, arms and specialist training would be offered to a select band of young men who were truly committed to the cause. 'Initially, when the regiment – or battalion, depending on numbers – is fully trained, you could expect to be sent to Spain to work with the falangists under General Franco. They need our help if they are to advance on Madrid. Your enemy there will largely consist of communists, including Soviet agents. But you would have better armaments and better training than those you face.'

'And how would that help us win back the Motherland?'

'First we must stem the tide of Bolshevism. In doing so, your men will become battle-hardened soldiers and will hopefully grow in numbers. As for the next step, well, I cannot speak for the Führer, but it is no secret that he considers Stalin and the Bolsheviks to be our most bitter enemy.'

'And our part in this campaign?'

'You will be the conquering liberators of your homeland. You will be the heroic vanguard and, as such, the new rulers of Russia. You have been selected not just for your courage, Herr Rybakov, but your intelligence and qualities of leadership.'

There was a fine line between praise and flattery and Rybakov was no fool: flattery always came with a price tag. Mann left him with a telephone number to call.

Later that evening, as they were sitting down to their meagre supper, Rybakov's old mother finally spoke. He had expected her to tell him to leave well alone, but she didn't. He must accept the German's offer, she said. He must avenge his father's cold-blooded murder. He must take her home to St Petersburg, to their wonderful old house. Whatever it cost, he must do this; for even death was better than this exile in the wasteland of the west.

CHAPTER 28

There is nothing colder than a burial on a winter's morning. Wind and sleet blew in from the east, wrapping the pile of earth dug for the grave in a winding sheet of dirty white.

No overcoat or scarf could keep out the chill. Wilde barely listened to the words of the vicar. They were meant to bring comfort to the family and friends, with promises of eternal life, but there seemed little consolation here within the ancient walled graveyard of St Wilfred and All Saints Church. How could there be hope in this cold acre, when a young woman's decaying body lay in a box of wood, waiting to be covered in earth?

As the coffin was lowered, Lydia's gloved hand sought out Wilde's and clutched it tight. Her head moved into his shoulder. He was half a foot taller than her. His arm instinctively brought her closer. Together, there was at least the semblance of warmth.

'Peace is in the grave,' she said, her voice barely a whisper. 'The grave hides all things beautiful and good.'

'Shelley.'

'Do you believe it, Tom, the peace? It all looks cold and cruel to me. I pray she is at peace, but I don't feel it.'

The church had been packed for the service. Some of the mourners were friends, like Lydia and Dorfen and various others of her generation from Girton and further afield, but many more were locals who knew her from childhood, and friends and acquaintances of her father. Wilde half expected to see Sir Oswald Mosley and Lord Londonderry among the great men, but there was no sign of them, although Slievedonard was there. Dave Johnson had not put in an appearance, but Horace Dill had. He stood alone at the back of the church, avoiding any chance of an encounter with the dead woman's father.

How many of those here were on the list that Nancy had found locked away in her father's office? Wilde and Eaton had spoken about *North Sea* at length. 'Perhaps it was merely a distribution list for the magazine,'

Eaton suggested. 'Perhaps,' Wilde said, 'but I would very much like to see it.'

They had talked, too, about Dorfen. 'He told us he lived in Pimlico and worked for a London company,' Wilde said. 'Claimed he was on the first train out of Germany when Hitler came to power.'

Eaton had laughed. 'He has a villa in the southern suburbs of Munich and is a Sturmbannführer in the Leibstandarte-SS Adolf Hitler, the Führer's own bodyguard.'

'Good God!' Wilde was appalled. 'Then what is he doing here?'

'Perhaps he's mourning his old friend and lover.'

'And why would he lie to us?'

'Because he's hiding something.'

Eaton had not come to the funeral. 'I didn't know the girl. I don't know the family. Don't think I'd really be very welcome, old boy. You be my eyes.'

At last the coffin was lowered into place and the gravediggers prepared to shovel the mound of rich East Anglian soil back into the gaping space from which it had been dug.

Horace Dill sidled up to Wilde and Lydia, dead cigar in the corner of his mouth. 'I've never seen anything like it,' he said without removing the cigar. 'There are more Nazis here than your average Nuremberg rally.'

Wilde could smell the alcohol on Dill's breath. 'This is not the time, Horace.'

Lydia took Dill's arm and tried to walk him away, but he shook her off. 'I'm not bloody leaving, Lydia!'

'You shouldn't have come. You'll upset Sir Norman.'

'I was more of a father to her than that fascist swine.' Dill spat on the ground, then looked up and caught Dorfen's eye through the crowd of mourners. 'And what's that fucking Nazi doing here? Thought we'd got rid of him years ago.'

Wilde gripped Dill firmly by the arm, marched him into the church, pushed him inside the vestry and slammed the door shut. The key, heavy iron and perhaps hundreds of years old, was in the lock, so he turned it.

From inside, he heard the sound of hammering, but the door was thick oak and immovable. There were muffled shouts of protest and then, after a minute, silence. Dill would be there until the vicar said goodbye to the mourners and returned. More than long enough to keep him out of trouble.

Lydia was at Wilde's elbow as he walked out into the cold air. 'Can we go now, Tom?'

'We should pay our respects to Sir Norman.'

Hereward, Sawyer and Lord Slievedonard were walking slowly along the narrow flagstone path to the lychgate. Slievedonard's jowls wobbled like a water-filled balloon. He bulged inside his vast fur coat. At his side, in a more traditional coat and a great deal more slender and six inches shorter, was Hereward, stooped and ragged. He looked, thought Wilde, as if he'd already consumed a bottle of brandy for breakfast. Briefly, Slievedonard put an arm round his friend's shoulder, almost enveloping him. On his other side, Sawyer had the swagger of a young lion waiting his turn to lead the pack.

Wilde moved in. 'Sir Norman, if I may . . .'

'Professor Wilde.' Hereward's voice was weary, resigned and somewhat slurred.

'We wanted to offer our condolences, sir. This is a day of great sadness.'

'I'm so sorry, Sir Norman,' Lydia said.

'Thank you.'

'I understand this is probably not the time or the place, but could we meet again to discuss the circumstances of your daughter's death?'

'Good God, what is this?' It was Slievedonard. He pushed Wilde in the chest. 'What are you doing? Have you no respect? How dare you press yourself onto a father who has just buried his daughter?'

Hereward put out an arm to restrain Slievedonard. 'It's all right, Peter.'

Sawyer decided to take control. 'Now, be a good fellow . . .' he began, trying to guide Wilde away. Wilde shook him off, his attention focused on Hereward. His cheeks were tear-stained, his eyes bloodshot. No man could feign that sort of grief.

Sawyer looked down his nose at Wilde. With Slievedonard, he manoeuvred Hereward out of the intruder's path. 'Come along, Sir Norman. This man isn't worth a moment of your time.'

From the church porch, Hartmut Dorfen watched the proceedings with curiosity. He lit a Players cigarette, drew deep on the familiar tobacco, then exhaled a cloud of smoke and vapour into the cold air. Margot would be going frantic, desperate to know his whereabouts. His eyes drifted to Lydia Morris and he nodded.

Lydia nodded back to Dorfen and he raised his hand in greeting. He started walking towards them and she nudged Wilde.

'He scares you, Lydia.'

'What scares me is that he has lied to me. To both of us. He's a member of Hitler's bodyguard, for God's sake.'

'Unfortunately, there isn't a law against that. And one can understand why a man might wish to keep such a fact to himself when in England.'

Dorfen looked grave as he approached them. He stamped out his cigarette on the stone path, then took Lydia's right hand between both his. 'I can't bear this, Lydia. This is all far worse than I imagined.'

'Yes, Hart. Yes, it is.'

He turned to Wilde. 'Professor.'

'Good morning, Herr Dorfen.'

'Did I not recognise Professor Dill earlier? You seemed to be man-handling him.'

'You know him?'

Dorfen laughed. 'How could I forget the darling old boy? When I was an undergraduate, he wanted to recruit me for the Bolsheviks, of course, but I am afraid I had other things on my mind. Wine, picnics, motor cars and dancing . . .'

'It seems that where he failed to recruit you, he succeeded rather too well with poor Nancy.'

'Is that so? I am shocked.' Dorfen ploughed on. 'But then she was always a little mad, wasn't she?' His eyes lit up. 'Tell me, are you both going now to St Wilfred's Priory? Perhaps I can offer you a lift.'

'I have my motorbike, thank you. Lydia? I'm sure you would prefer the warmth of a car.'

'No, I'm fine. I'll come with you, Tom.' There was an air of panic about her.

'Herr Dorfen would enjoy your company. You have all those years to catch up on.'

What was Wilde up to? 'All right.' Lydia pulled herself together and smiled graciously. 'Thank you, Hart. I would be very happy to accept your kind offer.'

Wilde watched them wander down the path to the cars that lined the road outside the churchyard. Slievedonard's bright red Maybach was just pulling out, and Sir Norman Hereward's chauffeur was opening the Rolls Royce to admit his master to the cream hide luxury of its interior.

As Lydia and Dorfen passed on the way to his little red MG, Wilde saw him nod to Sawyer, who was about to climb into the Rolls beside Hereward. Friends from Munich in an English churchyard. Gritting his teeth, Wilde returned to the church to release Horace Dill from his makeshift prison cell.

CHAPTER 29

Margot Greenway, née Langley, was not used to being imprisoned.

Not that this house in Grünwald, Bavaria, looked remotely like a jail. It was a large villa in the southern suburbs of Munich, with heavy panelling and walls decorated with the trophy antlers from long-forgotten hunts. A comfortable family home, abandoned by its previous owner, a wealthy Jewish doctor. With the coming of the Nuremberg race laws he and his Aryan wife had felt the cold wind of the new Germany and made their exit to healthier climes. And so, with a miminum of fuss, their property had been confiscated and signed over to Hartmut Dorfen. A little gift from the Führer to a favourite.

Now, though, it was indeed a prison; Margot was not allowed to leave and she was barred from using the telephone. The one time she had got through to England, to speak to Nancy Hereward of all people, she had been cut dead. Since then, the telephone had been unplugged and removed from the house.

'You must not think of this as a prison,' Wilhelm Brückner had said. 'It is merely a security measure while Hart is on a special assignment. I'm sure you understand. It is as much for your own good as for his.'

'But for how long, Willy?' She understood that this must be something important – the Führer's private office would not have sent Hitler's chief adjutant to console her otherwise – but she really didn't see why she should have to stay at home, even if she couldn't make calls.

'A few days. No more than a few days. There are too many foreigners in Munich, too many spies with inquisitive ears. That is why you must stay here. You are well looked after, are you not, Margot? The food is good?'

'I don't want food,' Margot wailed. 'I want Hart! And I want to go out. It is almost Christmas – I must buy presents for my family.'

She had run away to Munich because she could not live without Hart, whatever his terms might be. She had told no one, not even Lydia, whom she knew would disapprove. 'God, Margot,' she would have said, 'he'll only betray you again. It's in his nature.' But Lydia didn't understand the power of passion.

It had been hard enough calling her mother eighteen months ago. Since then, their relationship had been severely strained. How could her mother understand that if she had to live with Hart's infidelities, then so be it? There were things he knew about love and a woman's body that Jeremy Greenway, her husband of a few cold months, could never begin to know. Her mother was mortified, of course, couldn't bring herself to tell any of their friends. As for Jeremy, she'd heard he had retreated to his estates. Perhaps he was still waiting for her to come home, although her letter had made it abundantly clear she never would.

And so, after a long, solitary train journey she had arrived here in Munich in the summer of 1935. Hart had been pleased to see her, but his mother had not been at all welcoming.

'You must go home, Miss Langley,' the older woman had insisted the first time they were alone. 'You are English; we are German. I sent my son to Cambridge for his education, not to find a wife.'

Hart had not told his mother Margot was married. Goodness knows she was disapproving enough as it was. He brushed away her concerns. 'Take no notice of Mutti. Things will settle down.'

But so far, they hadn't. Frau Dorfen remained icily distant. And now Hart wasn't here.

Brückner shrugged his shoulders. 'I understand your distress, Margot, truly I do. But you must see it is out of our control. We must do what we are told. Once this is all over, Hart will take you to a spa. It will be like a honeymoon.'

'But it's almost Christmas, Willy.'

'If you have things in mind for your family, I can telephone the big stores to send you a selection of their wares.'

'You can trust me, Willy. You know I won't talk to anyone.'

He raised a sceptical eyebrow. She had already tried to call England before the telephone was disconnected and taken away. He tried to put a sympathetic arm round her, but she shook him off.

'Hart will come home and you will have the best Christmas celebration ever.'

'Willy, please.'

'And Frau Dorfen is sure to come tomorrow to keep you company. She misses her son as much as you do. You can commiserate with each other.'

'She doesn't like me. She's very cold towards me.' Margot pouted.

'Perhaps, like you, she is worried for Hartmut.'

'Can I just make one telephone call? Just one. It's my mother's birthday. Please, Willy. Just to let her know that I'm alive and well.'

St Wilfred's Priory was welcoming and warm. All the fires had been lit; broad, open fires with slow-burning ash logs. The hall was abuzz with the muted voices of eighty people, all dressed in black, all with a glass in their hand. Footmen were circulating with trays of drinks. The heady fug of midday gin hung over the room. Outside, cars crowded the forecourt.

Wilde stood in the hall entrance and spotted Lydia. He signalled to her but, deep in conversation with a woman he didn't know, she didn't notice. He took a glass of whisky from a footman, then approached another servant. 'Can you tell me where I might find the lavatory?'

'Follow me, sir.'

Dorfen lounged back in Sir Norman Hereward's desk chair. He had been trying to get through for ten minutes. The damned English couldn't build roads; it was no surprise that their telephone system was also a laughing stock. God help them if they ever had to fight a modern war.

'Hello?' At last. Her voice was wary.

'*Grüss Gott*, Sophie.'

'Ah, Hartmut, where are you?'

'You know where.'

'And all is well?'

'Well enough, depending on what information you have for me.'

'I have good news . . . a communication from my friend the major.'

The door was opening. He tensed. 'Wait, someone is coming in.' He put his hand over the earpiece.

When Wilde emerged from the lavatory, still clutching his tumbler of whisky, the corridor was clear. No one was likely to come up here while the funeral drinks were under way. With any luck Hereward's study would be unlocked.

As he pushed open the door he heard a voice from within. He looked round the door. 'I'm sorry,' he said hurriedly, 'I was looking for the lavatory. Ah, Dorfen, it's you.'

'Professor Wilde?' Dorfen kept his hand over the receiver. 'I am just on the telephone. A business call to my firm in London. Sir Norman has allowed me use of his office.'

'Forgive me. My error.' Wilde bowed his head and backed out.

'Who was that?' the Gräfin asked.

'Professor Thomas Wilde – you remember? Don't worry, Sophie. He's gone now. So they will meet today, you say. Time? Place?'

'Evening. That is all I know at the moment. Call me later. The major has promised me more details. He *will* provide them. He would rather cut out his own eyes with a scalpel than fail me in this.'

'I understand, Sophie, but there are problems here, too. The longer we wait, the more dangerous it becomes. We cannot rely on the weather.'

'Patience, darling. Trust me. Call Bremen.'

'You are certain, then? Tonight?'

'They will be together and they will have minimal security.'

He smiled to himself. This might yet be easier than Bad Wiessee. '*Servus*, Sophie.'

'*Servus*, Hartmut. And good luck.'

With his ear pressed to the door, Wilde could make out nothing but the muffled hum of Dorfen's voice and a woman's name: Sophie. Everything Dorfen said was built on a mountain of untruth. Whoever Sophie was, she certainly wasn't a business associate in London, because Hartmut Dorfen didn't work in London.

A click. The telephone had been replaced. Wilde moved along the corridor, folded himself into a doorway and waited.

Dorfen emerged from Hereward's office. Wilde pressed himself back against the door, heard footsteps on the stone floor, moving away, and then peered out from the doorway to watch Dorfen striding down the corridor back to the hall.

'Can I help you, sir?'

The voice stopped Wilde in his tracks. He turned to find Hereward's chauffeur.

'Ah, I'm afraid I got a bit lost.' He smiled. 'These old English houses – so many passageways and rooms. We don't have anything like this in America.'

'Are you trying to find your way back to the hall? Let me take you.'

'Thank you.'

'My pleasure, Professor Wilde,' the chauffeur said, leading the way. 'I would have thought you'd know your way about by now. You seem to be in and out of the priory.' He halted at the entrance to the great hall. 'Well, here we are, sir. Shall I find a footman to replenish your drink?'

'This will suit me fine, thank you.'

The chauffeur bowed and backed away.

Wilde strolled into the throng and made a mental note of the faces and names of the great and the good, storing them away. No sign of Slievedonard; he must have made his escape straight after the burial. Dorfen, meanwhile, had joined Lydia by the far window. Wilde wove his way towards them. 'Forgive me for interrupting your call, Her Dorfen.'

'Please, it was nothing.'

'And is your business difficulty resolved?'

'Oh, indeed. We had a delay in loading a ship. Frantic telephone calls to the buyers. As you must know, any sort of hold-up means a stop in production. The import–export business is always fraught with uncertainty. Rough seas, bloody-minded stevedores, late arrival of cargoes for loading. I'm afraid the trade unions have much to answer for.'

'Where exactly are your offices?'

'A little to the east of Tower Bridge. I'm sure you wouldn't know the company. It's not famous.'

'Try me.'

Dorfen laughed, then gripped Wilde's shoulder and nodded across the room. 'Isn't that chap one of Mosley's lieutenants?'

'Possibly. I've no idea.' Wilde wasn't even sure who Dorfen was indicating.

'Well, I know that he's a damned Blackshirt. I've seen his face in the newspapers giving the fascist salute alongside Sir Oswald. What is a man like that doing here?'

'I don't think he's the only admirer of Adolf Hitler here.' Wilde glanced at Lydia and saw her eyebrow rise.

Lydia sighed. 'What Tom is trying to say, Hart, is that you are in the middle of a nest of Nazis. Nancy was appalled by her father's sharp turn to the right.'

Dorfen's eyes widened. 'Is this true? I had no idea.'

Wilde gave a short laugh. 'I apologise,' he said. 'My American sense of humour, I'm afraid. Now then, where did you say you were staying?'

'A little inn not far from here. The Bear. I remembered it from my Cambridge days. I might stay another night. Now that I'm up here, it would be pleasant to visit old haunts, perhaps drive up to the North Norfolk coast. It has a strange beauty in winter, does it not?'

'I find this whole area a little strange at the moment. I imagine you heard of last night's tragic events.'

Dorfen nodded. 'My landlady told me all about it at breakfast. Shocking. And coming so soon after the death of Nancy and the Langleys . . .'

'One of the killers is in hospital even now. He's already talking, apparently, so I'm sure the whole thing will soon be resolved.'

'Then that is good,' said Hartmut Dorfen.

But Wilde had the feeling that Dorfen was not at all pleased with the news. And the sudden thought flashed through his mind that the German could have been the other killer. He dismissed it. Dorfen had been drinking with them until quite late. And what possible motive might he have had? He didn't like Hartmut Dorfen and he didn't trust him, but that was no reason to think he was a murderer.

Around them, the room was emptying rapidly. It would be an opportune time to go.

'I hope you'll excuse me, Herr Dorfen, but I must take my leave. I don't think bereaved families need guests to remain too long at these things. Lydia, are you staying or coming back to Cambridge?'

'I'll come with you, Tom.' Lydia turned to Dorfen. 'Let's not leave it so long now we know you live in England.'

Dorfen bent down and kissed her cheek. 'If you are not careful, Lydia Morris, I shall be up to see you every weekend. You are even more beautiful than I recall.'

'Don't you have enough hearts to break in London?' Lydia asked tartly.

His smile turned into a grin. 'Never!'

Outside, as Wilde kicked the Rudge into life, Lydia said, 'I saw Hart talking with your friend Dr Sawyer. They were speaking German.'

'He's not my friend. Sawyer's subject is German literature. He speaks German as well as Dorfen speaks English.'

'I want to watch them, Tom.'

Wilde turned in his seat. 'What are you talking about, Lydia?'

'Drop me off halfway down the drive.'

As the hall emptied and the stragglers were hustled away, Dorfen signalled to Sawyer to follow him to Hereward's study.

Dorfen leant on the edge of the desk and Sawyer settled back in one of the leather armchairs.

'It's tonight,' said Dorfen. 'Is the vehicle ready?'

Sawyer nodded his head in a vague direction towards the far side of the house. 'In the garages. An old Crossley once used by the Black and Tans in Ireland, suitably adapted.'

'Good. And the police? They are convinced Comrade Kholtov is the killer?'

Sawyer laughed. 'Indeed. His presence in town was most fortuitous.'

'What's not so good is that Wilde came in here while I was on the telephone. Said he was lost. But I have a feeling he was looking for something more than a water closet.'

'What do you think he wanted?'

'I think we'd better have words with Hereward.'

Sawyer pulled himself out of the chair. 'I'll get him.'

CHAPTER 30

From his seat behind Hereward's desk, Dorfen gazed out of the study window down across the parkland to the trees, the lake and what lay beyond. Himmler, in his final briefing, had told him he must be sensitive to the feelings of the English. Their aims were not necessarily the same as Germany's. Some were driven solely by a love of King and country, others by the hope of personal gain.

The door opened and Sawyer reappeared with Hereward.

'Has everyone gone?'

'Just about. The servants are pushing the last ones out,' Sawyer said.

'I've told the servants to keep to the hall and kitchens,' Hereward added. He had a large brandy in his hand and was drinking it in gulps.

'I think Wilde came in here looking for something,' Dorfen said. 'What could he want?' He shuffled through the papers on the desk, and then tried the drawers.

'Nothing,' Hereward said flatly. He had been drinking steadily. His eye twitched. He didn't like this German, never had done, even when their paths crossed during the younger man's undergraduate days. God knew why Sawyer seemed so fond of him. Clearly, Dorfen was the man for the job, but there was something about the creature that made Hereward feel ill-at-ease and out of control here in his own home. 'Nothing that I know of. There's nothing here.'

'Your desk drawers are locked.'

Hereward bridled at Dorfen's tone. 'Force of habit. I keep a revolver in there, an old Colt.'

'Open the desk.'

Hereward had never expected all this to be quite so *unpleasant*. He thought back to that last bitter row with Nancy. Of course, the Nazis were ruthless, but unlike the communists they did not threaten the very existence of landowners like him. Why had she not been able to see that? He walked across to the bookshelf and took down a German-English dictionary. He opened it and removed a small key from the hollowed-out pages. 'Here you are.'

Dorfen took the key, turned it in the lock and began rummaging through the drawers. He held up the Colt, pointed it at Hereward, raised an eyebrow, then laughed and lowered the barrel. Looking down into the drawer once more, his eyes lighted on a piece of paper. 'This.' He waved it. 'Why is this here?'

'I didn't know it was there. It's just a list of names. An invitation list, perhaps.'

'It says *North Sea* at the top.'

'Meaningless to anyone not in the know.'

Sawyer snatched the paper from Dorfen's hand, and held it in front of Hereward's face. 'Wilde knows something. I told you to have nothing to do with the fucking man, you doddering halfwit.'

'How dare you talk to me like that?' Hereward lurched unsteadily backwards. 'After all I've done for you!' *Sacrificed poor bloody Cecil Langley, for one thing. For England and the King. Someone always had to be first into the fire, but God it was a heavy price to pay.*

Sawyer looked at him with contempt. 'Everything you did was for yourself. The games have stopped now, Hereward.'

'I wanted to find out who killed Nancy! I thought Wilde could help. He's a clever man. You were doing nothing, the police were doing nothing!'

Dorfen ignored him. Whatever the Reichsführer-SS might have to say on the matter, he had no intention of offering sympathy to this drunken English fool. He turned to Sawyer. 'We have other business. Wilde said Braithwaite is talking.'

'I don't believe it,' Sawyer said. 'He was as good as dead.'

'We can't risk it,' Dorfen said. 'You know what to do.' He got up from behind the desk and walked over to Hereward. Without warning, he shot out a hand, grabbed the older man by the throat, and with his other hand forced the muzzle of the Colt against his face. 'Clear the house. Get rid of all the servants, all the gardeners. Now.'

Hereward started shaking. This was not how it was supposed to go. He fought to regain some command of the situation. 'Is it tonight then? What is to happen? What is the next step?'

Dorfen let go of him and pushed him towards the door. 'You'll find out.'

In the woods, Lydia shivered. Her black wool dress, donned for the funeral, was covered by a smart, long coat that was a great deal less warm than her duffle coat and the biting cold seeped into her small, slender body. Her hands and feet were the worst. She could hardly feel her fingers to hold the binoculars steady.

Wilde's binoculars were a finely crafted German instrument with powerful lenses, and gave her a direct line of view into the study of St Wilfred's Priory. She could see three men there: Dorfen, Sawyer and Hereward. They seemed to be arguing. Then, to her horror, she saw Hartmut Dorfen grab Hereward and press a gun to his face. The older man recoiled and for a moment she thought he had been shot, but the gun was lowered and Hereward was still standing there, slumped as if in shock, but unharmed.

Tom had begged her not to put herself in danger. She laughed silently, her teeth chattering with cold, not fear. Since finding Nancy's body the idea of danger had taken on a new meaning. Now she felt nothing but anger. She began to move forward, towards the house.

The secretary knocked at the door to Stanley Baldwin's Downing Street study.

'Come in.'

The secretary, a stiff young man with thin shoulders, entered the smoke-filled room. 'There is a telephone call for you, sir.'

'Yes? Who is it?'

'Sir Walter Monckton, sir.'

'Ah. Well, put him through if you would.' Monckton, a barrister by profession and an old friend of the King, was now His Majesty's only real confidant. Edward no longer trusted his official aides.

The telephone call was brief.

'Mr Baldwin, I have been commanded to convey a message from the King.'

'Yes, Sir Walter?'

'His mind is made up. He will abdicate the throne next week.'

'Then there is no more to be said. Thank you, Sir Walter.' Baldwin replaced the receiver. There was one more task to perform. He had to secure the succession – and he had to do it this very day. He called his secretary back in. 'Place a call to Royal Lodge. I wish to speak to the Duke of York.'

Addenbrooke's Hospital stood a quarter of a mile south of the college on Trumpington Street. The facade was a strange and rather magnificent affair, with colonnades along all three floors, almost like latter-day clois-ters, the idea being that patients could be wheeled out on their beds and bathchairs to take the fresh air. At the centre of the frontage was a gate-house topped by a clock that told the right time only twice a day.

Wilde parked the Rudge at the kerb and strode to the main entrance.

'I'm looking for the prisoner,' he told the man at the desk.

'Police, sir?'

'I'm working with Superintendent Bower. Which ward is the man on?'

'Third floor, at the rear. He's got a room to himself. You'll see the con-stable outside.'

Wilde walked up three flights of stairs, then took the corridor to the back of the building. A police officer was standing outside a closed door. As he approached, the constable stiffened his shoulders and his right hand went to the truncheon at his belt.

'Is Superintendent Bower here?'

The young constable went yet more rigid in the presence of authority. 'No, sir. He left half an hour ago.'

'Is Braithwaite talking yet?'

'No, sir. Taking a long time to come round. Out like a drunkard. I have been informed to contact the superintendent as soon as he's in a condition to talk.'

'Are you armed, constable?'

'I have this.' He touched the haft of the heavy black truncheon. 'Don't worry, the prisoner is bound. He won't get away from me.'

'I'll just take a look at him.'

'May I ask your name, sir?'

'Wilde. Professor Wilde to you, officer. I'm part of the wider investigation.'

'Thank you, sir.'

Braithwaite was secured to the bed with straps buckled across his ankles and chest and one wrist cuffed to the metal bedstead. The other was bandaged and had a splint up along his wrist and forearm. His eyes were closed, his battered mouth was open and he was snoring. His head, which had borne the brunt of the fall, was wrapped in bandages. His skinny chest was bare and there were dressings on the abdomen and side of the torso. Like his face, now sallow and blotched, there were the blue markings of a collier etched into his hairless chest skin. Blood was still seeping from his wounds, into the bandages.

Wilde looked on dispassionately. Braithwaite still carried the marks of the injuries Wilde had caused him when he attacked Lydia. The torn ear, the broken teeth. Wilde hoped that underneath the hospital sheet the man's balls were still swollen and blackened from his kick.

The constable, who had accompanied Wilde into the room, looked with curiosity at the patient. 'He doesn't look at all well, sir.'

Wilde leant forward and spoke firmly into the patient's ear. 'Braithwaite?'

The wounded man moved as though he heard, trying to turn on his side, but he was restricted by the straps and cuff. Wilde was not sure whether he was responding to the voice. He displayed no sign of waking.

'Braithwaite, we need to talk.'

The patient emitted a rattling groan. His body was covered in a film of sweat. The room was warmed by a cast-iron radiator and was as hot as a Kew glasshouse.

Wilde patted Braithwaite lightly on the cheek to rouse him, then a little harder. The man's eye twitched. 'Braithwaite, wake up. I need information.'

The wounded man turned away again, still comatose.

Wilde turned to the constable. 'Is this the best he's been?'

'As far as I know, sir. I stayed outside when the superintendent was here with him.'

'Did Mr Bower say when he'd be back?'

'No, sir.'

'Well, be careful, officer.' He turned to leave. 'And remember, whoever harmed him might want to finish what he started.'

The constable appeared startled. Had he really not thought of that, wondered Wilde. How was this poor sap to protect himself or his charge when the only weapon he had was a wooden cosh? Something had to be done to keep Braithwaite safe. If they were to get any information from him, there was little time to lose.

At the reception desk, he used the telephone to call the police station. Eventually Superintendent Bower came on the line.

'Yes, professor?'

'I'm at the hospital. Braithwaite has only one unarmed officer outside his room.'

Bower gave an irritated sigh. 'What's it to do with you, Wilde?'

'I found the man. I'd very much like to hear what he has to say.'

'Well, I don't think he's going anywhere.'

'That's pretty much what your constable said. Has it occurred to no one that Braithwaite might be a target?'

Silence.

'Well?'

'You have a vivid imagination, Wilde – but your point is taken. I'm going down there myself shortly. I'll see the man is well protected.'

Wilde looked in at the Bull Hotel, and immediately spotted Philip Eaton, talking on the concierge's telephone. Eaton saw Wilde, put up a finger in acknowledgement. 'Filing copy,' he mouthed.

Wilde ordered a whisky and sat down on a large leather sofa to wait. In a couple of minutes, Eaton put down the telephone and came over. 'Sorry about that. *The Times* pays my wages, so needs must.'

'What have you got?'

'The events of last night at Brandham Hall. The deeds of the hero professor . . .'

'You haven't mentioned me?'

'Not by name. Anyway, by Monday, my next publication day, there'll be wall-to-wall Edward and Wallis. In the meantime, what have *you* got?'

'I've just been to the hospital. Braithwaite's still unconscious, but I have to tell you, Eaton: one constable, no firearm, I walked straight in.'

'That's bad. We need to keep him alive for the hangman. I'll speak to Bower.'

'I've already done so. He sounded less than interested.'

'Don't worry, I'll put pressure on him.' Eaton paused. 'One thing – are you convinced Braithwaite was English?'

'Yes. No doubts. If he's an actor, he should be in Hollywood. Why?'

Eaton nodded. 'I'm just surprised there's no trace of him in any records . . .' He changed tack. 'What happened at the funeral?'

Wilde went through the morning's events. 'Sawyer and Dorfen cosying up to each other like best buddies. Apparently they met at the Ludwig Maximilian University in Munich.'

'Sounds plausible.'

'It also seems conceivable that they might have met in some Munich beer cellar frequented by the National Socialists. Dorfen claimed he knew no one at the funeral – apart from Sawyer, Sir Norman and Horace Dill – yet he was clearly very much at home there. And why is he not telling the truth about his position in the SS? I think you should get Bower to bring him in for questioning.'

'Won't happen, old boy. Kholtov's the man they want.'

Wilde looked at his wristwatch; time to pick up Lydia at their appointed rendezvous. He threw down the last half inch of his Scotch. 'I've got to go.'

'I'll go to see Bower, try to get the guard on Addenbrooke's ramped up, then I'm going to talk to a man about a great deal of gold.'

CHAPTER 31

Vladimir Rybakov smoked another cigarette. It was mid-afternoon. It looked as if, at last, things were moving.

They called themselves the SS Romanov Division. He smiled to himself; it was a grandiose name that had more to do with ambition than reality, for with fewer than fifty men – and only twelve of them here at Bremen – they were not even a company, let alone a battalion, regiment or division. 'We will grow!' Rybakov declared. He had been appointed captain, his old rank in the Kornilov Battalion, and had been granted the honour of a face-to-face interview with Himmler in his offices at Prinz-Albrecht-Strasse in Berlin before they were flown to Spain. That had been a stiff encounter; Himmler was a difficult man to warm to.

So far, they had seen only one small action – a skirmish with republican forces along the line to the north-east of Zaragoza, where the nationalist advance had become bogged down. Their taste of warfare had not lasted long. Shortly after they arrived in the line, they were visited by an SS officer. Sturmbannführer Dorfen told them they would be given work of far greater importance than shooting at a ragtag army of Trotskyites, anarchists and Stalinists. He said their valour had been much admired; now he was offering them the chance to strike a blow for God and monarchy.

'Who could have admired our valour? We have done nothing.' Rybakov was suspicious.

'You did enough. More than enough. Now you will perform an even greater feat. Your task will be to preserve England from the Bolsheviks.'

Dorfen pulled the SS Romanov Division out of Spain and had them flown back to Germany, to the Lichterfelde academy, south of Berlin, where they were allotted barracks in a corner unused by the Leibstandarte-SS Adolf Hitler, whose home this was. For the next few weeks, they received guerrilla training in the use of specialist weapons and explosives from Dorfen and SS instructors.

Rybakov had been taken aside shortly after he arrived in Berlin. 'The King of England is in grave danger,' Dorfen said. 'There is no one more suited to the task of saving him, no one more motivated than a group of men whose own royal family was slaughtered without mercy.'

'But I know nothing of this king,' the Russian said.

'But you know of his close cousin, Alexandra, wife to Tsar Nicholas II, last Empress of the Russias.'

It was the overthrow of the Tsar and Tsarina in 1917 that had opened the door for the communists in Russia. It was the exile of King Alfonso XIII fourteen years later that had heralded the Republic in Spain and the ascendancy of the socialists and communists. Every blow to a monarchy, whether in Russia or Spain or England, was a blow to the Church of Christ. God forbid the same should happen in England. Rybakov was exhilarated. However sketchy the details of the operation were, he knew it would involve the destruction of those who threatened the British King. In God's name, they were doing something at last. This was a thousand times better than Paris, taxi driving and the twice-daily tolling of the Renault factory bell.

The training was more intensive than anything they had so far experienced. They worked with pistols, sub-machine guns, mortars and hand grenades. They learned stealth and speed. This was a commando attack. Fast in, fast out. This was nothing like the trenches and rocky redoubts of Huesca. Their tactics in England would be overwhelming might, sudden strikes and ruthlessness. The SS instructors were harsh and unforgiving, but Rybakov's small band emerged from their training lean in body and expert as fighting men.

They had been transported to Bremen to this grim messroom where they ate, smoked and drank shit-like coffee, waiting for the order to collect their arms and board a Junkers JU-52. So here they were, still waiting, but at least the pilot had arrived and they had an aeroplane.

Only Rybakov had any idea what they might expect in England, and even he was uncertain of the actual target or targets. Dorfen would be in charge. All that the other eleven men selected from the SS Romanov Division knew was that they would be using Soviet weapons, and, if captured, would claim that they had been sent by order of the Kremlin. Stalin could take the blame.

Wilde parked the Rudge in the trees, twenty yards from the road, then walked along the path to the rendezvous point and waited for Lydia. He checked his watch. It was nearly half-past three. He was a little late; she should be here by now. He cursed. What was she doing? They had agreed she would watch for two hours. He was no more than five minutes late. She should be here.

Above him, he heard the buzz of an aircraft. He looked up through the bare branches and saw the bright yellow biplane he had seen on his previous visit, circling, playing in the cold winter air.

After ten minutes, Wilde walked further into the woods along the path he thought Lydia would have taken. He trod softly, ever watchful for gamekeepers, until he came to a place at the edge of the woods with a good view of the back of the house, including Sir Norman's study. A small area of undergrowth was pressed down: this was where she had lain to watch.

He peered through the bushes. Whatever there was to be seen, there was now no discernible activity up at the house. Not even any servants in evidence. He stayed for a few minutes but saw no movement.

With care, he moved westwards along the north side of the park, circling towards the front of the house but remaining under the cover of the trees. Now he had clear sight of the gravel forecourt. The only car was Hereward's Rolls Royce. So all the funeral guests had gone.

Wilde was angry with himself. He should never have left her watching the house on her own. She had been so bloody sure of herself, so insistent that she was smaller and quieter, could more effectively find a hiding place to observe. Where the hell was she?

Above him, the sky was grey and gloomy. In places, the sleet of last night lay as isolated patches of white, but mostly the land was a scrubby brown. It was mid-afternoon and darkness would fall soon. He moved further round the house, keeping to the trees wherever possible, looking for any signs of Lydia's presence, but there was nothing. He retraced his steps back to the place where they had been supposed to meet, and waited a few more minutes. Then he returned to the Rudge in case she had gone straight there. Nothing.

Wilde stopped to gather his thoughts again. He was moving in ever increasing circles further from the house, deeper into the woodland – bare branches of ancient oak and ash and sycamore and birch, the promise of broadleafed English splendour, buried deep in winter nakedness. By now he guessed he had strayed at least a mile, probably more, from the priory. The only focal point was the biplane buzzing and swooping overhead, its yellow wings and fuselage stark and bright against the gathering dusk. For a moment he thought its single engine was about to stall, but he saw that it was, in fact, preparing to land, somewhere beyond the trees.

He followed its trajectory and came to the edge of the woodland where an open, flat space of grassland ranged before him, with two rows of white pegs marking out a landing strip. The biplane was coming in slowly against the northerly breeze, touching down to a smooth and balanced landing, then bouncing and wobbling as it turned left, off the runway, braked and drew to a halt.

The pilot clambered out of the cockpit: a small, slender man in a battered leather cap and jacket, goggles pulled up on to his forehead.

Wilde walked across the greensward towards him and noticed a green car parked in the shadow of the woods, near the road at the northern edge of the clearing.

When they were about twenty yards apart, the man turned and saw Wilde approach. He smiled and raised a hand in greeting.

'Hello?'

'I was having a stroll and noticed your plane. Well, I couldn't really miss it – daffodil yellow, I'd call it.'

'Buttercup, actually. Not a bad kite. An old Sopwith fighter from the war. Good for tricks and shooting down the Hun. I'd have stayed up but the light and cloud beat me.'

'I'm looking for a friend. We were walking together and somehow got split up. I think I was too slow for her. She likes a brisk walk. Don't suppose you spotted her?'

The young man had started fixing a tarpaulin over the cockpit. He turned to Wilde. 'I saw a girl up near the priory, but that must have been over an hour ago. I rather thought she must have been playing some sort of game. You know, hide-and-seek or sardines or something.'

'Where did she go?'

'Couldn't tell you. Perhaps you'd better ask up at the house. It's Sir Norman Hereward's place. Do you know him? He allows me to use his airstrip and park my kite here. Help me with the tarp, would you?'

Wilde took the other end of the tarpaulin and together they secured it. He put out his hand. 'I'm Thomas Wilde. I teach history at Cambridge.'

The young pilot took off his right gauntlet and they shook hands. 'Pleased to meet you. I'm Geoffrey Lancing, physicist, St John's.'

Wilde estimated the young man's age at twenty-five or twenty-six; probably a research graduate.

'I believe there was a funeral up at the priory today,' Wilde said.

'Sir Norman's girl, Nancy. I didn't know her, but I knew of her. Ghastly business. Overdose of something, I believe. Should have taken up flying. A spin in the blue will lift your spirits better than any dope.' He seemed to be sizing Wilde up. 'Look, I've got my motor car just over there. Can I give you a lift somewhere? I'm going back to town. Your friend's probably made her own way home by now.'

'No, thank you. I have transport.'

He turned to go, but the young man stopped him. 'Actually, there was something, Mr Wilde.'

'Yes?'

'It's probably nothing, but on one of my turns, I saw a couple of people climb into a little red two-seater parked in front of the priory and then scoot off down the drive. Didn't see where they went after that.'

'Could one of them have been a woman?'

'No idea, I'm afraid.'

Harold Middlemass sat in his office at Royal Lodge. He felt a sense of calm. He knew what he had to do.

It was late afternoon. There were no sounds to intrude on his thoughts, none of the squeals and laughter of his children at play. The boys had broken up for Christmas and had gone off to the family home in Herefordshire. The plan was that he would join them in a week's time.

He had locked the door to the office. There was a note, of course, but it did not speak the whole truth, nor anywhere near it. It spoke in general terms about his unhappiness, his failure to recover after the war. No mention of Sophie or the photograph.

He was calm because there was nothing left. He was as immune to sadness as to joy.

On the old desk, his grey-black service revolver, a Webley .455, glared at him. Its harsh, functional metal edges offered no comfort, but the nicely rounded bullets within contained the promise of warm oblivion. Six of them, though he would need only one.

Surely the bitch would not send the photograph to the family or friends of a dead man? How could you take revenge on a corpse? There was no point in piling extra misery onto the grieving widow and children. Even Sophie, blackhearted Sophie, would not stoop to that. He had convinced himself that she would spare them the ignominy. And yet . . .

He reached out for the gun, but his hand did not obey his brain and he picked up the telephone receiver instead. He held it for a few moments in his right hand but then he put it to his ear and, with his left hand, dialled the Mayfair number of the Dorchester Hotel and asked to be put through to the apartment of the Gräfin von Isarbeck.

'Hello?'

'Sophie, it's me.'

'Hello, Harold. I was hoping you would call. Do you have the final details?'

'When will you give me the photograph?'

'As soon as the information is confirmed, the photograph will be yours. Come and pick it up any time. Or I could send it to you in the post.'

'No, no, I'll pick it up.'

'So, tell me what you know.'

'I . . . explain to me again *why* you want this information.'

'Silly boy, I told you, it is not me. It is Wally Simpson. She's mad with panic that the King is going to give up his throne for her. She is desperate for information. All she wants is to know what's going on, so that she can warn Edward and try to persuade him to stand firm. But look, Harold, I really don't think we should be talking about this on the telephone. Just give me the time and the place – and then our deal is done.'

'And you swear that I will have the original photograph, that you will give me the negative to destroy and that there are no copies?'

'I swear it. You know, I hate doing this to you – but Wally is my friend. I must help her.' There was a silence. Then, 'Harold? Are you there?' The soft voice had begun to harden.

Middlemass closed his eyes. 'I have been told that the King has made his decision. He is to abdicate early next week. Baldwin will be here to meet the duke this evening.'

'The time, Harold, the time.'

'Midnight.'

'And *here*?'

'Royal Lodge. Privately. The hope is that the press will be drunk or asleep.'

In the comfort of her hotel apartment, Sophie von Isarbeck felt a warm glow of pleasure. *Royal Lodge.* Just as they had thought. Ministers of the crown went to princes, not the other way round. Royal Lodge, home to the Duke and Duchess of York, was one of the most isolated and private of the royal houses and palaces. But it was well known to those who mattered in Sophie's circle. 'And this is tonight. Midnight? You are absolutely certain?'

'Midnight. I am staking my family's happiness on it, Sophie. Do nothing to harm them, I beg you.'

'Harold?' Her voice was soft again. She had what she wanted.

He was silent.

'Harold, I know you feel as though you are somehow betraying your master, the Duke of York, but your first loyalty must be to your King. This is every Englishman's duty, is it not? If Wally has asked for this informa-tion on his behalf, then it is your duty to provide it.'

'Goodbye, Sophie.'

He hung up the telephone and picked up the Webley, pushing the sharp-edged hexagonal muzzle into his mouth. He thought better of it, put the gun down and took off his jacket. Wrapping a sleeve around the barrel to deaden the sound, he held the weapon to his right temple. His finger trembled on the trigger, but he couldn't pull. Disgusted with himself, he threw the gun to the floor, put his head in his hands, and wept.

CHAPTER 32

Kholtov kept the curtains closed. They were dirty yellow, blotched with mould. The house was remote, down a farm track deep in the Fens, the sort of place where you could see for miles in all directions, but only on days when there was no mist to obstruct your vision. And only if you cared to gaze on such a desolate landscape.

Today, before dusk set in, the visibility had been dull but clear, with an icy northerly. Kholtov put more coal on the fire and sat on his haunches in front of the small hearth, warming his hands. The cat who had been keeping him company these past hours rolled over and he rubbed her belly.

The little house was single-storey and riddled with damp. A poor farm cottage, poorly built for a poor labourer by a grasping landlord, just as the kulaks sucked the blood of the peasants in Russia. At some stage, perhaps a hundred years ago, the house had been rendered and painted white, but now much of the mortar had fallen away, exposing soft, crumbling brickwork. Beneath his feet, the floor was nothing but packed mud and stone. What a place to come back to after digging the fields twelve hours in the day; it was bad enough just hiding out here. The damp drained into his bones.

Eaton had been apologetic. 'It's the best I can do at short notice. Every police force and port official in the country is after you.' Kholtov began to protest but Eaton had shrugged. 'Your innocence or guilt is entirely irrelevant at the moment. They want your blood.'

Every so often during the day, Kholtov had gone to the window and looked out along the mile-long farm track that cut through dark, ploughed acres of thick, rich soil. When he saw that it was clear, he went outside and looked across the fields in other directions. The only signs of life were gulls and crows and the occasional buzzard or harrier. He shook his head. The Russian countryside in midwinter had a stark beauty; this was desolate and ugly. Now, at least, it was shrouded in darkness.

The fire, the cat, his coat and his bedclothes were his sources of warmth. He huddled close to the glowing coals. There was plenty of coal, enough to last weeks. Not that he had any intention of being here more than a few days at the most. If the worst came to the worst, he would steal a car and make his way back to the coast and hope that the *Gaviota* and Ferreira were still there, their cargo undiscovered. Cut and run. Make another plan.

The cat had appeared late in the night. In the early hours, this house was the loneliest, most forsaken place on earth, but he had heard scratching and mewing from outside. Tentatively, he had unlocked and opened the door and a little black and white cat had slunk in, snaking her way past his legs as she headed for the embers of the fire. He had given her water and a little meat and she had found a bed in his lap and, later, on the pillow beside his head. In the morning, he had opened the door for her, but she hadn't left.

He thought he heard a sound and the cat's ears pricked up. Kholtov went again to the window. In the far distance, he saw the lights of a car, turning into the farm track. Was that Eaton? His whole body tensed. In the Soviet Union, he had driven down rural roads, deep into the countryside, to some dacha or farmhouse with a pistol, a pair of colleagues, and a death sentence. A bullet in the head for a general or department director or commissar. All of them traitors, of course. He had no qualms about such matters. They were big boys; they knew what they were doing when they betrayed the revolution. They could have no complaint. No complaint at all.

And yet he *did* have complaints. He had never betrayed the revolution and he had never said a word against Comrade Stalin nor disobeyed an order. He had done everything required of him, whatever the cost to his own conscience. He had recruited throughout Europe and he had killed traitors in France and in Spain. He had never slandered the Communist Party, nor its leadership. He was guilt-free. But that was not the same as being innocent.

He knew what NKVD director Genrikh Yagoda had planned for him with his summons to return to Moscow. He knew, because he himself had summoned men to their deaths on Yagoda's orders. But he and Yagoda had been friends, hadn't they, as far back as the early days of the Cheka? In which case the order must have come from above, from Stalin himself. And now Yagoda was gone, replaced by Nikolai Yezhov. The poisonous one. There would be no mercy there. He turned and spat into the fire.

The hold that Stalin had over him, of course, was his family. If he did not go back to Moscow, what would become of them? Dirty little Yezhov, the new head of the secret service, would kill them without blinking. If he was in a good mood, he might consign them to a labour camp, but that was a very small reprieve. They would have little hope of surviving the winter. Kholtov understood the logic well enough; the families of the condemned tended to harbour resentment against the state.

The car was approaching, its lights bouncing as it bumped slowly along the rutted track. Kholtov thought he could see two men in the front seats. Was there anyone else behind? If they were coming to kill him, how would it be done? Garotte? Bullet in the head? A syringe full of one of the new undetectable poisons from Moscow's Special Office? Or would they make it look like a suicide by hanging? All things were possible; he had done them all himself, and more.

And now it was too late to get Maria and the children out of Moscow. He should have prepared for this, when he still had the power and influence. He stroked the cat. Predators are so busy hunting, he thought, they never think they will in turn be prey.

Philip Eaton came to the door alone. Kholtov opened it cautiously, and Eaton could see that he was afraid. The Englishman smiled and held out a basket of provisions – two bottles of vodka and some food. 'Yuri, I have good things for you.'

Kholtov's smile was forced. 'Vodka? I want a buyer for my gold so I can remove myself from this stinking hole and you bring me vodka?' He tilted his chin in the direction of the car. 'Who is in the car with you?'

'A man who deals in gold. Just as you asked.'

'What is his name? Does he have the money with him?'

Eaton sighed and stepped inside the room, depositing the basket on the small table. All pretence at civility was gone. 'You don't need to know his name. Call him whatever you like. But first, the information. You have held out long enough, Kholtov.'

'You will have your information when I have a buyer and the deal is sealed.'

'I have a buyer with me. When a deal is agreed, you will give me the information. Do you understand?' Eaton's tone was icy.

Kholtov understood. They had reached the end point. 'I will tell you,' he said. 'Everything.'

'Good.' Eaton pulled out a napkin and unwrapped three small glasses. Then grasped the neck of one of the bottles.

'This dealer, he will pay me a fair price?'

'He is a professional and extremely wealthy. He is not here to cheat you.'

'Because a man always has options, Philip. A man can die with dignity or begging.'

'Well, I don't have anyone else to offer you.' Eaton began to pour vodka. 'I'm sure you will understand why he wishes to be discreet. And he, in turn, will not ask questions of you – such as how you came by all this gold.'

Kholtov hesitated. 'Is he armed?'

Eaton laughed. 'You have lived among murderers too long. You think everyone wants to kill you!'

'Well, is he?'

'If we wanted you dead, you would already be dead.'

The Russian shrugged. He believed it. He flicked his fingers. 'Bring him in. Let me hear his price. This is fine gold, eighteen carat, twenty-two carat, and so I want a great deal of money. In dollars.'

Eaton went to the door and opened it. 'Come in. He's ready for you.'

Peter Slievedonard pushed his bulk through the narrow doorway. In his hand he had the gold coin that Kholtov had given to Eaton at the Bull Hotel in Cambridge. A golden dollar with the head of Liberty on one side and the date and denomination and the words *United States of America* on the reverse. He held it up between his right thumb and forefinger. 'This is yours, I believe, Mr Kholtov.'

'You have tested it, yes?'

'Genuine US gold dollar, 1861. The year the Civil War began. Twenty-two carat fine gold. I am told you have many of these.' Slievedonard put the small coin into the Russian's hand.

Kholtov pocketed the gold and looked at Slievedonard. 'You have no bag. Where is your testing kit, sir, your nitric acid?'

Slievedonard ignored the question. 'Is the rest of the gold here?'

'No, of course not.'

Those who thought they knew Peter Slievedonard well would not have recognised him here in this remote house. His voice was soft, not loud and hectoring, the bombast gone. He was wearing his gold-dealing face; gold men were hard, but quiet and reasonable. The deal was about weight and quality and potential profit, not clever sales techniques.

'So why would I need a testing kit? Why would I waste my time testing only a portion of it? Anyone can bring me a few coins that are genuine. For all I know the rest of your stock might be base metal. I need to test it all, when you show it to me. Do you think me a fool, Mr Kholtov?'

'There are thousands of coins – countless thousands. You could not test them all.'

'Where is the gold?' Slievedonard repeated.

'Here, in England. You will not see it until a deal has been agreed. I will bring it to you in stages.'

'Seven and a half tonnes, I am told.'

Kholtov nodded. For the first time, he gave a genuine smile. 'Seven and a half. I think it must be worth a lot of money.'

'Well, Mr Kholtov, I have no idea how you laid your hands on such a quantity of treasure, but I must see it to make a judgement. From what you say, I would like to own it, so let us merely charge our glasses, make a dent in these bottles – and attempt to conclude a deal.'

*

Just before twenty past four, Sawyer picked up the telephone. 'Sir Norman Hereward's residence.' He listened for a couple of seconds, then smiled and handed the receiver over to Dorfen.

'Sophie?'

'Midnight, darling. Royal Lodge.'

'Thank you, Sophie.'

'My pleasure, *liebling*.'

Dorfen replaced the telephone receiver carefully. 'And so it begins,' he said.

Duncan Sawyer stood at the rear of Addenbrooke's Hospital and looked up to the third floor, counting along until he came to the window of what he had been told was Braithwaite's room. It was slightly ajar. No untidy ends, Dorfen had said. Simply a matter of good housekeeping. Nothing to tie the operation to Germany.

Sawyer had taken great pleasure bludgeoning Braithwaite's head with a heavy wrench and sending him sprawling onto the road. His one regret was that he hadn't killed the man outright, but it was better to have it look as if he had fallen from the car. Braithwaite had played the part of being a communist agitator well enough. The police would have no reason to believe he was anything but a Bolshie troublemaker in the pay of the Soviets. This series of killings was Stalin's work.

Sawyer lit a cigarette, drew deeply and continued to watch the window. A face appeared for a moment, grey and indistinct in the dim glow of an electric lightbulb. It was enough. Sawyer dropped the cigarette, grinding it to a pulp with his heel. One little telephone call had ensured that the way would be clear.

He was wearing a working man's cap, pulled down over his brow to shade his eyes, and a faded old boiler suit; the arms and legs were slightly on the short side and he couldn't do up the buttons all the way but no one noticed working men in blue overalls any more than the fixtures and fittings they maintained. He picked up his toolbag and made his way towards a rear entrance, careful not to appear hurried, or unduly keen to do his work.

No one even appeared to notice him. Starched nurses strode briskly past. Doctors with slicked hair and stethoscopes about their necks conferred with serious faces or swapped dark jokes. Sawyer walked unchallenged up to the third floor.

A figure at the end of the corridor paused. Their eyes almost met but then the figure slid away, like a silverfish between the boards, leaving Braithwaite's room unguarded. Sawyer turned the handle and walked in, closing the door behind him. For a few moments he looked down at the unconscious form on the regulation iron bedstead. The wounded man was no bigger than a twelve-year-old child, far too small for the hospital cot. Apparently he was a good member of the NSDAP and helped run the local Hitler Youth in Möhlau as an adult leader, but Sawyer had no sympathy for him; such creatures were there to be sacrificed for the greater good. Sawyer put the toolbag on the end of the bed.

He slapped Braithwaite's blue-veined face to see if there was any response. When there was none, he lifted the wounded man's bandaged head and grabbed his pillow from underneath. Braithwaite's head slumped back onto the sheet. Sawyer held the pillow over the pinched face, then thrust it down. Hard.

How long did it take a man to die of asphyxiation? After two slow minutes, Sawyer pulled the pillow away. Braithwaite was breathing fitfully, unconscious, but still alive. There had to be a better, quicker way. He took a rag from his toolbag, prised open Braithwaite's lacerated mouth and stuffed it in, deep into the man's throat, provoking an involuntary gagging reaction. Then, with his powerful thumb and forefinger he clenched the man's nostrils shut, while the other hand clamped his jaw.

Braithwaite's eyes suddenly opened wide and bulged, brimming with instinctive panic. He began to thrash against the straps holding him to the bed. Without releasing his grip, Sawyer climbed onto the bed and knelt on Braithwaite's scrawny chest, pressing down firmly on his face with his hands. The kicking grew feeble. Then stopped. A minute more, then another. Leslie Braithwaite was dead.

Duncan Sawyer removed the gag from the dead man's mouth, then wiped the film of sweat from Braithwaite's face with it. He put the rag back in his toolbag.

Using his fingers as a comb, he untangled the corpse's ruffled hair where it protruded from the bandages, brushing his fringe back from his forehead. He set the head just so on the pillow and smoothed down the bedding. Sawyer cocked his head to study his handiwork; Braithwaite looked almost serene.

Taking a last look round the room, Sawyer picked up his toolbag, opened the door and walked down the empty corridor. He was even tempted to whistle.

CHAPTER 33

They drank and talked for almost two hours. The coal fire glowed and threw off a good heat. With the fire and the vodka, a man might almost find some cheer in this dank peasant room. Kholtov was becoming steadily drunker but he didn't care. He could handle himself as well drunk as sober. Every time one of them demanded to see the gold, he stalled. He noted the cold, clever manner of the gross, fur-clad dealer and the silence of Eaton and wondered which of them would first mention a figure. Who would blink first?

Eaton had a dark frown fixed to his sleek, bourgeois face. He was a good agent, Kholtov thought approvingly, gave nothing away and was almost always affable. But not today. Today he was impatient. Today he demanded information, kept trying to move the conversation away from the gold, and made threats.

The vodka was taking its toll. Even Kholtov was beginning to feel it. And it was he, at last, who blinked. 'You haven't made me an offer yet,' he said.

'Suggest a figure,' Slievedonard said. 'A notional figure. Notional until we have sight of the gold.'

'You don't trust me? There was more gold in Spain at the end of the war than in any other European country. You and Germany and France and Russia – you all sold your gold to pay for millions of tonnes of iron to throw at each other across the trenches.'

'I am well aware of that,' Slievedonard said patiently. 'And that is why the coin you are offering interests me. That is how I can give you a good price. That is why we need to see it.'

Kholtov drew deeply on a western cigarette. His Russian batch had run out. He turned to Eaton. 'Who is this dealer? Some capitalist fascist, I suppose?'

'Just get on with it.'

The Russian laughed. 'You fascist capitalist swine are all the same. Eaton, you name a price.'

'Five million dollars.' Eaton had done his homework; he knew from Slievedonard that the gold should be worth at least that much.

'Conditional on testing of the gold,' Slievedonard said.

'Then we have a deal,' Kholtov said, grinning.

Eaton stood up. 'You have wasted our time long enough. I have brought you a gold buyer. You have agreed a deal. Now you will tell me about the White Russians and about what they are planning. I want to know the target and the time – and how they intend getting into England. I am worried that something might be imminent. No one leaves this house until you have told me what I need to know.'

Kholtov shrugged. 'I don't know.'

'What do you mean, *you don't know*?'

'The White Russians? I have no idea. I told you everything I had learnt in Barcelona. You must make your own inquiries.'

Eaton was standing over him now. 'Not good enough, Kholtov.'

'Forget them. Take your cut of the gold, Philip. We will all be rich – all three of us here in this room. We can even make my friend the cat rich.'

'I offered you safe passage to England in exchange for this information. God damn you, Kholtov . . .'

Kholtov was not listening. 'You did say five million?' He had expected a fight, a stupid offer like a hundred thousand. It never occurred to him that he could truly lay his hands on such a sum. Five million . . .

Slievedonard put out his hand. 'A deal then. I can't stay drinking vodka with you all evening. I need to drive down south. I have an appointment at my club. Shake on it – and we will arrange a meeting when you can show me the gold.'

Kholtov stumbled to his feet, his hand outstretched. But Eaton got there first and seized Kholtov by the throat in a powerful grip.

The Russian gasped as he was pushed back against the wall. 'Now then, you treacherous shit,' Eaton said, his face in Kholtov's. 'You are going to tell me. I know there's an attack planned. Where and when is it happening?' His knee came up sharply into the Russian's balls. Kholtov cried out, a rasping squeal like the sound of a shot hog. He doubled up. In the same movement, Eaton released his grip on the man's throat and crunched his fist into the side of his head.

Kholtov crumpled to the floor.

'If you want to be alive to enjoy your gold, then you had better talk. I ask again: when and where are these White Russians landing? Are they already in England?'

'I don't know, I tell you I don't know.'

Eaton took an iron from the fireplace and smacked it with bone-crunching force into Kholtov's left ankle. Kholtov screamed, and Eaton hit him again.

Eaton pointed the iron at Slievedonard, its blackened point an inch from the man's face. 'And you?'

Slievedonard was shaking in his fur coat. He had never seen such violence and had had to turn away. He was twice the size of Eaton, but he was scared. 'I promise you, I've told you everything I know. I just obey orders. I'm to go south for a few days, to my home in Berkshire, and wait by the telephone.'

'And then what?'

'I don't damn well know, Eaton. If a call comes through in the next day or two, then I do what I'm told.'

'Then you'd better go, hadn't you?'

Cornflowers was in darkness, but the door was unlocked. Typical of Lydia. No one was at home. Tom Wilde switched on the lights, looked in all of the rooms, then went to Lydia's drinks cabinet and poured himself a whisky. Despite the cold, he was sweating. He had searched the woods again and had ridden the motorbike along the roads in all directions from St Wilfred's Priory. He was frantic.

He raised the glass to his lips, but put the glass down again without drinking. His hand was shaking. He needed to keep a clear head this evening. Lydia might indeed have returned to Cambridge safely, but if it had been her the young pilot had spotted in the red sports car, she might have left St Wilfred's Priory against her will.

He would look in at her office in Bene't Street. It wasn't far from Addenbrooke's. Then, if he had still heard nothing, he would have to bring in the police.

Wilde wrote a hurried note outlining his plans in case she came home before he had found her, and left it by the telephone. *Call the police station. Leave a message.*

Ten minutes later, he ran past her office and saw that it was in darkness, so he carried on to the hospital. The policeman outside Braithwaite's room had been changed, and he looked nervous.

'What is it?' Wilde demanded.

'The doctors are in there,' the constable said. 'He's taken a turn for the worse.'

Wilde pushed open the door. Two doctors were examining Braithwaite. A nurse stood by the window, shaking her head.

'What happened?' Wilde addressed the question to the elder of the two doctors, a man in his fifties.

'Who are you?'

'Professor Thomas Wilde.'

'You knew the patient?'

'Yes. I was the man who found him on the road.'

'Then you saved his life,' the senior doctor said. 'But not for long, I'm afraid.'

'What happened?'

'Bleed in the brain probably. A fall from a car? Head wounds that look as if he's been hit with a blunt instrument? God knows what the damage was inside. I thought we had saved him, but you never know with these sorts of injuries.'

'Are you sure that's what happened? No one could have got in here?'

The doctor looked over Wilde's shoulder at the policeman in the doorway. 'Constable?'

The policeman shook his head.

'Let's leave it to the post-mortem examination,' the doctor said. 'There's a bit of bruising about the face I don't like, but I suppose that could have occurred when he fell. Thing is, I hadn't noted it before.'

Damn you, Bower; damn you, Eaton, Wilde cursed. The police were supposed to have doubled the guard on the hospital. Braithwaite was dead and Wilde was as certain as he could be that someone had helped him on his way. And where the hell was Lydia? And Eaton?

Wilde ran the short distance to the police station in St Andrew's Street where he found Superintendent Bower eating a steak and kidney pie at a desk. His tie was alive with fresh gravy stains. He looked up through his thick glasses at Wilde.

'Leslie Braithwaite is dead.'

'I know.'

'How did the killer get past your men?'

Bower waved his fork at Wilde. 'Calm down. I had officers there at all times, in shifts. I was even there myself shortly before he died. It seems the man simply didn't come round. It happens with head injuries. A bleed on the brain is likely, so I'm told.'

'Are you not the least suspicious, given the circumstances?'

For a moment a flash of anger passed across Bower's usually benign eyes, somewhere deep behind the heavy Bakelite spectacles. 'Be careful, professor. Be very careful. I could already have had you arrested for impersonating a police officer during your last visit to Addenbrooke's. Don't try me.'

Wilde fought to keep his temper under control. 'It's too late for Braithwaite, I suppose, but I am very concerned for the whereabouts of Miss Lydia Morris. We were due to meet at three thirty and she's been missing now for three hours.' Wilde told Bower about the funeral, Lydia's excursion in the woods, the rendezvous point.

'Perhaps she was invited in for cocktails or a cup of tea? You don't seem to be thinking very clearly, professor. Did it not occur to you to knock at their door and ask after her?'

'And say what? "Oh, are you holding Lydia Morris captive?" *You* raid the house, superintendent. Get your men to search the bloody place!' Wilde had begun to shout.

'Do you not think Sir Norman Hereward might take umbrage at being treated in such a manner, especially on the day he has buried his only daughter? Do you not stop to wonder what in the name of God you were both up to, spying on people in their own home, on private land? You've taken leave of your senses, Wilde!'

Wilde took a deep breath and forced himself to speak calmly. 'There have been four murders, probably five, including Braithwaite. You know as well as I do, superintendent, that there is something bigger here.'

'There is certainly a conspiracy – but if you think it involves St Wilfred's Priory, you have to give me evidence. We have no reason to connect Braithwaite, a known communist, with the place. Kholtov is another matter – and we will find him. Now, I've been patient with you long enough, professor—'

Wilde interrupted. He had nothing left to lose. 'Nancy Hereward left a letter. She found something in the desk drawer in her father's office – a list of names, senior members of the ruling class. Members of something called North Sea.'

Shock registered in Bower's eyes. 'What? Where is this letter? What does it say?'

'I have it safe. She was spying on her father. I suspect she was *sent* to spy on him by her communist friends. I take it you know of the *North Sea* newsletter, Mr Bower?'

'It's some sort of Nazi publication. But you're talking about National Socialists, Mr Wilde. All the evidence we have points to a communist conspiracy. Kholtov, he's the man we want. The search for him has gone nationwide.'

This was going nowhere. 'Get back to your bloody steak and kidney pie, superintendent.' Wilde headed for the door.

Bower's parting shot rang in his ears. 'Don't even think of trespassing on Sir Norman's land again or I'll have you in a police cell.' He pointed a warning finger.

Wilde stopped. 'And that's the sum of your fears?'

The policeman sighed, and lowered his voice. 'I know you're not stupid. Something *is* going on and we're all worried. But you and your friend Miss Morris flailing around like a topsail in a squall will do no one any good. I suggest you go back to her house – and you'll probably find she's already there. This is England, Mr Wilde, not Germany or Russia. People do not get lifted off the streets and carted away to a Moscow prison never to be heard of again. Have a whisky with Miss Morris and I'm sure things will all look a great deal more rosy in the morning.'

'Superintendent?'

'Yes, professor?' His voice was weary now.

'Go fuck yourself.'

CHAPTER 34

By 7 p.m., the sky above Cambridge was dark, overcast and biting, with the threat of snow in the air. Menace hung heavy, the shadows among the old houses and majestic university buildings sinister rather than comforting.

Where in this baleful town could Lydia be? He'd already been past her office and seen no light on. Now, he hurried back to try again. In Bene't Street, he caught his breath as he gazed up at her window. It was in darkness. The door at the side of the shop was locked. He tried the bell, but there was no response. She wasn't at home; she wasn't here. He strode to the college and found Scobie in the porters' lodge. 'Have you seen Lydia Morris?'

'No, professor, I'm afraid not.'

'Has she left a message?'

'Not to my knowledge, sir.'

'Let me use your telephone.' He called Dave Johnson but the call just rang and rang. Then he tried St Wilfred's Priory.

The phone was answered by Hereward himself.

'Sir Norman, this is Tom Wilde. I was wondering – is Lydia Morris with you?'

'Why would she be?' The voice was curt and defensive; an edge of suspicion.

'Is she there? Have you seen her?'

'No to both questions, Wilde.'

The line went dead. Wilde looked at Scobie. These men missed very little.

'Is everything all right, professor?'

'No, Scobie, no, it's not all right. Is Horace Dill in his rooms?' Perhaps Dill would know where she was. If he was sober. He cared for Lydia. A man like Horace Dill might just know what was going on.

'I'm afraid you've just missed him. He left an hour since on the London train. Won't be back until Epiphany. A lecture to deliver in London, apparently, and then Christmas in Scotland. Left in a bit of a hurry, so we had no notice of his going.' Scobie sniffed. 'Funny thing is, sir, an old pupil of his, German gentleman by name of Dorfen, was asking after him only ten minutes ago.'

'Dorfen was here?'

'Indeed, sir. I told Mr Dorfen exactly what I told you and off he went.'

'Thank you.' Wilde fished in his pocket for a florin. All he had was a shilling. He placed it in the man's proffered hand. 'Forgive me, I'm a little short just now, Scobie.'

'Very kind of you, sir. Seasons greetings to you.'

As he turned away, Wilde swore beneath his breath. Horace Dill leaving in a hurry. Escaping. But escaping what? Dorfen, perhaps . . .

With Dill gone and no help forthcoming from Bower, he'd have to return to St Wilfred's Priory. If Lydia wasn't here in Cambridge, then she had to be there, whatever Hereward said. She had to be there, because that was where he had left her.

And where was bloody Eaton?

Sir Norman Hereward sat in his study, alone in the empty house, staring blankly at the dark, uncurtained window, his right hand loosely gripping his brandy glass. Should he go to her? Not yet. She'd be all right.

He had spotted Lydia from his bedroom window creeping about behind the garages. He had left the house by the side door, moving silently across the grass and she hadn't seen him until he reached out and grabbed her by the arm.

'Oh!' she exclaimed. 'I was just going for a walk.'

'You were spying,' he said.

'What do you mean? I was just—'

He was close to her now, breathing alcohol fumes in her face. 'You were spying. Come with me.' He dragged her by the arm away from the garages into the woodland behind.

'Please, no!'

He tugged her even harder, bruising her arm. 'God damn you! You have no idea what you're dealing with here. Do as I say or things will go a great deal worse.'

'Is that what happened to Nancy?'

'Move, damn you.'

In the woods, not far from the house was an old ice house, a cellar, half buried in the ground, where ice had been shovelled in winter for use by the kitchens in summer. Now it lay hidden beneath a century's growth of ivy and brambles and roots.

Lydia struggled, but she was small and Sir Norman was still strong and he managed to propel her easily through the undergrowth that curtained the narrow entrance. Thorns and twigs scraped her face as he pushed her deeper into the dark space, eventually flinging her to the floor. He lit a match, then another. Above her, rusty hooks once used for game and fish were embedded in the ceiling. On the stone floor, there was an old ragged coil of rope. Taking a ball of heavy garden twine from his pocket, he bent down towards her and tried to grab her wrists. The match flame died. She scrambled back in the dark, away from him, but he struck her face a sharp blow with the flat of his hand.

She screamed. He hit her again.

'If you scream, they will come here and they will kill you. Do as I say and you will live. Hold out your hands because I am going to bind them and save your life. The choice is yours.'

'You know they killed Nancy?' Lydia said desperately.

'I know what they'll do to you.'

'Let me go, please,' she begged. 'It's not too late. We have to tell the police . . .'

He grabbed her hands roughly and pulled her closer. 'The problem with your generation,' he hissed, spitting his words directly into her face, 'is that you don't understand duty and honour. Loyalty to the King, observance of vows made, whatever the cost. My sons died for those beliefs. Do you think I would put your life above theirs?'

'Sir Norman, I beg you, it's not too late . . .' Lydia pleaded.

But he said no more. He bound her wrists and ankles and secured her with the rope to an iron ring embedded in the wall. He thrust a handkerchief into her mouth and wound more twine around her face so that she could not spit it out. She could barely breathe.

He lit another match and held it close to her face. 'I will come back for you when it is over. When the King is saved from the ungodly traitors.

And then you will thank me. You will thank me for saving your life. And, God willing, you will thank me for saving England.'

The match died, and he was gone.

It was dark now. No moonlight or starlight penetrated the ice house. How many hours had she been here? She lay curled up, barely able to move, struggling for every shallow breath, choking on the handkerchief. She still wore the clothes she had worn to the funeral: black dress, smart coat, gloves. Cold. So cold: she could not survive here long. A bullet in the head would be a more humane way to die than this.

She tried to think of something else, anything to soothe and slow her need for air in her lungs. She thought of Tom Wilde and how he would be worried about her. Tom would come to find her, she told herself. Would it ever start between them, she and Tom? she wondered. He was so dry; she was so passionate about everything she did. No, it was unfair to call him dry. He concealed his passions: a melancholy man, a man who had lost his wife and child, a man seeking some salvation. But he had loved before; perhaps he could love again.

And then there was Hartmut Dorfen. They had always known of his dark side. When they found him between Nancy's legs on the banks of the river, with Margot close by, she wondered whether he had wanted Margot to see. Had enjoyed her distress.

Hartmut had been their friend, their lover, their destroyer. Lover to them all, she acknowledged to herself, here in this dank, dark hole, with the air in her lungs thin and painful. Of course she hadn't admitted it to Nancy or Margot. But Hart had had them all that summer. One by one. Perhaps Margot had suspected. Perhaps that was what drove her insane. She hadn't understood that a man like Hartmut Dorfen couldn't be faithful to one woman. It wouldn't even occur to him. Why not? You all want me? Why would I not have other women if I want to?

Her breathing shortened by the second. What would happen first? Panic and then unconsciousness, she imagined. She must not panic, because that would consume oxygen. She must keep her eyes closed, not even try to move. Ignore the cold. Try to sleep. You are a cat trapped in a cupboard, she told herself. Curl up, relax, wait. Hereward will come back. He said he would come back.

In the shadows on the other side of the road from the college, Hartmut Dorfen smoked a cigarette and watched Thomas Wilde going into the porters' lodge. He was still smoking, still watching, as the professor came out.

Horace Dill's absence had saved his life. Dorfen had arrived at the college intending to kill him. The settling of an old score, a small strike for National Socialism against the insanity of Bolshevism. A balm for Sir Norman Hereward's vengeful soul. Wilde would not be so fortunate. Dorfen considered his next move.

He nodded towards a car parked fifty yards down Trumpington Street. Sawyer, in the driving seat, nodded back. Dill might have escaped temporarily, but they had killed Braithwaite, and now they would do for Wilde.

Wilde made his way to the Bull in case Eaton was there. He left a message and began loping through the cold streets home.

He heard footsteps behind him, the sharp tap of metal-toed shoes on paving stones. He looked round, alert for danger, to see the familiar figures of Roger Maxwell and Eugene Felsted, on the other side of the road. They crossed the road, weaving slightly.

'Merry Christmas, professor!'

'Not now, Maxwell.'

They were dressed as private eyes: thin ties and fedoras.

'We're on our way to a fancy-dress party. You told us to think like detectives, so we thought we'd dress like them.' Felsted was unsteady on his feet.

Wilde tapped his wristwatch. 'Look, I must go.'

'Actually, sir,' Maxwell said, 'we're going your way.'

They attached themselves to him like limpets to a ship's hull. Keeping pace with him. Quickening their strides as he quickened his.

And then they were outside his house. Next door, Cornflowers was still dark. Wilde turned, held up his hand to say this is really where we part ways, and was confronted by a pair of guns.

For a brief moment, Dorfen had thought of abandoning his plan when the two young men accosted Wilde. But word had come through that all loose ends must be tidied up, and this interfering professor was undoubtedly a loose end. He had been snooping at St Wilfred's; he had tried to force himself on Hereward, he had even been to Kilmington – and he had been a great deal too interested in the link between Dorfen and Sawyer. Wilde could not be allowed to return to St Wilfred's Priory. Tonight nor any other night.

'Through the gate.' He swivelled the pistols towards Maxwell and Felsted. 'And you.'

'What is this, Dorfen?' Wilde was horrified.

'Nothing to concern you.' Dorfen extended his arm and thrust the hard, dark barrel of one of the guns into Maxwell's face. 'Now. And you'll all be safe.'

Wilde knew Dorfen would have no compunction in shooting all three of them once they were out of sight in the passage between his house and Lydia's.

'You have no argument with these two young men . . .' Wilde began, but Dorfen's finger began to close on the trigger. 'OK, OK . . . we'll do what you say.'

'I say, this is past a joke,' Felsted said, not even trying to laugh. 'Those guns look real.'

Wilde gripped Felsted by the shoulder. 'It's no joke,' he said. He thought of blood, of bone fragments and brain tissue. 'Run,' he said in Felsted's ear, then louder. 'Run – for God's sake!' He pushed at the boy, but Felsted was frozen. Maxwell, too. Trapped by disbelief and fear. A car pulled up, a little red two-seater, and the driver emerged. 'Sawyer!' Wilde shouted. 'Get help!' But Sawyer, too, had a gun.

The two young men looked at Sawyer in shock. They knew him well from college. But it was Sawyer who, without a word, grasped their arms and pushed them, struggling, through the gate.

*

In the darkness of the garden, in the lee of both houses, they were invisible from the road.

'Tie them up,' Wilde pleaded, as Dorfen pushed him roughly behind them. 'Gag them. Leave them here. They're nobodies – they can't harm you.'

'Face the wall, in line. Nothing will happen.'

The voice was neither sharp, nor curt. Soft, reassuring.

'Does Margot know what you're doing? What you've already done?'

'In line, please. Face the wall.'

What do you do when a man holds a gun to your head and orders you to do something that will render you helpless, utterly at his mercy? Like the condemned man on the scaffold, you submit, even though you know death is coming. By submitting you might remain alive a few seconds or minutes longer, perhaps make death less painful; you hope, too, for a reprieve, that the killer might have a change of heart, that the police might arrive. But they won't, and you know it. There are no heroics when a man holds a loaded gun to your head.

'In the name of God,' Wilde begged again, 'spare the lives of these boys. They can't hurt you.' Except he knew they could. They could hurt Sawyer very badly.

Maxwell and Felsted were shaking, uncomprehending, but they did what they were told, standing on either side of Wilde. The three of them faced the dark brick of the side wall along the concrete pathway to the overgrown back garden of Wilde's pleasant house. Wilde smelt the sudden hot whiff of urine from his right. Felsted. Two seconds, then the crack of a gunshot. Maxwell crumpled. Wilde turned to plead again. A second shot, a sharp pain and he felt himself collapse in a heap. A third shot and Felsted crumpled.

'One bullet apiece,' said Sawyer.

'A bullet costs three pfennigs.' Dorfen thrust the pistol into his belt. 'With such economies, an empire might last a thousand years.'

It took a few moments for Wilde to realise he was alive. The movement of his head as the shot came had saved him. He could smell blood and cordite and burning and piss. His hair was burnt, the side of his head was scoured by the trace of the bullet. He could hear little but a savage ringing in his ear.

Someone gripped him by his hair. Wilde imagined them peering at the back of his head, before releasing it. Wilde allowed his head to drop, lifeless.

He waited, still as death, expecting the *coup de grâce*. Through the metallic thunder in his head, he heard their footsteps recede, then the car roared into life and sped off along the road. When he was sure it was gone, he clambered onto all fours, then to his haunches. He felt his head. Blood poured through his fingers.

'Felsted,' he said. 'Maxwell.' He touched their slumped bodies in turn, but there was no response, no pulse at their throats or wrists or chests. No breath. Two private eyes out for some fun at Christmas. He began to weep.

Hauling himself upright he stumbled along the passageway, up the steps to his front door, fumbling for the key as he ran. Inside he grabbed the telephone receiver. What in God's name was the number? It was there in pencil on a pad in front of him. He had written it himself when Lydia had first gone to the police station after finding Nancy's body. He dialled, his hand surprisingly steady. A desk officer answered. He shouted the address – told him to send an ambulance, doctors, anyone. Then he dropped the telephone; it clattered to the floor.

His motorbike goggles and gauntlets were on a shelf beside the coat-rack. He kept an electric torch there, the same one he had taken to Brandham Hall. He picked it up. It was dead. He kept matches and candles somewhere in the kitchen. Where?

He was in a hurry. The police would arrive soon, and he didn't want to be here. They would only hold him up. Behind him he heard someone trying the front door. It swung open. Too late. Not the police: Philip Eaton.

'You left a message . . .' Eaton tailed off and his mouth fell open, appalled. 'What's happened to you, Wilde? You look as if you've been shot.'

'I'm fine, but . . . Outside. Two bodies. Undergraduates. Wrong place. Wrong time. Sawyer and Dorfen shot us.'

'*Dr* Sawyer?'

'Yes, and Dorfen.'

'Good God, your head . . .'

'Don't worry about me.' Wilde let out a long, low breath of despair. 'God in heaven, Eaton, they were on their way to a Christmas party. Those poor boys. Their parents. What will I say to them?'

'Take it easy. We'll have a look outside. Show me.' Eaton was surprisingly calm.

'They stuck to me like glue. Jesus, I should have told them to fuck off.' Wilde put his head in his hands, combing his fingers through the tangle of hair and sticky blood. He recoiled when his finger touched the raw wound. The bullet had carved a furrow in the bone.

'Do you want me to look at that first?'

'No, but you'll have to speak up. My head's thundering.' Wilde began to open the front door, then stopped. 'My torch batteries are dead. I was looking for candles.'

'You're in shock. Take deep breaths. I have a torch.' Eaton took it from his coat pocket and switched it on.

Wilde ran along the passageway, Eaton behind him, his torch casting erratic light as he moved. The scene that met them was carnage. Blood on the wall; two lifeless bodies, one kneeling forward, his head against the wall, one splayed to the right. Eaton bent to check the pulses. Shook his head.

'This is it,' Eaton said under his breath.

'Come on,' Wilde said. 'My motorbike.'

'It's happening. Tonight. But where?'

'St Wilfred's. It must be. They wanted to stop me going to the priory . . .'

CHAPTER 35

The Rudge surged and roared beneath his body. Wilde pushed the motor-bike to the limit, sliding into the slippery bends and accelerating out; he had never ridden faster or with darker intent. He was riding for Lydia and Nancy and Maxwell and Felsted. Hartmut Dorfen and Duncan Sawyer would pay.

Eaton sat behind him on the pillion seat, his gloveless hands clasped round Wilde's waist. Within a hundred yards of St Wilfred's Priory, out of sight of the front windows, Wilde killed the engine. In his pocket he had a penknife for sharpening pencils. Nothing more.

Eaton dismounted, removed a pistol from his pocket and held it up to show Wilde.

Two windows were lit; otherwise the house was in darkness. The two men went to a side door and tried the handle. The door opened. They slipped inside and listened, but there were no sounds. The house seemed empty. They moved through the bootroom, the game room and the kitchens into the main body of the house. In the hall, portraits glared down at Wilde.

'I'm going upstairs,' Wilde said. 'You search the downstairs rooms.'

Eaton nodded, then moved on almost silent feet along the corridor in the direction Wilde had taken earlier in the day.

Wilde climbed the grand staircase to the first floor, his head pounding with pain. He didn't care any more. If Lydia was in the house, he would find her, and if he ran into Dorfen or Sawyer, then he could kill at least one of them. Wilde flung open door after door, switched on lights, wrenched cupboards open, then moved on. Bathrooms, bedrooms, laundry rooms, boxrooms were opened with a crash; he cared nothing about noise or disturbance.

He was in a bedroom, pulling at the cupboard doors. He turned at a sound. A maid stood in the doorway, mouth open in horror. His hand went to the knife in his pocket.

'What are you doing here?' She was a stout woman in her late twenties or early thirties. She was shaking with fear. 'Who are you?' Her eyes fell on the clotted and seeping blood at the side of his head oozing beneath his cap and goggles. She let out a gasp. 'Your head . . .'

He put his hand to the wound. 'This? I had an accident on the way here. Fell from my motorbike. It's nothing.' He forced himself to slow down. 'Look,' he said more gently, 'I'm not going to hurt you. My name is Professor Wilde. I think I saw you at the funeral reception earlier today. Weren't you serving drinks?'

'Yes, I was. But all the guests are long gone.' Her eyes strayed around the shambles of tossed bedding and open doors.

'I'm looking for a missing woman.'

'There's no woman here, only me.' Her voice was still nervous.

'Who else is in the house?'

'No one. All the servants have been sent home for the weekend. We all worked overtime at the funeral reception. I'm not supposed to be here, but I had to finish off.' She tensed; she had told him she was alone.

He held up his palms. 'I promise, you're safe with me. Did you see the young woman I was with at the funeral? Did you see her later, after we left?'

'Miss Morris, sir? I remember her. She was a friend of Miss Hereward.' She had stopped trembling. 'I haven't seen her here.'

He thought she was telling the truth. Lydia was unlikely to be in the house. Not if she was alive. 'Where has Sir Norman gone?'

'He didn't say, sir.' She was gaining in confidence. 'Now, please, you must go. I don't want to have to call the police.'

'Was he with Dr Sawyer? And the German?'

Her eyes were wide. She was afraid. If she didn't know what was going on, she certainly suspected something. 'Please, sir . . .' She was close to tears. 'I don't know anything about anything. I'm just the housemaid.' She put her hands to her eyes, sobbing.

Wilde ignored her. From somewhere to the east of the house, he heard the distant drone of an aeroplane, but the sound was deeper, bigger, more powerful than the yellow Sopwith that had landed earlier that day. He went across the corridor into Nancy's childhood bedroom, and looked out across the parkland.

There was little to see. The sky was dark. All he could make out beneath the clouds was the skeletal line of winter trees. Charcoal lines on black canvas. Then the clouds broke, revealing a waning moon, a little over half full, like a clipped silver coin. Out of the clouds, coming straight in his direction but still two or three miles distant, were the lights of a low-flying aeroplane. It came from the east. His first instinct was that it was too low, that it would crash into the woods. But the aeroplane began to turn in a gentle arc to make its descent to the hidden airstrip.

Wilde found Eaton in the hall. Together they ran from the house, mounted the Rudge and rode into the woods, along the paths he had taken earlier in the day. Low branches loomed, ghostly, from the darkness into his headlights and they had to duck and swerve.

A quarter of a mile from the landing strip, Wilde cut the engine and ditched the motorbike and they ran in silence along the pathway. Wilde no longer thought of the injury to his head or the blood caking his face. Nor was he afraid. There was only the need to find Lydia and the desire to avenge two innocent lives.

Stopping at the edge of the woods, they looked down across the greensward. Two lines of flaming torches lit the runway for the approaching plane. The aircraft was low in the sky, altitude less than a hundred feet, almost suspended in the air. In the light from the cockpit they saw two pilots. Two faces, a world away. Hanging there like a great unwieldy moth searching for a place to drop down between the blazing lines. The flames of the torches dashed and leapt in the wind.

The plane had three propellers, one on each wing and one on the nose cone, a trimotor passenger plane; no apparent markings.

'Junkers JU-52. German built. I rather think we're about to meet a band of heavily armed White Russians,' Eaton said in a low voice.

'White Russians?'

'Ssh. I'll explain later.'

In front of them three people stood watching the approaching aircraft: Dorfen, Sawyer and Hereward. Parked alongside the airstrip were two vehicles: a Rolls Royce and a closed truck. A welcoming party.

The plane landed smoothly, bumped along the grass, made a full turn, and came to a juddering halt dwarfing the tarpaulin-covered biplane parked nearby. At last, Wilde saw markings – a white cross on a red background on the tailplane and sides of the fuselage. Swiss.

The side door opened and a small flight of metal steps was lowered to the ground. Men in old leather jackets and Lenin caps, working-men's clothes, began to emerge. They may not have worn uniforms, but this was a fighting force. A dozen men in all, then the two pilots, accompanied by two men armed with sub-machine guns. There were raised-arm salutes, clicked heels, some shaking of hands.

Sawyer brought a tray of drinks from the back of the Rolls Royce and offered it round. All but the two with sub-machine guns drank quickly, then threw the glasses to the ground. Hereward drank in nervous, quick gulps. Did he have any concept of what he was dealing with here? Wilde wondered.

'Your gun,' Wilde whispered to Eaton. 'I don't think it's going to help us much against that crew.'

'No. All we can do is watch.'

Dorfen had taken aside one of the new men, a huge man with a bushy black beard. He had the look of a ragged animal, leader of a pack. Under his orders, the men formed a line from the door of the plane and began to unload a stream of weapons: automatic rifles, sub-machine guns, a heavy machine gun, and some bulky wooden crates. Dorfen, meanwhile, was conferring with the pilots.

The back of the truck was thrown open to reveal a partially lit cabin with bench seats on either side. It looked nothing like any vehicle Wilde had seen. Low and broad, it had the appearance of a dark metallic war machine, a tank without cannon, the sort of vehicle H. G. Wells might have imagined. Once the weapons were loaded into the back, the men themselves clambered in. Dorfen went over to them and said something quietly, finger to lips – silence.

Wilde spotted a stash of heavy jerry cans near the Rolls Royce. The two remaining men helped the two pilots haul them across to the aircraft, and lift them to pour into the fuel tank. Without a pump and line, it would be a slow process; perhaps just enough to get them back to wherever they had come from.

'As I said, they're White Russians.' Eaton spoke under his breath. 'A mercenary squadron linked to the SS. Call themselves the Romanov Division, I believe.'

'You knew about this?'

'I didn't know when they were coming or how or where, but I've been trying to discover their plans for quite a while. I need to call in the army.'

'Where are the bastards going?' Wilde whispered urgently.

The back doors of the vehicle were slammed shut. Dorfen went to the front and climbed into the driving seat. Sawyer and the bearded man went round the other side and climbed in beside him. The bonnet shuddered and the vehicle began to crawl away from the clearing towards the path through the trees, leaving the two pilots and their armed guards standing next to the plane.

'Hereward will know. I'll choke the truth out of him. I'll call for help from the priory.' Eaton looked at Wilde. 'I need you to follow them.'

'But what about Lydia?'

'If she's here, Hereward will know. I'll throttle it out of him. I'll find her.' Eaton fished out a scrap of paper and thrust it at Wilde. 'If you get a chance, call that number. Ask for Terence Carstairs. Say these words: *I'm calling for Eaton. The Russians are here.* Those words exactly. Then give him as much detail as you're able. I'll keep in touch with him; he'll know what to do.' He held out his pistol. 'Walther PP. Full magazine. Hope you don't need it.'

Eaton watched as Tom Wilde rode off into the night and then raced back to the priory. In the study, he grabbed the telephone. They would need roadblocks and alerts on all vulnerable points. He was not hopeful. There could be hundreds of targets in Cambridgeshire and thousands more beyond the immediate vicinity. How far would the White Russians travel on their murderous mission? How many troops could his superiors muster at half-past eight on a Saturday night in December?

In the distance, he heard the muffled roar of the JU-52's three motors firing up, then the receding hum as the aeroplane took off and disappeared into the night. The study door opened and Hereward walked in, cigarette in one hand, brandy glass in the other. He stopped, swaying slightly, and looked at Eaton.

'Do I know you?'

'Philip Eaton.'

'I've heard of you.' Hereward pointed at the brandy decanter. 'Help yourself. It's my best Cognac.'

Eaton ignored him. Hereward shrugged and sank into one of his leather armchairs.

'This has all got a bit out of hand, hasn't it, Hereward? Correct me if I'm wrong, but it wasn't supposed to involve the death of your daughter, was it?'

'What exactly are you implying?'

'She found out what you and Sawyer and the others were up to. She had to be silenced, didn't she?'

Hereward said nothing.

'Well?'

'You're North Sea, aren't you? You're certainly on the list. I thought you were with us. I've nothing to say to you.'

'You've been duped all along – and you've paid a price no man should have to pay.'

'Get out.' Hereward's words were slurred. 'You're too late anyway.'

'You can still go some way towards making things right, you know.' Eaton approached him and leant over. 'Tell me now where they're going, and you may yet find some peace. This is for your King and country, Hereward.'

'King and country?' The older man gave a bitter laugh and threw the contents of the brandy glass down his throat. 'We turned our children to dust for King and country. My boys, both of them shot to hell. And we're still fighting. Didn't you know, they're planning to get rid of him? Baldwin and Dawson and Chamberlain and Lang and all the other treacherous, sanctimonious bastards are plotting against the King. All those damnable words: *oust, depose, usurp, treachery, treason, cheat.* Slippery, slimy, dirty words, all of them, Eaton. And they apply to Baldwin and company. Traitors every one.'

Eaton ripped the cigarette from Hereward's hand and threw it to the floor, grinding it into the rich Persian carpet with his heel. 'If Sawyer and Dorfen are your friends, then who are your enemies?'

'It looks very much as if *you* are, Eaton.'

Eaton put his hands out to grasp Hereward's well-fed neck. The door opened. A shambling, bespectacled figure shuffled in, hat in hand.

'What the hell are you doing here, Bower?' Eaton demanded.

'Come to do my job, Mr Eaton. Come to do my job. Now, Sir Norman, is this man bothering you?'

On the road the truck was even more menacing than it had seemed at the airstrip: squat and windowless. Wilde kept well back, feeling the weight of the pistol in his coat pocket. He was glad to have it, but what use was one gun against a heavily armed squadron?

Up ahead, the dark vehicle was turning right. Wilde followed it, holding the Rudge as far back as he could. He hoped there was enough fuel in the tank.

Vladimir Rybakov sat perched on the truck's front seat between Sawyer, who was navigating, and Dorfen, at the wheel. They stank of cordite and blood. This was a great deal less comfortable than the three-and-a-half hour flight from Bremen. Fears of bad weather closing in had proved unfounded. During the early part of the journey, Rybakov had flown up front with Hans Baur and his co-pilot.

'The stillness of the night sky, Mr Rybakov,' Baur had said cheerfully. 'Beneath us the vast expanse of the North Sea – the water that links us to Britain.'

'And keeps you separate.'

'Indeed. You know, I love the dark hours. I flew the Führer by night across Germany during the election. I loved to show him the lights of the cities beneath us.' He laughed. 'The great man had a fear of flying.'

'Hitler?' Rybakov was surprised.

Baur laughed. 'Don't tell him I told you.'

Rybakov had spent the rest of the flight trying to calm the nerves of his men. Half of them were silent, the other half agitated. The fuselage smelt of gasoline and vomit; two men were airsick. Spain had been one thing; this was quite another. During their training sessions at Lichter-felde, there had been arguments about the operation. Great Britain was a friend to the White Russians, was it not? Could it be right to launch an attack in such a country even if it was to save the King? Only those who had not expressed these reservations had been selected for the mission, but still there were doubts. Doubts that, in his heart, Rybakov himself shared. But thus far, this was their best hope.

He was edgy. Dorfen kept saying the same thing over and over again. 'You must speak Russian at all times. No German, no English. Only Russian. Do you understand, Rybakov?'

'I understand. You have told us all this before. But, you know, some of my men are more fluent in French than Russian. They have grown up in France . . .'

'Well then, tell them to keep their mouths shut. And if by misfortune any man is taken, he must say that he was landed by boat on the east coast of England, he does not know exactly where or from which port in the Baltic he left. He must say that you were met by an Englishman who spoke some Russian who had transport waiting. And that is all he knows.'

'They understand. I understand. It was drummed into us.'

'And all the weapons? No one has slipped a Mauser or Luger into their jacket?'

'Only Tokarevs and PPDs. And this operation . . .'

'Patience.'

'At least tell me the target.'

'Two English traitors. Two men who would depose their king, to whom they have sworn allegiance. This will be your most glorious night.

The SS Romanov Division will be hailed by good men throughout the ages to come.'

'Who are these traitors?'

'Baldwin, the British prime minister, and the Duke of York, the King's brother. Can you imagine any creature more loathsome – a man who would conspire to topple his own brother? Who would not wish to shoot such a dog?'

CHAPTER 36

They were winding their way through a series of country roads in an intricate, southerly direction, edging round to the west of Cambridge. It was a slow, complicated route, one that had been picked out to confuse: even if Eaton had succeeded in calling in the army, they would never find them. Wilde was alone. From the certainty with which each turn was taken, he guessed that the route had been rehearsed. Duncan Sawyer was nothing if not meticulous.

The vehicle ahead was going thirty to forty miles per hour and often slower than that, for the roads were mostly narrow and not in good repair. Wilde had no difficulty keeping in touch with it; the problem was how to remain unobserved: there was little other traffic. He kept a steady distance behind the truck, as far back as he could manage without losing it. At times, on a long stretch with good visibility ahead, he pulled into a layby and waited twenty seconds, even half a minute. Whenever he had the chance, he allowed another vehicle to overtake him. The cloud had mostly cleared, leaving the dull light of a half-moon. On certain stretches of the deserted road, he switched off the headlight.

He glanced at the fuel gauge. He'd been going for nearly two hours. Still over half full. Despite his heavy gauntlets, his hands were frozen. It was agony merely to grip the handlebar.

Yuri Kholtov lay curled up on the floor of the farm cottage. Every time he tried to move, he cried out in pain. His ankle was shattered. He was sure, too, that at least three of his ribs were broken. His head was throbbing where Eaton had beaten him again and again.

He was bruised and bloodied, but he had not been left for dead. Eaton had known he was alive, for he had said he would be back; there was unfinished business between them.

The little cat licked his face, savouring the salt. He no longer wanted the damned thing and pushed it away, but the effort sent a searing pain down along his arm into the side of his torso. And the pain was becoming worse, for the effect of the vodka was wearing off. How many hours had he been here? How long before Eaton returned to finish him off?

Think, he told himself. Steel yourself. You have been through much in your life. There is a way out of this. You are a survivor; you will survive this and look back on it and laugh.

Yet even if he could escape from this filthy cottage in the middle of nowhere, how long would it be before he was picked up by the police to face a murder charge?

But he had to try because waiting here was not an option. If a man cannot run, then he must walk. If he cannot walk, he must limp. And if he cannot limp, he must crawl.

And so he crawled, and somehow he made it to the open door.

Prime Minister Stanley Baldwin and Prince Albert, Duke of York, were unlikely men to be involved in a palace coup. Neither gave the impression of desiring more power than he had; neither seemed to have a reason to bear a grudge against the King. What they did have in common was an intense patriotism, a belief in doing the right thing for Britain and the Empire and the Church of England. And in the eyes of both men, the as-yet still uncrowned King Edward VIII was doing the wrong thing in wishing to marry the twice-divorced Mrs Wallis Simpson.

Now, this winter's night, Stanley Baldwin was preparing to travel to Royal Lodge in Windsor Great Park, the home of the Duke of York. It had been a particularly trying year for Baldwin: a succession of crises in Europe, and a series of health problems. His doctor had told him he was suffering from nervous exhaustion. Not this night, though.

His fingers tightened round the glass. How could the King not understand? His wish to marry Mrs Simpson was irreconcilable with his position as head of the Church and Empire: right-thinking men and women were horrified. Those old enough to remember her wondered how the dear old Queen Empress would have viewed these goings-on. God's teeth, even the humble marchers of the Jarrow Crusade were said to be appalled that a King of England could consider marrying a divorcee.

There were others, Baldwin acknowledged, who believed the King should be free to marry the woman he loved. Prominent members of the establishment: Winston Churchill, David Lloyd George, popular newspapers like the *Daily Mail* and *Daily Express*. Baldwin ground his teeth in frustration. It was *he* who held the reins of power and he was determined the King must either give up Mrs Simpson or renounce the throne. In this, he had the backing of his Cabinet. There could be no compromise.

Baldwin sipped his whisky as he considered Prince Albert. He was a shy, sickly man, his timidity accentuated by a speech impediment, a heavy smoker; but biddable enough. Although he had no desire to take the throne, he was driven by an old-fashioned sense of duty: please God, he would accept it. But nothing could be taken for granted. Baldwin knew he would have to exercise all his guile and charm to ensure that the transition went smoothly. The upheaval over Mrs Simpson was quite enough on its own; the country would be shaken to its core by an abdication. Baldwin could not afford any hiccoughs.

He lit his pipe and considered the words he would use. *Duty to Empire. Duty to God and country. We must put aside our own misgivings, Your Royal Highness. No one can take pleasure in your brother's decision. In some respects, we are similar men, you and I. Neither of us seeks glory or fame. And yet there are times when a man must step into the breach. We must, indeed, steel ourselves to the task ahead.*

Above all, he knew, he must use the duchess's influence. Elizabeth was his greatest ally. She was wrought from iron. She knew her husband would make a greater sovereign than the undignified Edward could ever make. More than that, she knew that her place was at Albert's side, as Queen and mother to his heirs, the little princesses, Elizabeth and Margaret Rose.

Baldwin finished off the whisky. He had a flask in his coat pocket for the journey. He turned to his aide.

'Do we know what his thoughts are?'

'I believe he has been quite calm since returning from Edinburgh, prime minister.'

'Doesn't tell us much. If I know him, his stomach will be churning.' He nodded towards the window. 'Any newspapermen about?'

'No, prime minister,' the aide said. 'The coast is clear.'

The meeting with the duke had to be secret; the King must not know. He would see it as conspiratorial. It might even stiffen his resolve, make him turn away from abdication at the last moment and fight to remain monarch as bloody Wallis Simpson wanted him to do. Although Baldwin hated to admit it to himself, Edward had considerable pockets of support among his subjects, and even some support in parliament and the colonies. Word of this meeting must never get out.

'How long will it take?'

'Depends on the state of the roads, sir. About an hour. Perhaps less. There will be next to no traffic.'

Baldwin looked at his wristwatch: 11.00 p.m. 'Call the duke and tell him we're on our way. My apologies for arriving at such an ungodly hour. And tell him I would be grateful if the duchess could be in attendance.'

'Yes, prime minister. I have already told them we would like her there.'

'And fill my tobacco pouch for me, if you would. I fear this will be a long night.'

Wilde was bitterly cold. He had been looking at the fuel gauge with increasing concern. There was little petrol left, certainly no more than a gallon, and he would be lucky if he managed another twenty miles.

By now, he knew that he was deep into the south of England. The countryside suddenly changed dramatically. This was nothing like the villages or country lanes through which he had passed. On his left, high walls loomed out of the darkness, but the truck carried on and he found himself in a wide-open parkland of oaks and bridleways. Suddenly, he recognised where he was. He had been here once before, researching his Walsingham book. This was Windsor Great Park. The cold knotted and twisted in his belly. The King had a home near here: Fort Belvedere.

Ahead, the dark truck took a sharp left turn up an incline. It accelerated, crashing through a wooden fence, and continued lumbering up the hill.

Wilde brought the Rudge to a halt at the side of the road and killed the headlight. The numbness of his hands and feet, the aching cold in his cheeks and eyes consumed him. He looked about him for a telephone kiosk or a house from which he could call, but there was nothing. He waited and watched as the black vehicle trundled, tank-like, up the grassy slope. Instead of disappearing into the copse ahead, it halted just before and extinguished the headlights. No more than half a mile away.

Just as Wilde was about to slide from the saddle, a car appeared, driving slowly along the main road.

Baldwin's journey to Windsor Great Park from Downing Street had been as smooth as expected through the suburbs of west London, along the new stretch of the Great West Road, past thousands of brand-new houses costing £500 apiece and new factories bringing popular brands of bathroom products to the masses. Now, if anything, they were a little early.

In the back of the Rolls, Baldwin had a small electric torch. He checked his wristwatch: nearly midnight. He infinitely preferred meeting Prince Albert to his brother. They had similar tastes: liked the quiet life, hated flash; as did their wives. Both men were appalled by the louche set that surrounded the King and his dreadful American concubine. Baldwin sniffed. Too dignified a word for her, concubine. Tart was better. She was a tart.

The interior of the car was a rich fog of tobacco smoke. Baldwin drew on his pipe, but the glow had died. He fished in his pocket for his pouch, drew out a few strands of aromatic tobacco and tamped them into the bowl. He hadn't touched the whisky in his flask. He might need it for the journey home. It had been a bad forty-eight hours. His spies had told him that Winston bloody Churchill had been meddling; he had visited Fort Belvedere yesterday to see the King. Two hours later a letter arrived at Downing Street from Winston begging the prime minister to delay the abdication. The King, he believed, was just a young man in love; he must be given leeway. Today had only made matters worse, with Winston issuing a statement to the press pleading for 'patience'. Patience? What good would that do? This thing had to be dealt with as quickly as possible. Lance the boil before the poison leaks into the body.

Now the Whips were telling Baldwin that forty or more Conservative MPs were willing to back a King's Party. Winston was already drawing up plans for an alternative Cabinet at his flat in Westminster. Meanwhile, in darker corners, the fascist-leaning Lord Londonderry was said to have his own designs on the premiership. Was that Churchill's ulterior motive, too? You never could tell with Winston. One thing was certain, there had to be something in it for him; altruism and Churchill were words that did not sit well together.

At the last moment before they set off, Royal Lodge had told him that the duchess wouldn't be there, that she was laid up with influenza. But as the car glided silently through Windsor Great Park, Baldwin still felt a glow of warmth. Albert would undoubtedly talk to her by telephone and her response was certain. 'You must do this, Bertie,' she would say. And he would not demur. Elizabeth always knew what was best for him.

By night, the world of the park was one of shadows. Nothing like it existed anywhere else in England; this was the country's ancient heart. It was dark, but he could sense the thousands of undulating acres and its history all around him. It had been a vast forest, the hunting ground of monarchs through the centuries, a recreation ground for the royal and the great. The woods were thinned out now, but great trees still loomed all around, many decked with large, perfect bundles of mistletoe, ready for Christmas picking. Beneath them, the red deer huddled together, seeking warmth.

Nature nurtured, thought Baldwin. A little like myself. The rough edges smoothed off. The affable assassin.

Wilde watched the car coast by. As it passed, a match flared and momentarily lit the interior. Good God, Wilde thought. Stanley Baldwin. Where was he going?

He ran now, loping across open land following the direction taken by the truck. As he ran, he thrust his hand into his coat pocket and felt the cold steel of the Walther.

The half-moon gave him just enough silvery light. At first it seemed the ground was firm, but it soon became boggy underfoot and his shoes squelched into deep, cloying mud, up to the ankle.

He could see the truck up ahead, and slowed down. The terrain was littered with deadwood and old trunks blown down by the winter winds. They gave him some cover, but also impeded his progress. He was no more than a hundred yards from the vehicle when its rear doors were thrown open and light flooded out. Almost as quickly, the light was extinguished, but he had seen what he needed to see: a dozen or so men disgorged, all of them carrying arms.

Below him he could hear the sounds of the prime minister's car sweeping on up the road, past the men and their truck, oblivious to their presence.

To the left, across parkland, Wilde saw the lights of a big house. That must be where Baldwin was heading, unaware of the desperate danger he was in. Wilde gripped the little Walther, leapt from his cover and began running towards the house. He no longer felt the throbbing of his injured head. He ran low and fast and when he was thirty yards from the vehicle he stopped and caught his breath. Ahead of him, the militia had formed into a concave arc and was moving off, down the slope.

There was no time for choice. No time to do the sane thing and dodge past these men. No time to reach the house to warn those inside. He thought of his Harrow classmates. Half of them had died in the trenches. They had done their duty. They had known the terrible risks. Who was he to fail them now?

The sharp crack of the Walther shattered the night. The recoil jerked his right arm backwards. He fired again, and again: three times, in rapid succession. Gunshots in the night to alert a royal house to danger.

CHAPTER 37

Almost hidden away, very close to the centre of Windsor Great Park's five thousand acres, sat the soft pink, almost white, walls of Royal Lodge, home of Prince Albert, Duke of York, his wife Elizabeth and their two daughters, Elizabeth and Margaret Rose. The duchess had presided lovingly over its restoration. Now it was full of light and life. A Hollywood house, fit for a Fairbanks or a Pickford. More than anything, it was a family home.

At the heart of the house was the saloon. Forty feet long, lit by three great chandeliers of Waterford crystal, it turned the building from a large, pleasantly appointed country house into something a little more palatial. This was where the duke received Stanley Baldwin. This was the room where it had been decided they were to die.

The Russians moved down the incline towards the house's perimeter fence, dark shadows in the dull shine of the moon. They walked two metres apart, weapons at the ready.

At the sharp report of Wilde's pistol, they instantly stopped and dropped to one knee. Their leader made frantic motions with his right hand for them to get lower. With a flick of his other hand he detached two men and pointed uphill in the direction of Wilde and the gunfire.

They were coming to get him. A guttural voice, barking an order. He crouched low beneath a fallen oak bough. A burst of sub-machine gunfire shattered the chill night air. A thousand birds flew from their perches in wild, uncomprehending panic. Wilde hugged the soft, leafy ground.

Two men came back up the slope, sub-machine guns slung low.

From his cover, Wilde fired again and again. How many bullets did he have left?

The advancing gunmen recoiled at the sound of his shots. Another burst of bullets spewed from their muzzles.

Below, he could see the militia moving again, their semi-circle fanning out so that the flanks were twenty yards ahead of the centre. They had reached a pond, no more than a hundred yards from the big house. Without pausing, they broke down the tall, chestnut fence in front of them, passing through the gap to open land. Wilde pulled the trigger again and his shot rang out, harsh and short. He heard another shouted order.

The only advantage he had was that they had no idea what weapons or ammunition he had; no idea that he was alone. He pulled the trigger again. Nothing. The magazine was empty. Had they heard the telltale click? If so, he was done for.

From down below, on the far side of the pond, there was a sudden manic hail of gunfire. But it wasn't aimed at him. A hand grenade exploded, then another. The crack of more gunshots. Wilde crawled to the left, through the thick layer of leaves. From below, the sound of bullets and explosions came in intense bursts. There were groans, a few screams. Then silence.

Joseph Saddlesmith and his wife lived in one of the new houses, in the area of Great Park known as the Village, beside the Crown Estate Office and the workshops. Like everyone else who lived there, he was an estate worker, and like most men of his generation, he had been a soldier. He knew the sounds of war.

It was just after midnight. Like every night, whatever the weather, he was out walking his fox terrier before turning in. As usual, he strolled up past the little village store, then turned south until he reached Dark Wood, allowing the dog to run free. As he entered the copse, he stopped abruptly and called her to him. From across the Great Park, perhaps a mile or two, perhaps less, came familiar sounds, echoing from the trenches, down the years. Saddlesmith's heart began to race. He couldn't breathe. He started to tremble; then his whole body shook, his legs began to buckle. He put a hand down to steady himself on the dog's back, and fell to his knees.

He had no idea how long he knelt there. When he regained his wits, he got to his feet and stumbled on. What was happening?

*

Vladimir Rybakov and the other men of the Romanov-SS Division never stood a chance. They were cut down like corn before a scythe. Most of them died very quickly. With a bullet in his left leg and two in the left shoulder, Rybakov fell to the ground and survived a little longer. Long enough to see a British officer standing over him, pointing a revolver at his face.

'*Russki*,' he said, and raised his own Russian-made pistol in a shaking hand. The British officer's bullet blew a hole in Rybakov's heart.

From his cover, Wilde watched with a strange mixture of horror and relief: horror at the brutal, shattering rattle of sustained gunfire, the screams, the deaths; relief that the attack had been so swiftly countered.

By now, the whole area was bathed in floodlight from the back of a pair of army trucks. In the glare, he could see the ground in front of them, littered with dead. The attackers had been completely outgunned; met by an overpowering onslaught of fire.

But the attackers were *not* all accounted for. Wilde had watched as two men slipped away into the dark of the trees and the thick covering of the rhododendron bushes. He had seen them go and he knew who they were.

He stayed crouched in darkness, away from the harsh electric glare of the army floodlights. He considered emerging from the bushes with his hands up, but there was no guarantee he would not be shot in the aftermath of such carnage. Instead, he slid back further and crawled towards the bushes into which Dorfen and Sawyer had disappeared.

His thrust his empty pistol in his pocket. He had no torch, no way of signalling to the troops below the danger that remained. His only weapon was a blunt penknife.

He moved through the night on pale moonlight and instinct. He had seen Dorfen's torch, before it disappeared into the undergrowth. From the arc of the chestnut fence that marked the boundary of the private land, Wilde guessed they were heading towards the house. Not far ahead he could hear the rustle of leaves, the spring of young branches. Whispered words.

*

Hartmut Dorfen was two steps ahead of Duncan Sawyer. There was still a chance to salvage the operation. If he and Sawyer could get to the other side of the house, it might not be guarded. A bullet through a window. There was still hope.

Blood dripped from Dorfen's left hand where half his thumb had been blown away by a bullet. The pain was burning through his hand; he ignored it. His tongue went to the false tooth made of glass; one hard bite and the cyanide would kill him in seconds. It was a fallback; he could not afford to be taken alive. No one must have proof of German involvement in this operation.

On the other side of the maze of bushes and to the right was a chapel. The main building, lights blazing in the windows, stood in front of him. In the driveway, a black Rolls Royce was parked among other cars, and a pair of army troop carriers. The whole area was swarming with soldiers.

Dorfen switched off his torch and halted. Sawyer stopped behind him. Ahead of them was a small garden complete with a tiny cottage: the little princesses' playhouse.

'What now?' Sawyer whispered.

'We wait. They will appear. Then we will kill them.'

'It's suicide.'

'Does that worry you, my friend?'

'You know me better than that.'

There was a sound behind them. Dorfen gripped Sawyer's arm with his uninjured right hand.

'Behind us,' whispered Sawyer. He looked down at Dorfen's left hand, thick with blood. 'I'll go.' He thrust his Russian-made Tokarev TT-33 pistol into his jacket pocket and, taking a long-bladed knife from his belt, crept slowly back along the path through the rhododendron bushes.

Crouched in the undergrowth a few yards away, Wilde's eyes had become accustomed to the cloying gloom. He heard a rustle of undergrowth, then saw the flash of sharp steel. He was already twisting sideways as it came thrusting down like a bolt. The blade missed his body and plunged into the soft earth.

He had never known himself capable of such anger. He knew now how men, in the rage of battle, could maim and scalp. Killing alone was not enough. His right fist hammered into the side of Sawyer's head. The blow caught Sawyer square on the temple and he fell awkwardly, stunned, yet still holding the haft of his dagger. Wilde was up now. He leapt on his assailant, knees on his chest, desperately trying to break Sawyer's grasp on the knife. Sawyer's fingers were slippery and he was dazed from the blow. Wilde tore the weapon from him and raised it, gripped in both hands.

The point hovered for a split second above Sawyer's startled face. Wilde faltered. Sawyer momentarily regained his senses and began scrabbling at his pocket. A pistol? Wilde's hand continued its journey, diverted downwards from the face, and thrust the blade deep into the exposed throat. Blood gushed out in a fountain. Sawyer's mouth gaped open as though crying out, but it was nothing but a gurgle of blood. The rattle, panic and fury of imminent death.

Wilde pulled the blade out. In the dim moonlight, he felt down the dying man's body until he found the gun. He began to crawl forward again.

The prime minister and the Duke of York were leaving from a doorway at the side of the house where the official cars were parked alongside the army vehicles. At their side were two servants in the soft green livery of the Windsor household. But others surrounded them: men in military uniform. Within a few moments, Stanley Baldwin, pipe in mouth, and Prince Albert, with cigarette in hand, would both be in the line of fire of Sturmbannführer Hartmut Dorfen.

They were twenty, perhaps thirty, yards away. Dorfen raised his PPD-34 to his chest, his shredded thumb thudding with pain. It was a Russian sub-machine gun, a new design, captured in Spain, fitted with a 71-round drum magazine. Seventy-one bullets, to be fired in six lethal seconds. A spray of lead that would certainly kill both the prince and the prime minister and all of those around them: the armed soldiers, the grey-suited officials, the chauffeur bowing as he opened the back door to the Rolls Royce for Baldwin. And then, perhaps, he would make his escape. If not, then so be it. He would have done his duty.

He sensed something behind him. He turned to motion Sawyer down and came face to face with a ghost, a man he had already killed in a little side alleyway in the town of Cambridge.

'Put your weapon down.' Wilde aimed Sawyer's pistol straight at Dorfen's face.

Dorfen laughed, turned back and pulled the trigger.

Wilde fired, but he was too late. Dorfen was down, tumbling forward, the PPD-34 discharging its drum of bullets into the earth beneath him, his molars crunching involuntarily into the cyanide pill. Wilde's own bullet went over the German's head and smacked into a tree some seventy yards away. Dorfen was already dead, a neat little bullet hole in his head from the scoped rifle of a British Army sniper on the roof of Royal Lodge.

Wilde dropped the pistol and threw his hands up in surrender. 'Don't shoot!' he yelled. 'Don't shoot!'

Twenty or more soldiers had their guns trained on him. They remained silent. Wilde looked down at the body by his feet. A rectangular scrap of paper lay in the mud. It must have fallen from Dorfen's pocket: a photograph of a man and three young women, happy and smiling on a summer's day, outside the majestic, turreted stones of a Cambridge college.

It was over.

Except it wasn't. Lydia Morris was still missing.

Just before half-past midnight, on Timberlodge Hill, not far from Royal Lodge, Joseph Saddlesmith was stopped by two men in army fatigues, carrying Lee Enfields. They glanced at his flat cap and his dog, and told him to go home and say nothing to anyone.

Had no one else heard the shooting? Why was no one else about? In the morning he would tell his wife what had happened. No doubt she would nod as she made his breakfast and got the children off to school, but she wouldn't believe him, not until she read it in the newspaper. A gun battle in the middle of Windsor Great Park? Soldiers with Lee Enfields? Just another bad dream, Joe.

Perhaps no one would believe him. Perhaps he had dreamt it. Better, perhaps, to say nothing. He'd keep his counsel as the soldiers had said he should. A soldier still at heart, Saddlesmith obeyed orders.

SUNDAY DECEMBER 6, 1936

CHAPTER 38

Kholtov tried to lie still in the cold, heavy mud. He could hear the car on the long farm-track from the main road and he could see its light. He was a hundred metres away from the track; even so, he wasn't safe.

The car stopped at the cottage. He could hear the car door opening and shutting and then Eaton's footsteps entering the half-derelict building. It would not take him long to discover it was empty.

There was nothing to be done but to stay still, endure the savage cold and the never-ending pain. He could not run, nor could he hide. In his pocket, he had a pistol, but Eaton, too, would be armed. He would only use the gun if he had no option. Until then, all he could do was lie here in the thick, fertile earth of this desolate field and hope that the Englishman did not find him.

Philip Eaton cursed. God damn this night. For hours, he had been engaged in frantic telephone calls at the Bull, both to Terence Carstairs at the office and with more senior men. It was only when word came through from Carstairs that an attack had been foiled at Royal Lodge that he could relax. He had told Carstairs to go home and get some sleep. Meanwhile he would tend to his other business: the bloody Russian and his gold.

He swung his torch in a great arc, its beam sweeping across the landscape. A low mist hovered barely a foot above ground. He moved away from the track into the muddy field. The soil was thick and at each step his shoes seemed to accumulate more mud.

God in heaven, how had Kholtov managed to get away? He had left him unconscious, his left ankle a wreck, his body broken. Had someone come to him and taken him away?

Walking back to the cottage he shone his torch low, looking for footprints, but there were none. At the edge of the field he thought he detected flattening of the earth, as though someone or something had dragged itself, slug-like, across the surface. But after a few feet, he lost the trail amid the furrows.

Dawn was hours away. Even if Kholtov was still here, there was no chance of finding him until then. If he was already gone, he couldn't wait to find out. He switched off the torch and strode back to the car. Carstairs would have to get back to his desk. A bit of old-fashioned detection was called for.

When Kholtov heard the car driving back along the farm track to the road, he began to crawl again.

To dull the pain he tried to empty his mind, but the memories came anyway. He thought of Barcelona where he had first met Philip Eaton. Everyone knew *The Times* journalist worked for the British secret service, sending reports from Catalonia back to London. Slutsky had been told by Moscow that an eye was to be kept on him, but he was not to be harmed. No one wanted to provoke the British; their Royal Navy was already patrolling too close to the coast for comfort.

The British Consulate had told Kholtov that Mr Eaton would most probably be found at the Continental, one of the city's grand old hotels. Kholtov found him in a sumptuous suite, drinking good brandy and eating a meal in solitary splendour. This was not a place for the masses, even in a town supposedly ruled by the proletariat.

Eaton had invited Kholtov to sit down. 'Why have you come, Mr Kholtov?' he asked after Kholtov had introduced himself. 'Do you have a story for me?'

'A story?'

'As you know I am a correspondent for a British newspaper.'

'I do not have a story,' Kholtov had said. 'But I am going to England. And it is possible we might be able to help each other when I am there.'

'I doubt you will be very welcome in England.'

'That is where you can help me.'

'Are you going to tell me more?'

'In my own way. I need to make certain contacts before I go.'

'You already speak English.'

'Yes, I learnt it well. I have spent a good deal of time in your country.'

'Not killing people, I trust. There seems to be an awful lot of killing here in Barcelona these days, and you Ogpu or NKVD men – whatever you call yourselves these days – always seem to be in the vicinity of the bloodshed.'

Kholtov had laughed. That was the curious thing about the British: you could actually find yourself being charmed by their upper classes. Such a thing could never have happened in Russia. That did not mean, of course, that he trusted Eaton. One thing the NKVD had taught him was to put your trust in no one unless absolutely necessary. 'My hands are as clean as any man's, Mr Eaton,' he said. 'And I am sure we can forge a relationship of mutual benefit. If you help me with a certain matter, then I will reveal a secret of great import to your country.'

'What sort of secret?'

'A conspiracy. I hear things – from both sides, republican and nationalist. The lines are porous. An old man with a donkey can pass from fascist territory to ours, and back again. I have been in Cartagena recently. I heard something there. And I have heard more here, confirming it.'

'Yes?'

'There is a Russian militia.'

'Well, of course, there are whole battalions of Russians here in Spain, including you and your friend Abram Slutsky, Mr Kholtov.'

'No, not here with the republicans. On the nationalist side, with Franco's rebels. The Nazis have sent a White Russian militia to them. They are in the region of Huesca.'

'That is certainly vaguely interesting.'

'But there is more. This militia is being withdrawn. My source tells me they have another mission, a secret mission. In England.'

Suddenly, Eaton was listening. 'What would White Russian fighting men be doing in England?'

'I will tell you when I have safe passage to England.'

'Not good enough. If you have any information about this militia's mission, I need to know it now.'

Kholtov shrugged. 'And then I have no bargaining tool.'

'If we wait until you arrive in England, it may be too late.'

'No, there is time enough. And before that I will give you a name. Just one name.'

'Yes?'

'It was overheard in a discussion between two SS officers. It is a name I have never heard before, but perhaps it will mean something to you.'

'Try me.'

'I will call you as soon as I am sure you have arranged entry to England for me.'

'Tell me now.'

Kholtov had grinned. 'All I will tell you is that there is a link to your great university town, Cambridge. I know it well. Let us meet there – I can see friends, do some business perhaps.'

Eaton was not entirely happy, but the smile still hovered around his eyes and lips. 'I will do what I can. See if I can pull a few strings. But I will expect that name *before* you arrive – and the full story when we meet.'

'Then you have a deal.'

They clinked glasses. Eaton would get Kholtov into England, but he would expect much in return. It was not a perfect solution, but it was the best he could do.

'Do you need a train ticket to Perpignan?' Eaton asked. 'I can help you with funds.'

Kholtov laughed. He would never get out alive if he went by train. 'Very generous, Mr Eaton, but I think I will go through the mountains. Up to Prats de Mollo, then down the Tech Valley, then it will be easy through France. I will call you from Dover – and you will help me with another little matter.'

'Oh yes?'

'It is not much. A little service. It will be easy for you. I will explain everything when I arrive.'

'Leave a message with *The Times*.' Eaton had handed him his card.

But, Kholtov thought bitterly, Eaton had failed him. Neither he nor the fat gold-dealer he had brought was to be trusted. He raised his head from the furrow. Somehow he had to get out of this field and reach the coast where the *Gaviota* and the gold awaited him. He would head for the open seas: there was no trade to be done here.

From Windsor Great Park, Wilde was taken across country to a dull military office in an army garrison on the eastern margins of Salisbury Plain.

Men came and went, some in uniform, some in civilian clothes. None of them identified themselves. He guessed they were military intelligence, possibly MI5. He said the same thing to each of them. 'I need to get out of here urgently. Call Philip Eaton. Please.' He had handed them Eaton's card with Carstairs's number on it. To no avail.

Fighting exhaustion, he gave them the story, as he knew it. He told them again and again about Lydia, begged them to call Eaton, and got no answer. He was suspected of involvement in the deaths of two young men found at his house in Cambridge, he was told. He indicated his bandaged head. 'And do you think I did this to myself, too?'

Sometime before dawn, he lay down on the floor and fell asleep. He dreamed that his long-dead father came to him and held him in his arms, a thing that had never happened while he was alive. His father told him that the boy in the Winslow Homer picture was him, young Tom. *You were the boy with the longing in his eyes.* It was a dream so real that when he awoke later, he still felt the warmth of the old man's arms about him and he wanted to cry.

At about six o'clock, they brought him bacon and eggs, toast and marmalade, and a mug of very sweet tea.

The questioning started again and continued throughout the morning. And then, just before midday, Philip Eaton arrived and the mood changed.

'You look a state,' were the first words Eaton uttered. 'We need to get you cleaned up.'

'You don't look so good yourself. But to hell with that – what about Lydia?'

'Ah, yes, that's not good news. Come on, let's get you back to Cambridge.'

CHAPTER 39

Tom Wilde had not come for her. And nor had Hereward. She had found that death came slowly, that if you suppressed your hysteria and the horror of having a gag in your mouth, you could take in just enough air through your nostrils to keep you alive.

Now the thirst had taken hold. Hereward hadn't even had the decency to give her water. Even on the field of battle, you would put your flask to the lips of a dying enemy. She needed badly to pee and held out as long as she could and then gave in. The warm sensation of the urine on her legs at least told her she was alive and the relief of emptying her bladder was almost pleasurable.

Later, a glint of light entered the gloom. Morning. Dawn should be a harbinger of hope, but the pain of her bindings and the unforgiving stone beneath her body, the thirst and the lack of air allowed no room for hope. Drifting in and out of consciousness, the end, she knew, was very near.

Sitting in Eaton's black Austin Ten as they hurtled along the long road back to Cambridge, Wilde finally exploded. 'You didn't find her? God damn you, where is she?'

'I'm sorry. Bower's men are supposedly scouring the priory inch by inch.'

'And Hereward?'

'I was about to beat the truth out of him when Bower turned up.'

'Bower? What was he doing there?'

'Protecting Hereward.'

'Surely you don't think Bower is involved with North Sea?'

'It's possible.'

'Good God, then there's no hope for Lydia. Put your foot down, God damn it.' Wilde retreated into a murderous silence.

Eaton glanced at him. 'You realise you saved the life of the duke and the prime minister?'

'I didn't,' said Wilde shortly. 'The marksman did that.'

'But he hadn't seen Dorfen until you disturbed him. Snipers, like hawks, seek out movement – and you made Dorfen move.'

'And your role in all this?'

Eaton smiled. 'All in good time, Wilde. All in good time.' He accelerated into a bend. Beside him, Wilde chewed his fingernails and looked out of the window. The weather was deteriorating.

'One thing still puzzles me,' Wilde said, as they approached Cambridge. 'If you got nothing from Hereward, how come the troops were waiting at Royal Lodge?'

Eaton gave Wilde a quick glance. 'MI5,' he said slowly. 'I'd known for quite a while that something was going to happen. It was the reason I was in Cambridge.' Trying to bribe, blackmail and beat it out of Kholtov, he thought. 'I just didn't know what or where or when. Five were going about it another way. They learnt from a wire tap that something was going to happen at Royal Lodge and sent in the army at the last moment.'

'Who was being tapped?'

'Wallis Simpson – but that information goes no further than this car. Strange tale. Have you heard of Sophie Gräfin von Isarbeck? She's extremely wealthy and rather exotic and a good friend of Mrs Simpson – and a favoured chum of Adolf Hitler. When the abdication crisis was coming to a head, our friends in Five realised she was communicating with Mrs Simpson every day – and by Friday they had decided it might be wise to listen in to her other telephone conversations. Yesterday, they discovered that she was blackmailing one of the Duke of York's aides. He told her where and when the prime minister would be meeting the duke. Baldwin was actually on his way to Royal Lodge when the decision was made to send in a company of men, just as a precaution.'

'And you knew nothing of this?' Wilde was incredulous.

Eaton made a face. 'Five and Six don't always communicate very well.'

'But how did you hear about the White Russians? What sent you here to Cambridge?'

For a couple of minutes, they drove on in silence. 'All right,' Eaton said at last. 'I knew something about the White Russian plot from Yuri Kholtov.'

'How did he know about it?'

'The Russians were in Spain. He heard it there.'

'And called MI6 to tell you?'

'No, I was in Spain too. Kholtov gave me information in exchange for safe passage and help with a deal involving gold. Unfortunately, he didn't give me nearly enough.'

'You didn't mention you'd met Kholtov in Spain. Why didn't you tell me any of this before?'

'Look.' Eaton's voice was sharper. 'I knew *something* was going to happen, but I didn't know *what*. I had no idea a bloody Junkers JU-52 transport plane was going to land in the middle of Cambridgeshire. I had no idea what the target was. Nor was I sure who was involved at the English end.'

If Eaton hadn't been driving, Wilde would have punched him. While he had been playing his spy games, innocent men and women had been slaughtered – and now Lydia was missing. 'Damn you, Eaton, what have you done?'

It was past three o'clock in the afternoon by the time Eaton brought the car to a halt on the forecourt of St Wilfred's Priory. Two uniformed police officers stood to attention outside the front door. Four police cars and an ambulance with its rear doors wide open and its engine running were parked side by side on the gravel. There was a buzz of activity among the ambulance men and plainclothes officers.

'Christ,' said Eaton in disgust. 'It's Bower.' He turned to Wilde. 'Say nothing about last night. We don't know what he knows.'

Superintendent Bower, in a suit that would have shamed a tramp, was talking with a uniformed police inspector. He nodded to Eaton and Wilde without removing his pipe from his mouth. Smoke billowed forth, mixing with the vapour trails from his nostrils. The man-made cloud dispersed, to be followed a few seconds later by another.

'Still no sign of her, superintendent?' Eaton demanded.

'None.'

'What have you done with Hereward? I left you with him last night.'

'Indeed you did, but as he had no knowledge of Miss Morris's whereabouts, I had no cause to detain him. It seems everything has changed today. Unfortunately, Sir Norman has also gone missing.'

'Someone must know where he is.'

'The servants don't know where he is, or Miss Morris. I think we're probably looking in the wrong place. My men have been through the house with the proverbial fine-toothed comb but there's no sign of the young lady. Now they're fanning out through the estate, but it's one hell of a size.' Bower turned to Wilde. 'I have to warn you, professor, we're thinking of getting divers in to search the lake. . .'

As he spoke, a pair of officers emerged from the north side of the house, half-dragging, half-marching Sir Norman Hereward onto the driveway. His head was slumped forward and it looked as if he was having difficulty standing up.

The officers stopped in front of Bower. 'Dead drunk, sir. Found him down by the lake, trying to wade into the water.'

'Let him go,' Eaton said.

The officers removed their supporting arms. Hereward lurched forward but managed to keep his balance. Eaton shook him hard. He grunted but did not raise his head.

Wilde strode forward and gave Hereward a vicious smack to the head with the palm of his hand. 'Where is she?'

Hereward's head snapped back, mouth dribbling. Wilde hit him again.

Bower tried to pull Wilde away. 'That's enough, sir.'

Wilde shook him off. 'Where's Lydia, God damn you?'

Hereward opened his eyes. 'Don't know what you're—'

Eaton pushed Wilde aside and gripped Hereward by the throat. 'Get this into your brain, you fool. You have one chance of escaping the noose. One chance. If you don't tell us where Lydia Morris is, you will be charged with murder and high treason and you will be hanged.'

Hereward pushed ineffectually at Eaton. Eaton tightened his grip.

'*Where is she?*'

'The ice house, damn it!' Hereward slurred the words. 'She's in the ice house.' He clasped his hands to his head. 'She'll be all right . . .' Eaton released him and he fell back into the arms of the two constables. 'They would have killed her.'

'My God,' Wilde said. 'It's freezing. She's been there twenty-four hours . . .'

Hereward closed his eyes again. The officers had released his arms and he was standing on his own two feet. He ran a hand across his grey, sweat-slick brow to gather himself. 'I'll show you,' he said. 'She'll be all right,' he repeated.

They frogmarched Hereward into the woods. He stumbled and vomited several times, but they pushed him on. A police sergeant and a doctor had joined them; the ambulance on the forecourt was ready. Wilde's stomach was churning. He had seen too much death in these last hours.

Hereward stopped by a thicket of twisting vines and sharp-thorned brambles.

'This is it.' He was beginning to sober up. His voice was little more than a whisper. 'She's in there. My God . . .'

The brick building was almost invisible from the path. Wilde clawed his way through the brambles into the darkness. At first he could see nothing, only smell the damp. 'A light,' he demanded. 'A torch or a match, someone.'

The sergeant switched on his torch and they peered in. In the far depths of the cold brick interior, a bundle of old clothes was the only sign of human habitation. But the bundle was not clothes; it was Lydia.

Wilde climbed in and fell to his knees by her side. Her body was cold. He ripped at her bindings, tore the gag from her mouth, fought to release the cords that held her to the iron ring. He clutched her to him and she was as limp as an old doll. He put his hand to her cold throat, trying to detect some pulse, some warmth. Nothing. He held her wrist, desperate for even the faintest sign of life.

The doctor was at his side, pushing him away. He held up a hand. 'Keep that light focused in this direction, sergeant.'

Wilde backed off as the doctor cupped his hand behind Lydia's head, then shone a penlight at her eyes. 'That's good, Lydia, that's good,' he said. Then he pressed two fingers lightly on her neck.

'Oh Christ,' Wilde said. 'Is she . . .'

'There's a pulse,' the doctor said. 'It's faint, but it's there.'

They carried her on a stretcher to the waiting ambulance. Wilde tried to get in beside her, but Eaton gripped his arm. 'Leave it to the experts, Tom.'

The doctor climbed in, the doors closed and the ambulance lurched forward.

'Drive me to the hospital,' Wilde said. 'I've got to be with her.'

Eaton turned to Bower. 'Take Sir Norman Hereward into custody and when he's sobered up you can question him to your heart's content. You can talk to Professor Wilde later. Come on, Tom.'

Eaton was saying, 'Stay close to her, because there might not be another chance.' He was saying that she might not come out of this. Wilde's blood ran cold.

CHAPTER 40

He sat in the waiting room for hour after hour. At times he paced. Sometimes he confronted a passing nurse or doctor and demanded information. Very little was forthcoming. And when they offered to look at his own head wound he wouldn't let them near it.

Day turned to night and still no word. At last, the doctor who had been with them when they found Lydia came out. He looked exhausted.

'She's going to be all right.'

'Are you sure?'

'Yes, I'm sure.'

'Can I see her?' He had to see for himslf.

'Just for a moment.' He hesitated. 'Her body temperature was very low when we found her. She's done well to survive.'

For a few moments, Wilde simply looked at her. Her eyes were closed, her breathing hardly noticeable. He had never realised before quite how beautiful she was. And she was alive.

She opened her eyes when he said her name. A small smile crossed her lips. 'Tom?'

'Yes, it's me.'

'Your head . . . what's happened?'

'My head's fine. Don't worry about anything.'

'I want to sleep.' She closed her eyes again.

'Yes, sleep.' There was a lot to talk about. It would wait. 'Sleep, Lydia.'

He leant over and took her in his arms. She was limp and yielding and warm. Her breathing was soft and steady. He kissed her forehead. He released her gently and she sank into the pillow.

He couldn't face going home. Instead, he walked the short distance to the college. He would have a large Scotch and sleep the night in his rooms, in preparation for the grim hours of questions and answers that lay ahead. Like the loyal college servant he was, Scobie nodded him through, eyeing the rust-coloured clots of blood in his hair and on his clothes without comment. Who knew what he'd heard about the events of the previous night? Rumours would be rife in this small university town.

Even as he dragged himself up his staircase, Wilde could smell the tobacco smoke. He pushed the door of his rooms open but did not step inside. The light was on.

'Who's there?'

A faint shuffling noise, then silence.

Wilde kept an old walking stick by the door, one that he sometimes took with him when he went birdwatching. He grabbed it.

Yuri Kholtov was by the window, standing on one leg, supporting himself against the sill. He, too, had a stick, a bit of wildwood.

'Professor Wilde, I have nowhere else to go. You must help me. Please, I beg you.'

Kholtov moved to the centre of the room. His face was bruised and cut, and he was limping badly. He couldn't put any weight on his left leg.

'What's happened to you?' Wilde kept the stick in a firm grasp.

'It's nothing.'

'Someone has beaten you.'

Kholtov shrugged his shoulders. 'You don't look too good yourself, Professor Wilde.' He slumped down heavily on the sofa, flinching. 'I need your help. My ankle is shattered.'

'What's happened to the safe house?'

'Look at me.' He tried to laugh. 'Do you think it was safe? I had to get away.'

'And how did you manage that?'

'I crawled to the road. It was painful and slow. And then I was fortunate. A beet wagon stopped and gave me a ride.'

'You realise, of course, you're wanted for a series of murders? Give me one good reason why I shouldn't simply turn you in?'

'Professor Wilde, you have to believe me. I have committed no crimes in England. I was invited. I am a guest. And now I merely want to leave the country in peace.'

Wilde took the peseta coin from his pocket and flicked it towards Kholtov. It span through the air and landed at his feet. 'Explain that then. It was found in Nancy Hereward's house.'

Kholtov snorted contemptuously. 'It is a Spanish coin, that's all.'

'Is it yours?'

'I had never met Miss Hereward. I did not go to her house, so no, it cannot be mine.'

Wilde did not bother to pick up the coin. As clues went, it was worthless. He changed the subject. 'Shouldn't you be asking Horace Dill for assistance?'

'His rooms are locked and he's not there.'

Very convenient, Professor Dill. There was only one man to deal with this: Philip Eaton. How had he allowed the Kholtov situation to spin so far out of control?

'You can talk to no one. I trust no one.'

'I'll talk to Philip Eaton.'

'*No!*' Kholtov began to rise from the sofa. 'Not Eaton. He is the devil.'

Wilde shrugged. There was more than one side to Philip Eaton. 'So why don't you tell me what's been happening, Mr Kholtov? I'm afraid I have no vodka, but I can give you a glass of Scotch.'

'I kept my side of the bargain. I told him all I knew.' Kholtov touched the bruises on his face. 'He tried to kill me.'

'Oh, I doubt very much that he tried to kill you. Why would he want to?'

'Because I had no more information to give him. You know he is a spy? British Secret Service. MI6.'

Wilde handed the Russian a tumbler of whisky. 'Here, drink this.'

Kholtov drank it down in one swallow. 'That is good.' He held out the glass. 'One more, yes? Thank you.' He sipped this one. 'Mr Wilde, if you help me, I promise it will be worth your while. I will make you a very rich man.'

'Now why would a communist wish to give money to a filthy bourgeois enemy of the masses?'

'In exchange for your help. I think you are honest. I need you to drive me.'

'I don't have a car.'

'Don't worry about the car.'

'And where precisely do you want me to take you?'

'A river inlet. It is on the coast of Suffolk. You know of it?'

Know it? Oh, he knew the Suffolk coast as well as he knew these rooms. 'What do you want to do there?'

'We will find a boat, laden with treasure like a Spanish galleon. Spoils of war. You will share it with me.'

'My inclination right now, Kholtov, is to call the police, who will probably want to hand you over to Mr Eaton who, I am sure, will know exactly what to do with you.'

Kholtov put his hand into the inside pocket of his jacket and pulled out a pistol. 'This is a Tokarev TT-33,' he said. 'She is a fine weapon. I do not wish you harm, but she has no safety catch, so please do not try to take her from me. I would hate her to go off unintentionally.'

'I'll take that as a threat.'

'Persuasion. To concentrate your mind.' Kholtov waved his left hand. 'I have her because I want you to be clear that you will help me – and there must be no Eaton. If he finds me he will kill me. I am not ready to die.'

'What nonsense. He doesn't go around killing people.'

'You think not? You have spent too much time with your nose in old books, Professor Wilde. You are looking for a murderer? Look twice at Philip Eaton.'

'If he wanted you dead, how is it that you are still alive?'

'He thought he had me trapped and he still has hopes of getting information from me. He believes I will work for him.' Kholtov sighed. 'Listen. I met him in Spain. We did a deal. I told him that I had heard that Germany was planning an attack in England, using Russian exiles. I even gave him a name.'

'A name?'

'Harwood . . .'

'Hereward?'

'Hereward, then, however you say it.'

So that was Eaton's link to Cambridge.

Wilde looked down at the Tokarev and then back at Kholtov. 'If your ankle is broken, you should go to hospital.'

'That is the same as handing me over to police. I will be charged with killing the girl, a crime I did not commit and of which I know nothing.'

It occurred to Wilde that the official view on Nancy Hereward's death might have changed in the light of recent events. But the Russian would be arrested regardless. And why not? He had plenty to answer for, in this country as well as abroad.

And yet . . .

'Let's find a splint for your ankle then you can tell me precisely where we are going.'

'If you help me, Mr Wilde, it will be to the advantage of us both, but,' Kholtov waved the pistol, 'I will not hesitate to kill you if you move against me.'

From a drawer in his desk, Wilde pulled out a long shoehorn. Then he went to the corner cupboard and pulled out a spare shirt and ripped it into strips. He knelt on the floor beside the sofa and examined the Russian's ankle.

Kholtov leant forward, the pistol at Wilde's head. 'Be careful,' he warned.

'More whisky?' Wilde asked. 'This is going to hurt.'

'Just do what you need to do.'

Slowly, Wilde manipulated the broken ankle back into something like its normal position. He placed the shoehorn along the outside of the ankle, down to the heel, and secured it with cloth ties. Kholtov gasped with pain, swearing in English and Russian.

Wilde stood up. 'Best I can do, I'm afraid.'

'Good. Now we wait until the early hours.'

'And the car? I imagine you will have to steal one.'

Kholtov grinned and pulled a coil of wire out of his pocket. 'Borrow, Mr Wilde. Not steal, borrow. Remember, property is theft.'

MONDAY DECEMBER 7, 1936

CHAPTER 41

The car was parked on Trumpington Street. In the event, they didn't need the wire because the key had been left in the ignition. 'The English are trusting people, professor,' Kholtov said as he climbed into the passenger seat, his pistol trained on Wilde. Wilde fired up the engine, put the car into gear and they drove out of Cambridge towards the gathering dawn.

It was a long, difficult route, first due eastwards towards Bury St Edmunds, then on a winding series of small roads, most of them single track, some little more than bridleways or farm trails.

'Why am I doing this?' Wilde's eyes were heavy. The road was difficult to follow.

'Maybe you are afraid I will shoot you.'

'Do I seem afraid?'

Kholtov laughed. 'No. Death is nothing. It is the same as the time before we were born – and we have no fear of that, for it too is nothingness. Anyway, I will not kill you. Why would I?'

Wilde laughed, too. Kholtov would kill him without blinking if he felt it necessary. There would be nothing personal. There never was with men like Kholtov.

'Keep on talking, Kholtov. Keep me awake, otherwise I'll wrap this thing round a tree.'

It was curiosity that motivated him. He had come this far, seen so much death and horror. He needed to know how this piece slotted into the jigsaw. 'Tell me about your love for Lenin and Stalin and all that Marxist tosh. You don't really believe any of it, do you?'

'Tosh? Why do you call it tosh? It is man's best hope. If you ask me whether it is working perfectly, then I would have to say not yet. But give it fifty years, a hundred years, and you will see it achieve its goal.'

'And in the meantime, countless people must starve, be worked to death or shot on the vague promise that their children or grandchildren might one day find Utopia. By which time, someone will probably have come up with some other crazy idea anyway. It's all bullshit – and you know it.'

Kholtov snorted. 'We must try to do better. This is for the good of the human species. This is enlightenment.'

'Darkness for those who cross you.'

'I have never intentionally caused pain to any man.'

'Just killed them.'

'Anything I have done I have done for the many, for the poor and dispossessed. And think on this: when you kill a man with a bullet to the head it is quicker and less painful than any death your God doles out. No gasping for breath, no foaming and vomiting, no lingering paralysis . . .'

Eaton tapped his finger on the table in the empty reception lobby of the Bull, the telephone receiver clamped to his ear. The early morning concierge brought him coffee and Eaton nodded his thanks. What he really needed was to plunge into cold water to wake himself. But he didn't have time. At last, the receiver was picked up.

'Carstairs?'

'I think I've found it, Mr Eaton.'

Eaton allowed himself a long breath. 'Go on.'

'As you said, there must have been some record of a Spanish vessel arriving in British waters.'

'And?' Impatient now.

'No mention of a Spanish vessel, but the shipping reports did mention a French trawler that came in at Orford Ness and then disappeared. The skipper told the harbourmaster they were resting up before making for Yarmouth. But Yarmouth had no record of it arriving.'

'What makes you think this was our Spanish boat?'

'Its name was *Gaviota*, Mr Eaton. That's Spanish for seagull.'

'Carstairs, you're a genius. Go home and sleep until Christmas.'

'Thank you, sir.'

When dawn broke, they were still a few miles from the coast. Kholtov had a scrappy map. As they crossed the flatlands down to the sea, he followed their progress with his finger.

'There is a byway to your left, professor. It is like a farm track, but it is not a farm. A house for summer holidays, for boating and swimming and watching the birds. No one will be there.'

'How do you know of it?'

Kholtov smiled, but did not reply. Wilde did not need to know that it had been bought in Horace Dill's name in the late twenties. Useful for bringing illegals into the country from the sea.

The track to the house was pitted and muddy, but led, finally, to a screen of leafless trees, partially shading a shabby blue and white clapboard house.

'A nice place, don't you think? Come, let us find my friends. Then together we will make a fire, you can sleep and I can rest my ankle a while. Maybe they have some Spanish brandy to ease the pain.'

Kholtov had told Wilde something of the gold, but not the whole truth. 'If I can sell it, I can buy arms. Eaton was supposed to bring me the gold buyer and then an arms dealer.'

'And he failed?'

'He brought a man about the gold, but it soon became clear to me that there was no deal because they could give no guarantees. They would have cheated me. When I saw this, that is when I was beaten. Eaton was impatient and short-sighted and so was his fat rich friend in furs, for in time I could have brought much more Spanish gold to them – hundreds of tonnes. Better to change it into dollars and guns than allow it to fall into the hands of Franco and the Nazis. Five hundred tonnes of pure gold. Think of it, professor. Enough to buy an army.'

'So this is nothing to do with enriching yourself or fleeing Stalin's death squads?'

'I am a revolutionary and must do whatever it takes to further the cause. I must even do deals with capitalist pigs. And *you* will help me. You will find a way to change the gold into currency, won't you, professor?'

Wilde had noted the description of the gold dealer: *Fat rich friend in furs*. One name sprang to mind: Slievedonard. And he had no illusions. He hadn't been brought here because of his ability to find a gold buyer. Kholtov needed someone to drive him. A bullet would be his lot, so the longer he could play along with the Russian's game, the better.

Most likely he was still alive as insurance – in case Kholtov needed to get away in a hurry.

The house was open and empty, save for three thin roll-up mattresses, some tangled blankets and a telephone. It was dusty and cold. In summer, thought Wilde, it would indeed be a fine retreat, but no one would come here at this time of year, except to look out across the marshlands to the mud-grey sea. He would, though. He'd come at any time of year to watch the birds. In the distance, he could see a lighthouse, red and white striped, which he knew to be the one near the town and port of Orford, guarding the shingle spit that presented such a hazard to shipping and provided such a rich refuge for the waders and gulls.

Kholtov was watching him. The Tokarev was loose in his hand, but Wilde was well aware that the Russian's languid indifference was a front; Kholtov was alert behind the easy-going exterior. Why would he need to exude menace when he had total control? His finger never left the trigger.

As they left the house, they did not bother to shut the door behind them. Stepping down through the ill-kept gardens to the marshy farm-land beyond, Wilde could hear the wind banging it shut, then open, then shut again. They walked slowly, Kholtov leaning heavily on the walk-ing stick he had taken from Wilde's rooms, groaning with every yard he advanced.

The *Gaviota* was well concealed at a mooring in a small turbid broad, hardly bigger than a decent city lido. No one was on deck, but a thin trail of smoke from the cabin door and the smell of burning tobacco told them that the crew was aboard the vessel.

Kholtov called from the bank. 'Juan, are you there?'

A noise from within. In seconds, the Spanish skipper appeared from the wheelhouse.

'Yuri, you have come.'

'Indeed. Did you not expect me?'

The Spaniard looked ill at ease. His eyes darted from Kholtov to Wilde.

Kholtov gave him a hard stare. 'Where is your crew?'

'They – they are in the cabin.'

'Things are very hot, Juan. Very hot. England will not work for us. We need to move on. I will come with you.'

'Where can we go?'

'Norway. We have friends in Norway. There are fjords where our little boat can more easily be concealed.'

Ferreira laughed nervously. 'No chance! We are stuck fast. Even if we can lose ballast and somehow make our way to the sea, I do not believe we can get this wreck across the North Sea in the middle of winter.'

'We have no alternative.'

'We will sink.'

'It is a risk we must take. Make preparations.'

Kholtov turned to Wilde, smiling apologetically. 'Forgive me, professor.'

So this was it. The death bullet from Stalin's man, where Hitler's had failed. Was this the way the world would end? He looked away from Kholtov, didn't want to see the gun raised. A gull soared lazily south across the horizon, buoyed by the winter wind.

The bird flew on. Perhaps Kholtov wanted him to go down on his knees and kiss his feet in supplication? He wouldn't do it. Better to die on your feet than live on your knees, as someone once said.

A blast of cold air made him shiver, and then he heard a familiar voice. He turned back to see Eaton standing next to the Spaniard on the deck of the fishing vessel. He was carrying a Thompson sub-machine gun.

Kholtov shrugged, dropped his pistol and held up his hands in surrender.

'So the gold is all yours, Mr Eaton,' Kholtov said.

'The gold, as I understand it, is the property of the Spanish government. It will be returned to them.'

'And me?'

'That all depends how useful you prove yourself to be, Mr Kholtov.'

Even at the worst moments of the war, Harold Middlemass had shaved each day. When they went over the top into the enemy fire that was likely to kill him, he was clean-shaven. On this Monday morning, he was not. His eyes were haggard and tired, the lines of his cheeks were heavy, his mouth set, his jowls stubbly. But his infernal tic, mysteriously, had gone.

He had been awake for the best part of two days. No one had slept properly at Royal Lodge except His Royal Highness the Duke of York. There had been much clearing up to do outside. Most of it was down to the army, but they had made an unholy mess of the removal of the bodies and other evidence of the firefight and it had fallen on the major to organise the restoration of the gardens.

'No one wants the duchess and the princesses to come home to this,' the duke had said. 'In fact it would suit me if she was never to know that it happened.'

Middlemass had bowed. He had understood implicitly. He and the other royal aides and servants would be sworn to secrecy.

Now, in the Dorchester Hotel, Middlemass was beyond exhaustion. Surely it was only a matter of time before the trail of evidence led to his door? Perhaps they were watching him now, looking to see where he led them. He was resigned. Whatever happened, his reputation was surely done for.

The butler opened the door to the Gräfin's apartment. 'Major Middlemass,' he said, eyebrows raised. 'I didn't know you were expected.'

'I was on my way to my club. Wanted to pay my respects to Sophie.'

'Wait here if you would, sir. I shall see if this is convenient.'

'Oh, it's convenient enough.' Middlemass pushed past him and opened the door to Sophie von Isarbeck's office. She was at her desk on the telephone. She immediately put her hand over the mouthpiece. 'Harold, what are you doing here? It is too dangerous.'

'I've come to see you, Sophie.'

'I'm in the middle of a rather important call.' Her voice was cold. 'Give me ten minutes, would you?' She nodded to her butler. 'Hansi, offer Major Middlemass some refreshment.'

Harold Middlemass, a large and powerful man, turned round and pushed the butler out of the door, slammed it shut and locked it. 'You're always on the damned telephone,' he said. He went over to the desk, took the receiver from the Gräfin's hand and hung up.

'Harold, you can't do this!'

'You know what I want, Sophie. Hand it over.'

'You can have the picture. I don't have the negative yet.' She pulled an envelope from her top drawer. 'Here, take it.'

He slid out the photograph and took out his lighter. As the flame reached his fingers, he dropped the hateful picture, still burning, to the carpeted floor.

'Does that make you feel better, Harold?'

'No.' He took the Webley .455 from his coat pocket. 'But this will, Sophie.'

Before she had even registered what he was doing, she had slammed back in her chair, staring stupidly down at the bullet hole in her chest and the blood that pumped from her ruptured heart.

The sound of the gunshot in the enclosed space of the apartment was deafening. Major Harold Middlemass heard the sound of hammering at the door outside and then the cracking of wood as something heavy was slammed against it.

He put the muzzle of the revolver between his parted lips, pointing the cold metal upwards into the roof of his mouth to ensure a clear passage to the brain. This time he would do it. This time he had the courage. His last thought was that he should have done it long ago. If only a German sniper had saved him the trouble at Passchendaele.

Then he pulled the trigger.

On that same Monday, 7 December, Edward VIII confirmed to his brother Albert that he was surrendering the throne. The prime minister, meanwhile, told the House of Commons that he had nothing new to say on the matter. Winston Churchill made an ill-judged attempt to plead once more on the King's behalf but was shouted down and took his seat utterly humiliated.

The following day, Baldwin bade farewell to the King for the last time. Edward's mood was lighter and more positive than it had been for some time. In a private moment with his prime minister, he said, 'I know that you and Mrs Baldwin don't approve of my action. It is the view of another generation. My generation doesn't feel that way.'

As he took his leave of his sovereign, Baldwin simply said, 'Well, sir, I hope that whatever happens, you will be happy.'

Two days later, on Thursday 10 December, at ten o'clock in the morning, Edward signed the Instrument of Abdication. His reign had lasted three hundred and twenty-five days. As the next in line, Albert immediately became King, taking the name George VI.

Later that day, five hundred Blackshirts from the British Union of Fascists protested angrily outside Buckingham Palace. They gave the Nazi salute and demanded that Edward stay on as king. The following day, their leader Oswald Mosley demanded the people of Britain be allowed to decide on who should be monarch by plebiscite. He was ignored.

AFTERMATH

CHAPTER 42

Ten days later, Eaton took Wilde to lunch at his club where they had Dover sole and a good Pouilly Fuissé. 'You look like a war hero, old boy,' Eaton said, indicating the bandage around Wilde's head.

'I don't feel like one. Look, Eaton, I think you owe me answers.'

'Fire away.'

'You've seen the North Sea list, haven't you?'

Eaton nodded his head slowly.

'So how did you get it?'

Eaton laughed. 'Ever been fishing?'

'Once or twice.'

'Well, I've done a great deal of freshwater fishing and I've learned one thing above all others. To catch a pike, you've got to think like a pike. So I joined the Anglo-German Fellowship and got as close as I could to Slievedonard. Made myself useful to him.'

Wilde did not mention that he already knew of Eaton's membership from Jim Vanderberg.

'A lot of the members of the fellowship simply have a penchant for *bratwurst*, Wagner, foaming steins of beer and young men in *lederhosen*. But there are those within the organisation who have darker ideas . . .'

'And they were the ones recruited for North Sea? You infiltrated them.'

Eaton laughed again. 'I suggested to Lord Slievedonard that he might like to invite me. Peter Slievedonard was never much of a Nazi. A lot of Jewish gold-dealers are being forced out of Germany. Slievedonard has been buying up their businesses for a song. And if he's anti-Jew, it's no big thing in his mind, simply a way of making money. I made him a simple deal – work with me or I'll bring you down.'

Wilde's hands were gripped into tight balls. 'Why didn't you tell me any of this before?'

'I wanted to see what you could find on your own. Anyway, it's my business to discover secrets, not reveal them.'

Wilde lowered his voice. 'And Sawyer? Why am I not in jail? I killed him.'

'Self-defence,' said Eaton. 'His own knife, I believe. Anyway, that's all for the birds. Play your part and there will be no charges. I think we'll say he was lost at sea, something of that ilk.'

'Play my part?'

'You don't say a word about this. To anyone. It dies with you.'

'Why would you want this kept a secret?'

'Come on, Wilde, you're not naive. We don't want a civil war, that's why. Hereward's a former Cambridge master and a former MP. There are others. Think of the North Sea list . . . this is the ruling class we are talking about.'

'So they're above the law?'

Eaton sighed. 'The realm is already shaky. Just think of the new King and his brother – do you imagine it would be healthy to pitch brother against brother? You're a bloody historian, Tom – it would be like the damned Wars of the Roses all over again.'

'You English haven't really moved on much from the Middle Ages, have you?'

'The world hasn't, Wilde. Hitler, Mussolini, Franco – they're medieval warlords.'

'Don't forget Stalin.'

'You can include him if you like.'

'What precisely was the significance of the list?'

'I've a pretty sound idea. With Baldwin and the Duke of York dead, Slievedonard would have received a telephone call ordering him to go to Fort Belvedere to tell his chum the King that he had to declare a state of emergency and appoint a new prime minister – probably Mosley or Londonderry. Perhaps Edward would have taken the reins of power himself; it's certainly an idea that has been mooted in some corners. Anyway, the abdication would have been called off, Stalin would have been blamed and the men on the North Sea list would have sealed the coup by securing parliament, the courts and the armed forces. Germany would have kept her best friend on the throne. Perhaps a mutual defence alliance might have followed.'

'You have proof of this?'

'Do you have a better theory? Everything – the murders of General Carr and the Langleys, perhaps Nancy too – was about building a tale of

Bolshevik terror so that when the big event happened, the killing of the prime minister and the heir, no one would be in any doubt that Stalin was behind it. Stalin might be guilty of many things, but in this instance his hands are entirely clean. This has Hitler's fingerprints all over it.'

'So what will happen to those on the North Sea list?'

'Well, apart from Hereward, they are *guilty* of nothing. That list is *proof* of nothing. In Germany, appearing on such a list would be enough for a one-way trip to Dachau, but in England there is no case to answer. Slievedonard would never have carried out his orders anyway – if the call had come through, he'd have been straight onto my man Carstairs at the ministry.'

'So that's it. A band of would-be traitors walks free.'

Eaton smiled. 'Not exactly. They have all been talked to.'

'Ticked off by the headmaster? And who gave them this telling-off? You?'

'In some cases. Others too far above my pay grade are receiving friendly summonses from their superiors. In the next few days and weeks some notable men will quietly retire from public service. Parliamentary seats will become vacant, judges will decide they prefer golf to the bench, senior civil servants will go on that transatlantic cruise they have been considering for years, officers will resign their commissions, policemen will retire to their gardens.'

'Policemen? Bower. Was his name on the list?'

'No. But that doesn't mean he didn't have links to North Sea.'

'Can I see the list?'

'No,' said Eaton shortly.

Wilde thought back to the death and mayhem that night at Royal Lodge. So a nearly successful coup was to be buried beneath a mound of silence. How very British.

There were still questions he wanted answers to. 'Were those soldiers I followed through the night really White Russians?'

'Oh, they were Russian, all right. Recruited from the emigrés in Paris. Their leader was a man called Vladimir Rybakov.'

'How can you know that? I assume they didn't carry identity cards or passports.'

Eaton lowered his voice. 'One of them survived. A man named Ivan Chernuk. Says he wants to stay here and fight *against* the Nazis. We could put him in prison, but, well, we have other plans for him. He's going back to Paris to keep an eye on the Russian exiles.'

As the meal ended and they were enjoying a glass of Château d'Yquem, Wilde's eye was caught by two new arrivals being shown to a table. 'Do you see who that is?'

Sir Norman Hereward and Lord Slievedonard did not look in their direction, but Wilde knew they had spotted them.

'Perhaps I should wander over and tell Hereward how much assistance his old friend Slievedonard has been giving me,' Eaton said. 'That might put the dampers on their meal.'

'Hereward should be in jail. Or the Tower. It stinks.'

Eaton smiled. 'Sir Norman has been persuaded that his future lies in foreign fields. Frankly, I don't care if he drinks himself to death in the gutter. Meanwhile, Baldwin has what he wanted – Edward VIII gone and his biddable brother on the throne. All the prime minister desires now is a period of calm to settle the nation's nerves. An image of national unity. So no trials, no newspaper stories . . .'

'What of Kholtov? Where is he and the gold now?'

'Classified, I'm afraid.'

'He gave you Hereward's name, didn't he?'

Eaton frowned. 'What makes you say that?'

'He told me. You see what interests me is this: if you wanted to infiltrate Hereward's world, why didn't you use his daughter? You knew enough about her – the trip to Berlin for instance – so why didn't you introduce yourself to her?'

Their eyes met, searching. This, thought Wilde, was the man Kholtov had said was the devil.

'I didn't need to,' Eaton said with an easy smile. 'Slievedonard was easily turned.' He looked at his watch. 'Come on, Wilde, drink up. Some of us have work to do.'

A little way along Pall Mall, in another gentlemen's club, three friends in their mid-forties sat in their habitual armchairs beside the high windows, looking out over a bleak, grey day.

'These modern men, they don't get it,' the Foreign Office mandarin said. 'How can anyone in England complain about Signor Mussolini's ambitions in Albania or Abyssinia when we have already colonised a quarter of the globe? Italy looks at us and of course she's going to want a little empire. Same with Germany. If Adolf gazes covetously at the Sudetenland and Poland as potential colonies, are we really in a position to condemn him when we have our own?'

'Damn shame about Sawyer,' the general said. 'I served with him in Mesopotamia.'

The landowner poured port from a decanter for all three of them. 'All is not lost. We can still forge a peace with Germany. Chamberlain will be in Number Ten soon and he won't want war. I think he'll get his way.'

'One can only hope.' The civil servant sipped his port.

'Since when was hoping enough?' The general growled. 'We'll have to make sure of it, won't we?'

Later, in his cab back to King's Cross station, Wilde thought of the long lunch and their parting. As they stepped out into the bustle of Pall Mall, Eaton had said, 'I hope I've answered most of your questions. There are things I *shouldn't* tell you, old boy. And things I can't tell you. You'll have to be content with that, I'm afraid.'

Wilde had nodded, but he was far from content. And there was still one overriding question. The one that had first drawn him into this web of death. Who had killed Nancy Hereward?

At the start of Lent term, a memorial service was held for Eugene Felsted and Roger Maxwell in the ancient college chapel. The place was full, of course, and the choir's singing touched the soul. Light streamed in through the high, south-facing stained-glass windows. There were tears and a fine tribute from the master of the college. He spoke with regret of lives cut brutally short, of the need to bring their killers to justice. It was widely supposed that the young men's murders were linked somehow to the deaths of Mr and Mrs Langley and General Carr, but these also remained unsolved. The trail had gone cold. 'We must believe that justice will prevail. The killers, whoever they are, will face judgement in this world or the next.'

He spoke, too, about another loss the college had recently suffered: Dr Duncan Sawyer, killed in a tragic yachting accident. A man of fine qualities, he would be sorely missed by all who knew him.

Afterwards, the fellows and guests proceeded to the Combination Room. On this sombre day it was a place of unusual abstinence. Wilde was there to pay his respects to Maxwell and Felsted. He thought of the terror of their last disbelieving moments. And he thought about Sawyer, about the way the blood had spurted from his throat, and the way it had drenched his face and hands and clothes.

Outside, the bells of the town chimed the hour. In the dark-panelled room, dimly lit by yellow electric light, they were muted, a distant accompaniment to the murmuring voices and grave faces of the fellows in their gowns, and their guests, as they sipped their modest glasses of sherry.

The parents of both Felsted and Maxwell were standing together, beside the table, stiff and awkward, grief lines etched into their faces. Wilde introduced himself. Their eyes, inevitably, went to the scar gouged in the side of his head. They knew who he was and what had happened from the police reports and the inquest.

'They were fine young men,' he said. 'Their deaths are not only a tragic loss to you, but to the college, to Great Britain and to the wider world. I am sure they would both have done great things. They will certainly be remembered with fondness and admiration by all who knew them at Cambridge.'

They thanked him, inquired after his own health and said their sons had both spoken highly of him in their letters home. Then they asked him whether he had any theories to offer about their sons' murders.

Wilde bowed his head. What could he say to these good people? He cleared his throat. 'Clearly the man Braithwaite was involved in some way, but your sons and I were attacked by two men *after* Braithwaite's death. Who they were or what they were trying to do is yet to be discovered. I rather think we were simply in the wrong place at the wrong time.'

Like every family in the country, the Maxwells and the Felsteds had suffered enough in the war to understand the fickle nature of life and death. There was nothing to be done but endure and carry on. Wilde shook their hands and moved away.

Horace Dill sidled up to him.

He pointed at Wilde's head. 'It was that fucking Nazi Dorfen who shot you, wasn't it?'

'I didn't see their faces, they were masked.'

'What happened to him? Where did he go from here?'

Wilde shrugged.

'Well, what was it all about, Tom? Those two poor boys, the general and the Langleys? What was going on?'

'Keep your voice down, Horace. We'll probably never know – except that the deaths were clearly all linked.'

'It must have been Dorfen. He always was a dirty piece of work. His father was a pal of Hitler.'

'Well, then, you know as much as I do, Horace.'

'As for that weasel Braithwaite, I knew he was a bad 'un as soon as I saw him at Lydia's place.' Dill drew deeply on his fat cigar. 'Ah,' he said as he exhaled. 'The pleasures of life. This is a *Romeo Y Julieta*, I'll have you know, a gift from Comrade Stalin himself. Sent me a box of fifty of the things. Damned fine of him.'

'For services rendered, I suppose, sending young men to their deaths on his behalf.'

'Uncalled for, Wilde. I loved him like a son.'

'I know. I'm sorry.' Wilde bowed his head. Word had recently arrived that John Cornford, the young Cambridge poet who had gone to fight in the Spanish Civil War, had been killed.

Dill perked up. 'Not quite so fond of Duncan Sawyer, however. Nasty way to go, drowning. Damned foolish of him to go sailing in rough weather in the middle of winter.' Dill raised an eyebrow. 'Have they found his body yet?'

'No,' said Wilde. 'And I doubt they ever will. Went down in the North Sea, somewhere east of Great Yarmouth.'

'So it's said. Well, he won't be here to see the scholarship he fought so hard for come to pass. Perhaps now Slievedonard has agreed that his name doesn't have to go on the fucking thing, they could call it the *Duncan Sawyer Scholarship*.' Dill grinned slyly.

Wilde had been surprised by the way the vote was going; evidently the bursar would get his way. 'I thought you would be worried about the college accepting the fat capitalist's money.'

Dill stabbed the butt of the smouldering cigar in the vague direction of Wilde's face. 'I wasn't worried a bit. Not a buggering bit. I don't happen to believe that money has a conscience. If they're ill-gotten gains, then why not put them to virtuous use? The cleansing power of charity. Anyway, the college will have complete control over who benefits.'

The bell clanged to summon them to Hall.

'Will you be joining us at High Table, Professor Wilde?'

'You know, Professor Dill, tonight I think I will.'

'Well, glory fucking be.'

Margot arrived home a week later. Hart had died heroically on a secret mission behind the lines in Spain, she had been told. The Führer had sent his condolences on the loss of a fine man and regretted he would not be available to meet Miss Langley personally. It was important, he had said, that she return to England, to be among her own people. Margot knew enough about the new Germany to realise that it was futile to try to argue.

'Yes,' Frau Dorfen had said. 'Go home. There is nothing for you here.'

It was only at Croydon Aerodrome, where she was told the terrible truth about the murder of her parents, that she discovered there was nothing for her in England, either.

CHAPTER 43

Lent term wore on. Wilde was busy with lectures, with marking essays and with supervisions. He was making good progress with his biography of Sir Robert Cecil.

The winter chill had taken a firm hold. The countryside was coated with ice and snow and there was even skating on the Fens, just outside town. Wilde spent long hours in the college library and in his rooms, huddled over papers and books, the fire and his other needs tended throughout the day by Bobby, who kept the outside world at bay.

Early in February Wilde got a telephone call from Jim Vanderberg.

'How you doing, old friend? Been worried about you.'

'Trying to get back to some sort of normality, Jim.'

Vanderberg snorted. 'It's overrated. Look – I heard something on the sly that I thought might interest you. Your pal Yuri Kholtov has turned up in Moscow.'

'Really?' Wilde was instantly intrigued, and puzzled. 'Last I heard, Eaton had him under lock and key, pumping him for information. And Kholtov gave me the impression he was afraid of what might await him in Russia. How the hell did he end up there?'

'No idea. But it seems he has been consigned to a Lubyanka cellar. I wouldn't give a dime for his chances.'

'Are you absolutely sure about this? I can't believe Eaton would have let him slip his grasp.'

'Maybe he shipped him home deliberately. Because I've also heard that Moscow is awash with Spanish gold just now. More than five hundred tonnes, aboard four ships. Came in through Odessa . . .'

The *Black Work* cell, the place of execution. The stench of blood was strong. There was no window, no bed, not even a table and chair. There was only one purpose to this room deep in the unholy bowels of the Lubyanka prison.

Perhaps he should have taken a cosy desk job? But Stalin liked to keep people doing what they were good at – and with his command of languages and easy manner, Kholtov had been the obvious choice to run the Soviet espionage networks in France, Spain, Scandinavia and England, the obvious choice to recruit men like Horace Dill. And now this, not even a trial. Not even a visit from his wife or children. How would they survive the inevitable labour camp?

He should be angry. He should be raging against his old friends: Stalin and Slutsky, against NKVD chiefs Yagoda and Yezhov, but he no longer had the energy. Not even against Philip Eaton.

The door opened and a figure emerged from the dark corridor, filling the doorway. Vasily Blokhin. The brute beast.

Even as Blokhin entered, the smile did not leave Kholtov's eyes. He nodded to his executioner, noting the pistol in his hand, a German-made Walther. Blokhin had never trusted the Soviet-made Tok. At least Blokhin was a professional, the veteran of hundreds if not thousands of killings. It would be quick and easy. No nervous beginner to leave you half-dead and paralysed in a pool of your own blood. Kholtov turned away to face the wall and waited for the darkness. He did not close his eyes.

Blokhin said nothing. It was just the work of a moment for him. He held the automatic pistol to the base of Kholtov's skull, and pulled the trigger with the indifference of a slaughterman dispatching cattle.

Over the next few days, Wilde found himself wondering more and more about Philip Eaton. The peseta coin sat on his desk and he would pick it up from time to time, turning it in his fingers. Yuri Kholtov was not the only one to have gone to Spain: Eaton had been there, too. Wilde thought about Eaton's youthful flirtation with communism. Could it have been more enduring than he cared to let on? That might go some way to explain why Kholtov had been flung back to the wolves in Moscow. It was certainly a strange thing for a British secret service man to do.

A fortune in gold coins hidden on an old trawler . . . and a single, pathetic peseta coin found in the room of a dead girl. If an undergraduate had come to him with this sort of flimsy evidence to back up a piece of historical research he would have sent him packing.

And yet . . . and yet it was part of a narrative that had begun to form in his mind since the lunch in Eaton's club, a narrative that was beginning to make sense of many things.

If Sir Robert Cecil or Walsingham had been running Soviet secret intelligence, what would they have said to a man of Eaton's potential? It was obvious: *Forget the Communist Party, Mr Eaton, work for the Comintern in other ways. Secret ways. You will be a thousand times more useful to the cause than any rabble-rouser with a banner.* The implications of such a possibility were chilling. And who had been Eaton's mentor? Horace Dill.

Wilde abandoned caution and let his imagination run riot. What if Eaton had learned of Nancy's work in Berlin from Horace Dill? Berlin might have been Dill's idea, but perhaps Eaton realised he could get Nancy to find out what her own father was up to. Who better?

He paused for a moment. What if Eaton had gone one step further. What if he had tried to recruit Nancy not just to work against the Nazis but to work *for* the Soviet Union. Nancy was clever, one of the brightest of her generation. And what if that had gone badly wrong? What if Nancy saw the distinction immediately: working for a foreign power was not the same as working for a political movement. Working for a foreign power was treason.

Wilde pulled out Nancy's letter to Dave Johnson from beneath the pile of books on his table, He read through it again. One sentence, one question stuck out: *is there a line between fighting for a cause and fighting for the enemy?* Berlin was an honourable undertaking, helping a renowned scientist. But the letter to Dave Johnson was written months later. What had gone wrong in the meantime? Had Eaton indeed tried to recruit her – or had she seen his name on the North Sea list? What if Nancy had become seriously rattled? Eaton would surely have worried that she would expose him. He would never be safe while she was alive.

It would have been a simple matter for Eaton to call on Moscow for something undetectable to slip into her heroin dose while visiting her in Chesterton, perhaps? Something she could slide, unknowing, into her own arm with her silver syringe. And what if a forgotten peseta had fallen from his pocket . . .

But if any of this was true, why had Eaton befriended *him*? Why did he suggest that Nancy had worked for the Comintern in Berlin? Why draw attention to himself in such a manner? Wilde thought again of Sir Francis Walsingham and Sir Robert Cecil, Elizabeth's great masters of intelligence. A little truth goes a long way in concealing a more damning truth. And Eaton was a professional. He knew of Wilde's connections with the US diplomatic service. Meeting men like Wilde would have been part of his job – whether for MI6 or the NKVD. Eaton saw an opening – and he was in.

The kettle was boiling. Wilde took it from the hob; he didn't want tea. He wondered where he had left the bloody whisky. His mind was taking him to dark places. Too much Machiavelli. Too much Walsingham. And all utterly futile, because in the case of the death of Nancy Hereward there was no proof that a crime had even been committed. Nor was there ever likely to be.

He found the whisky and poured a small shot. Then thought better of it and put it aside, untouched. Instead he stretched his arms and looked out of the window.

The days were getting longer. A little more light. Intimations of warm days to come.

He put on his coat and boots and gauntlet gloves and left his rooms, nodding a greeting to Bobby.

'I've got another horse, professor.'

'What happened to the last one? Winter Blood, wasn't it?'

'Fell at the first fence, sir. But this one's a certainty. Golden Miller.'

'Half a crown each way then.'

'Put it on the nose, professor.'

'Whatever you say, Bobby.'

Wilde walked out into the brisk February air. Lydia would be waiting for him, huddled into her duffle coat up at Cornflowers. Together, they would ride out into the countryside aboard the Rudge and she would wrap her arms round his waist and nestle her head into his shoulder. In bed last night, she had told him she wanted to see some snowdrops, some sign of new growth. New life. And he had promised they would.

ACKNOWLEDGMENTS

I could not have written this book without the tireless help of my editor, Kate Parkin, and agent, Teresa Chris. I like to think of them as my Lendls.

Nor could I have survived the long, difficult days without the support of my family, who always bore the brunt of my ill temper when things weren't going quite as planned.

In addition, I would like to mention Andrew Neall of the wonderful Norfolk Motorcycle Museum in North Walsham. Andrew is a motorcycle enthusiast who introduced me to the delights of the Rudge Special, a bike he has lovingly re-commissioned and made fit to ride once more.

Last, but certainly not least, I am immensely grateful to Greg Fisher, who lent me many books on the 1930s and assisted me with his knowledge of Cambridge University life.

If you enjoyed *Corpus* – why not join the Rory Clements Readers Club by emailing me at rory.clements@bonnierzaffre.co.uk?

Turn over for a message from Rory Clements. . .

Dear Reader

Corpus is different from anything I have tried before, but I hope that those of you who have supported the John Shakespeare series so enthusiastically have enjoyed reading it as much I enjoyed writing and researching it.

For all its international background, *Corpus* always returns to Cambridge and an unconventional history professor named Tom Wilde. As a character he intrigued me from the very start and I knew he had many other stories to tell - and so this has proved. Even as I was finishing *Corpus*, my next novel, *Nucleus*, had begun to evolve. It opens in June 1939, the period in the build-up to the 'Phoney War', a summer during which England partied like there was no tomorrow, with gas masks at the ready. In Cambridge, the May Balls were played out with a frantic intensity, but only the most optimistic believed that the good times would last. Germany had invaded the free Czechoslovak territories, with flagrant contempt for the 1938 Munich Agreement. The persecution of the Jews in Occupied Europe had gathered pace to such an extent that desperate parents were sending their children to safety in Britain aboard the *Kindertransport*. Closer to home, the IRA had launched its S-Plan campaign, perpetrating more than 100 terrorist outrages around England.

However, in hindsight, perhaps the most far-reaching event of this time went largely unreported: in Germany, Otto Hahn had discovered nuclear fission and an atomic device was now a very real possibility. In the immediate wake of his breakthrough, the Nazis set up the *Uranverein* group of physicists. Its task: to build a superbomb. Aware that there were scientists working on similar lines in England and the US, the German high command needed to discover how soon the West might be able to produce such a bomb, and prevent that happening. Only then would it be safe to go to war.

The obvious target was the famous Cavendish Laboratory in Cambridge, home to the world's greatest physicists and the place where the atom was first split. Scientists there were alert to the dangers posed by the *Uranverein*. So were the British secret services. And when one of the Cavendish's finest brains is murdered, Tom Wilde is once more drawn into an intrigue from which there seems no escape. In a conspiracy that stretches from Cambridge to Berlin and from Washington DC to the west coast of Ireland, he faces deadly forces that threaten the fate of the world.

If you would like to hear more from me about *Nucleus* and my other future books, you can email me at rory.clements@bonnierzaffre.co.uk where you can join the Rory Clements Readers Club. It only takes a moment, there is no catch and new members will automatically receive an exclusive e-book short story that throws a little more light on to Hartmut Dorfen and the background to *Corpus*. Your data is private and confidential and will never be passed on to a third party and I promise that I will only be in touch now and again with book news. If you want to unsubscribe, you can of course do that at any time.

However, if you would like to be involved and spread the word about my books, you can review *Corpus* on Amazon, on GoodReads, on any other e-store, on your own blogs and social media accounts, or, of course, by actually speaking to another human being! You'll help other readers if you share your thoughts and you will help me, too: I love hearing from readers about what they experience from my books – and I always read my reviews!

But for now, thanks again for reading and for your interest in Tom Wilde and his Cambridge world. I'm lucky to have had so many committed and intelligent readers for my John Shakespeare series and I look forward to hearing from you about my new venture.

With my best wishes